TRUTHERS

GEOFFREY GIRARD

TRUTHERS

carolrhoda LAB
MINNEAPOLIS

Carolrhoda Lab™
An imprint of Carolrhoda Books
A division of Lerner Publishing Group, Inc.
241 First Avenue North
Minneapolis, MN 55401 USA

For reading levels and more information, look up this title at
www.lernerbooks.com.

Cover and interior images: © Oleg Osharov/123RF; © iStockphoto.com/loops7;
© iStockphoto.com/ismagilov; © iStockphoto.com/maciek905. Jacket flaps:
© iStockphoto.com/Gruppo_Teatrale_Universitario. Illustrations © Laura
Westlund/Independent Picture Service.

Main body text set in Janson Text LT Std 10.5/15.
Typeface provided by Linotype AG.

Library of Congress Cataloging-in-Publication Data

Names: Girard, Geoffrey, author.
Title: Truthers / by Geoffrey Girard.
Description: Minneapolis : Carolrhoda Lab, [2017] | Summary: "When her veteran
    dad is committed to a psych ward, one girl must unravel a conspiracy that
    connects her past and the terrorist attack on 9/11" —Provided by publisher.
Identifiers: LCCN 2016007899 (print) | LCCN 2016033569 (ebook) |
    ISBN 9781512427790 (th : alk. paper) | ISBN 9781512430004 (eb pdf)
Subjects: LCSH: September 11 Terrorist Attacks, 2001—Juvenile fiction. | CYAC:
    September 11 Terrorist Attacks, 2001—Fiction. | Conspiracies—Fiction. |
    Fathers and daughters—Fiction. | Mystery and detective stories.
Classification: LCC PZ7.G43948 Tr 2017 (print) | LCC PZ7.G43948 (ebook) |
    DDC [Fic]—dc23

LC record available at https://lccn.loc.gov/2016007899

Manufactured in the United States of America
1-41504-23365-3/15/2017

Dedicated to Elliot K.

The El, Kelly Kidd
boogie-woogier, orc slayer
Kamchatka defender, rook master
heartbeat of The Shire
thinker, dreamer
searcher of truth
best friend

1

They killed her. Killed all of them.

This is what her father said.

Half a dozen times that she could remember.

When he was very tired. And high.

They killed her. Killed all of them.

I'm sorry.

He'd said it again two nights before they took him away.

The police car that pulled up to her house that night didn't surprise or alarm Katie.

It wasn't the first time; neighbors could be so nosy. She'd even seen her father arrested once (misdemeanor marijuana). But this night, there were *two* police cars. And a specially-marked SHERIFF'S OFFICE car.

And now a black car and a weird yellow van pulling up her driveway.

Her immediate guess was that her father was dead. Reeking of pot and/or beer and wrapped around some telephone pole. Or, worse and more likely, smashed into an SUV filled with some family who'd been racing on the tangled pathways of destiny toward this unhappy man for years. *It finally happened,* she thought.

And now, all these cars. All these people. Huddled in small circles up and down her driveway. People talking. Pointing. Organizing to fully include her in today's tragedy.

Katie stepped back from the window, the world quiet and still as she deliberated how to behave when they officially told her. Cry? Scream? Act surprised? She felt too disconnected from herself for real thought. Her brain unexpectedly empty, This-Space-for-Rent, entirely without the solutions that always came.

Finally, a knock at the door. *Thank God*, she thought. Because a knock was a sound and sound was something real and hinted at next steps. At least *a* next step.

She opened her front door slowly and a tall shadow filled the space behind.

"Kaitlyn Wallace?" the tall shadow asked.

She managed only a nod. It was as if Death himself had come to her door. Dropping by to explain all the complexities of the universe. She almost found the idea funny and might even have laughed if she weren't also so terrified.

Death leaned forward and, of course, became a man. Round face, gray goatee. No scythe or glistening black eye sockets. But a leather folder and a black baseball cap that said SHER-IFF. "Sheriff Mathieson," he confirmed and asked if he could come in. More shadows hovered directly behind him. There was some discussion regarding whether she was a Kaitlyn or a Kate or et cetera, and she may have answered but wasn't really listening yet. Merely staring.

Outside, the nasty rainstorm that'd swept through had passed, its gloom and dankness trailing after. Some cops stood posted in her driveway. A half dozen neighbors confirmed their nosiness, their faces flush and hellish in the lone red light revolving slowly atop one of the police cars.

The sheriff had entered her house, and then a half dozen other equally tall dark shapes—several men in suits, another cop, and a woman in plain clothes—followed him in and crowded her hallway as Katie was led to her living room. Already a guest in her own home.

"This is Gloria Dorsey," the sheriff said, introducing the woman. She was middle-aged, dressed like a modish schoolteacher, and had short, jagged blonde hair. She looked eager to take over. "Ms. Dorsey is—"

"Is he dead?" Katie asked. She also wanted to take over, but still felt weirdly apart from her own words and movements.

The sheriff sighed, almost chuckled. "Oh, little lady, no, no. No."

"Your dad is fine," the Dorsey woman said. She'd taken a spot beside Katie on the couch, though Katie had no recollection of even sitting. Struggling for the reaction to the idea her dad was still alive proved as elusive as what she might do if he were dead. "He's perfectly fine. We should have told you that right away." The woman shot a look at the sheriff and his whole face tightened some.

Katie asked, "Is he in jail?"

"He's at a hospital," the sheriff replied. "Ventworth."

She'd never heard of it. Behind the sheriff, the others scurried around her house. Around it, through it, over it. Doing what, she had no clue. The cop had stayed back in the front hallway. And one man . . . This guy she'd not noticed before, now stood off to the side, in the entrance to the kitchen, watching. Watching her. And while all the others moved in a sort of intense frenzy, this guy looked perfectly calm. Chewing gum, even. Almost amused. Smiling?

"I don't understand," Katie said, looking away. Reality returning fast now, pursuing something they'd said. "You said he was fine. So why is he at the hospital?"

The sheriff and the Dorsey woman shared a look.

"There was an incident at work," Dorsey explained.

Work? Her dad was a maintenance-groundskeeper type for Park Services: cutting out honeysuckle, putting in new picnic tables, etc. What kind of incident would he—

"The doctors believe your father had a panic attack of some kind," said Dorsey.

"Nervous breakdown," the sheriff amended.

So, nothing to do with the honeysuckle. Of course not . . .

Katie thought about some of the things her dad had said to her recently. Stranger than usual, even. And, because it was tricky to separate them all, she also thought about some of the things he'd said for years. A "breakdown"? His whole damn life had been a breakdown.

"They don't know for sure what it was," Dorsey said, interrupting Katie's racing thoughts. "But he's going to spend at least tonight at the hospital." Pause. "Maybe longer. And he was worried about you here alone."

Katie made a face, calling Dorsey's lie. She'd spent most of her life alone in the house—this one and all the others before— while her father was off fishing or holed up in some nasty bar after work or God-knows-what. He wouldn't give one shit if she spent another night alone.

"We were worried," Dorsey corrected and then presented her most professional I-know-what-you're-going-through face before her next words: "You're a minor, Katie."

Finally, Katie realized what was going on.

Her dad was already at some hospital. They hadn't come for him.

They'd come for her.

There was no known next-of-kin.

No grandparents or aunts or second cousins. No one. Only her dad. A.k.a.: the man imprisoned in some psychiatric hospital called Ventsomething.

So the Dorsey woman helped Katie collect her schoolbag and fill a county-supplied gym bag (said *BUTLER COUNTY SOCIAL SERVICES* right on the side) with some clothes, then led her to the weird yellowy van. The sheriff followed.

Katie had gone on autopilot again. She had little memory of stepping outside or moving down the rain-stained driveway with Dorsey or getting into the van. She sat alone in the middle row of seats, while Dorsey shut the side door and then got in to drive. The night still swirling red. Neighbors still watching. Mrs. Lindhorst and Gary the Grouch. Their stares.

As the van pulled away with her in it, she noticed all the lights in her house were still on, the front door wide open, strange men still within.

"I want to see my father," Katie said.

"Soon," Dorsey replied from up front.

But she was lying.

2

Katie spent that first night with total strangers called the Claypools.

The Claypools lived all the way across town. The Claypools had two other foster kids. "Other" being the key descriptive word here, the implication being that she was now a third. The Claypools were goddamned do-gooders.

"My cell number is on the back," Dorsey explained, giving Katie a business card. They stood in the do-gooders' kitchen. There were ceramic roosters everywhere. Mr. and Mrs. Claypool hovered anxiously out in the front hallway, waiting to get on with saving the world one kid at a time. Their "other foster kids" reportedly were in their rooms and sound asleep. At one in the morning, it was just the roosters.

"What about school?" Katie asked Dorsey, and her own voice sounded too far away. "How will I—"

"You'll take tomorrow off. I'll handle it with the school."

Katie imagined what Gianna and Alexis would say when she didn't show. Or her teachers. How could the school keep any of this quiet? It might be on the news. Her dad's arrest and picture on TV. On the Internet. The "crazy guy." Her house and the flashing lights. Katie Wallace being led to a yellow van like some kind of criminal. How would Dorsey even begin to explain tonight?

"Oh my God!" Katie's hands went to her mouth. "Winter! I left . . . our cat, Winter. I wasn't even . . . How could I?"

"Hey." Dorsey touched her shoulder. "It's been a stressful night. Winter will understand. Tomorrow, we can—"

"Can she stay here?"

A quick glance toward the Claypools out in the hall. Nervous smile. "We'll see. For now, I could—"

"Never mind," Katie snapped, quickly solving this new problem herself. Something she was quite used to. "It's fine. One of my friends will watch her. I'm sure of it."

Dorsey breathed outward in genuine relief. "Perfect. We'll take care of that tomorrow, okay? I'll be back first thing." She stepped closer and hugged Katie briefly, like a coach after giving a participation trophy. "It's all going to be okay."

Katie stood frozen. Unable, unwilling, to move or reply. Convinced that tomorrow was only going to get worse.

Dorsey was gone.

With careful and short words, Mrs. Claypool showed Katie to her new room. Each girl—*Thank. You. God.*—had her own. There was a freshly-made bed and an empty dresser for her things and a lame painting of a girl riding a horse. Katie may have cursed under her breath, but Mrs. Claypool pretended not to notice. There was a small shelf of books. There was a bag with a new toothbrush and toothpaste. There was a stale can-produced lavender smell to everything.

Throughout the settling-in routine, Mrs. Claypool did about as well as someone could, given the situation. She was kind and supportive and practical about it all. *Here is This* and *Here is That*. And *If This* and *If That*. All with the same reassuring smile and energy the Dorsey woman had hoped to convey with her reassuring smiles and energy. Katie was both astounded and sickened that Gloria Dorsey, a woman she'd met less than four hours ago, was now actually missed and somehow so much better than this even *stranger* stranger.

"Good night, Katie," Mrs. Claypool said finally and gently, and equally gently shut the door. "Try and get some sleep."

But Katie didn't sleep at all that first night. She didn't cry either.

Sleep and crying came later.

That first night was all about hate.

Her father was a child. A monster? For sure an asshole.

The constant pot-smoking, the rambling talk, the long bouts of depression. These had been only a private irritation before. A tolerable cross to bear. He'd merely *stained* her life. Not yet *ruined* it. But this? This was different.

I'm sorry.

This was not eating alone. Or dealing with some past-due utility bill because he'd let them pile up again. This was not odd looks from neighbors, friends' parents, teachers. This was not having to stamp out another cigarette when he fell asleep. Or cramming in earbuds to help ignore his stoner mumblings.

This was real-life stuff now. Very direct and very real consequences. This was being packed up and shipped off in front of everyone like some freak. Spending the night in a stranger's house. Staring up at the painting of some stupid girl on some stupid fucking horse. Her life uprooted. A "ward of the state." Practically an orphan. Something out of a Charles Dickens novel.

And so, all that first night, she hated him.

And wished that she'd been right.

That the police had come to tell her he was dead.

The man was looking for one thing more.

"Sir, we already checked those."

He simply lifted a hand and the others left him, heading for the front door while he casually opened more cabinets.

Their job was done here. They'd found nothing in the house. But this wasn't a surprise. The work location had also turned up empty. Here, they'd discovered only a couple of guns (properly licensed) and a single file folder of old news clippings (all on the usual suspects and subjects). The lone desktop computer they'd seized had nothing of value; looked like the daughter used it mostly. This guy, unsurprisingly, clearly used other online avenues. No flash drives found. No smartphones. Nothing. The girl had an archaic iPod, which she'd taken with her, but they'd first quickly copied its contents and found only groups he'd never heard of.

His team waited in the front hallway. It'd been a long night for all of them. He leaned over to open another cabinet. Finally found what he'd been looking for.

The man emptied the whole bag of Meow Mix into a large salad bowl and laid it on the kitchen floor. He'd already filled the water dish and opened the toilet lid. The white-haired cat weaved around his feet and he squatted down to scratch its neck. It purred in thanks. The man stood to leave.

"Good luck, soldier," he said.

3

The next morning, Katie's new best friend Ms. Dorsey
returned as promised. The woman had thankfully left the
weird yellow van behind and pulled up in a normal car. Dorsey
was overly cheerful, even more than Katie remembered, and
had brought Katie a mocha from Starbucks. That cup sat
untouched between them throughout the long drive to the
hospital as Katie deflected Dorsey's questions with polite one-
word answers.

Did you sleep okay? *Yes.* (A lie.)

Did you get to meet the other girls? *No.* (And hoped she
never would.)

Ventworth Hospital was split unevenly by an ornate glass
and red brick entranceway. On one side of this entry was a
long five-story white building with hundreds of windows. The
shorter side was only two stories high, with fewer windows and
more red brick. The lawn and trees behind were private and
blocked by a high fence.

Katie knew right away which side her dad was on.

Sure enough, they parked and she silently followed Dorsey
toward a door on the shorter side.

"How you feeling?" Dorsey asked for, seemingly, the
tenth time.

"Good, thanks," Katie tried again (the tenth?), hoping the

answer would stick, that the woman with the Starbucks and overly-empathetic eyes would just drop it.

Dorsey held up her ID to a camera and the door buzzed open.

Inside was a desk area with a security guard and a small bank of monitors. Dorsey stopped to sign them both in and then led her into the next room, which looked, at first, like any doctor's office Katie'd ever seen. Not that she'd been to a real doctor in years, she realized. Maybe not since her vaccination shots when she was little. Her dad didn't believe in doctors; said it was a total waste of money.

Dorsey sat in one of the chairs and indicated Katie should do the same. Now, in case she'd somehow forgotten the security guard, she also noticed the cameras in each ceiling corner, and the big locks on the one door, and the bars running vertical along every window, and the nurse encased entirely behind Plexiglas.

Okay, maybe not so much "any doctor's office" after all.

My dad is really here?

"Someone will be out to talk with us in a minute," said Dorsey.

They waited in silence for another ten, twenty minutes. Finally the only other door in the room buzzed open and a man appeared. Not her dad.

But Katie recognized him all the same.

Smiling Guy who'd been at her house. Chewing Gum Guy. Mr. Cool.

He moved to shake Dorsey's offered hand, but his eyes never left Katie's alarmed stare. "Paul Cobb," he said and now offered his hand to Katie.

"I'd like to see my dad." She'd crossed her arms.

"Of course, I understand. Katie, right? Okay if you and I talk first?" He turned back to Dorsey. "Give us a minute," he said. It wasn't a request.

Talk about what? Katie bristled. *What's there to talk about with THIS guy?*

She watched Dorsey consider objecting and then stiffen. "Sure," Dorsey said, tapping Katie's arm supportively. "I'll be here if you need anything."

Katie couldn't imagine what she might "need," or where she was even going.

"Thanks, Gloria." The man winked and held up a hand for Katie to move toward the door he'd come out of.

Her dad was somewhere back there. Behind all the bars and fences and security guys. And if the admission price to see him was a little talk with this loser first, so be it. Whatever hate for her father she'd felt the night before, whatever anger she still carried, didn't matter at this moment. She just wanted to see him.

Katie went to the door, which buzzed loudly. The Paul Cobb guy pulled it open and motioned for her to step through first. She found herself in a long hallway with several side conference rooms. At the opposite end of the hallway, there was another door and another security guard.

"You're okay," Cobb said, following her. "We'll grab the first room on the right."

Then the main door behind them closed and locked with a thunderous and final clank.

"You were at the house last night," she said.

The room had too many chairs but only one window, which overlooked the parking lot. Paul Cobb, the Smiling Man, freed one of the chairs and turned it, indicating she should sit. Seemed to be a lot of that going on today.

"Yes." He pulled his own chair around the table to be closer to her.

"Why?"

"I work with Veterans Affairs," he replied, sitting.

"Doesn't really answer the question."

Paul Cobb did what she already suspected was his favorite thing: he smiled. "I'm here to help, Katie. We want to make sure your dad gets the best care."

"If you guys want to help so much, where've you all been all these years? Why now?"

Cobb's brows lifted, his smiling eyes seeming somehow disappointed. "There are more than twenty million veterans in the United States, Katie."

Katie blinked. "I meant—"

"You brought it up, so let me finish. Of those twenty million veterans, more than three hundred thousand are suffering from PTSD and another two hundred thousand from traumatic brain injuries. I am sincerely regretful it took us this long to reconnect with your father. You'll admit, I hope, he hasn't exactly gone out of his way to keep in touch with us either. Fair?"

She nodded. Embarrassed. Mortified. Lectured like a third grader.

"What's past is past," he continued. "Our best strategy moving forward is to focus only on what we can do for him today."

"Fine. I'd like to see him." She'd stood again. To hell with this guy. "So, let's go ahead and do that."

"Not today." He'd held out a hand, indicating she should

sit again. Worse, he kept talking. "His attending psychiatrist believes, at this time, that any outside visitors would create distress and perhaps impede your father's recovery."

"'Outside visitors'?" Katie gripped the back of her chair. "I'm his daughter."

"Yes. Still, it's the doctor's call. I'm sure it's only for another day or so."

This was all so wrong. She could feel her whole body shaking. Nails digging into imitation leather. "Why drive me down here then?"

"We'd hoped there'd been more improvement overnight, but by the time Dr. Ziegler ruled out visitors, you and Ms. Dorsey were already on your way. And I wanted to talk with you anyway."

"He's not crazy."

"No one's saying he is. Just a temporary thing. It happens. Katie, do you know what he might have been upset about?" Cobb asked, fishing a packet of gum from inside his jacket pocket. "Something that might have triggered this episode?"

They killed her. Killed all of them. I'm sorry.

"No," she said. And meant it. She had no clue what'd set him off. This time, or any other. And, quite honestly, didn't want to know either.

"Nothing at home? Work? Something out of the ordinary he might have talked about? Someone stop by the house? Anything, even something small?"

They got their war, didn't they?

"No," she said. "Nothing. He's been really quiet, but, you know, he's always kinda quiet. That's just the type of guy he is. So, then, when can I see him?"

He offered her the pack of gum and she shook her head. "Let me ask you this . . ." Cobb leaned back again, putting the gum away. "Do you know why he was brought in?"

"They said—last night they said he had a . . ." She didn't want to say *breakdown*. Sounded too much like *crazy*. A label for people who stayed locked behind barred windows and security guys, wore straitjackets, got shock therapy and stuff. People who never came home again. "They said he had a panic attack of some kind."

"Something like that." Cobb nodded. "Apparently got pretty upset. Started shouting, making threats. His coworkers couldn't get him calmed down. He even knocked a guy out. So they eventually called the police."

Knocked a guy out? For all his faults, she'd never once seen her dad violent. Couldn't imagine him even knowing how to throw a punch.

"What kind of threats?" she asked.

"He threatened to kidnap and torture someone."

"What?" Katie's shock seemed to fill the whole room. She'd heard her dad's rants on politics and "backroom deals," the wars in Iraq and Afghanistan. War profiteering. Corporate greed. *Follow the money.* And so on. She'd heard all that a hundred times before. And ignored it well enough before too. Lots of dads shouted at the TV, calling people morons and criminals and worse. But kidnap and torture?

"Who?" she managed. "Who'd he threaten?"

"Well, threatening to torture anyone would be problematic, I hope you'd agree. But he specifically talked about Dick Cheney. You know who that is?"

"Bush's vice president. I'm not an idiot."

"Never considered it once. See, threats against a vice

president, even a retired one, are a class D felony. That's real jail time, Katie. People have been imprisoned for years."

She hated that he kept using her name. Wanted to shout "STOP IT!" Then the words he spoke *after* her name pinged against her brain.

Imprisoned for *years*? Wait, what?

"A stupid threat," she countered, the magnitude of her dad's situation sinking ever and ever deeper. "A joke, maybe. What does it matter?" Deeper. "I see stuff like that online all the time. So what? It's people being stupid." Deeper. "What· about freedom of speech?"

Paul Cobb gave another smile. This one somehow different from the others. She could practically smell the gum's peppermint between his teeth. "Some pretty extreme speech. Now, I hope, you'll understand why there were so many people in your house. He ever talk like that at home? The threats, I mean."

Katie stiffened. "Is the idea for me to help you put my father in jail?"

"The idea's for you to tell the truth so we can help him."

She stared at him. He let the silence (and peppermint) remain between them for too long. "No," she said finally and looked to the door for escape. "He's never mentioned Dick Cheney at home. Or Joe Biden or John Adams either."

Cobb laughed. "Okay, got it. Ever talk about the service? His time in the military?"

"Does he need a lawyer?"

"Probably. Can you afford one?"

It was a shitty question. He surely knew the answer already.

"I don't think so," she admitted. She really had no idea how much money they had. For all she knew they were millionaires or fifty grand in debt. Her dad always called it "enough." He refused to do online banking—one more way to "stay off the grid," he always said—but never stayed on top of using old-school checks either. When Katie forged his name on checks to keep the lights and water on, she always paid the minimum and hoped the check would clear. It always had, too. "I doubt it."

"That's okay. The state will provide legal counsel," he explained. "We'll help make sure they assign the right man for the job."

"Or woman," Katie amended, almost automatically.

Cobb studied her, his smile back in place. Waited.

Katie didn't mind. She'd spent a whole lifetime in uncomfortable silences.

"What does he do?" he said finally. "I mean, other than work. Friends? Hobbies?"

She thought. Nothing came to mind, really. He went for long walks and smoked pot in the woods. Fished. Watched lame TV and fell asleep on the couch. Beyond that, she had no real idea how the man spent his free time. No more than he knew about her.

"Anything you can think of?" Cobb prodded.

They killed her. Killed all of them. I'm sorry.

"Sorry." She echoed her father's words. "No."

"No apology necessary. He ever talk about his years in the service?"

She noted it was the second time he'd asked. "Not really," Katie replied carefully.

"So he does sometimes."

She wanted to scream or curse. Both. This guy was awful. "No," she said again instead. "Not something he likes to talk about, I guess. 'What's past is past,' right?" She wanted to tell him how her dad was when he got high *and* drunk, or when he couldn't sleep for days, the things he sometimes said: Slurred. Cryptic. Fucking dumb things. But she knew anything she admitted to would only make him seem all the more unbalanced.

"It's not easy on a lot of veterans," Cobb said, as if reading her thoughts. "Unresolved pain can sometimes come out in rather curious and extreme ways. Paranoia. Even violence. He's been out of the service, what, ten-plus years?"

"More. Before I was born."

"That's right. How about TERNGO? He ever mention a company called TERNGO? Place he used to work for. How about Fuenmayor? A guy named Gary Fuenmayor."

She thought, tried to remember having ever heard of either. Nothing. She shook her head. "Sorry, no. What would—"

"Okay," he stopped her. "And you can't think of anything he might have said that could help us here? Might help get to the core of what's really bothering him. Could be the first true step in his recovery."

"Okay. I'll . . . let you know if something comes to mind."

He stared at her some more.

"Can I see him tomorrow?" Katie broke the silence this time.

"No promises. But as soon as possible. We're all here to help you, Katie."

"Just help get him out of here."

Cobb nodded. "There'll be a hearing later this week where the doctors will talk with a judge to determine when he can be released."

"He's not crazy," she said again.

Because saying it again and again, and out loud, made it more real each time.

Didn't it?

Tomorrow. After school.

Ventworth had finally approved visitors. It'd been three days since her meeting with Cobb. She could see her dad in a little more than twenty-four hours. And then . . . Then, she didn't know what. No idea.

Katie stood with Gianna and Alexis on the sidelines of a gym game called trench ball, an overcomplicated version of dodgeball they all loathed. The good news was you could pretend you were "out" at any time and walk off the court. The bad news was Alexis had just said something.

"What?" Katie turned, tried to refocus. Something about Winter.

"Why's your dad being such a dick?" Alexis asked, her voice half lost beneath the background noise of squeaking sneakers and hollering cave boys.

"Who knows?" Katie shrugged. "Just said I needed to get her out of the house." It was a totally believable lie. She turned to Gianna. "You're sure your parents don't mind?"

"Please." Gianna narrowed darkly-lined eyes. "Momzilla already acts like it's *her* cat."

Katie wanted to cry. Again. But at least this time, it was out of genuine relief. Winter was clearly being taken care of. Even if she was stuck in another strange house, like everyone else in her family.

"And your dad'll come around," said Gianna. "Mr. Moody."

Katie nodded. Tried harder to stop thinking about

tomorrow. About finally seeing him after four, soon to be five, long days. Absently watched the stupid game as she tugged at her oversized CLARA BARTON HIGH gym shirt and thought of the alternate reality she'd so easily managed to bring to life.

Her friends didn't know her dad wasn't actually "being a dick" or acting the part of "Mr. Moody." He was locked up in a mental hospital. For how much longer was now the big question. (Days, years?) When they last spoke, Dorsey told her the criminal charges were being dropped. The man her dad hit at work—*hit* as in shattered the guy's nose and knocked him unconscious—was one of his few friends there. Wasn't pressing charges; good friend. And the bigger, more serious charges for the threats about Cheney would likely be dropped too. All that remained, apparently, was determining his mental state. Deciding what level of danger he was to society. And to himself.

So rather than try to explain all this to her friends—the hospital, the foster home, the police—she'd lied. Or, rather, simply had withheld the whole truth.

And why not? Despite her fears, there'd been nothing in the news about her father, and none of the neighbors' gossip had made it to the school yet. Only her friends had even asked why she'd missed a day of school. "Not feeling well," she'd answered honestly. That was all. So simple. The lies. Too simple.

"Hey, Wallace? Parker! Little help."

Katie's mind came back to gym class and followed the voice calling out to them.

Doug Jessberger. Hottie. Loudmouth. Tried to hook up with her at Joey Meyer's Halloween party. Epic fail all around. Worse yet, she knew Gianna was still maneuvering to put Doug and her together for prom, which absolutely wasn't going to happen. He grinned. "Someone toss me that ball?"

"*This* ball?" Alexis said, glancing at the ball behind them.

"Go away," Gianna replied.

Doug Jessberger laughed and, backing away, lifted up the bottom of his shirt to reveal his renowned abs—sadly, the solitary thing he had to offer.

"Idiot." Gianna shook her head. "It's a room full of idiots." Her remark was shockingly restrained compared to her usual language; G's sentences were typically bejeweled with body parts or the F-word as adverb, adjective, *and* noun. She must really think she still had a shot at that prom setup. *Yeah*, Katie thought, *NO*.

Still, "idiots" totally worked. A room of people throwing spongy balls at each other as if any of this mattered. Gym classes and proms and taking quizzes and homework and planning weekends. In a world of divorces and suicides and cancers and dads locked away in padded cells.

Katie picked up the ball at their feet.

And hurled it as hard as she could.

Later, Gianna would swear that, for one whole second, "that silly fuck's head" literally separated from his "fucking shoulders." Well worth, G said, her now-dented matchmaking schemes.

Katie couldn't say for sure what Doug's head had done. She'd been already halfway to the lockers by the time the ball connected. The laughter of her friends and the gym teacher's squealing whistle at her back.

4

She noticed the handcuffs first.

Even though she hadn't seen her father in almost a week, and even though someone had tried covering them with his blanket, it was the padded cuffs—a single pair that joined his right arm to the railing of the hospital bed—that first caught her eye.

They'd propped him up, the top third of the bed lifted so he was almost sitting. A tray of food positioned on a wheeled table over his middle. The blanket tucked tight, reaching from his toes to below the top of his chest. For all she knew, his feet were bound with restraints too.

They'd freshly shaven him. Washed and combed his hair. And it'd changed nothing. Despite the declarations she'd been making throughout the week, he sure *looked* crazy.

His eyes were only half open, and what she could see of his gaze was vacant, glazed over. His whole face loose. She'd seen him high before, sure. But this was beyond ripped on pot. His mouth was open a little. Not enough to turn him into a drooling monster, but still disturbing. Gross. Wrong. He looked, in fact, a little like a displayed corpse.

"Is he . . . Is he drugged?" she whispered to Dorsey, who stood in the doorway beside her. The nurse looked up from whatever she was doing.

"He's probably still sedated," Dorsey confirmed.

Katie approached the bed slowly. Tried to get in his line of sight. "Hi, Dad." Her voice sounded like some other girl's voice. The voice of a four-year-old, maybe. "How are you doing?"

A stupid question. Handcuffed to a bed, drugged, shaved by someone else. *That's* how he was doing.

"It's good to see you," she managed. Amazing, really. Saying the exact opposite of what she was actually thinking.

There was no recognition on his face. None at all. Might as well be talking to one of the Claypools' ceramic roosters. She studied the tray hovering above his waist to avoid having to look again at his ghoulish expression. The food was untouched. "He's not eating," she said.

The nurse shook her head. "On and off," she explained. "We had him on IVs for the first few days. Don't you worry, beautiful. He's being taken care of."

Katie glowered at the nurse. No real reason. Someone to blame.

"Why don't we leave you two alone for a little while," Dorsey proposed. "Would that be okay?" She was asking both the nurse and Katie.

Will you be okay if we leave you in a room alone with your own father?

What a horrible, horrible question.

Worse, Katie didn't know the answer.

"I suppose that'd be okay," the nurse said, looking between them.

Katie's very next thought was to run from the room.

"Ssss . . . ta." Her father mumbled something. That didn't help put her at ease.

"What's that?" the nurse asked, turning to him, leaning in.

"Saaalta," he tried again, his voice like wind in dead trees.

"Salt," Katie translated almost soundlessly.

Her dad looked at her for the first time. Half lidded. High as the stars. Relief flooded her. *This* she knew. *This* she could deal with. It was not the first time she'd had to play "mother."

"You need some salt, Mr. Wallace?" the nurse asked, smiling. A terrible smile, by the way. Phony. Another one of those *it's-my-job-to-smile* smiles.

His gaze drifted back at the nurse and he nodded slowly.

"Back in a jiff." She left the room while Ms. Dorsey dragged over a chair for Katie to sit. (Why was everyone always trying to make her sit?)

The nurse returned with a handful of salt packets and handed them to Katie. "I'll check back in about ten minutes," she promised.

Katie honestly didn't care if she ever saw the woman again. Unless she was the one who could unhook her dad and let him go. The one who could end this.

Dorsey leaned in and whispered, "I'll be right down the hall if you need anything."

Katie nodded. Watched as the two women left the room together.

Leaving her alone with her dad. *Shit!* she thought. *Now what?*

"Are you hungry?" she asked and dropped the salt packs onto the tray.

What else to say? Did he want to hear about the damn Claypools or the last week at school? Would he care or even comprehend? How far gone was he?

His left hand pulled the blanket down, exposing his chest and right arm fully. The handcuffs. Now she could see them completely. The faint marks they'd left on his forearm.

Her dad was reaching for the tray and Katie pulled the roller closer for him. Glad to look away from the cuffs. His fingers stretched toward the cup of water.

"Here," she said, irritated, embarrassed for them both, grabbing the Styrofoam cup. "Let me do it."

His fingers slid down *into* the cup.

"Dad! Hold on." She pulled the cup back.

He'd dragged his left hand down and over his right forearm, his fingers leaving a trail of water behind. "Sssssallt," he said.

"What?" Katie turned around, hoping the nurse had somehow already returned.

"Salllt," her father repeated.

She grabbed one of the packets.

"Alllll," he said. "Opennn themm all."

"Dad, I—" Katie sighed, picked all five packs back off the tray. "You don't want to use all of it."

His left hand latched onto hers and Katie jumped back. Cursed. His fingers gripping so tightly around her hand. So much it hurt.

"What the hell? Here!" She let go of the salt packs and he clenched them. Brought his fist slowly to his mouth, showing teeth. He bit down, slowly turned his head. "Dad, hey, Dad, I can—"

The paper dribbled from his mouth, one piece dangling disgustingly off his lower lip. Before she could react—and, really, what would she have done anyway?—he'd dumped the salt, all five packs, onto his right forearm. The tiny mound now collected above where he'd wet it. Directly above the handcuffs.

He IS insane, she thought for the first time.

Anyone could see that. Anyone would be forced to admit it.

Even me.

She reached to brush the salt away.

"NO!" he growled.

Katie recoiled. It was not a sound she'd ever heard him make before. She'd heard him weak and sad and she'd heard him tired and short, but never this. This . . . this *rage*. She looked for some kind of phone or button to push near the bed. Something to call the nurse. Dorsey. Someone. Anyone.

His left hand lifted again, fingers dangling over the tray once more. A low groan escaped his lips, fingers twitching. Reaching again for the cup.

And once more, his hand dipped into it. Sloshed it. The water and ice spilling over the whole tray. His fingers coming away with only ice. A whole handful.

She watched helplessly as he pressed the ice onto his arm. Onto the salt pile waiting there.

Ten seconds, twenty.

"Dad, what are you . . . Let's get you cleaned up." Katie went into Fix-It mode. A role she knew well, one she'd learned many years before. Some water trickled from beneath his pinkie and collected along the rim of the handcuffs. She pulled free a handful of paper tissues from a box beside the bed. Tried to clean away the mess. But his top hand would not budge.

She gently touched his shoulder, hoping to . . . to what? To get him to acknowledge she was in the room. But he never looked at her once. And the arm was locked; fingers dug into his other arm. The ice and salt trapped beneath.

Maybe she heard it first. The sound of salt melting.

Or maybe was it the smell? The smell of flesh . . .

Burning?

She grabbed her dad's left arm. Struggled to pull his hand

away. The right arm trembling. The cuffs rattling against the attached railing. "Dad?" With each second, the sound, the smell, grew worse. "Dad!"

Nothing. She couldn't pull the hand away. Thirty seconds, forty-five . . .

He was too strong. And growing stronger. His face red, eyes watering.

She kept wrenching at his fingers. Nothing. A minute . . .

His breath hot and quick against the back of her head.

"Dad, please . . ."

Suddenly, she felt the left arm loosen. Let go. She tried again, tried to pull his hand back. This time, she could.

Katie opened her mouth to scream, but no sound came out. There was a hole in his arm.

More like a divot, gaping and red. Maybe an inch scooped out of his flesh as if someone had pressed a large marble into it, melting away the skin and muscle down to . . . Was that glistening bone? She lurched back, knocking the tray, stumbling away from the bed. Getting away from the insane man there.

She had to find help. *The nurse! Dorsey. Help!*

She'd somehow made it to the door.

"Katie . . . wait."

The voice from behind. His words clear and strong, now. Normal.

She stopped. Turned.

Her dad sat up in the bed, his face tight in agony, but his eyes alive again. Awake. Lucid. More lucid, more *alive*, than she'd seen them in a very long time. And staring straight at her.

"Dad?" She'd dropped her hand away from the door.

"Listen," he said, his next words clipped. "We don't have long. You need to know the truth right now."

5

**Katie staggered to his bed. "No, Dad, my God! Dad, you
need to—"**

His arm.

"Please," he said. "Drugs. They've got me on . . . The
pain'll help me focus for maybe another minute. So, just listen."

Katie nodded, stepped closer still. His arm. Tried not to
look at the gaping red hole where flesh once was.

"I should have told you," he said. "I wanted to." His whole
body shuddered with pain. "I love you, Katie, I do."

"I love—"

"Please," he hissed, the words so low she could barely hear
them. "Listen. I'm so sorry. You're—I'm not your father. Not
your biological father, I mean, I . . . There's no time. Please,
Katie. Christ, I don't even know your real name."

Katie watched his mouth moving, his lips forming words.
She knew they were forming words, yet they weren't coming
out in any way she could possibly understand. "Dad?"

"That day—that day I was—I was working. TERNGO.
Covert security detail."

"Wait, did you say TERNGO?"

"But we weren't the kind of guys—not the kind you bring
in to secure an empty hangar. So we knew it was something.
Something. We just didn't—Your mother gave you to me. She

handed you, she . . ." His voice broke, shattering on the edge of words that made no sense to her. "Cleveland. She begged me to save you. And I did. I did, Katie. Dear God, I finally did."

All he was saying hit her at once, a roar of sound, and Katie reared back. "What?" she exhaled. "What in the hell are you talking about?"

His face scrunched in agony, both eyes wet, his teeth clenching. "She knew what was happening. She knew. Even if we didn't, not yet. Not yet. But they took them off the planes, and—" He gasped, his eyes going wide.

"Dad, stop."

"They took them off the planes," he continued gruffly. "All of them. Part of the plan, the lie. And she knew. Your mother. What they were going to do. And she begged me to take you. I was—I couldn't. But she begged me, *begged* me, to save her baby. To save you. And I did, I did, I took you. Hid you. Until it was over. And then, after. Gave you a new name. New documents. A new life. And they just . . . Killed her. Killed all of them."

"I don't understand."

"You're not my daughter, Katie. You . . . You're more important than that. You're the truth the whole world needs to learn. They'll tell you I'm crazy, I know they already have. But trust none of them. They wanted their war and they got it. No matter what the price. No matter." He leaned forward. "Only reason we're still alive is because they fear me, what I know. What I saw, the things we did. What I'll tell everyone. You need to get me out of here. They'll eliminate both of us soon if you don't."

It was the first thing he'd said that made any sense at all: Get me out of here. *That* she could wrap her head around. Not psychotic phrases like "eliminate us" and "you are not my daughter." Her gaze skittered over the terrible wound in his arm once more. The wound he'd put there so he could reach her. So he could talk to her.

"How?" she asked, her mouth dry. "How do I get you out?"

"Keep the pressure on them. You and me, we . . ." His eyes were flickering, and she could almost see consciousness beginning to blur at the edges. "We stick together, we . . . Keep pressure . . . so we can walk away and settle this on our own terms. Not theirs. You got it?"

"Yeah." She had not one single idea what he was talking about.

"Listen." He'd said this last word as a full whisper and she leaned closer to hear the rest. "Listen. The room . . . The room is bugged. Do whatever is necessary to get me out. I . . . If you need help, find Benevolus. Benevolus, five. Five. Two. He'll . . ."

"Who?" Katie couldn't yet make any sense of it.

"Tell him—tell him nothing yet about what I've said. Only that I need help. He'll . . . He'll figure out something. You may, you may . . ." His voice trailing off. The whispers becoming more broken, his head falling back as the drugs drowned out the pain once more. "The dragon may come for you, Katie. He—you can . . . Your father should know you're alive."

"Dad?"

"He . . . he needs to know."

Fully slipping back into his medicated daze again.

Good, she thought.

But before he did, she needed to actually hear one thing more.

After years of half-grumbled accusations and offhand comments directed at the TV, she knew the answer well enough. She'd guessed where his major fears and anger and demons lived.

No, not a Where. A *When*.

And she wanted to hear it. Really hear it.

"Dad? Dad!"

He looked at her. His eyes half closed.

I'm not your father.

"When?" she said. Her voice no more than a whisper. "The planes. My mother. When?"

"You know," he replied, croaking like some dead thing.

Katie felt herself, the room, the hospital, the whole world, shudder to a complete halt. Waiting for her answer, the answer for both of them.

"Nine-Eleven," she said.

Then the door burst open.

There was shouting and alarms buzzing and people pushing her out of the way. Katie was whisked—or, more accurately, herded like livestock—down the hallway and away by Ms. Dorsey and one of the security guards. Every step one step farther from him. From the madman. *(I'm not your father.)* From the explosion of accusations and instructions and nurses and security that had stormed through the door. From padded handcuffs and melted skin. From doctors injecting more and more sedatives.

Dorsey led her back out to the empty waiting room. "We won't leave until we confirm your dad is okay. I promise."

Okay? Katie didn't know what the word meant anymore. She'd seen her father chained to a bed, half drugged out of his mind. Burning his own flesh. And then saying such ridiculous things. Horrible things. Could a man like that ever really be "okay" again?

Sitting in the chair, catching her breath, she replayed in her mind everything he'd said. Or every word that she could remember. (Had he really said *that*? Had he really meant *that*?) All the pieces reassembling in her mind, she pulled the biggest takeaways she could. TERNGO. Something about "Benevolent" or "Benevolus" and a bit about a dragon. People she should look for or who might be looking for her. But the core of it all.

I'm not your father.

I'm not your father. The atomic bomb in the room.

I'm not your father. Her dad honestly believed that some fifteen years before . . .

On 9/11.

THE 9/11.

It was not—admittedly, even with her dad's freaky and sporadic interest—a subject she gave much thought to. Probably *because* she'd always associated the event with her dad being drunk and high, she preferred to avoid thinking about it.

She knew radical Islamic terrorists had hijacked planes and smashed them into the Twin Towers in New York City and that, on a third plane, the passengers fought back and the plane crashed. She knew lots of people died but honestly wasn't sure if it was hundreds or ten thousand. She knew the name Osama bin Laden, and that he'd planned it or something, and that America eventually found and killed him. But that was about it. It really wasn't something covered in any class.

And in any case, it'd happened more than *fifteen* years ago, when she was maybe two, and she had no personal memory of that day, or of the weeks or months that followed. So, yeah, it was tragic and all that, but from a completely selfish, and honest, point of view, 9/11 was ancient history. It had about as much effect on her as Kennedy getting shot or the *Titanic* sinking. None.

Unless . . .

Unless her dad's "freaky and sporadic interest" was more than that. Much more.

Unless somehow, some way, her "real" mother had been involved with that historic day. Something about the planes. And people who *weren't* Islamic terrorists . . . And many deaths, deaths the world didn't yet know about and, and, and that—could that be right?—Her mother . . . And she, Kaitlyn Wallace *(I don't even know your real name)*, had been some kind of survivor of that day. A toddler, plucked like Moses from a huge, terrible conspiracy. *(Don't even know your real name.)* Stolen, hidden away with a fake identity, raised by a random guy. *(I'm not your father.)*

Yeah, right.

So then, here it was again. More evidence of the possibility she'd managed to avoid until the salt, until this bizarre outburst.

Her dad *was* insane. For-real insane.

And he would spend the rest of his life locked away. Zombified with drugs. And she would live in foster homes until college, and then . . . And then, who knew? Both their lives ruined. For what? This ridiculous, delusional bullshit.

Katie sat in silence considering what had happened to them. Allowing the total disinterest of the universe to enfold her. She and her father were just two of thousands swept aside every day in similar fashion. She—they—were now the "other," the ones locked up in institutions with hospital charts and child-services reports, categorized and registered and footnoted. Something to watch from a great distance. Herself slung into a chair like a broken doll—Dorsey sitting patiently beside her, a million miles away—officially branded into this other world of misfits and losers.

But in that strange silence, that distance from all else—from her dad and Dorsey and the doctors and the Smiling Guy and her friends and the whole world—Katie started considering an even worse possibility.

That her dad was somehow telling the truth.

6

Over her graph, she'd drawn an airplane:

It soared over the looping first and second derivatives, the x-axis many, many miles below. Mr. Ward's lecture and the accompanying assignment were lost to her own rambling thoughts. Chin in hand, barely responsive at all anymore. Living only on instinct.

It'd been three days since she saw her father. Tomorrow he would have his court hearing, where a judge would decide if he was a danger to himself and society or if he was free to go home. And what would *her* vote be? This strange broken man who believed in massive global conspiracies and magical disappearing airplanes.

Disappearing passengers.

Yes, she'd looked into it. Used the school library's computers to get on the Internet and type a few simple words: 911 PASSENGERS 911 PLANES MYSTERY

Yes, she'd read enough of the websites and posts to understand her father was not alone in rejecting the official story. Other people believed something far stranger and more sinister than Osama bin Laden was responsible for that day. The

US government somehow recast in the role of "bad guy," supposedly orchestrating the whole event. Passengers invented as part of some giant deception. Or, even worse, real passengers made to vanish during the cover-up of what "really" happened. Passengers forced off the planes . . .

They killed her. Killed all of them.

Yes, other people were crazy too.

But because of her dad's special brand of that same crazy, she now lived with the Claypools and their ceramic roosters and this one girl named C.J. who was afraid of her own shadow and another named Zoe who just wanted to talk about Wicca and anime all the time. Their breakfasts and dinners over forced small talk, every clatter of a spoon or fork like the clanking of a Victorian factory. Katie didn't even like breakfast. She already hated the smell of lavender. And she especially hated nighttime.

She imagined her dad again. *His* nights. *(I'm not your father.)* Restrained to his bed. Both arms now, probably. A nurse coming in to sponge off his face, pull up the blanket, inject some more medication and kill a couple more brain cells. His room cold and barren. Low light spilling in from the hallway beyond his locked door. *(I'm not your father.)* The faint echo of patrolling security boots stepping closer, moving past. Maybe the faint gibbering of some nearby patient in the dark, alone and—

"Kat . . ."

The muttered sound of her name broke through the fog of thoughts. She looked up toward Gianna's voice, but G was gazing straight ahead, a clear sign their teacher was watching both of them. The next voice was not Gianna's.

"Miss Wallace?"

"Yes?" She hadn't even remotely heard Mr. Ward's question. Worse, she hadn't even finished the first problem on the worksheet. "That was . . ." She pretended to read her work, hoping he'd move on. He didn't. Mr. Ward never did.

"Question three," he prompted. "The points of inflection."

"Oh, yeah." She rescanned the problems, looking for the third, tapping her pencil on imaginary work. "Um, x equals, ahhhh, negative two, one, and, um, three."

Katie looked up victoriously. Knew it was right. Entirely right.

It was nice knowing.

"And why?" Mr. Ward asked, folding his chalk-dusted hands together. Gianna shot her a sideways glance. Smiling.

"It's where the derivative changes sign," Katie replied.

"Points of inflection"—Mr. Ward nodded and turned his attention back to the rest of the class—"are located at values of x where the second derivative changes sign. Good. Thank you, Miss Wallace. Now, Mr. Bugada, for what values of x is the graph . . ." Katie tuned out the rest of his question and answer. She was likely safe again until next class.

They killed her. Killed all of them.

Who, exactly, were these "killers" her dad was talking about? He clearly hadn't meant the terrorists. This TERNGO company, maybe? She'd checked them out online and they were just another boring corporation. And the Gary Fuenmayor guy whom Paul Cobb had mentioned. Nothing special, just a business guy. So, then, who else to blame? The US government somehow? That was horrible to even think. Why would they?

She didn't care what people online were saying. The Internet was chock-full of idiots and liars. Anyone could post anything, and an event as enormous as 9/11 was sure to draw a ton of stupid comments and opinions. Sure to draw a ton of weirdos.

Weirdos like my dad.

"Hey," Gianna whispered beside her. "You okay?"

Katie looked at her friend.

Gianna had first appeared at the start of last year, a job transfer forcing her family down from New Jersey into western Maryland. They'd become friends almost immediately. Gianna had declared, "You're not full of shit, Wallace," believing Katie was someone who stood beyond, or even above, The Games. Katie had just smiled, not even sure she'd know how to play such games if she wanted to. But that the exact same could be said of Gianna was probably the biggest draw for Katie, too. No secrets with G, you knew exactly what she was thinking at any given moment. A capacity that, combined with borderline-Kardashian looks and her acknowledged ambition to be valedictorian, had made her some quick enemies but mostly propelled her to the top echelons of the Clara Barton food chain. Eighteen months and four hundred complaints about the local pizza options and "pussy Maryland boys" later, she remained the most honest person Katie knew.

And yet . . . In return, all she'd given her best friend was a week of lies. Even in response to the simplest of Gianna's questions. Was she "okay"? Come to think of it: Katie didn't think she was.

"Yup." Katie turned back to her desk, started quickly filling in the rest of the answers. Knowing that Mr. Ward frowned on doodles and clutter, she turned her pencil and erased the drawing.

It took four or five gentle strokes. Then it was gone.

As if it'd never been there at all.

Almost.

The court-appointed attorney was a guy named Schottelkotte.

The first time Katie met him was right outside the courtroom a half hour before the hearing. From movies and TV, she'd expected a harried dipshit six months out of law school with an armful of folders representing his hundred other cases, several spilling from his arms as he stumbled down the hall toward them. Schottelkotte was not that. He looked maybe fifty, and polished. Whatever folders he had were carried in a single briefcase.

He shook Katie's hand first, then Dorsey's. "We're on at two," he said, checking his watch. "So I wanted to—"

"What's your plan?" Katie asked.

"Excuse me?" He indicated they should follow him down the hall, where they could talk more privately. "My 'plan'?"

"Yes, sir," Katie pressed, matching his steps. Mrs. Claypool had bought her a new dress (her only dress) for the court hearing, and while she'd felt awkward putting the thing on, she was glad now that she had. She felt formal and serious walking down that hall. Suitably outfitted for court. "Your plan to get him out?"

He put his case down on an empty bench. "We're going to file for voluntary admission. That means—"

"That he's locked up 'voluntarily,'" Katie interrupted again. She'd spent almost an hour online researching these cases as best she could. "And can leave when he chooses."

Schottelkotte looked at Dorsey, smiled politely, and then looked back at Katie. "Precisely," he said.

"But if the doctors—"

"*If* the doctors successfully prove your father is an immediate danger to himself or others, then the judge can rule an *involuntary* admission and he's potentially looking at another thirty days minimum. There's a third-degree assault charge to consider. And also the, ah, threats."

"All those charges were dropped," Katie said.

"The *criminal* charges, yes," the lawyer confirmed. "But they're still part of his case history for a mental-health investigation. The doctors will certainly mention it. Then there's the stunt with the ice and salt."

"It wasn't a 'stunt.' He was trying to counteract all the drugs they'd put him on."

"Yes, well . . . Not sure how sensible all that's going to sound."

Katie's heart thumped a little hard in her chest. She straightened her shoulders. "Isn't that for the judge to decide?"

"Yes, it is," he nodded. "But combined with your father's other behavior and the threats to Vice President Cheney, it *is* problematic. It's best we simply leave out the 'I was drugged' angle *and* all the conspiracy business. It doesn't help."

Katie half scowled at a group passing by, concerned they'd slow their pace enough to hear what he said next. But they kept walking to or from their own scandal.

"What 'conspiracy business'?" she asked. What, if anything, had her dad said to them? What had he been saying about 9/11? About her?

"Paranoia is likely going to be brought up. So, the less focus on, um, personal historical views, the better we are." The court-appointed attorney sighed heavily, regrouped. "Look, Miss Wallace—Kate, it's a routine hearing. They give their report, we make our counterargument. Prove your dad's been a pretty good guy the last twenty years, all and all. I've got an affidavit from his employer saying he's been a model employee until this one incident. And Veterans Affairs sent along the info on him being a war hero, et cetera, et cetera."

Katie blinked at him. "War hero?"

"Absolutely. In the Army. Got a whole bunch of medals, in fact."

"My dad?" Impossible. This guy trimmed bushes and fixed swing sets for a living. Spent hours watching *Bar Rescue* reruns and game shows about tattooing people.

Katie waited as the man retrieved a folder from his bag and deftly opened it. "Distinguished Service Cross, two Bronze Stars for Valor, Kosovo Campaign Medal, Valorous Unit Award."

She didn't know what a Bronze Star for Valor was, but it sure sounded good. And her dad had *two* of them.

He kept reading: "Purple Heart, Southwest Asia Service Medal, Armed Forces Expeditionary Medal."

"And you'll bring that up at the hearing."

"First chance I get. We'll hear them out, get a feel for the judge and so on, okay? This is not my first rodeo. You're just going to have to trust the system, and we'll get him home as quickly as possible."

"It's going to be fine, Katie," Ms. Dorsey added beside her.

"Fifteen minutes to showtime," the lawyer said. "Okay if I drive for a bit here?"

"Yes, sorry. Go ahead." Katie eased off, crossed her arms in thought. When had her dad gotten those medals? How?

"The judge may want to ask you some questions. She may not. If she does, yes and no answers only, when possible. When not, try to keep your answers simple. No need to ramble on. Understand?"

"Yes, sir."

"If I object or interrupt you, you stop talking. Okay? If I do, it's not because you did anything wrong. It's because I don't like something they did. Don't look so worried. You'll be fine."

"I'm not worried," Katie said. Not about herself, no. Maybe some about the guy who got excited for some reason whenever he saw a blue jay or cardinal. The one who always made a point to crouch down and pet a passing dog. Maybe about the guy who laughed at *South Park* until tears ran down his face. The guy who looked truly relaxed only when he slept, his face loosening its hold on all those lines and ridges and sliding into some place beyond imagined shouts . . . or whispers.

About *him*, maybe she was worried. Maybe a lot.

"Last thing," Schottelkotte said. "And the most important." He fixed her with a stare. "No matter what the judge may ask, you tell the truth."

"Sure."

"I mean it. Don't try to answer what you think she wants to hear. The truth is simpler, required by law, and almost always comes out in the end anyway."

Is it really? she wondered. *Does it really?*

"How'd it go?" the man asked.

"Ninety days. There'll be another hearing then."

"Then we've got our cutoff date."

"How's it coming?"

"Nothing yet. Hell, we may know even less than when we started."

"He'll talk."

"Maybe."

"They always do, sir."

"Maybe. He's not a 'they.' He's an 'us.'"

"Well, worst case, if the ninety days isn't enough, another year or two can be easily arranged to deal with all that magnificent training."

"What we're seeking will appear on the Internet long before then. He'll have time triggers going off soon. A week, month, ninety days. He'll have made those preparations."

"You think?"

"He's an 'us.' And a man like that doesn't live in peace for all these years unless he takes the necessary precautions. Any day now, some preset trigger will activate and information *will* be leaked to some website, some reporter. Only a taste. Enough to scare us. Probably won't even make sense to anyone but us. Like the routine with his daughter the other day at the hospital. He knew we were listening."

"Yes, sir. Well, he didn't have too much to say this morning. He tried to make a statement but couldn't get four words out with all the crap we got him on."

"How'd she take it?"

"The girl?" The second guy shrugged. "How do you think?"

"Yeah."

"Don't worry about her, sir. She's barely seventeen. Too worried about foster care or some looming zit on her chin to cause any trouble for us."

"Maybe."

"You think we might need to watch her too?"

The first man said, "We already are."

7

Katie drifted through her empty house like any other ghost.

Alone. Kinda lost. Only partially aware of what she was doing as she slowly passed from this room to that on sluggish reflex and fading memory.

It had been barely one week since she'd come to collect Winter to bring the cat to Gianna's, but that week was enough. The air inside the house was already motionless and thick, the silence muffled like, she imagined, the sound in crypts. One week. She already felt like a trespasser.

To reinforce this, Gloria Dorsey waited outside. Giving Katie some space, but not exactly free rein over her own home either. This wasn't a casual stopover. Far from it. This was "custody-of-belongings" protocol. Procedure. This was a line item somewhere in Dorsey's fancy leather daily planner. An hour, maybe, for this poor pathetic girl to collect the rest of her shit for the long haul in foster care.

Ninety days. Three more months. With the roosters and breakfasts and stares and the two weird girls who were nice and all, but *THREE MORE MONTHS*. School would be over and it'd be well into summer before she'd be done with the Claypools. Out of Dorsey's planner. And that was the *best-*case scenario. Worst case, the next hearing would turn out similar to the first. Her dad drugged out of his skull, drooling all over himself in front of the judge, babbling incoherently, heartbreakingly pathetic.

And, if what Schottelkotte had said was true, those three months could be extended another six months. Or even two years! Years. She couldn't bring herself to imagine what two-years-from-now would look like. Where she would live. If she'd even be in college. If everything.

Katie realized she'd wandered into her dad's bedroom, and her thoughts refocused. She couldn't remember the last time she'd stepped inside. This was *his* space. He never went snooping through her room, so why should she intrude on his privacy?

And yet, here she was. Possibly not as much on autopilot as she'd first thought. Maybe there was something here. Something to . . . explain.

This man she hardly knew at all, who'd been more or less a mystery her whole life, was now somehow, suddenly, even *more* of a mystery. Who had she really been living with all this time?

When she was old enough to first notice the drinking and pot stuff, she'd blamed herself. If only she scored more goals when he came to games, or got more As at school, or needed less attention at home. If only she could unlock the secret right words to say at dinner or find the perfect time to stay absolutely quiet. If only she'd been a better baby and her mom had stayed and . . . But the more soccer goals and As she collected, the more she took over caring for herself, always moving around him on pins and needles, the more unhappy he seemed to become. Every year, somehow sadder than the last.

In junior high, she'd started to understand he was "broken" somehow. Maybe it went back to her mother, her leaving them.

Katie couldn't say. But she finally realized his sadness would never go away and had nothing to do with her. Which meant she could not fix it, fix *him*. Only help keep him as stable as possible. That, at least, she could do.

Or so she'd thought.

His room was sparse and tidy. Bed, a single dresser, a lawn chair in the corner with some folded shirts and pants for work. A paperback on the carpet beside the bed. One of his *Star Trek* novels.

On the dresser, there was a lone framed picture. One she knew well.

The two of them together. An older photo. Dull colors. Taken on one of those Polaroid insta-things at some park event a good ten years before. Katie up on the gray pony, her dad standing stiffly beside her. She had no real memory of the day beyond the picture. Based on their smiles, especially his, she'd always told herself it must have been a good day. (There had been some.) Katie picked up the frame and studied the photograph more closely.

Herself as a child. Freckled and ponytailed. Purple dress. Smiling so big at the camera that her eyes were squinted almost totally closed. Her dad in brown plaid, rigid like one of those guys in Civil War photographs. Hair buzzed tightly as usual, but still sporting that straw-colored goatee he'd once had. His angular face even more razor-sharp in his youth, his narrow eyes even more dark and piercing.

Katie studied these two people again.

Her face ghosted the frame's glass. All those freckles had faded, but her face was still rounded like the little girl's. Short plump nose, not pointed. (Not like his.) Her eyes still big when not squinting in a smile. Big and brown. (While his eyes . . .)

Her hair thick and straight, pulled back in the same ponytail from ten years before. Revealing the higher cheekbones, the small cleft in her chin.

She looked nothing like him.

It wasn't something she'd given any thought to ever before. But now, literally staring her in the face, there it was. She had none of her father's facial features. Not a single one. In fact, the more she looked at the photograph, the more it looked like two strangers standing next to each other. Like he was simply the guy hired to hold the pony still.

I'm not your father.

There were lots of kids who didn't look like their parents. Sophie Padgett was the prettiest girl in the whole school and her parents both looked like trolls. Jay Brotnitsky was their All State linebacker and a foot taller and fifty pounds heavier than both his parents combined.

I'm not your father.

She'd never seen a picture of her mom. Never even asked to, either. Before he'd dropped all this 9/11 business on her, she'd been told only that the woman had "taken off" one day, said family wasn't "what she wanted," and that was that. Katie didn't care one bit what the bitch looked like.

But now . . .

I'm not your father.

"Katie."

She spun around.

Gloria Dorsey stood behind her in the hallway. "Is everything fine?"

Katie shuddered, closed her eyes to gather herself. "Yeah," she said. "I'm just . . . yeah."

"Sorry to startle you. We should probably get going."

"Yeah, okay." Katie wondered what the next pressing line item in Dorsey's fancy leather planner was. "I'm done."

"May I?" Dorsey indicated the photo.

Katie looked at it again, thought of dropping it on the floor. She handed Dorsey the frame.

"Ohhhh. That's a nice one," Dorsey said, and then did that smile thing.

Katie squeezed past her down the hallway. In the living room, she grabbed hold of the two gym bags she'd filled with her stuff. There was also a small cardboard box.

"I'll get it," Dorsey said, following her into the room. Dorsey placed the framed picture inside and lifted the box.

Katie almost put down her bags to take it back out. Again, she let it go.

"Anything else?" Dorsey asked.

Katie surveyed the house. Mentally going through every room. Looking past Dorsey into the kitchen, Katie again pondered the bowl of cat food on the counter. She'd found it on the floor a week ago when she and Dorsey swung by to pick up Winter. Hadn't given it any real thought then, just picked the damn thing up and went on with her life. Now, more curious. Had she put food out for Winter in all the commotion the night they'd come for her? And totally forgotten? Katie blinked the questions away, turned to leave. "Let's just go."

She desperately wanted such questions, all questions, to stay behind in the house when she left. There, they could wander the empty hallways. Alone. Dead. Lost. No longer weighing down her every thought, plaguing her days at school and running into single-digit times each night as she lay awake in bed. She didn't need to understand the past so much as, well, get on with her own future. Start over.

And so all that other stuff—all that shit that came after, with her dad and 9/11 and Max—it likely never would've happened.

Except for Mrs. Lindhorst.

Mrs. Lindhorst was one of the neighbors.

One of those standing courtside the night the police and everybody came. Katie couldn't forget that face. That totally-engrossed, offended, giant Lindhorst face. Watching the night's events unfold with the same fascination as she probably felt watching some actress she didn't care for finally get voted off *Dancing with the Stars*.

This woman lived two doors down. Had three yippy dogs and a husband who pulled out their dandelions one at a time to spend as much time working on the yard as possible. (Hint, hint.) She was one of those generic adults somewhere between forty and seventy and built like an oversized pear. Katie's dad always called her a Weeble, but Katie had no idea what that was.

In any case, the Weeble was coming this way.

Suddenly, Katie's lone goal was to make it to the car. Quickly as possible. Get the bags loaded and get the hell out. Now. Excruciating pleasantries with a nosy neighbor were definitely not on the program. She wedged one of the bags between her hip and the car to open the door. Locked! Trapped, a meager foot from sanctuary. Willing Dorsey to walk faster. To get in the goddddddamnnnnn car!

"Hello. Hello?" The woman's voice demanding attention behind her, no doubt the same voice she used when seeking assistance in Macy's.

Katie finally heard the doors unlock. She fought to open the backseat and toss everything in as quickly as possible.

Not quickly enough.

"Everything okay?" Lindhorst's voice close behind. Breathing hard. Really pushed it, apparently, to cover the distance between them. If only Dorsey had been as nimble. "I wanted to see how your father was doing. No one seems to know."

Katie loaded the second bag. "Fine, thank you."

"Is he?"

"Yes."

Dorsey finally arrived. "Hello," she said. "All set?"

Katie nodded and opened the front seat to get in. She could feel the sweat collecting between her shoulder blades.

"I'm Scott and Katie's neighbor," Mrs. Lindhorst explained to Dorsey. "We live right there. And you are?"

"A friend of the family," Dorsey replied.

"Is she staying with you, then?" Mrs. Lindhorst asked. "Where *are* you staying, honey?"

"It was nice to meet you." Dorsey *finally* recognized the situation, urging a quick end as she loaded her box and got in the car. "We'd better get going, Katie."

"Thanks, Mrs. Lindhorst," Katie managed robotically. "I'll let my dad know you—"

"So, so sad."

Katie froze, half sitting, holding the top of the car door. "What's that?"

"It's very sad, is all. Very—well, I'm sure it's all for the best."

Katie stood again. "How do you mean?"

"Katie?" Dorsey's voice from inside the car.

Mrs. Lindhorst hesitated, smiled. "Well, your father and all."

"Yes?"

"He's just . . . We always knew something like this would happen."

"Something like what?" *We?*

"Oh, I only meant, your father, he's . . . Oh, honey, everyone's a little whackadoo in their own way, I suppose. We're happy he's getting the help he needs, is all."

Whackadoo? But that wasn't the word that had really stung.

"We?" Katie pressed. She was afraid to check but felt as if her one hand had unconsciously drawn into a fist. "Please let 'we' know my dad has two Bronze Stars for Valor, and a Distinguished Service Cross. Oh, and a Purple Heart. Which is a hell of a lot more than anything 'we' has probably done."

Mrs. Lindhorst narrowed her eyes.

"And he earned it putting his life on the line while he served our country. So, I'm not really sure what you—"

"Happy to hear you're now both doing so well." Mrs. Lindhorst turned as if to leave, smiled a little too brightly. A smile Katie wanted to rip off her stupid Weeble—whatever that was—face.

"Katie." Dorsey's voice again, more urgent.

Katie found she'd taken a step after the woman, and then stopped. Heart pounding. Her entire body filled with shame. And outrage.

And Grade-A hate.

She turned to Dorsey, who waved her back into the car.

Katie got in slowly.

"You all right?" Dorsey asked.

"Fantastic."

They drove past Mrs. Lindhorst on the way down the street. Katie glared out her window, psychically daring the old bat to look her way. She didn't.

Dorsey drove quietly for a while. Maybe she talked, Katie didn't know. Her head was too full of all the things she could/should/would have said. If she ever saw that despicable woman again, she would—

"—almost there, Katie. You need anything?" Dorsey's voice finally registered. Something she'd just said that was useful.

"Yeah," Katie said. "A fucking lawyer."

8

Katie handed the folder across the desk to Marilyn Wren,
and the attorney smiled politely (they always did at first) as she
opened it to scan the documents within.

While the woman read, Katie checked out her office: the
chrome and black-leather chairs and avant-garde paintings, the
fish tank/bar thingy, floor-to-ceiling windows overlooking the
entire Inner Harbor from thirty-some stories above. It was,
Katie decided, the chicest room she'd ever been in. More the
pity that Wren would kick her out in about three minutes.

Dorsey hadn't been any help finding a new lawyer. *Au
contraire*, she'd gone out of her way to convince Katie it was an
unwarranted, and unrealistic, idea.

And, based on the past week, Dorsey was probably 100
percent right.

"First thing you'll need to do is contact the circuit court."
The attorney flipped through a couple more pages. "Pick up
what's called a 'petition for emancipation' affidavit. That's a
basic description . . ." She flipped back a page, her burgundy-
colored lips scrunched in thought.

Katie sat forward, preparing for the next part. She didn't
know much about high fashion but suspected Wren's suit, no less
chic than her office, had cost a month's rent. Not a woman who
would appreciate being deceived, her time (i.e., money) wasted.

"But you're not really here for emancipation from your father, are you?" Marilyn Wren said at last.

"No," Katie admitted.

"You're here to get him out of Ventworth. Why did—"

"Most lawyers hung up on me in less than thirty seconds. When I changed my story to wanting to file for emancipation, I sometimes got a whole minute. Four even agreed to actually meet me. You're number four."

"Nice. How'd those other three meetings go?"

Katie shrugged.

"Got it. And your court-appointed attorney? Mr. . . ." She searched. "Schottelkotte. What happened to him?"

"Oh, he's gone. I fired him, acting as an advocate for my dad."

Wren laughed. "Not sure a minor can be an official advocate. That requires a guardianship order, or an advance directive that—"

"Then help get me emancipated and we'll get all that stuff and *then* I'll fire him. My father—"

"Ms. Wallace . . ."

"My father needs a new lawyer. One who can appeal the first ruling, or at least conduct a more complete defense at the second hearing in sixty-three days. I was thinking maybe even a lawsuit that—"

She stopped talking. Wren was shaking her head and had closed the folder.

And that's that, Katie thought. Exactly where two of the other lawyers she'd managed to meet had also quickly, albeit politely, shooed her away. Maybe it was the deception that pissed them off. Katie half stood, ready for a quick, chic dismissal.

Instead, Wren said: "Tell me about the first hearing."

She sat back down. "What do you mean?"

Wren got up from behind her desk and came around to join Katie, repositioning the chair beside her. Katie watched her fixedly—always extra drawn to the strong women she met in real life, much as she was fascinated by those she saw on TV. And she didn't need Dr. Freud, or Dr. Phil, to explain why: surrogate role models for her own piece-of-shit mother.

The lawyer was super tall, even more so standing above her like this, maybe fifty, and basically model pretty with an explosion of silvery-blond Go-To-Hell hair atop her head. "I mean," Wren said, sitting, with the folder still in her hands, "what happened, exactly? You were there?"

Katie perked up, sat taller. None of the other lawyers had asked about that day, not even the cheeseball who'd let her keep talking after discovering what she'd really come for. "Yeah, I was there," she said. "It was mostly the doctor talking. The judge only asked him a few questions. Then Schottelkotte talked about my dad's military service and how he had letters from my dad's work. Character witness stuff. It's all in that file. I asked him for the copies."

"Were you called as a character witness?"

"No. No one ever asked me anything. You'd think the judge would want to know if I thought my dad was a threat to himself or me or—or whatever. But she didn't even ask. I sat in the back. The whole hearing took, like, ten minutes."

"What about your dad? Did he give a statement?"

Katie suppressed a snort. "Please. My dad . . ." The image came back again, too strong to disregard. Her dad listing to the side. Slobbering like a beast. Awful. "My dad was a total zombie," she said. "They had him on all these hospital meds again. Couldn't get two words out. But I think if he'd had that chance,

I mean if he could just talk to the judge . . . See, I found this case online, *Fraley v. the Estate of Oberholtzer*, and I thought—"

Wren leaned closer, seemingly genuinely interested. "*Fraley, Oberholtzer*. What's that?"

"Involuntary-admission case in Ohio. This old lady, Mona Fraley, was involuntarily committed for being a danger to herself. So some inheritance thing got put in a trust controlled by her six nephews because they all said she was crazy and the doctors agreed. But all she had to do was prove in court that she wasn't crazy. Despite this big funny-looking hat she wore all the time or the fact she slept in the bathtub and sometimes carried this antique Prussian sword around."

"Interesting. How'd she convince them that wasn't crazy?"

"She explained to the judge how the big hat kept her head warm because she saved money by keeping her heat down and had read that, like, 80 percent of your body's heat escapes through the top of your head. And she slept in the bathtub because she lived in a rough neighborhood and was afraid some stray drive-by bullet might get her when she was sleeping."

"And the sword, I imagine, was also for security."

"Exactly. Protection after her husband had died. She was afraid of guns. The judge ruled Mrs. Fraley competent and set her free that same day because she was able to explain her 'crazy.'"

The lawyer smiled, impressed. "You believe your dad's competent?"

"I think he can *explain his crazy*," Katie said carefully. "That it's possible that he can . . . well, *justify* his views, prove they're not completely outlandish. Mrs. Fraley's lawyers didn't have to prove 80 percent of your body heat escapes through your head—"

"Because it doesn't. That's a myth."

"Exactly. They just had to show it's a myth many sane people believe."

"I've got to be honest, Katie. This is not something I'd—"

"Also," Katie blurted, using her last card: The Money Card. "I was also thinking a lawsuit of some kind. A big one. A civil case beyond the psychiatric stuff. Maybe an emotional-distress lawsuit against his former employer for PTSD. He used to work for this big international corporation, TERNGO Global Security and Risk Management. We could sue them for lots of money. Like, a class-action thing. Or, I read about these lawsuits called, ah, Bivens actions, where you can sue agents of the federal government. You know?"

"For violations of constitutional rights," Wren replied. "This case involves the federal government? How, exactly?"

Katie shivered inside. Unable to say the words. But if she couldn't say them here, now—how in God's name would they sound in a courtroom? "I'd prefer not to say yet," she said.

"Are you doing this for the money, then?"

"Oh, no. Not at all. You can take 100 percent of any settlement."

Wren waved the idea away, literally, with a hand. "Thank you, but 40 percent is the most allowable, and don't trust any lawyer who asks for more than thirty. In any case, lawsuits against the federal government can go on for years. Decades. And they're rare to win."

But we don't need to win, Katie shrieked inside. They only needed enough proof to show her father wasn't completely insane. "I understand," she said aloud. "And one thing you also need to know . . ."

And now to where the third and final lawyer had sent her away. The one who'd sat there with such a dumb smirk on his face, finding her oh-so-amusing, until she'd gotten to this: "Aside from a settlement, the case would need to be, well, pro bono."

Katie'd just asked Wren to work for free. She'd learned that all lawyers were encouraged to provide hours of charitable service to their community, a little help every so often for a couple poor wretched souls. As good a description of her and her father as she could think of.

Wren stared back silently.

"So," Katie said. "I guess, would that—"

"How many lawyers did you call before me?"

Katie looked for a gracious answer.

"Found a list online, right?" the lawyer asked, lifting her perfect brows. "*A* to *W*. How long before Dan Zapanta gets a call?"

"He's, um, not taking on new clients."

Wren smiled again.

"Do you think that . . . ," Katie started, hopefully. Pitifully. After Wren, that was it. She'd have to start at the top of the list and try again. Or give up. "What else can I do?" she murmured. The question more for herself than Wren.

"For starters," Wren said, "you can tell me about 9/11."

Katie blinked at the tall, pretty, crazy-haired attorney.

She'd planned to avoid the specifics—all that 9/11 conspiracy stuff—for as long as she could. Another few years would have been nice. Now, for sure, her time with Wren was over. No words came. Katie stared past Wren at the harbor's dark waters below.

"It's in the file, Katie," Wren said. "I can read."

Katie cleared her throat. Gathering the right words. Words she'd run through her head a thousand times but not dared utter out loud to anyone yet.

"The medical report claims," Wren prompted, "he's suffering from schizoaffective disorder and persecutory delusions. How so?"

"Well," Katie started, "my dad believes there's more to 9/11 than we've all been told."

"Many people believe that."

Katie felt her heart lift some. Other than anonymous weirdos on the Internet, she'd never before heard a single adult admit this. She kept going. Cautiously. "Specifically, he believes the attacks were carried out by people other than the terrorists. *American* people, I mean. The actual government, even. And he was involved somehow."

"He, your father, was involved?"

I'm not your father.

"Yeah. That's what he says. Anyhow, he, ah, worked for this TERNGO company then. On, you know, that day. And . . ." She trailed off, looking out the window again, but Wren didn't let her off the hook.

"And?"

"And, I think, I mean, he says maybe he saw something. Something he shouldn't have." Her hands were clenched in her lap, forming tight fists. "Maybe even *done* something."

"What, Katie?" Wren's words a little more distant-sounding. "What did he see? What did he do?"

"He, um, claims passengers were taken from the planes. The planes that supposedly crashed on 9/11, I mean. He says they actually landed safely in Cleveland. And then, as part of some big conspiracy, that he was there and . . ."

Katie stopped. There was no more she could say. Even saying this much to someone sounded absurd. How could she possibly begin to explain what he'd claimed about her mother?

Or about her.

Wren gathered a huge breath: her turn to look out her own window at the harbor.

Just go, Katie told herself. *Walk out with your tail between your legs. Let him do his time. Let him get the help he needs. You'll be fine. You'll figure out college or a job or something. You'll . . . You'll just never know the truth.*

Never 100 percent know if he was insane. And never 100 percent know what had happened to her. Her mom. Her "real" father . . . *How bad is that? Isn't 90 percent truth good enough? Just go!*

Wren turned back. "That's an extreme allegation," she said. "Far beyond the norm."

"I know."

"And do you believe him?"

No, she didn't.

"Does it really matter what I think?" Katie replied.

"It matters to me," Wren said. "Very much."

"I—find it hard to believe his claims are true. But we don't need to prove that they're true, just that they're . . . reasonable."

"Well, that's where this gets a lot trickier than the Fraley case. Your dad doesn't just think there was a 9/11 cover-up; he thinks he *participated* in that cover-up. You're not dealing with common myths that plenty of functional people buy into. You're dealing with a story no judge is going to consider sane at face value. Unless you can back it up somehow. So that's why I'm asking what *you* really think."

Katie reflected before responding. "I know something bad happened that day," she said eventually, her words slow and careful. Like they might break if she spoke too loud or too quickly. "We all know that. And maybe only a few people on Earth know exactly how bad. Maybe my dad is one of them. If he is . . . if he is, and that's, you know, really, it." She tried to make her answer sound intelligent, rational, but only gibberish filled her mouth; words that didn't dare address the woman's specific question. "Then maybe with a lawsuit, if he can call real witnesses, get some government people under oath, and prove, somehow prove, that he was ordered to do something terrible that day . . . it might help get him out of that place." Katie stopped herself, swallowed hard. "You think it's ridiculous, huh?"

"I think you're flailing some."

"I guess so."

"Look, Katie, I respect the work you've obviously done on this. You're going to be a hell of a lawyer yourself someday if you want."

Katie knew then the conversation was over. Wren had started the polite wrap-up. Katie felt her whole body deflating, imagined the smallest breeze from the AC carrying her off the chair and back down the hallway. To get this close. To finally get someone who'd listen to her and—and nothing. She'd blown it.

"You're not going to take the case, are you?"

"No." Wren pointed a well-polished fingernail. "But I'm going to make you a deal."

The monitor on the left wall filled with the list.

A list of web searches ran the full length of the screen, the letters enormous, the typos glaring. Mostly search terms related to 9/11, the planes, passenger manifests. Expected. The man scanned the rest, very relieved to not find certain words.

The kind of words that could do a lot of damage. They weren't there. Yet.

But, now, these last half dozen or so:

bivens actions
consitutional tort law
federal tort claims act
ssuing the government for negligence
freedom of information act
how to nake a FOIA request
beverly eckert lawsuits
september 11th litigation cases

"Looks like Wren gave our girl some homework."

"Looks like," agreed the agent who'd uploaded the list.

"This from the house?"

"Yes, sir."

"Who is Beverly Eckert?"

"A 9/11 widow. Activist. Thought too much was being swept under the carpet and so refused any settlements. That way she could retain the right to sue the airlines, the FAA, the World Trade Center, et cetera."

"As suing equals subpoenas and testimony under oath. Fantastic. Just what we need our girl looking into." The first man returned his attention to one of the monitors on his right, reading about the lawyer again. "Is Wren really taking this case?"

"She's evidently a fan of controversial trials. High-profile stuff. Likes to get her face on TV. Good-lookin' babe like that has—"

"But there've been no further calls or e-mails between the two?"

The agent rechecked his own tablet. "No, sir. Only the two outings to Thurgood Marshall."

"Yeah." The man scratched his cheek in thought. Thurgood Marshall was the library at the University of Maryland law school. Wren was an adjunct professor there, taught one course a year. The girl had already visited the library twice for several hours. Doing what exactly, he could only assume. Not a word he much cared for. "No sign of Wren?"

"Don't know. We didn't go in."

"Okay. We'll probably have to do something about that." He scrolled through some more info, the data changing on the screens. "I've got an idea."

"And how is Daddy doing?" the agent asked with a bit too much amusement in his voice. He'd been staring at another screen altogether. "Has he cracked any more yet or—"

The first man cut him off. "Anything else?"

"No, sir."

"Thank you," he said curtly and watched the agent's quick retreat from the room.

He closed the list of web searches and dragged the file into his folder on the daughter. "Katie, Katie, Kaitlyn . . . ," he muttered to himself. Glanced at the screen the agent had been caught looking at: the live video feed of Scott Wallace and the two men skillfully questioning him. "How much has Papa Bear told you?"

He sought the half-eaten packet of gum on his desk. Watched the video a moment more as he pulled a stick free, folded it into his mouth, and then got back to work.

9

Turns out a law library is just like every other library but with more law books. Major letdown. Katie had imagined something dark and gothic like when Morgan Freeman goes to the library in *Se7en*. Something definitely more interesting, less generic than the reality.

This visit, she'd claimed one of the empty workstations closest to the computers. Easier to get up and search for archived e-articles or whatever next book she might need. An endless process, really. Like that Sisyphus guy pushing his rock in the Greek myths. Every time she thought she had some law or case figured out, there was always another judicial ruling, another legal definition, another law review article to decipher. Statutes, court reports! Bivens actions led to articles on constitutional torts, torts led to "sovereign immunity," which led to "punitive damage," and punitive damage led to absolute and qualified immunity, to *Harlow v. Fitzgerald*, 457 U.S. 800 (1982), which led to *Pierson v. Ray*, 386 U.S. 547, 554 (1967) and *ordre public* and "petitioner's claims" and the same sort of twisting path of documentation, with infinite variations. Every time!

So, while it had *seemed* like Wren was being super cool at first—she'd even given Katie the name of the head librarian and called ahead so she could get a guest account and access to books and databases only available to Maryland University law students—maybe Wren was basically messing with her. Because, while the lawyer's proposition had been straightforward and simple and fair, it was also proving effing impossible.

Katie had only six weeks to present her case to Wren. Wren: judge, jury, and likely hangman. Katie would only get one chance. One meeting. No running back to Wren's office with insufficient evidence, getting shot down, and then asking for second or third chances. She had to go in with the whole show. Lay out the case from beginning to end. And if she could somehow convince Wren there was *any* plausibility to her dad's claims—and, really, what were the chances of that?—the lawyer had promised to take the case.

Before any of that, Katie would have to sort through all the timetables and claims and news and government reports, and the legalities of who her father might call as a witness and how he could do it. She'd have to submit Freedom of Information Act requests. Track down old coworkers, get someone other than her dad on record. Somehow substantiate as much of her father's story as she could. All by herself.

Katie sat back, disgusted. The 9/11 stuff aside, did Wren really expect her to become a legal expert in six weeks? Was that even possible? For anyone? It took *years* for college graduates to become lawyers.

Was it Wren's intention, from minute one, that she'd grow confused and frustrated? Unable to navigate all the legal shit and eventually give up? Wren gets the weird girl out of her office, even looks magnanimous doing it, and yet never hears from weird girl again. Win-win-win. Not a bad plan. A dozen times already, a hundred, Katie'd thought of packing it up.

Yet here she was in this library for the fourth time in a week. Surrounded by several piles of enormous books she'd collected from the reserves and off various shelves. Sample Freedom of Information Act request letters beside her own drafts. Printouts of law review articles that seemed almost readable. Almost. Fighting through all the new words and arguments. Excited when an entire sentence or especially two in a row made sense. Because maybe, just maybe, Wren wasn't brushing her off. Maybe Wren was genuinely testing her, seeing if Katie was someone worth helping. Worth fighting for.

And are you? Katie wondered, dropping her head into both hands for a minute. *Is he?* She closed her eyes, beckoned the library's silence and new blackness to enwrap her.

"'Truly songs and tales fall utterly short of the reality . . .'"

Katie opened her eyes, looked up.

It was a guy.

She'd gotten a couple curious looks from some of the other students, the guys mostly, and one legit nod and "hey" standing at the printer, but no one had started a true conversation yet. This one seemed younger than the others, an undergrad for sure. The hopeful, half-finished beard and mustache on his boyish face weren't helping hide that much. Lightweight blue hoodie, hipster black T-shirt, jeans, book bag over one shoulder like most of them. Wavy, messy hair. Impish Peter Pan look.

"Excuse me?" she asked.

"Smaug, the Chiefest and Greatest of Calamities."

Katie turned to confirm he wasn't speaking to someone behind her. She found only the walls of her workstation. She looked back. "I'm sorry. I'm not—"

"The dragon," he explained. "Smaug. Sitting on his piles of treasure, the gold. And you're . . . The books, you know? *The Hobbit.*"

"I honestly have no idea what you're talking about. I haven't seen *The Hobbit*." She stared up at him, confused, and then something shifted inside her, fear and panic warring together to freeze her solid.

The dragon may come for you.

What her dad forewarned in the hospital. Was this guy a messenger of some kind? A threat? There was no way this was a coincidence. This guy was working with her dad or an enemy of her dad's, or . . . he was trying to tell her something. But what to say?

Her voice shook as she spoke. "What do you know about the dragon? Are you . . ." She could imagine the expression on her face. Waiting for his response. Waiting for him to reveal everything. Whatever "everything" was.

"What? No, no. I mean the piles of books. It was a stupid joke, I'm sorry. I need . . ." He shook his head.

Katie let herself breathe again. Laughed. Relieved. So stupid. Freaking out because some guy says the word *dragon*.

"Hi, okay," he continued. "That's just, wow, I'm always doing—Let me try again." He took a deep breath too, smiled. "I'm Max Thompson. I'm a student here, and I'm terribly sorry to bother you. But if you don't mind, I'd like to please borrow a few of your books for a bit. Hour, tops." He was blushing. It would have been amusing if she wasn't so shaken up. He tapped one of the piles. "You've got a bunch of the reference books signed out. There, that probably made a whole lot more sense."

"They said I could have them for six hours," she argued, suddenly annoyed by the intrusion.

"Yeah, I know, and you can. And if you're using them, that's cool, I'll go away faster than positronium hydride. But, I've got this paper due and I promise to sit right over there"—he pointed to another workstation—"grab some quotes, be on my way. *If* you're not currently using them, is all."

"Oh," she said, regretting her reaction. "Sure, of course. Sorry, I guess I have been hogging them all day."

"No 'sorry' necessary. I'm the one infringing, and you're being very sympathetic. I just need to look up a couple—Freedom of Information Act, huh?" He'd diverted attention to the stuff on her desk. "Always fun. I remember this one time I needed—"

"Yeah," she quickly collected the materials as politely as possible. *Some privacy, please.*

"Is this—Sorry." He'd looked away, then back to her. "You pre-law?"

"Um, no. Still in high school, actually. This is for . . . we're doing this mock trial thing. Team-school thing. And I'm . . . I'm doing something for that." Time to change the subject. Go-to solution: get people talking about themselves. "Are you? Pre-law, I mean?"

His mouth scrunched into a half-frown. "Not exactly. Working on my JD."

"What's that?"

He shrugged. "Graduate degree, technically. *Juris doctor.*"

Katie grunted, sorting him out. *Graduate degree?* He looked no older than the guys in her classes at Clara Barton. "Oh. Okay."

"The marvelous beard didn't fool you, huh? It's okay. I'm used to it. From a traditional standpoint, I'm a tad young for grad school."

"I see. How young?" she asked, smiling. Curious. Interested, for the first time in way too long, in something that had nothing to do with her dad.

"Eighteen," he replied. "Well, I'll *be* eighteen in September."

"No shit."

"No shit."

"Wow." She'd knuckled a fist up under her chin, elbow on the desk. "So you—"

"Graduated high school at thirteen. College at sixteen."

"You some kinda genius or something?"

He shrugged again. "That's what they tell me."

Katie watched the genius guy work from across the room.

Max. His nose down in the books he'd borrowed from her (one monstrosity on tort law and another even bigger tome on constitutional law). Flipping through pages like he knew them by heart and then tapping away on his laptop at an absurd speed. Once he'd caught her looking and given her a short wave/salute from over his keyboard. Then it was back on task.

An example she needed to follow, actually. But he'd totally gotten her off track. It hadn't taken much. Simply by existing, he'd managed to make her reevaluate her whole situation. Here was this genius kid in his first or second year of law school and she'd been at it for about a week. People like him were equipped to deal with the stack of books on her desk, all the legal intricacies and expectations. People like Wren and Schottelkotte. Not people like her, some junior in high school with a handful of books she could maybe half read. There was no way.

Unless . . .

So she waited and waited. Pretending to read and take notes herself but really only dawdling till he finished his own work. He'd said an hour, tops. And he proved true to his word, back in less than forty minutes. "Thanks again," he said, stacking the two books on her workstation's shelf. "Really saved my bacon."

"No problem," she smiled, immediately recognizing she'd just used her best flirt smile on a guy whose T-shirt read *MAY THE (m × a) BE WITH YOU.*

"Okay." He shifted his book bag to the other arm, deciding his next words. "Well, see ya. Good luck with everything." He patted the side of the workstation and spun to leave.

Katie watched him go for a few steps and then called out. "So what's your paper on?" Had to give it a try . . .

He turned back. "What's that?"

"Your paper due tomorrow. What's it about?"

He'd walked back toward her slowly, almost cautiously. "Oh, well, it's on digital media law. Defining liability for likeness of celebrity avatars. Arguments of misappropriation and whatnot."

"Okay . . ."

"For, like, video games and so forth. Exploiting the names or likenesses of public figures. For instance, a game where Justin Bieber fights vampires or, say, Oprah Winfrey and Amy Schumer lead opposing clans in some postapocalyptic America."

Katie's laugh was completely unforced. "*That* could be a cool game."

"It is a cool game." He pulled a card from the front of his backpack. "Total old-school MMO built on modular scripts from a customized Lua script. Speaks web top to bottom, you know. Anyhow, you can download it for free here."

"No shit."

"No shit."

She had no idea what he was talking about. "Junction Entertainment," she read off the card, hoping for a clue. "This is you?"

"Yup. Started that company when I was . . . younger."

"Uh huh. How young?"

"Well, ten, actually."

Katie grinned.

"Goofy, I know. Anyhow, my undergrad work, my real interest, has always been in software engineering, coding, algorithms, et cetera. The international law thing is another little piece of that, really."

"International?"

"Ultimately."

"Look," she started, searching for the next words. *How to ask another total stranger for help?* It was not an option she'd ever wanted to take. But: "I was wondering if . . ."

"What's that?" He looked genuinely interested.

"Well, this school thing I'm working on. There are a couple of parts I'm struggling with and—"

"Sorry," he stopped her. "Can't."

"Oh." She sat up straighter. "Okay, I . . . sure."

"Like I said, you totally saved me today, and I should totally be Rumpelstiltskined here and owe you my firstborn or something. But I have to get this paper done and I'm going to be up all night as it is."

"I understand, really." Katie smiled as politely as she could. It had been a long shot anyway. "It was nice meeting you."

"Plus, I—" He was making an uncomfortable face. Like he'd sucked a lemon. Or several. "Never mind."

"What?" Katie said. *What is this guy's deal?*

"Nothing."

71

"Okay. Seemed like you had—"

He sighed. "I don't like the 9/11 stuff."

"The what?"

"I'm not a big conspiracy guy is all."

Anger flared hotly. "You have no idea what my project's about."

"Sure I do," he replied. "Your FOIA letters."

"My . . ." She looked down at her desk. Oh. He meant the Freedom of Information Act requests she'd written. He'd glanced at them for barely a second. "How did you—?"

"You're requesting official flight manifests on the one, and classified commission interviews with Cheney and Bush on the other and . . . sorry. I read fast. I happened—"

"Oh yeah. The genius."

"Again, apologies. Didn't mean to snoop. I, when I look at something, anything, I . . . kinda analyze it. Always in on-mode, I guess."

"Got it." Whatever. "Okay, well, take it easy."

"Sure." He pointed at the card in her hand. "Check out the games sometime."

"Not really a gamer."

He smiled in reply, turned again to leave. More slowly this time.

"Hey, tell me something." Katie stopped him again. Couldn't help herself. "Why do you assume I'm not proving the official story? That it was terrorists."

"Why would you? That's already been done."

"Okay. But I would think a guy who likes to 'analyze' things so fast would be all over huge global intrigues and convoluted cover-ups and all that."

He paused, genuinely thinking about her question. "I don't

know. I guess I'm not comfortable with people thinking the United States had something to do with it. Nine-Eleven, I mean. Or killing Kennedy. Or Sandy Hook. Or anything like that. That we intentionally let these things happen or, even worse, planned them. I believe Americans were at our *best* on 9/11."

"Some would say that's being closed-minded. Naive, even."

"Agreed," he said. "But if that's the price for not walking around all day thinking I live in some shitty evil country, well, that works for me."

"Fair enough." She was done with the discussion. Certainly done with Max—she glanced back down at his card—Thompson. A teenager with his own business card? She set it down and turned back to her books, hoping he'd get the message.

"See ya," he said weakly above her.

She didn't raise her head but held up a hand to say goodbye. Felt him move away. Waited until enough time had passed to know for sure and then looked up. He was gone. The library appeared almost entirely empty.

She was alone.

Again.

That night, Katie stared up again at the painting.

The one of the girl and the horse.

Her room was dark, everything surrounding her quiet and still. Well past midnight, she figured, and the house's various night noises—its many creaks and pops and hums—were all familiar and strangely comforting now. Too much so. How quickly we settle into new truths, new places. New cages. *Is he already settled in his new cage?* she wondered. Was her dad even now lying in a dark room, familiar with and even comforted by the psychiatric hospital's various night noises? The murmurs and babbling. Doors locking. The creak of leather restraints. The occasional scream.

Katie couldn't think about this. Wouldn't.

So, instead, she focused on the girl and, now, the horse. Because, as she'd gathered after a few nights, the girl in the stupid painting wasn't really *on* the horse at all. She was a good couple of inches *off* the horse, suspended in midair against a deep blue sky. White stars in the distance. Falling up and backward. The animal was bucking her, and she was maybe another half second from falling on her ass or maybe even breaking her damned neck.

Now that Katie thought about it, it looked like the horse was going to wipe out too. She tried imagining what the very next frame would look like, the painting never painted. The horse, the girl, knocked out flat. Or, maybe, this girl somehow landing right back on that saddle again and then maybe a whole other picture. Because there was this one little detail. The smile on the girl's face. This terrific and also irritating smile. Like she knew exactly what was going to happen next and wasn't worried about it one little bit.

How nice for you, Katie thought and tried closing her eyes again. Maybe in sleep—even in troubled sleep—she could absorb, through some kind of osmosis, the confidence of the girl in the painting. She needed every positive vibe she could muster. No matter where it came from.

Tomorrow she'd be back on the web, maybe back in the library. *To find what, exactly?* she wondered for the hundredth time. *Nothing*, she countered again. *Nothing*. Poring over books she couldn't possibly understand. Collecting bizarre online takes on what "really" happened that day. Unable to see her dad again, no chance to get useful information beyond the cryptic words he'd spewed at her. Words no one else believed. Even if he could tell her more, where would words like that ever truly lead?

I met a genius today, she thought, half remembering the boy's face. *One who thinks 9/11 conspiracy talk is stupid. A genius. But I'm apparently going to continue. No matter what the world tells me. Why? To maybe save him. To save myself.*

Katie crossly turned sideways, yanked the sheet over her whole head.

What's the opposite of a genius?

10

"This yours?"

Katie looked up, only half aware, at best, of where she was. She'd totally spaced out. Again. "What?"

"Is. This. Yours?"

Reality resumed. Focus. She recognized that it was Zoe talking—the older of the other "fosters"—and that Zoe was standing above her, okay . . . and Zoe was holding something. A notebook. *Wait, SHIT!*

The notebook.

"Yes." Katie reached out her hand. "It is."

"Figured as much. What's it for?"

She must have gotten distracted, left it lying somewhere by mistake. So dumb. And, no surprise, someone else had found it. That's what happens. Not staying on top of things. Running around all week like some chicken with its head cut off. Juggling homework, trips to the Maryland University law library, and incessant 9/11 web surfing. Getting lousy sleep thanks to nightmares she couldn't remember (still, the kind that wake you up). Add all that up and you get someone holding your secret stuff, asking questions.

Katie sat up fully, her hand still strangely empty. Seemed she'd been quite clear on her wishes. Anger woke her whole system in half a second. Fight-or-Flight set totally on Fight.

Her hand stabbed out again. "Do *I* go through *your* shit?"

"Geeeeeeze," Zoe chuckled, handed the notebook over. "You don't gotta get all World War Three about it. You left it up by the computer. I peeked at maybe one page to see whose—"

Katie yanked the book free and set it beside her hip. "Okay. Thanks."

Zoe looked down at her, smiling. But not a shitty smile. More of a genuine friendly smile. Comforting. She'd only been playing. Katie smiled back as best she could.

Zoe was a junior too, but she went to Tilghman High across town. She was on the heavy side, with these spectacular eyes hidden behind thick black glasses and short purplish hair that stopped right under her chin. Around her neck was a small silver necklace in the shape of an ankh—some kind of Egyptian symbol—and a beautiful blue-green golf-ball-sized stone called labradorite that was, she claimed, supposed to provide protection and heighten psychic abilities. Katie hoped Zoe wasn't successfully mind reading right now.

"Didn't mean to pry." Zoe held up her hands in apology (maybe she *could* read minds), then turned her attention to the third girl in the room. "Anything good on?"

C.J. shrugged. She'd been sitting there the whole time, cross-legged directly in front of the big basement TV, watching her foster sisters sort it out. Too petrified to get up and leave the room, most likely. A fourteen-year-old ninety-pound pixie with sad eyes and long, straight brown hair who spoke in one or two words at most. Watched TV mostly. Pretty much the exact opposite of Zoe. Katie had no idea what had made her shut down so badly—probably far worse trials than anything she herself was dealing with.

While the two girls navigated the cable guide together, Katie pondered her reaction to Zoe and the notebook. Why'd she been so mad? Why so scared?

Because you know it all sounds so, so stupid.

Katie clutched the book tightly again in her hand. For a week she'd been filling it with scribbled notes, numbers. All about the different flights on 9/11. Her dad might have other ideas about what happened to those four planes that day, but she needed to know the *real* story first. Or at least, the most accepted story, the official story, whatever she was calling it.

She now knew the two different airlines involved, and the four planes' specific call numbers and sizes and types. Times of takeoff that morning and, well, times of each crash. She'd found passenger lists. Seating charts. Even personal details about every passenger. Ages, jobs, photos. It was amazing how much information there was online. Even specific stuff on how most of them had ended up on the plane that morning. So many seemingly only by chance; missed flights or early flights, last-minute plans. Just regular people flying from or to some business trip or family visit. It was all so unbelievably sad.

If she'd been expecting one of these sad names or pictures to jump out, to shine more brightly than all the rest as if to say: I AM YOUR MOTHER . . . Or even a picture of a little girl, all freckles and dimples and dirty blond hair. If she'd been expecting any of that . . .

And, truth be told, she really had thought: *Maybe.*

Well, she'd been wrong.

Because no name stood out more than any other. No picture, either. Despite the ages and jobs and chance reasons for getting on those damn planes, it was still four lists of utter strangers. Was one of them *actually* her mother? Was such a thing even remotely possible? A question that hadn't gotten any clearer. Quite the opposite, in fact. The more she learned, the more confused she got about all of it.

Three thousand dead. The whole world changed forever. New laws. New wars. Everything debated. Everything a supposed "cover-up." Everything classified.

An endless swirl of claims and denials and confusion.

A missile—not a plane—had hit the Pentagon. Explosives—not jet fuel and structural damage—had collapsed the Twin Towers. The Air Force—not brave passengers—had brought down Flight 93. Specific politicians and businesses received advance notice. The four airliner planes were actually military jets. America's air defenses had been intentionally delayed that morning, allowing the attack to succeed. The nineteen identified terrorists were "patsies" and six of them were still alive and—and on and on.

With only two things holding it all together.

The date.

And the anger. Lots and lots of anger.

No matter what website she visited, eventually the thread of comments devolved into someone calling someone else a moron or racist or fascist or hippie or fag or bitch or much, much worse. Regardless of nationality, sex, race, creed, or age. After three or four lines of serious discussion on *any* issue, someone always declared how stupid everyone else was. It seemed as if anyone who believed, say, a missile had hit the Pentagon judged that anyone who believed otherwise was a brainwashed fool. Conversely, the majority judged those who suspected a missile, et cetera, as offensive assholes.

Katie had spent enough time online to recognize and ignore trolls, but this was on a whole new level. She'd read genuine death threats. Predictions of people lined up against walls and shot as traitors or victims of some Arab invasion or New World Order or some weird combination. Guys making lists. Threatening to track IP addresses and shit. It was crazy.

And smack dab in the middle of all this crazy: her father.

And now, by extension, her.

No wonder she was in such a shitty mood, jumping down Zoe's throat. The venom of these sites still clinging to her somehow. In only a week or two of searching. Imagine almost sixteen years of living in that world. How gone was he?

Her notebook was already half filled with dates and names and allegations. Where to even begin? Her best bet was to hold on to the most-accepted version of 9/11. Using that as the source she could always run back to if she ever wandered too far down some weird side passage. The kind of passages her father had obviously gotten lost in.

Because there could be no confusion. The next time she spoke to Wren, she needed to nail 9/11. To know as much about that terrible day as Osama bin Laden and George W. Bush combined. *All* sides of the argument, especially her dad's. No matter how fringe his claims were. And to speak all this with a confidence on par with some Harvard history professor. There was only one way to achieve that: practice. She had to get comfortable with the patter. Was Flight 93 out of New York or Boston? Was it a United flight? Was that the one where the flight attendants called or . . . ?

She could fill her notebook as much as she wanted. But until she could stand up and present everything—the accepted facts as well as her dad's allegations—as clearly and precisely as possible, she had zero business seeing the lawyer again.

And zero chance of helping her dad. Or herself.

Almost before she realized she was actually speaking, Katie's voice filled the whole basement.

"So," she said. "What do you guys know about 9/11?"

"You writing a report?" Zoe asked.

"Something like that. Curious what you know, is all."

C.J. asked, "Was I even born yet?"

"September eleventh, two thousand and one," Katie recited. The day—if she dared believe him—her father maybe helped orchestrate the greatest crime in American history. And maybe the day her mother died? *(Gave you a new name. New documents. A new life.)* "I was almost two."

"So, no, for me," C.J. said.

"And I would have been a baby," said Zoe, adding with a laugh. "Thirteen months, I guess. Don't remember too much."

"What about in school?"

"Are you kidding?" replied Zoe. "When's the last time you learned about anything other than pilgrims and the Civil War?"

"That's why I'm asking. What *do* you know?"

"There were, um, four planes," C.J. replied. "They crashed them into the Twin Towers and the Pentagon. And one crashed in Virginia."

Pennsylvania, Katie thought, even knowing the exact town. "Who crashed them?"

"George Bush," Zoe said.

Katie froze. "Why did you say that?"

"I don't know. Joke. I knew this kid who totally thought Bush planned it and stuff. Wanted me to watch these movies on Netflix. About how the buildings, the World Trade Center, got blown up by bombs. I never watched them. It was terrorists. They took over the planes."

"What country were the terrorists from?"

"Is this a quiz?" Zoe smiled.

Katie nodded. "Extra credit if you can spell *Al-Qaeda*." It was nice Zoe was playing along. So far, anyway.

"Iraq?" Zoe shrugged. "I don't know. Bin Laden guys. So, Afghanistan?"

"Saudi Arabia," Katie said. "Fifteen of the nineteen hijackers."

"What's the difference?" C.J. asked. "They all hate us the same, right?"

Katie shook her head. "I don't really know. I hope not. But Saudi Arabia is considered a US ally. And Bin Laden was from there. He moved to Afghanistan in the '80s to fight the Russians."

"Russians?"

This was actually kind of fun. Katie hadn't known any of this herself a week before. Then she'd researched Osama bin Laden, the man who ran the terrorist group accused of plotting 9/11. "Russia invaded Afghanistan in the 1980s, for oil. And as part of the Cold War, America gave weapons and money to radical Islamists to help fight off the Russians. Bin Laden was a billionaire from Saudi Arabia who joined that fight and became one of the leaders. Many claim he worked directly with the CIA back then."

"Weird," C.J. said and then glanced back at the TV.

"Whoa." Zoe grinned, her darkened eyes narrowing into amused black slits. "Now I get it."

"What?" Katie asked.

"You're a Truther."

11

Katie put on her best blankly-curious expression. "What do you mean?" she asked, hoping to cover up that she knew *exactly* what Zoe had called her.

A term she'd encountered a thousand times online the last few weeks.

TRUTHER.

The word used with absolute ridicule or intense pride, depending on who was using it. But there was no doubt which side had the clear numbers advantage.

Truthers were considered, by most, to be nutballs.

"Like the Netflix kid. Into all that conspiracy stuff, right?" Zoe persisted. "New World Order? Illuminati?" She put her hands into the shape of a triangle. "Jay Z, Rihanna, Bill Gates, right? Area 54 kinda stuff?"

Katie's face had scrunched, switching to her best mortified expression. "Um, noooooo." Why such a strong negative reaction? Was seeking "The Truth" really such an unusual thing? Was her dad really that far off center? "I'm just, you know, curious," she admitted.

And the real reasons for her curiosity would remain hers to keep. If Zoe's friend at school could be so interested in this stuff, why in hell couldn't *she* look into it? Without feeling so embarrassed? So weird. So repulsive.

"I mean, a lot of people think sketchy stuff happened on 9/11," she pushed. If she couldn't say these things with a straight face to these two, how could she possibly say them in front of someone like Marilyn Wren? "Stuff the government isn't telling us. I thought that was . . . *interesting.* The possibility that some shadow government orchestrated the whole thing. I don't know." The words sounded so dumb coming out. The argument completely half-assed. "You think it's stupid, huh? The conspiracy stuff, I mean."

"Me?" Zoe snorted. "I believe in feng shui and garden fairies. Not exactly the judging kind."

Had she just compared 9/11 conspiracy to believing in imaginary backyard pixies? "Well, I wouldn't go so far as—"

"Sounds weird," C.J. stopped her. "Too complicated. Isn't the simplest answer usually the best? Murphy's Law or something?"

Occam's razor, Katie corrected silently. A term she'd thought of a lot these last few days. A famous principle used in problem-solving, which argued that among competing possible answers, the one with the fewest assumptions should be selected. So then, the explanation for 9/11 with the fewest assumptions, the most straightforward explanation, was that a handful of well-funded Islamic fanatics learned to fly, made some test runs, bought tickets, and then crashed four planes as America was caught with its proverbial pants down. Simple. Done.

An answer that was, unsurprisingly, also the official answer. The one most of the world believed.

But *simple* and *done* wouldn't free her father. *(They killed her. Killed all of them.)* And it wouldn't even kinda explain the things he'd claimed. *(She begged me to save her baby. To save you.)*

Katie thought about the box upstairs in her closet. The old Polaroid of a man standing beside a girl on a pony.

"What would it take to convince you?" she asked.

She hadn't been out here in years. And even then, only once. It'd been a Saturday and he'd brought her along on their way to something else. (Whatever that other thing had been, she had no recollection.) She'd been maybe eight, nine. Didn't remember very much, just carried a faint memory of a huge garage with enormous trucks and equipment. Dark. Half remembered her dad waving to someone, talking while she looked around. Then climbing up into this weird truck with six wheels, and her dad driving them out into the woods where he did some kind of testing on mosquitoes for an hour or so.

Katie stood in front of the open bay doors at the back of the main shop where her dad worked. A giant boring red-brick building. She could only assume it was the same place she'd visited as a kid. Inside, the Park Services facility basically looked like a huge garage: one truck high up on a lift with its tires off, half a dozen mowers of various shapes and sizes, and a couple of vans. Somewhere, a radio played faintly.

She'd been waiting outside awhile. *Too* awhile. Waiting for someone to notice her and invite her in, or to know for certain no one was one around and, well, sneak in. But neither absolute had presented itself yet. It was almost four o'clock. Most of the workers would probably be out another half an hour or more. Probably. She'd come in through the back so she could avoid some snotty secretary turning her away, but now, she wasn't so sure. Maybe the risk of a snotty secretary was better than trespassing and getting yelled at or going to jail and having to explain: *Oh, yeah, I'm the daughter of the employee who recently beat everyone up. No, I'm not also crazy. I'm just snooping around for evidence about my dad and his secret past and the biggest cover-up since the sinking of Atlantis. Nope, no crazy here!*

She looked over her shoulder. Gianna sat in the car making her best WTF face, one Katie'd concluded people from Jersey received special training in.

Katie held up her hands to say "I don't know," and she didn't.

All the questions Zoe and C.J. had about 9/11, all the objections to the conspiracy stuff, always came back to the credibility of the sources.

And the credibility of *her* main source?

El Zippo. Nothing but cryptic statements uttered throughout a lifetime of drinking and substance abuse. Oh, and all the babblings made while burning his arm in a drug-induced haze. Not anything to build even a half-decent discussion, let alone a case.

What, then, did she *really* expect to find out here?

Some kind of evidence he was telling the truth? At least that was the stirring idea when she'd talked Gianna (sans questions, but not without some skeptical looks) into driving out here, right? Now, however . . .

She'd started back toward Gianna's car.

She begged me. Begged me. To save her baby. To save you.

Katie stopped, turned, found herself moving forward again until she was under the bay door and into the coolness and shade of the large building. Inside was this smell, a certain combination of engine oil and cedar that almost knocked her flat with memory. She didn't remember much about that Saturday all those years before, but that oil-cedar smell was an instant time machine, like she'd smelled it yesterday.

She stepped around one of the vans to find empty chairs and worktables beneath and endless tools running up the back wall. She stopped, looked around more. Nothing. Some sunlight spilled through a single window high in the vaulted ceiling. She found the radio sitting at the next workstation; small, playing some tinny-sounding old '70s song. She pressed forward and found the bathroom and then another door leading down a carpeted hallway.

Katie opened the second door. Listened. Still, nothing. Following the hall, she passed a water fountain and some pictures of the Chesapeake Bay, and then came to one of the things she was looking for: the locker room. Katie could see several lockers through the small window in the door. She pushed that door slowly. Didn't appear anyone was inside, so she stepped through.

She shuffled past several lockers, running her hands along each, looking for her dad's. How many times had he come into this very room? Checking in for the day, checking out. Maybe grabbing his lunch (one she'd pulled together for him the night before). Maybe grabbing his tackle box for a little fishing after work.

She didn't know. These people we live with, these loved ones we see for maybe an hour a day—how much do we *really* know about what they're doing the other twenty-three hours? Or what they did before we were even born?

There were no names on the lockers. Only numbers. Her hand settled on one of them and she carefully, slowly, opened it. Nothing inside looked specifically familiar. Jacket, thermos, a can of chewing tobacco sitting up on the top shelf. It *could* be her dad's. At the bottom of the locker, a pack of toilet paper, a dirty crumpled Redskins baseball cap. No.

Went to the next locker. Taped-up photos of kids she didn't know. Next one, some guy's skull-painted motorcycle helmet. Each time, she opened and shut the doors a little faster. She'd managed to cover an entire bank of lockers and still nothing looked familiar.

When something finally did, in the second row, against the other wall, she stood there for a couple of seconds, not knowing what to do next.

The ceramic candy dish on the top shelf. Yeah, she'd made that in second grade. And the worn flannel shirt hanging on the hook—the one with the blue and jade-green squares—she'd washed and folded it a thousand times. The one picture taped to the inside of the door: a picture of her, maybe seven years old. And another of her, one of those staged ones, in uniform, on one knee with a soccer ball. Junior high.

She reached into the locker, touched the shirt and then the worn mustard work jacket. Checked the pockets. For what, she didn't know. A "clue" of some kind. Maybe go Full 007 and find a key to a secret safety-deposit box, a hidden microchip. Big shock: nothing.

She moved on to the top shelf. Coffee mug. Half-eaten bag of Mike and Ikes (one of his favorites). She wondered if he'd started this bag the day he'd been arrested. Work gloves. Goggles. Another couple of *Star Trek* paperbacks and one of the Barsoom books by Edgar Rice Burroughs. She riffled through each book, looking for something, anything. A secretive note, mysterious scribbles in the margins. A name. A phone number she didn't recognize.

Anything that could lead to proof he was telling the truth.

Or even prove he was lying.

At this point, she really didn't care which.

There was a disassembled fishing pole in one corner. An old umbrella in the other. The locker was a bust. The entire idea had been absurd from the start.

What did she expect to find? Maybe some kind of top-secret folder crammed with pictures and classified memos he'd sneaked out of the Pentagon? Or maybe secret recordings of Dick Cheney admitting the whole plan for 9/11 and then bragging about his direct involvement? Yeah, right.

The only recordings in this locker were old cassette tapes. Def Leppard, Mötley Crüe, and—her dad somehow needing still more umlauts—some band called Queensrÿche on the bottom of the locker. Beside the tapes was an old radio–cassette player that was even nastier than the one Katie had seen in the garage.

She'd taken a seat on the long bench that ran directly across from his opened locker. Just staring at it. Thinking harder than she ever had in her life, it felt. Because if she couldn't . . . if she couldn't—

"Hey, girl," a deep voice growled behind her. "What the hell are you doing in here?"

12

Katie expected some seven-foot giant with a shaved head and neck tattoos. But this guy was no taller than she was and might have even weighed less. He was dressed in his light blue Park Services T-shirt and cap and had a thick beard that was half gray. "I said, what you doin' in here?" He took off his sunglasses and hung them from his shirt's collar. The eyes beneath were the eyes of a sleepy rat.

"I'm Scott Wallace's daughter."

"He don't work here."

"Sure he does." She stood and gestured at her dad's locker. "He's—"

"He don't work here *no more*, is what I mean."

"Okay." She didn't know what else to say. Didn't even know if what this guy was saying was true. Had her dad really been fired? After one mistake in like ten years? Pretty big mistake, though. She stopped thinking about it and realized the Rat Guy was staring at her. As he did, it looked like he was maybe tonguing some chew in his lower lip. *I've been in your locker, weirdo!* she thought. *What do you think of that?*

"So, why you here?" he asked.

To find clues. Yeah, brilliant.

"I was . . . My dad asked me to pick up some things from his locker."

"That so? How's he doing, anyway? Heard he was in the nuthouse."

She let the term pass, shut her dad's locker. "He's doing better, thanks. I also wanted to—"

"What's that?" He stepped in closer. So much so she could smell the tobacco breath. "You 'also wanted to'?"

"I was also hoping to maybe see Phil. Phil Lampert."

"I'll bet. What you want to see him for?"

None of your damn business! But she knew she was trapped. "He's friends with my dad."

"Not so sure. Your old man messed Phil up pretty good."

"Yes, sir. Anyhow, if you know where he could be . . . that'd be great."

He played with his lower lip some more. Said nothing.

"Okay, thanks," she said again. Why, she had no idea. What was there to thank this guy for? Totally creeping her out? Whatever. Her new goal was to get out of the room as quickly as possible. Jump in Gianna's car and be gone. This was all too bizarre.

"You didn't take nothing," the man said.

"What's that?"

"You said you were picking up stuff for your dad. But you didn't take nothing."

"Oh. He was looking for . . ." Thinking, thinking. Concocting what the hell he would have realistically sent her for. Her shoulders slumped in defeat.

The guy had pulled out his walkie-talkie phone thing. "Hey, Lampert!"

"Yeah?" A voice from the other end. Then a beep.

"Back at shop. Someone here to see you." Beep. He smiled at Katie. It was a terrible smile. There was brown gunk caught in his teeth. "Scott Wallace's kid."

Katie assumed nothing but silence would follow. Static. The colossal tobacco-stained asshole would probably even turn up the volume on his communicator to make the effect more devastating. None of this happened.

"Okay," the ghostly voice replied, "I'll be up in a couple minutes." Beep.

"Roger." He hooked the phone back to his belt. "Couple minutes."

"Thanks," Katie managed more sincerely.

"Sure thing, sure thing."

She'd already started moving the other way out of the locker room. It was the long way, but at least she wouldn't have to pass him. He stepped in behind her without a word and followed her out down the hall, back toward the big garage. She was terrified she'd make a wrong turn. It reminded her of being at the hospital with that Paul Cobb guy walking behind her. Not a good memory.

She successfully made it to the garage and the tinny radio and the promise of open bay doors and daylight. Then Katie stepped outside. Free. Gianna was still there—*Thank God*—her face squinted with confusion and worry.

"That your friend?" the guy asked, moving up beside her.

"Yes, sir."

He'd turned to spit tobacco juice next to his right boot.

"Pretty girl," he said, considering his own glob of brown spit.

Pervert, Katie fumed, creeped out again, wishing she could take back the thanks she'd just given. Her every instinct urged her to call the guy out, report him to the main office, call the police. Something. But she stopped herself. There was something about the way he was looking at her. *He's TRYING to piss you off*, she realized. *He actually WANTS you to be insulted. Who does that?* Then it hit her. *Is this who got my dad going that day? Pressed him, kept pushing until he'd had enough?*

"So," she said, turning. "Were you there?"

"Was I where?" he asked, and even smiled. Again, doing it on purpose.

"When my dad . . ."

"Oh yeah, you bet."

"Any idea what got him so upset?"

In reply, he retrieved a can of chew from his back pocket. Slowly put a fresh pinch in his mouth. Katie sneaked a look at Gianna, who'd turned both palms up in puzzlement.

"Were people arguing?" she pursued. "About politics, maybe, or . . . maybe something about 9/11 or—"

"Here's Lampert." He pointed to a dark blue pickup coming up the drive.

"Thanks." She'd started toward the moving pickup. It couldn't get here soon enough.

"I'm the one who called," he said behind her.

Katie turned. "What's that?"

"I called the cops that day." He made a slurp sound with his mouth. "Only thing to do, really." His little rat eyes squinted into the sun.

"I don't blame you," she said and quickly walked toward the newly-parked truck.

Or maybe ran.

Your old man messed Phil up pretty good.

Yes, he apparently had. The man who got out of the truck was probably thirty and built like he lifted serious weights. His dark skin couldn't hide the two black eyes with bruising running down into both cheeks, and he still had bandages and tape on his nose, a gauze cross running up into his forehead. The bruises made his eyes look like the two giant sockets of a skull. From weeks ago? Katie couldn't believe the damage her dad had done. What could she possibly say to this man? She looked back at Gianna, thought briefly about running to her car. Screeching away. Never thinking about any of this again.

"Hi." She held out a hand to shake. "Mr. Lampert?"

"Phil." He shook. "You Scott's daughter?"

"Yes, sir. Katie Wallace."

"Okay. What are you doing here?"

"I . . . my father wanted me to . . ." She'd instinctively started again down the path of *picking his stuff up*, which had gone nowhere fast. Best to stick with the truth. Right? "I had some questions about my dad."

"Huh, okay. Not sure what I can tell you."

Katie looked back to where the first man was still watching them from afar. "Who's he?"

"Ken? Don't worry about Ken. He's a dick. Come on." He started walking the other direction and Katie followed. "Didn't give you a hard time, did he?"

"Not really. He . . . Was my dad fired?"

Phil Lampert had slowed so she could catch up and walk beside him. "Not that I heard. Your dad's a good guy. I'm sure they'll figure things out."

"I'm sorry about your nose."

"Shit happens."

"I guess. Still, it looks . . . I'm sorry."

"It's fine. Second operation was a couple days ago. Only reason it looks so bad. That should be it, they tell me. I'll look like Denzel again in a couple weeks."

Katie laughed politely. *Second* operation? "Thank you for, you know, dropping the charges."

"No worries." He'd stopped walking. "How is he?"

"He's . . . he's okay."

"Yeah?"

"I don't know, actually."

He nodded, looked out over this wide grass field behind the complex. "So, what'd you want to know?"

"Was hoping to maybe figure out what set him off that day."

Phil Lampert shrugged. Laughed. "Who knows? 'Politics' is what I heard. But guys are always bullshitting about a hundred things so, you know, I don't know. It rained hard that afternoon and most of us came back early to get some work done around here. Your dad came back in around one, one thirty."

"You know where he went that morning? What he was working on?"

"Sure. Parker's Farm, I think. You know it?"

"The barns and stuff? Yeah, we went there in elementary school. Field trips. He go alone?"

"Almost always. The man prefers the solo jobs. Volunteers for 'em. Grabs Old Rusty, the nastiest truck we got, doesn't even have AC, and off he goes. Keeps to himself. I'm sure you know that."

"Yeah. You think anything happened out at the farm?"

"Not that I ever heard. He didn't come back pissed or anything. From what we could tell, it all happened back here. He wasn't making much sense. I mean, he was grumbling about this and that. Claimed someone was messing with his locker. Someone needed to go to jail. Someone was, you know, like, 'following him.' Then grumbling became yelling. He started on the politics stuff. Threats and that kind of thing."

"The Dick Cheney stuff?"

"You heard about that? Right, so he was gonna kidnap Cheney and waterboard the jerkoff." He chuckled. "Then, I don't know, everyone was gonna know everything. Nine-Eleven. Whole world gonna change and all."

"He ever get like that before?" She'd seen it enough times. Had they?

"Scott? Guy rarely speaks two words about *anything*. Maybe some shit he just saw on the nature channel. Keeps to himself. I knew your dad wasn't a big fan of the government, the wars, but he never got specific. That day, I don't know. Maybe a couple of guys didn't help. Messing with him too much when you could see he wasn't, you know, all right. Guys like Ken back there. All of a sudden your dad's in this Bruce Lee stance and folk are getting . . . uneasy. That's about when I showed up. Great timing, huh?" He smiled and gently tapped the bridge of his nose. "Couple of us tried to calm him down. He'd knocked a few down already. Tempers got going maybe."

"They get physical with him?"

He nodded. "But nothing serious. Honestly. I was one of the guys who 'got physical.' Trying to get him to chill, you know, a hand on his back is all." He put his arm out and patted the air to demonstrate how gently. "Let him know everything was cool. That's it."

"And he . . ."

"Shattered my damn nose. Don't even know how he did it. One second, I'm standing there with him, talking nice and all. Next thing I'm out cold and lying on my ass in a pool of blood. Other guys backed the hell off and he came out here to stand by himself. Cops came about fifteen minutes later. Hey, listen, I wish there was something more I could tell you. Really. But I think we just caught him on a bad day."

"My dad had lots of bad days."

"I guess." He considered further, then said it again but very differently. "I guess. I remember he, ahh, he and I . . . the two of us went out this one time after work."

"Drinking," she said for him. "What happened? What'd he tell you?"

He ran his fingers across the tape on his forehead. Thinking. "Again, nothing specific, but I remember he kept saying he was sorry. He was sorry and that there was nothing he could do. That kind of thing. At some point I realized he'd actually been in the military. Was he?"

Distinguished Service Cross, two Bronze Stars for Valor, Kosovo Campaign Medal, Valorous Unit Award.

"Yes."

"Well, when I tried asking him about it later at work, he ended the conversation in a second, you know? Like he didn't know what I was talking about. Private guy, for sure."

"Did you even know he had a daughter?"

"Yeah." He looked down at her. "But to be honest, I didn't know if you were seven or twenty-four."

"What about a wife? My mom? He ever say anything about her?"

"No, I, ahhhh. Not that I can remember."

"She'd dead." Why had she said that?

"Okay, yeah, figured it was something like that. I got the sense it was just you two."

Now just one.

He shook his head, thinking. "Like I said, he's a good guy, Katie. I hope he gets better soon."

She didn't know what else to say. It seemed he didn't either. "I really appreciate your time," Katie said finally.

"No worries," he replied again. "Hey, that night we went out. He, I could see it, he had this look. Something very real. More than his face, you know. Like his whole being. Like you could almost touch it. Saw it again the other day. It's why I don't take the nose thing too personal."

"How do you mean?"

"*Something* happened to your dad. I don't know what exactly and I don't know when. But something happened. Something bad."

"Yes," Katie agreed. "It's the one thing I'm sure of too."

The shadow people loom above her, enormous and black, moving a hundred different ways, then suddenly shifting all together in the same terrible direction, so fast, maddening, and she can feel them against her, touching, clutching, pulling, lifting, forcing her back down into the darkness like being caught beneath an enormous black wave, their stiff hands and thrusting fingers, their screams, these many voices, a clamor of threats and pleas and confusion and fear, and no words she can understand, only sound, and still the screams, crying, she is crying, can't breathe, and the shadow people are bobbing together in the darkness, flashes of colored light, reds and blues, like a police car, and blinding white light swirling in the darkness above her, above everything, and the light is screaming at them in air that is musty and cold, and one of the shadow people is squeezing her, too tightly, still can't breathe, and she's pushed forward and back, her whole face pressed against the blackness, shaking, and the shadow person is shaking against her, holding too tightly, and someone is watching them but she can't see who, and then she is floating in space, lost, cold, away from the others, claws digging into her back, and she hears a dog barking furiously, and a voice, a voice saying something, a voice crying and she is not sure if it is her voice or the shadow person's, and she does not understand the words but has never heard such a sound, such a genuine and terrible sound, and finally words she knows are said from the darkness surrounding them all: *I'm sorry.*

I'm sorry.

Katie woke, these two words still haunting the room's darkness. Lingering on the edge of true awareness. The dream already faded. Lost. She shuddered, trying to remember it at all. Half afraid she'd succeed.

Something happened to your dad. Something bad.

Okay, but what about *her*?

She sat up, clutched the blanket tight against her chin. Looked over this strange room that wasn't hers—would never be. Dark shadows hovered in its every corner. Inching onto the ceiling. Watching her.

She turned to the framed photo beside her bed, but it was too dark to truly see without turning on the light.

Katie forced herself to lie back down and close her eyes. Tried to sleep.

She felt the phantom sensation of being pushed this way and that.

She felt anxious. Alone. Powerless.

She felt crazy.

13

"And then . . . well, then, he claims, they murdered my mom."

Katie sat cross-legged on the floor. Gianna stared back down at her from the bed, saying nothing. For a long time now, she'd said nothing. Her face told Katie enough. It was a face that wanted to laugh, or maybe scream.

Katie'd told her all of it. The night the police came. The Claypools. The salt. Looking for lawyers. And then—finally, slowly—her dad's claims about 9/11.

"Anyway," Katie finished, "I guess all the other passengers too."

Gianna finally spoke. "That's totally fuckin' crazy. I mean, isn't it?"

"I don't know," Katie replied. "Probably."

"He really told you all this? Wow. I mean . . ." Gianna looked up at the ceiling to search for her next words. She found few. "Just wow."

"Yeah," Katie agreed.

"And do you believe it? Any of it?"

"I think he does."

"Yeah, but do—"

"Jesus, G, I don't know. I don't." Katie laid her head back against the bed. "I swear to God, I don't know what to think anymore. I know how it sounds, but . . ."

"But what?"

"I've been doing all this research and, well, let's say he's not the only one who thinks the US had something to do with 9/11. That it was staged. That there weren't passengers on those four planes. Lots of other people believe that too."

"Other crazy people?"

"No, I mean the kind of—" Katie stopped herself. Sat up straighter.

"I'm sorry," Gianna said quickly, realizing what she'd done, seeing the expression on Katie's face. "I didn't mean your dad. I meant—"

"It's okay." Katie sighed deeply. "Believe me, I know how all of this sounds. But, it's my job now to somehow make it sound *less* crazy."

"Isn't that, I don't know, like . . . disrespectful?"

"To who? The victims?" Katie nodded slowly. "Yeah, I think that a lot. I—I suppose it comes down to intentions. Are you coming up with wild theories for fun, for something to do instead of blogging about your cat or how much you hate the newest Marvel movie, or are you really doing it for—"

"The truth," Gianna finished.

"Right."

They sat quietly together for a while. Then Gianna slid off the bed and down beside her on the floor. "Were there any little kids?" she asked. "Babies? On, you know, the flights?"

Katie shuddered. "Yes."

"And do any of them, um—"

"Look like me? I don't know. How much does someone change in fifteen years? I've studied the pictures of every victim. *Every* one. Especially the women. Looking for something, anything, that feels—I don't know—familiar. Connected to me. And there's nothing. I'm left staring at complete strangers. Strangers I now know better than most of the people I've ever met. It's agonizing. Worse, it's ghoulish."

"Katie . . ."

"More ghoulish: there are thousands of people who believe the passenger lists are *fakes*. That some names are real, some not. Invented Americans who never really existed. Or maybe government agents, all living rich under new identities now. All part of this Big Plan. The Big Lie. So, you know, for all I know maybe five little girls died that day, or maybe none. G, I'm telling you, it's—"

"And you don't know anything about your mom?" Gianna asked. "I mean *anything*? Her name, even?"

Katie shrugged. "The name he told me, you mean? How do I know that was her real name? There's no one else around who knew her."

"It'd be on your birth certificate, wouldn't it?"

"If the birth certificate is real. He says he got me 'new documents' after he saved me on 9/11. So everything on those documents could be a lie."

"You could just do an Internet search for her name and see if you can find her . . ."

"I tried that. There must be forty people with that name in Maryland alone. Do I contact all of them and ask, hey, are you my real mom?"

"There's got to be a way to narrow it down. You seriously don't know anything else? Job? Where she grew up?"

She shook her head, admitting defeat. "No. She left when I was two, maybe three. Don't really remember her at all." Katie said this but wasn't 100 percent sure. There was a distant memory—a feeling, a smell, a face even—that came to mind anytime she slipped and thought of her mother. Of *having* a mother. Of hating her mother. A momentary hint lost as soon as she knew to chase it. "She couldn't deal," Katie explained quickly. "Trouble with drugs. Took off. Fuck her. End of story."

"Did she ever send you, like, letters or cards or anything?"

"End of story." Katie picked angrily at the carpet.

"Or maybe not."

"Or maybe not."

And there it was: the dim possibility her mom wasn't some druggie coward, but instead a brave woman who'd loved her deeply, who'd managed to save her life against incredible odds. The exact opposite of what she'd always imagined.

"Hey." Gianna reached out and grabbed her hands. "I'm glad you finally told me."

"Finally?"

"Hey, I knew something was up. I've known for weeks. Also knew you'd talk when you were ready."

"Had to." Katie looked up. "I think I was starting to . . . I had to tell someone."

"Well, I'm glad I was your someone."

Katie squeezed back.

"Besides," Gianna added, "can't have you relying on those weird foster sisters, can I?"

Katie shook her head. "They're pretty cool, actually."

Gianna blinked rapidly, once again realizing she'd over-stepped, trying to navigate this new terrain. "I'm sorry. I didn't mean—"

"No, no. It's okay." How quickly do we get used to the way things are now? How quickly do we start believing the new stories we tell ourselves, burying the ones we can't? "They're fine, that's all I mean. Could be a lot worse."

Gianna breathed out a long sigh. "So now what?"

Katie laughed. A very tired laugh. "Well, let me see. First, they won't let me see my dad. Second, I found out nothing at home or at his work yesterday. I can tell you all this shit about lawsuits, or about 9/11, about explosives and planes and phone calls and classified reports we'll never see, but the more I learn . . . the less I know. I honestly have no idea what I'm doing. I looked into this company where he supposedly worked before, TERNGO, the one he claims was somehow involved in all of this, and that didn't lead anywhere."

"What about the dragon thing and the Benevolent five-something?"

"Benevolus Five. Benevolus five-two. What about it? I told you, it was crazy talk, gibberish. He was drugged."

"Then maybe *all* of it was gibberish." Gianna's eyes widened. "Or maybe those are secret code names or like a military thing?"

Katie shook her head. "Didn't find anything when I searched. A glass door company, that was about it."

"But I mean, did you even look that hard? If it's some kind of classified info . . ."

"Then it probably wouldn't be floating around on the Internet at all. You're right, though—I didn't spend much time searching. I've been so focused on all this other stuff, and that's bad enough. God, I need to— "

"Let me do it."

"G, driving me out there to play Sherlock Holmes was bad enough. I don't want you—"

"Shut it. Seriously, I want to help. You focus on the legal stuff and I'll look into the Benevolus and dragon thing. If I don't find anything, what's the harm? But, if I do, so much the better."

Katie smiled uneasily, unsure what to do with the emotions surging through her. The relief, the gratitude. The feeling of being a part of something, instead of standing alone.

"No one else," she warned. "Not even Alexis can know."

"Aces." Gianna mock-saluted. "Dick Cheney better watch out now."

"I've created a monster, haven't I?"

"Nope. Just recruited one."

All that afternoon had been for Supreme Court cases.

Lockett v. Ohio and the role of mitigating factors. *Rennie v. Klein* and patient refusal of medications. *Jackson v. Indiana*. *Addington v. Texas.* The limits of involuntary civil commitments as determined via *O'Connor v. Donaldson*. Good old Ken Donaldson had been diagnosed with paranoid schizophrenia one weekend—like her dad—and had spent the next fifteen years in a mental ward with dangerous criminals. Fifteen *years*. Katie could hardly imagine fifteen *weeks*, only a little more than her father's prescribed confinement. And if she couldn't help him, maybe he was looking at more time than that. Maybe he *was* looking at fifteen years.

What more could she do? Unless she found another lead, she was pretty much dead in the water.

Katie yawned. Looked up from her book. The library was all but empty. A couple hours before she'd seen the boy genius, Max, crossing the library with a pair of fellow students. He'd waved briefly, politely, and moved on. She wondered if—

Wait. A couple *hours*? She looked for the nearest window.

"Shit." It was dark. *Dark* dark. Katie grabbed her phone and checked the time. 9:54. "Shit, shit." She jumped up to collect the reserve books, jammed printouts into her book bag. She'd lied to the Claypools about having dinner at Gianna's and caught a bus downtown instead. Totally lost track of the time. She'd be in for another lecture about curfews and "mutual trust."

Katie dropped the reserve books at the main desk with a quick thanks and was out of the building in under a minute. She checked her phone again. Ten minutes until the next bus. All in, she was looking at almost 11:00 until back at the Claypools'. Damn. Had to call.

"Mrs. Claypool? Hi—yes, ma'am, it's Katie. Yes, yes ma'am, I know. I'm sorry." The sidewalks were almost as empty as the library. Shops closed or closing. "Was studying with my friend and lost track of time." She watched a cab go by, wondered how much it would cost. Doubted the five in her back pocket would cover it. "Of course. I'll get home as soon as I can. Thanks, okay, bye." Closer to an hour than not. Oh well. Not a damn thing to be done about it now.

Katie tossed her book bag onto the empty bus stop bench. Paced back and forth like a caged animal. Nothing to do but wait. Get some shit from the Claypools, nothing too severe, nothing she couldn't sit through politely. If there was one thing she'd learned living with a stoner/drunk prone to random fits of depression and anxiety, it was how to settle in and let the dark cloud blow past.

She caught her breath and thought about Ken Donaldson again, the guy from *O'Connor v. Donaldson*. He'd grown convinced someone was poisoning his food, so his parents got worried and called the authorities. After fifteen years in a freaking mental hospital, the courts decided it was within his rights to be "crazy"; that thinking someone was poisoning your food was not dangerous to himself or anyone else. If you wanted to think the world was flat or you were the king of France, that was your business.

And so, if you wanted to think the United States orchestrated a phony terrorist attack by murdering three thousand of its own citizens—

I've seen him before. This thought came distinct and deafening, crowding out everything else in her head.

The man directly across the street. The one bent low against the wind, lighting a cigarette. The one who'd—a second ago—been looking right at her.

Looked away when . . . when she looked back at him.

I've seen that man before. Where? Her first thought, of course, was the night they'd come for her at the house. This guy was one of those men. Had to be. Except, maybe he wasn't. Someone from the library then?

He was tall with a buzzed haircut. Looked late forties, fifty. Where had she seen him?

An older woman joined Katie at the bus stop, eyeing Katie's backpack suspiciously as if it were a rabid pit bull. Katie grunted, moved to retrieve her bag.

The man, meanwhile, had actually gone down the street some. Away from the bus stop. The cigarette smoke trailed thinly above his head. He seemed to be looking now for something coming from the other direction. Waiting for a ride, for friends.

He has nothing to do with me at all, she thought. Talk about paranoid delusions. *Next I'll be thinking the Claypools are poisoning my cereal.*

Katie grabbed her bag and held it close, protectively. But still, she kept watching.

He'd moved farther away, never gave her a second look, and

now he turned down another side alley and out of sight. She looked the other way to check for the bus, saw it far down the street. She glanced once more toward the man but he—whether she'd really recognized him from somewhere or not—was gone. Lost beyond the darkness of that side alley and the night.

The bus pulled up and Katie waited while the old woman climbed onboard and paid. Katie followed, paid, found a seat as the bus pulled away. She checked her phone. Too late to ask Gianna to pick her up on the bus line. The Claypools were going to get their version of pissed, no way around it. She collapsed into her seat and tried not to think about that.

She peered out the window as the bus passed the dark alley where the man had disappeared. Curious as to where he might have gone or what was down that concealed road.

At first she saw only the darkness of an unlit street. Then a small orange glow flared in the middle of all that dark: the tip of a burning cigarette.

Someone standing there, watching her bus pass.

She turned back in her seat to see more, and the light vanished into the darkness.

"Ready to meet Benevolus552?" Gianna had turned her laptop so Katie could see. "Voilà!" she said, indicating the screen.

Katie recognized the type of website immediately. Had pored over hundreds during the last two weeks. Probably even visited this one at some point and simply didn't remember it.

Plain-Truth.com.

A "conspiracy site." Beside a single row of cheap-looking advertising, the page was broken into a dozen or more rectangles, each one with a picture, headline, and text leading to the full story. Little icons at the corner of each rectangle denoted the main topic, and today the home page featured *US POLICE STATE, NWO, WW3, FEMA, RFID CHIPS, CDC.*

And *9/11.*

"Keep going," Gianna instructed, and Katie scrolled past a dozen more articles to the bottom of the page. There, in small letters:

Contact Us   About Us

Katie clicked the "About Us" link and was brought to a page showing four headshots with bios and job descriptions.

Head #3 was titled: *Benevolus552.*

"Really?" Katie said, reading.

"Really," Gianna replied. "Wasn't 100 percent sure how to spell it, so I tried a couple variations. First, I discovered that Ben Franklin sometimes used 'Benevolus' as a pen name, so there's that. Eventually searched the name *and* several number combos *combined* and then added some 9/11 words and this site popped up. He's got posts all over it. A couple other sites too. Like, politics stuff. But this one is home base for sure."

Katie looked at the man's picture. It was black and white and his face was purposely turned so you couldn't really see what he looked like. "International Man of Mystery." The other pictures on the page were done in the same mysterious fashion. This Benevolus guy looked heavier, but youngish. She tried picturing the man from the bus stop. Looked at all four pictures on the page.

"Says he lives in DC," she noted.

"Could live in Turkey for all we know. My Twitter profile says I'm twenty-five."

"Of course it does." Katie stared at the veiled picture. "Why would my dad contact this guy?"

"To get information about 9/11, looks like," Gianna offered.

"Or to *give* it. Do I contact him?" There was no email beside his or the other profiles. "This guy could be—" As crazy as her dad. "It's weird to just contact the guy out of the blue, isn't it?"

"*All* of this shit is weird," Gianna said.

"Touché." Katie clicked the back button and then the "Contact Us" link. A standard email form appeared: Name. Email. Subject. Message. She typed in *K* for name, then tabbed and paused. "I don't want this guy to know my email."

"Give him one of mine," Gianna said. "It's a bullshit account I use for douche-bag retailers. I check it maybe once a year to delete everything."

"Thanks." Katie turned the laptop so Gianna could put in her email. Katie then typed *For Benevolus552* into the subject line. "Now the hard part." *What do I say?* Katie shook her head. "You know, fuck it. Right? What have I got to lose?"

She typed: *I am the daughter of Scott Wallace. He is now jailed. I have questions.*

Then—before she had time to second-guess what she'd written, or delete it, or shut the laptop and walk away from this forever—she clicked the Send button.

She looked at Gianna. "Think he'll reply?"

"You want him to?"

"I don't know. But my dad mentioned him specifically, and he's definitely into all this stuff." She tried imagining the information this man might have. Could he possibly know, or do, anything that could help? She clicked the back button a few more times to inspect the home page again. Up top was a tab leading to all the 9/11 stories. When she selected it, a list of fifty articles appeared. Everything from metallurgical studies to the disappearance of some plane in 2007. "You read any of this?" she asked Gianna.

"The 9/11 stuff? Some."

"What do you think?"

"I don't know. These guys all seem pretty serious, but then you start reading what they're saying and . . . it's an awful lot to accept."

"For sure." Too much, maybe. "You'll check your email tomorrow?"

"Totally. Here, if I can remember the password. Hopefully used my usual."

"MrsJacobBlack?"

Gianna sneered. "Haven't used that one in years, thank you."

Katie laughed, looked out the bedroom window. Another day dying outside. Another day her dad would spend locked in a mental hospital. But was she any closer to helping him?

"Yay, second try. And hey! Only four hundred some unread emails. I'm gonna wipe these out. Or, um, okay, never mind. Katie?"

Gianna had turned the laptop again.

At first all Katie saw was a bunch of junk emails, but she'd also seen the look on Gianna's face and her gaze scanned up accordingly.

The very top email was a reply from Benevolus552.

"It's probably one of those auto receipt things," Katie said.

It wasn't.

Click to talk.

The email from Benevolus552 was a three-word note. That's all.

Three hyperlinked words. Katie hovered over them for a look at where they might take her. It was a superlong link, different from the website they'd used to find him. Some kind of private chat or . . . ?

"Should I click it? What if it's a virus or something?"

"Please, you want to talk to this dude or not?" Gianna reached over the laptop and clicked the link for her. "Okay, then."

A separate browser window opened.

Something called Champion Arena. And a log-in box.

"What the hell?" Katie looked at Gianna.

Gianna's face was scrunched in disgust. "Weirdo."

"It's like a stupid game or something . . ." Katie stopped talking as, on the screen, both the Username and Password fields somehow filled themselves in.

"Ohhhkayyyy," Gianna sighed behind her.

"Seriously," Katie said. "What the hell?"

The screen changed immediately to a bigger, even more colorful home page, and then, as quickly, an image of what seemed to be monsters fighting.

"Told you," Katie fumed. "It's a virus. Shut it off."

"Shhh." Gianna pushed Katie's hand from the keyboard. "Who cares if it is? This laptop's old as fuck anyway. Let's see where it goes."

The browser window settled. They were definitely in a game of some kind. Brightly-colored graphics of a field, trees, clusters of shiny rocks, and smoking volcano stacks. Stacks of square icons representing various characters and powers. Two windows scrolling real-time gamechat and ongoing scoring.

"That's cute and all but—"

"YOU SENT ME AN EMAIL. PLEASE IDENTIFY."

Both girls screamed.

The weird computerized voice had come out of the laptop. It sounded like someone talking through one of those mechanized voice boxes that smokers with throat cancer sometimes use. Like Siri on crack.

Katie and Gianna turned and stared at each other. Gianna's hands were on her mouth, but the scream passed and she was clearly about half a second from laughing hysterically.

"What do I do?" Katie asked her in a half-whisper. "Do I type or—"

"JUST TALK. CAN HEAR YOU."

Gianna's hands stayed at her mouth but now she wasn't ready to laugh. Her eyes were saucer wide. "Dude . . . ," she whispered.

"Is this Benevolus552?" Katie asked out loud. She forced herself to look away from Gianna, back to the computer.

The voice blared out again: "YOU SENT ME AN EMAIL. PLEASE IDENTIFY."

Katie scowled. "Exactly what it says in the email." She placed her thumb over the laptop's built-in camera. Just in case.

"WHAT SHOULD I DO WITH THIS INFORMATION?"

"I have no idea," Katie admitted. "My father said to contact you. That you would know what to do."

Nothing but silence came back.

"Do you?" she prompted.

"NEED TO MEET."

Any impression of "weird" had now increased tenfold. In what unspeakable scenario could she possibly agree to meet this person in the real world? He was barely even a voice on the Internet. Could be someone who secretly hated her dad or a nine-year-old kid messing around or some kind of human trafficker or serial killer.

Or, was it someone who genuinely had the information she so desperately needed? Someone who had even one inkling about what the hell was going on.

"Yes, fine," she blurted. "Where?"

"CAN YOU FIND RENTCHLER WOODS?"

"Fuck *that,*" Gianna whispered. "You meet in, like, a McDonald's, and I'm going, too."

"I APOLOGIZE," the creepy computer voice said. "DID NOT MEAN TO SCARE YOU."

Too late for that.

"YOUR FRIEND IS RIGHT. PUBLIC WILL HAVE TO DO FOR NOW. THE ROOT BEER STAND IN BECKET RIDGE? TOMORROW. 4:00."

"Becket Ridge? I don't even know where that is . . ." She looked to Gianna, who'd already started checking on her phone and quickly gave the thumbs-up. Katie squinted at the map on the phone. "Oh, okay. Got it. 4:00? Is there anything I—"

"SEE YOU SOON."

The browser window closed. Behind it was the first window where his original reply email had been. Only now the email with the link was gone. It wasn't in her inbox or deleted emails, either. It'd vanished. Right along with the voice.

As if neither had ever existed at all.

Katie dropped her thumb from the camera.

"See you soon," she said to no one.

14

Katie checked her phone again.

It was 3:40. Gianna was a good twenty-five minutes late (not entirely surprising) but she wasn't responding to texts either (which was). Any extra time needed to find the place was completely chewed up now. Worst case, she told herself, they'd arrive a little late. But would he leave if they weren't there on time? He could. Benevolus552 could do anything.

Guy was clearly a weirdo. Exhibit A: he called himself Benevolus552. Exhibit B: he'd taken over Gianna's computer, set up a private chat with a fake voice, et cetera.

She still tried to give him the benefit of the doubt. Because: What If?

What If her father's accusations, even some of them, were legitimate? What If the United States government, or some powerful hidden group working within the government, was actually behind 9/11 somehow?

Then, Benevolus552 was right to be overly cautious. Protecting himself against the most powerful people on Earth. Something to perhaps consider herself. How careful was she being? What If Big Brother really *was* watching?

She'd looked for Max in the library earlier—had questions regarding the computer stuff Benevolus552 had pulled—but he hadn't been in all day.

It was 3:45 now. She didn't want to text Gianna again. That'd be obnoxious.

She wandered the library, still half looking for Max but mostly hoping to kill some time and take her mind off waiting.

She spotted him on the second floor. Wearing his backpack and talking animatedly to someone, an older girl, mid- to late-twenties for sure. Katie watched, deciding to leave him be. No need to disturb. But he'd noticed her, and she watched as he ended the conversation and gradually headed her way.

"Hey you," he said, his grin shy and awkward. "How's the project coming? You're in here more than I am now, I think."

"Yeah, maybe." She smiled. "I didn't mean to interrupt."

"We were done." He looked back. "She's the graduate assistant for my Strategic International Transactions class. Talking about this thing."

"I can't imagine. Hey, could I ask you something?"

"Of course. I still owe you my firstborn, right?"

"How hard is it to take over someone's computer? Like, use their mic? Open browsers? That kinda thing."

"It's a joke. Why?"

"Really? That easy?"

"If you know what you're doing. Even if you don't, it's not that hard. Why?" He was smiling. "What'd you do?"

She groaned. "I clicked this link and—"

"'Here endeth the lesson,'" he said in a deep Scottish-like accent. "That's one anyone can do. Whatever link you clicked afforded someone on the other end instant control. It's like super spyware. Hops on, gets a look at all your files, pulls your IP, everything."

"God. You guys are awful."

"'You guys'?" He reset his book bag. "Look, just because I know *how* to yodel doesn't mean—"

"Are you Benevolus552?"

"Do you want me to be?" Max asked.

Katie bit her bottom lip in thought. "I don't think so."

"Then, no, I am not he-she-they. Though, if that's the sarlacc who's messed with your computer and you'd like to get even, I can certainly assist with some shenanigans of my own."

"Ha," she grinned. *Sarlacc*? "I'll keep it in mind. I—Oh!" Her phone was buzzing in her front pocket and she pulled it free. *Yes!* "Sorry, I really need to take this!"

Max held up his hand in approval, stepping away but not leaving.

"Are you here?" Katie asked right away. "Tell me you're outside."

"Bad news," Gianna's voice admitted quietly at the other end. "Still at home."

"Oh. Will you be able . . ." Katie's head dropped in defeat.

"I'm really sorry, Katie. Got into this thing with Momzilla as I was leaving and it escalated. And, so, yeah, I'm really, *really* sorry." Gianna sounded devastated.

Katie wanted to be mad, but couldn't. Not when Gianna had actually listened to her. Not when Gianna had actually tried. "Don't worry about it," she said. "Go be nice to your mom. We'll try another day."

"Should I contact him with, you know, that webpage or something?"

"No, best keep away for now. We'll figure it out later."

"You're not still going out there, are you?"

"No," Katie said, almost meaning it.

"You can't, Kat. He's probably a serial rapist or something."

"No doubt."

Gianna moaned. "I screwed up everything."

"You," Katie corrected honestly, "are the only reason we even found this guy. And you were amazing to offer me a ride in the first place. It's not your fault I don't have a car."

"Well, it's your fault there's a cat staring at me."

"Is she? Hi, Winter," she spoke closer into the phone.

Gianna's voice now carried a smile. "She heard you."

"I'll stop by to see her tomorrow. I gotta go now."

"I'm really sorry."

"Don't be. You rock. Bye." Katie ended the call and stared at the ground for a while. There was still time to get an Uber out to Becket Ridge, but Gianna was completely right. Benevolus552 was a total stranger. Someone she'd literally met on the Internet. Textbook eighth-grade health class example of guys not to meet up with alone.

But, if she rescheduled, what if he got pissed? Got scared off? Lost interest? *Damn, damn, damn.* How many more days, weeks, would she have to go before getting this same chance again? The chance to meet someone who maybe actually knew something about what was going on with her dad. Was meeting him alone really that dangerous? She'd be in a public place. She could—

Katie blew out a breath, turning back to the doorway, half surprised to see Max still standing there. She focused on him, hope suddenly rekindling, her heart beginning to pound a little. It didn't hurt to ask, right?

What the hell would she do with his firstborn anyway?

Katie sat alone at a picnic table outside the Root Beer Stand.

She had a soda and a medium order of waffle fries, both untouched. The curbside restaurant was crowded. Lots of families, a few younger couples, and a pair of truckers who'd pulled over for a bite. There were also a couple of older random women and men sitting around by themselves. She studied each, trying to figure out which one was Benevolus552. The picture online didn't show much and could be a fake anyway.

Was he even there at all? Was he a *she*? Katie doubted it. Based on everything she'd found online, every book she'd flipped through: 9/11 conspiracy was primarily a "man's world." She couldn't recall more than a small handful of females cropping up in her 9/11 research. No idea why. Maybe something to do with guys' love for facts and figures, the same kind of guys who could talk forever about sports stats. So, probably not female, she decided, eyeing one woman again. Though she still couldn't rule it out.

Max sat on one of the end stools along the outside counter that ran along the back of the restaurant. He was turned so it looked like he was watching the cooks work, but he definitely had his peripherals on her. It was beyond cute. He'd been a champ from the get-go. After a brief explanation (leaving out *why* exactly she was meeting this guy) and several genuine apologies for asking, he was all "no-problem-understood-happy-to-help" and walking her to his car. An old faded four-door Saturn, and even that had seemed charming.

It was 5:11 now. He'd driven that Saturn as fast as he could, but they'd still been thirty-plus minutes late. The last fifteen minutes had been spent ordering and sitting and waiting and realizing Benevolus552 was long gone, probably never to be heard from again. She'd go until 5:30 and pull the plug. It had been a stupid idea anyway to—

Someone sat across from her.

A guy. Late twenties, early thirties. Hair pulled back in a ponytail revealing a giant forehead. He was wearing dark sunglasses and a cutoff plaid shirt over a black T-shirt with some band she didn't recognize. "You get the root beer?" he asked.

"Excuse me?" Katie looked around, made sure Max was watching. He was.

The man had a cardboard box with several chili hot dogs, onion rings, and a giant soda. "Did you get the root beer?" he asked again, looking around. "Best flippin' root beer in, like, the state. You order chicken at Red Lobster?"

"Uh, look, I'm kinda waiting for someone."

"Champion Arena," he stopped her. "I'm your guy. 552, okay?"

Katie narrowed her eyes, studying him more.

"Not what you expected?"

"I didn't know what to expect," she admitted. "Your online pic's pretty vague. How'd you recognize me?"

"You waited too long to put your thumb over the camera."

"Oh." So he had been watching. A shiver ran up her back. "That's some sketchy stuff you pulled on my computer."

"Yeah, well, only way." He took a sip of his drink. "Ahh, so good. So, yeah, if you are who you say you are, I couldn't have you sending more emails. NSA, FBI, DHS. They're all over those."

"Who else would I be? You want to see a driver's license or something?"

"No point, too easy to fake. I looked into some things. For now, I'll accept you're Wallace's daughter. How'd you get my name?"

She didn't want to imagine what he'd "looked into." Or how.

"I told you," she said. "My dad told me to look you up."

He took a bite of an onion ring. "And he's in jail?"

"Psychiatric hospital. I've only been allowed to see him once. That's when he told me about you. Said you could help. That you'd think of something."

Benevolus552 studied her. "You wearing a wire?"

"What? No. Dude . . ."

"Who's that guy?" he asked, pointing one greasy finger at Max.

"A friend. I didn't want to come alone."

Benevolus552 nodded. "Who else knows about this meeting?"

"No one. That's it. Oh, my other friend. The girl whose—"

"Gianna D'Eustachio. Clara Barton High. Yeah, I know about her."

"That's the creepiest thing I've ever heard. We should report you to the police or something."

"Just trying to protect myself. Again, know who I'm talking to. Dangerous business trying to find and share the truth, you know. I don't want to end up like . . ."

"Like my dad?"

"Damn straight. Patriot Act allows arrests for 'domestic terrorism' without trials, without lawyers. 'Domestic terrorism' is anyone who doesn't drink the Kool-Aid. You know you can be arrested—as a terrorist—for advocating the proven environmental dangers of the beef industry? If you refer to yourself as a constitutionalist or you're found to have more than seven days' worth of food stored in your house, you're considered a domestic terrorist. So, what'd they arrest him for? Your dad. Officially, I mean. *Eight* days' worth of food in your house?"

"He hit a coworker, made threats against Cheney. And, you know, all the 9/11 stuff. They're using that to say he's delusional, certifiably paranoid."

"Of course they are." He shook his head. "Citizens who 'believe in conspiracies' are on the top of the government's watch list of suspected radicals. Quickest way to shut us up. Just lock us away. No trial needed."

"Well, he had a trial. And will have another soon. So, here's what I want to know: is he delusional?"

Benevolus552 shrugged. "You know who we are? The Plain Truth?"

"Your website? Yeah."

"Lot more than a website. I admit, many Truthers are only doing it as a hobby, something to kill the time on a Saturday night. Or maybe a legit academic pursuit. Then there's the rest of us. Without genuine info, without the truth, humanity will never truly thrive. Franklin once said . . ."—Katie suppressed a smile: *Nice, G!*—"we'd founded a true republic, a nation of laws. Not another tyranny or the mob rule of democracy, either. A republic. 'If you can keep it,' he warned. Meaning it would take work, a committed and informed citizenry. The Plain Truth provides that backbone, a breathing archive of news, documents, and facts pertinent to the ongoing war between civil liberties and the modern world. No easy task when most people don't even realize they're in the middle of that war."

Was this the same secret—imaginary?—war her dad was still fighting?

"What's this have to do with my dad?"

Benevolus552 leaned in closer, his next words mere whispers. "Okay, guess I'm going all in. Your dad found me six months ago. Didn't send no email, either. Found me in person.

Scared the shit out of me, to be honest. Thought I'd covered my tracks pretty well. He said he had intel on 9/11. *Real* intel. The kind that'd change the world. I figured he was full of shit."

"Why'd you think that?"

"Most guys are full of shit." Benevolus552 leaned back again and made half a chili dog vanish in one bite. Wiped his mouth. "You know how many jokesters write me, tell me they have this secret info about this or that? All week, every week. But your dad was convincing, knew his stuff. The military. The private security work after."

TERNGO, she thought to herself. "What 'intel' did he have, specifically? I mean, did he show you anything?" Anything *real* she could bring to Wren?

Benevolus552 leaned closer again. "Yes."

Katie suddenly felt like she was standing outside her own body, watching herself not react to this chili-breath guy. Oh, look! There's the girl learning from a total stranger that maybe her dad isn't completely insane after all! Look how she's sitting with that serious smile and that serious stare and she's not at all about to lose her complete shit at—proof!?

"He showed me enough." The man scratched his chin, pondering his next words. "How much has he told you?"

"Nothing," she lied. Because he'd told her to say nothing.

"Nothing about TERNGO? The Cleveland airport? Said he knew about a survivor." Benevolus552 had pulled down his sunglasses to the bridge of his nose. "One of the passengers who'd been snuck away that day."

Boom! Once more, she was right outside her body, watching herself not react. It was like the most useless superpower ever, but she was nailing it.

"You believe that?" she asked. "His story, I mean."

"I don't know. Clearly, *someone's* nervous about what he claims. Why else would he be locked away?"

"And my dad was gonna use your site to get this information out?"

"That was the plan. He's been trickling us info over the last couple months."

"Sorry, but why you guys? Why not go to the real press?"

He smiled, grabbed his cup of root beer and lifted it up as if to toast her. "You're joking, right? The 'real press'? When's the last time those guys told the truth about anything? They been toeing the party line for Corporate America about 9/11, and everything else, since day one. Reporters who've tried to cover anything outside the official story have been fired. Legit news stories about explosives in the towers or government foreknowledge have been scrubbed like they never existed. Fox, CNN, right, left, it don't matter. They're all working for the same master. Six companies control 90 percent of all media. That's almost everything you hear, read, or know, controlled by six corporations. And I'm not talking media corporations. I'm talking GE, Goldman Sachs. Companies with only one purpose: to make money."

She could sense him revving up, about to launch into a longer monologue about American corruption. No thanks. "You said you and my dad started talking six months ago. Why is none of this supposed intel of his on your site yet?"

"That's on him. He said he wasn't ready. Wanted to get organized before we went live with everything he had. I respected that. Seemed worth the wait." He shrugged. "And now he's locked up."

"Very."

"Okay, I got an idea. Come to Philly in his place."

In his place? "What's in Philly?"

"Truther convention in two weeks. He and I were going to meet there with some others in the movement. Make final arrangements for how all this information should go out to the world. We agreed it had to be all at once or not at all. Otherwise—funny, he'd predicted it—we'd all end up in some psychiatric ward together. You could come and talk to the others. Maybe—"

Katie grunted. Like the sympathy of some underground cyber-radical group was going to help her in any way. She already had *one* nutjob to manage. "I don't think so."

"Together we could figure out a way to keep the pressure on these guys."

We'll keep the pressure on them, Katie. You and me . . .

Her dad's words echoed in her mind. Would it really put pressure on the right people? Help shake loose more info somehow? "What do you mean?"

"Just seems there are a few guys very interested in what your dad might know and they're all gonna be in one place in two weeks. They'll *want* to help you. Once you get the right people asking questions, you might be surprised what you find out."

This was getting out of hand. "I should probably leave," she said, smiling politely. "Thank you for meeting me. I appreciate it." Her hands shaking now, the not-reacting routine finally starting to crack.

Despite her brush-off, Benevolus seemed—happier now. Energized. He peered at her, excitedly. "Can I ask you something?"

She sighed, distracted, wanting to be gone. "Sure."

"Are you her?"

From somewhere far away, she watched herself again turn and look blankly at the stranger, not wanting to honor his question. Not wanting to believe any of this was happening, that any of it *could* happen. "Her, who?"

"The missing girl," Benevolus said, but his words somehow weren't a question. "The 9/11 survivor."

15

The man's eyes were wide with elation at whatever he now saw in her face. The surprise. The panic. "You *are*, aren't you?"

"I don't . . . No." Katie stood, slammed back into her own body. "I should go."

"Holy shit." He leaned back and ran the fingers of both hands over the top of his whole head, slicking back hair already in a ponytail. "That's real? *You're* real. He wasn't bullshitting about that."

"I really need to leave."

"Wait!" He reached out to take her wrist.

"Please." She'd stepped back. "I need . . ."

"Everything okay?"

It was Max. Of course it was Max. Standing beside her. And Max was smiling at her and it was the best smile she'd ever seen because somehow it said: *I got your back if needed.*

"We're good," she replied, then turned back to Benevolus552.

"You the boyfriend?"

Katie grimaced.

"I'm her, uh, regional mobility consultant," Max replied. His face had reddened again.

"Sure, okay." Benevolus552 smiled, looking down at his cell phone. "So, Philly. Be there. Anything come up in the meantime, no more emails, just enter 'Benevolus552' in your friend's browser and I'll know to send you another link."

Max reached across the table and took one of the guy's onion rings. "You can do that?"

"You have no idea." Benevolus552 grinned, looking up.

"Wow." Max smiled back. "That's really neat."

"Let's go." Katie tugged once at Max's arm. "Thanks again."

Benevolus552 nodded, then reached for his second chili dog as they walked away.

"Was it really necessary to take the dude's onion ring?" she asked Max once they were heading toward his car.

"'You have no idea,'" he replied.

"You okay?" Max asked again, driving.

"Yeah. Thanks."

"Respectfully, you don't look it."

"I'm a little weirded out, I guess," she admitted. "The guy back there . . . You know, never mind."

"Yup. So, what's in Philadelphia?"

"It's private."

"Yup."

"A Truther convention."

He laughed. "I knew it. You're really into that stuff, aren't you?"

"It's for a school—"

"School project, yeah, yeah. Okay. You didn't come all the way out here and meet that two-bit hacker for any school project."

She stared out the car window, watched the town of Becket Ridge fall away into the past with everything else. What could she tell him? "It's personal," she finally said. "Let's just say it serves my needs if I can prove the official 9/11 story has some holes in it."

"And talking to this Benevolus clown will help?"

"Maybe. I don't know."

"Mind if I ask you a question?"

"Go ahead."

"Why?"

"Why what?" She turned to look at him.

He watched only the road ahead. "Why would the US government kill three thousand of its own people?"

She knew the customary responses well enough.

Too well. Part of the tangled maze she'd spent weeks studying. Didn't mean she was comfortable repeating any of it out loud yet. Taking on the role of an actual "Truther."

"I'm not sure I want to get into all of that," she said.

Max shook his head, disappointed. "First stage of any criminal trial is to establish *mens rea*, legalese for—"

"The 'guilty mind' of the accused," she stopped him. Okay, if he wanted to do this, fine. "The *intent* of the crime."

Max smiled, glanced over. "Give the girl an A. So, was it the US government's specific intent to purposefully create this calamitous event or . . ."

"Or," she finished, recalling the exact terminology she'd studied a week earlier, "were they 'knowingly,' 'recklessly,' or, what-is-it, wait, 'negligently' involved in the actions of that day?"

He nodded, impressed. She was, admittedly, a little impressed with herself. "Question of the hour, yes?"

"Question of the century." Katie took a deep breath. "I assume you know the phrase *cui bono*."

"Who gains?" he replied.

"A-*plus* for the boy. And you also know what a false flag operation is?"

"Sure, like the Reichstag fire, right? Nazis deliberately burn down their own building, then blame the communists and use that as an excuse for seizing power. Cui bono? Hitler. You saying we're Nazis?"

Katie's body tensed. "No, but the United States hasn't been above using false flag operations in the past."

"Let me guess: Pearl Harbor."

"We can start there, sure. Many believe Roosevelt knew the Japanese were coming. He wanted the US to—"

"Wanted the US to get into World War II." Max shook his head. "That's why I hate conspiracy stuff. The Japanese killed three thousand Americans. You don't think Roosevelt could have gotten his war with better air defenses, some torpedo nets, and maybe only one thousand dead? A *hundred* dead Americans, you don't think we declare war on Japan? That's why cui bono can be real problematic. Sometimes people are simply making lemonade."

"How so?"

"When something bad happens, those in power do what they can to turn the event to their advantage. That's what you're *supposed* to do."

Katie frowned. This was not an argument she wanted to have. Not even one she completely believed in. And yet. She felt challenged. Dared. Almost as if Max was calling her stupid if she couldn't back any of it up. "But Roosevelt *pushed* the Japanese into it. He, like, refused treaties, cut off their oil supply."

"That's a far, far cry from intercepting specific plans for

a December 7 attack and not doing anything. I've read that Roosevelt cried that day."

"Maybe out of guilt." She pushed on to another famous example she now knew. "What about the Gulf of Tonkin?"

"You mean Vietnam?"

"It became America's excuse to enter Vietnam," Katie said frostily. "Yet it never happened."

Max scowled at her. "I'm pretty sure something happened."

"Look it up."

"I will. Go on."

"Well." Katie riffled through her memory, thinking of the other examples she'd scribbled down into her notebook over the past two weeks. "In the sixties, the CIA blew up buildings in Italy and Spain. Blamed the communists."

"That right?"

"It was called Operation Gladio. Look that up too." She paused. The next one trickier to discuss. "You know about Operation Northwoods?" she asked. Her voice had gotten so quiet, she wasn't entirely sure if she'd spoken the words out loud.

"Nope."

"In 1962, Kennedy asked the CIA and the Defense Department to come up with more plans to get rid of the communist government in Cuba." She paused, suddenly wanting to burst into tears. The similarities to her dad's version of 9/11 were too awful. "Part of their scheme involved painting a military jet to look like a commercial airliner and shooting it down near Cuba. Blaming the Cubans. Then the US could invade."

Max looked at her. "For real?"

Katie nodded, feeling a little sick. "Their plan was to use empty planes with fake passengers—or sacrificial travelers—on a flight *deliberately* sent off course past Cuba."

"No shit."

"No shit. Kennedy rejected the plan, but still . . ."

"Got anything not from the Stone Age?" he asked.

"Who'd know? The Kennedy stuff was only declassified in 2001. A lot of people think the Oklahoma City bombing in the nineties was a false flag event. Katrina, Ebola, ISIS . . ."

"Oh, right." Max rolled his eyes. "So *everything* shitty that happens is now manufactured by the government. Hurricanes, even. Let's stay on task. So if 9/11 was a false flag operation perpetrated by the USA, cui bono?"

"Weapons manufacturers, for one," she replied. "The wars in Iraq and Afghanistan have made a handful of companies trillions of dollars. *Trillions.* In American taxes, American debt. You and I already both owe the government more than a hundred thousand dollars to pay for those two wars. *Someone* got all that money. Haliburton, one of the biggest military companies, made sixty billion on Iraq alone. Know who Haliburton's CEO was right up until he became the Vice President?"

"Aaron Burr?"

"Funny."

"Dick Cheney."

"Yes. Haliburton didn't even have to submit bids to get the contracts. They were handed sixty billion dollars."

"Lemonade." Max shrugged. "We have to quickly go to war, of course the guy's gonna contact old pals. People he trusts."

"Or he was sent to Washington to get them their wars . . ." She paused, the last line sounding way too much like something her dad had said. "Well, defense spending was on its way down in 2001 but it's increased 2,000 percent since 9/11. Oh, and the Bush administration had plans to invade Iraq and Afghanistan *before* 9/11."

"So did the Eisenhower administration. So what? That's what these guys do. Somewhere, they have plans to invade Canada and the moon."

"Secondly, there's the pipeline in Afghanistan."

"Oil."

"Enough to secure the West for another hundred years. The United States was in negotiations with the Taliban—yes, the Taliban—to secure the construction of a major pipeline across Afghanistan. Working with this company called Unocal. When talks fell through, the Taliban were warned that they could be 'buried in gold or bombs,' their choice. This was in August, a *month* before 9/11."

"You ever hear of coincidence?"

"Some coincidence. American troops had trained and were on standby for an invasion of Afghanistan. We were going in that fall no matter what."

"Bingo. In which case, why kill all those innocent people? I mean, if we were really going in anyway?"

"Maybe Bush and Cheney knew they wouldn't have the public support needed to get it done. Needed an excuse. Maybe it wasn't Bush and Cheney, but some rogue group working for the oil companies. After the invasion, Unocal's CEO became the US ambassador to Afghanistan, and two members of the Unocal board became Afghanistan's prime minister and director of defense. Nice, huh? The pipeline's being built now. And American military bases 'coincidentally' line its route from one end to the other."

It was exciting to challenge Max, to answer his objections. But she was merely playing devil's advocate. Arguing for the practice. Not really believing. And yet, so much of what she'd just said was verified. True. And with the simplest conjecture, she could hold these facts in formation, make them coherent.

Isn't that all her dad was trying to do?

"Third," she said, "and *last*, I promise. Before entering the White House, Bush and Cheney were part of this group called the, ah, 'Project for the New American Century,' one of those Washington think tanks. This one was focused on America's shrinking role in the world and came up with a solution. The group argued specifically for three things: increased military, US military in space, and greater surveillance at home and around the world. In their most famous paper, they argued Americans would never have the stomach or pocketbook for any of those things unless . . ."

"Unless?"

"To quote them verbatim: 'Unless there was some sort of new Pearl Harbor.'"

"More lemonade. A woman's husband dies. She gets a five million dollar insurance payout, moves to Aruba with the pool boy. Did she murder her husband?"

"Is there really such a thing as a pool boy?"

"Or . . . did she merely take a horrible situation and turn it to her advantage as quickly as possible?"

Katie sighed, slumped back in her seat, any further arguments flowing out of her like air out of a balloon. "I guess that makes sense too."

Max nodded. "They wanted to hurt us," he said. "The bad guys. For complicated reasons. And for simple reasons too. So they attacked us and killed some of us and then . . . then we made lemonade."

"An awful lot of lemonade," Katie grumbled.

Max shrugged. "We're not in charge for nothing."

16

"Back in one piece," Max said, pulling up in front of the Claypool house. "Please check your overhead luggage rack for any personal belongings."

Katie stared at the house. Not yet wanting to go back inside. It was dark, but still before curfew. "Thank you so, *so* much for doing this."

"My pleasure." He bowed his head slightly. "I was going to stay in all night and hack video games. This was a far better use of my time."

"Well, thank you."

"Hey."

"Yeah?"

"You're going to Philadelphia, aren't you? See that Benevolus guy again?"

"No. Probably not."

He smiled.

"I don't know," she confessed.

"If you go, take your friends. If they can't make it, maybe call me."

"You're not my friend?"

Max's race reddened again. She loved how quickly it could do that.

"We'll see." She opened the car door. "I probably won't go."

"I could steal some onion rings for you. Act tough."

She smiled and stepped out. "I believe you could."

"Well, good night," he waved.

"Good night," she echoed, then shut the car door and watched him drive away.

The next morning, Katie stared in horror at the man standing in the Claypools' foyer. Gray slacks and a light blue shirt and tie. Plastic smile.

Paul Cobb. The gum-chewing Veterans Affairs guy.

When C.J. had come upstairs to get her, she'd assumed it was Ms. Dorsey or maybe even Max but . . . why this guy?

She took each step with a heavier thud, as if maybe, if she stalled long enough, he'd go away. Not happening.

Mr. Claypool was talking to the guy about God-knows-what. Probably giving him some kind of report. What time Katie came in each night, any mentions of her father at the dinner table, how many squares of toilet paper she used each day.

"Here she is," Mr. Claypool beamed. It was genuine, too. That was the really maddening part. You couldn't hate this guy if you tried.

"Hello again, Katie," Cobb said.

Him, however, you could hate with reckless abandon.

"Mr. Cobb," she said, hitting the bottom step.

"Was in the neighborhood, wanted to give you an update. Is now a good time for you?"

There'd been no new information on her dad in almost two weeks. And last night, after Max dropped her off, she'd lain awake for hours, her brain bouncing around the prospect of her get-together with Benevolus552, and any and all ways it might help free her dad. *You're goddamned right now's a good time.* Katie nodded.

"Would you two like to—" Mr. Claypool was offering up the front room for their talk.

"Gorgeous day." Cobb had already half opened the front door and waved her to follow. "Let's take a walk."

"I'd prefer to—"

He stepped through the door, ignoring her. "Come on."

Katie followed down the porch steps into the morning sun. Even that short journey felt more laborious than it should. *I'm working on four hours of sleep,* she reminded herself.

Paul Cobb put on sunglasses. Smiled again. "Just to the end of the street and back," he explained, turning. "Ten minutes tops."

"Okay." She walked beside him. "How is he?"

"I stopped by the hospital this morning," he said. "Why I wanted to see you."

Emotions surged through Katie so quickly she almost choked. Fear, first. What had happened? What had they done? Then worry. What had he said? And then anger, blind rage that they were holding him like some animal.

"They're making progress," Cobb said. "That's the main takeaway I got from Dr. Ziegler and his staff. Definite progress."

"I can see him again, then?"

"Soon." Even as he said it, she'd whispered the same word. He chuckled. "Guess we say that a lot, huh?"

"We could get a lawyer and demand to see him. He has rights."

"Oh, do you have a personal lawyer now? That's great."

"I want to see him."

"I'm sorry. Visitors are still prohibited."

"Even daughters?"

"*Especially* daughters. You're father has, in all likelihood, had a total nervous breakdown brought on by decades of untreated and acute PTSD. Hence, his delusions regarding evil government plots."

"Should those really be dismissed so quickly?" she asked. "What if he's telling the truth?"

"Katie, it's Paranoia 101. You're a smart girl, you gotta know that stuff's not helping him any. It's only getting in the way of real issues. Do I need to remind you what happened the *last* time you visited?"

She'd stopped walking. Stood, shaking her head.

"I knew this guy once." He'd stopped too and now turned away from her, studying the neighborhood. "Guy by the name of Crazy Harold."

"Look," she tried to cut him off. "Mr. Cobb, I think the best thing to—"

"A terrible nickname. Utterly politically *in*-correct, but we're talking thirty-some years ago, so, what are you going to do? I was a student at Georgetown." He glanced back at her. "This gentleman, Harold, was older—fifties, sixties—and he spent all week in the Library of Congress. Down in the stacks in this little work cube he'd reserved. Doing research. Thirty, forty hours a week."

Katie's lungs or heart, or both maybe, dropped somewhere deep into her stomach. Somehow, Paul Cobb knew about her hours at the library. *Her* research. *Her* cube in the stacks. How?

Of course! That man near the bus stop *had* been following her. Her dad was right; they were being watched. Right? This was the proof she needed.

"What was . . . what was he researching?" she asked. Her voice had come out strained and frail.

"The sinking of the *Lusitania*," Paul Cobb replied.

Katie shivered in the warm spring sun.

She knew all about the *Lusitania*. Hadn't a month ago, but she sure as shit knew it now.

It was the 9/11 of World War I.

The *Lusitania* was a doomed ship.

Torpedoed and sunk by the Germans during World War I. The attack killed a thousand people, including a hundred Americans, tipping American public opinion from years of neutrality into finally joining the first global war.

It was considered by many—back then *and* now—to be one of those false flag plots. One Katie might have brought up to Max the other night. A setup contrived by the British (a young Winston Churchill, in fact, who was in charge of the navy at the time) to nudge the slow-moving Americans to finally join the war.

There were letters from Churchill saying as much. He'd written: *It is most important to attract shipping to our shores in the hope of embroiling the United States with Germany. We want the traffic—the more the better; and if some of it gets into trouble, better still.*

The *Lusitania* had been sent into dangerous German-infested waters. Sent without military escort, even though dozens of military vessels were available. Ordered by the British navy to "slow down" while passing through these waters. And, when torpedoed, sank in less than twenty minutes, a speed that baffled shipbuilders. Had it secretly been carrying explosives? Had all the victims truly sunk to the bottom of the sea so fast?

Had the British government really sacrificed a thousand innocent souls to win World War I?

They killed her. Killed all of them.

I'm sorry.

"I'm sure you've heard of it," Paul Cobb said.

"What?" Katie's mind refocused. "Oh. Yes."

"Harold was convinced that the *Lusitania* was an 'inside job.' That the British government had somehow been behind the whole thing." Cobb paused as if to fully let the connection between her father and Harold sink in.

Katie wanted to scream.

"And even more so," he continued, "that the victims were still alive somewhere. That the British were too civilized for outright murder and the missing passengers had been spirited away to live out the rest of their days under some form of house arrest on a small Scottish island."

The similarities between this story and the one her dad told were . . . they weren't similarities. The stories were almost identical. Almost. Except in Harold's demented tale, there were many survivors.

Not just one.

Katie stopped thinking about it. Cobb was toying with her. Proving he knew exactly what she and her dad were up to. Pushing her. Why?

"That's all very interesting," Katie said carefully.

"No," he replied. "Wizard schools and zombies and Magneto are interesting. This is something else. This is a man's life we're talking about. Twenty-plus years chasing down a harebrained fairy tale. For what? So hundreds of grad students would call him Crazy Harold?"

"He probably didn't care about that." Katie glared. "Why would he? He was after the truth."

"The truth? The truth." He took off his sunglasses and folded them into his shirt pocket. "The truth, Katie, is the *Lusitania* didn't get a military escort because the British navy was terribly unorganized. The truth is the United States waited another two years before entering the war. Two years. If England's plan was to sink a ship and get us into the war, their plan sucked."

"Fine," Katie said. "What's your point?"

"The point is your father, and you, need to drop the 9/11 bullshit."

"What makes you think I care about any of that?"

Would he dare admit to spying on them? An even worse thought: what, if anything, could she do about it if he did?

"Not a minute ago," he said instead, "you asked me: 'What if he's telling the truth?' Quite honestly, we can't have you two meeting if that's how it's going to go. This conspiracy nonsense is getting in the way of your father's real mental health issues. If he can't get past it . . ."

Katie felt herself grow very cold, as if all the blood in her veins was slowly dropping in temperature, degree by degree. Maybe the feeling that she'd blown it; that if only she'd managed to say the right things—just this once—she'd unlock the secret code and Paul Cobb would drive her straight to her dad. That it could all be over.

"If he can't get past it, then what?"

He shrugged, squinting into the sun. "I'm not sure if he'll ever get out."

"How'd it go with the Wallace girl?"

"It went," Cobb replied into the phone. "She's no pushover, for sure. But she's been fairly predictable so far. The nudge will work. She'll be in Philadelphia next week."

"Good. Could be the break we're needing, sir."

"Could be." He watched the passing houses as he drove. Half wanted to pull up to one randomly. Knock on the door, go inside for a cup of coffee or a beer, and tell the people there what he and his team, and a dozen teams like it, were doing to keep them safe. If only it were that simple. "I think it's time we let them talk again," he said.

"Wallace and the girl?"

Only 20 percent of the country trusted its government anymore. In the 1950s, 75 percent had. But after Kennedy and Cambodia and Tuskegee and Watergate and Iran-Contra and Edward Snowden and . . .

"His daughter," Cobb corrected, putting away such thoughts. "Yes. Make sure he's presentable. Couple days enough?"

"Okay, if he's mostly out of it."

"It'll have to do."

"Yes, sir."

"Funny," he commented, thinking. "I told her about Crazy Harold."

"Right, the *Lusitania* guy. You thought you might."

"All those years looking for survivors on some Scottish island, and his entire theory was flawed from the start."

"How's that?"

"There'd have been no survivors," Cobb replied. "The Brits would never have taken the extra step to spare them. Not worth the risk."

"Would we?" the man on the other end asked.

Paul Cobb hung up, hoping the question was rhetorical.

17

The Truthers' thing in Philadelphia was proving a little disappointing, in the same way that the law library had. Smaller than Katie had expected, for one. A lot smaller, actually. One lecture hall and a hallway of seven vendors in the Cabrini Arts Center. Less than a hundred people, and a pretty low-energy hundred, too. She'd kinda imagined impassioned mobs with signs and petitions and pamphlets. Hundreds of interested citizens, standing room only; most of them unsure, coming out to learn more, to test and stretch their own positions. Reporters covering the event. Long lines.

Maybe there'd been more excitement, more people, ten years before.

Today, the room was almost half empty and everyone was pretty quiet. Mostly keeping to themselves or in pairs as they wandered in and out of the sloped hall during a short break, waiting for the next speaker. Sitting toward the back, Katie could watch.

Almost all men again. From twenty to sixty, all shapes and sizes. Hippies. Hipsters. Nerds. A couple soldier-wannabes. And a teenaged law student.

Max Thompson surfed his phone in the seat beside her.

Katie smiled, happy he was there.

She'd never even thought to ask Gianna or Alexis for a ride.

And if Max had said no, she'd have considered it a sign from the gods and skipped this madness altogether. Had she secretly been hoping he'd decline?

She checked her own phone for something to do. Still ten minutes before the next speaker. They'd seen two other panels so far. One about the Malaysian planes that'd vanished in 2014 and their possible links to Al-Qaeda with plans to strike the Petronas Towers (Asia's own Twin Towers) or deliver a dirty-bomb attack in the United States.

The second one, which Max claimed to have actually enjoyed some, was more like a chemistry class than anything. Two interchangeably generic white guys, one presented as an architect and one as an ex-military "explosives expert," went over the nano-thermite or super-thermite allegedly used (alleged, that is, by Truthers like her dad) to bring down the towers in New York. They'd shown pictures and charts of the residue found in the building rubble, revealing specific molecules only made possible when sophisticated explosives have been employed. By this point, Katie probably knew almost enough about this stuff to present the lecture herself.

"Your boy's back," Max said, not taking his eyes off his phone.

Katie turned.

Benevolus552 had finally reentered the room and was working his way down toward the front, trailed by two other men. She'd spotted him in the thermite-panel audience too, but when their eyes finally met, he'd quickly looked away—clearly no plans to walk over and say hello. This guy who'd invited her, practically begged her to come, hadn't said two words to her yet. Would he continue to ignore her? Had something happened? Either way, it would've been a lonely and rather dismal outing thus far except for the boy now smirking beside her.

"What's so funny?" she asked.

He put the phone away. "I'll tell you when you're older."

"Guess you think these guys are pretty stupid, huh?"

"*Au contraire.* Some pretty smart guys here today."

"You being serious?"

He nodded. "Not saying there aren't a couple dummies, too, but the vast majority is legit top of the curve. A lot of programmers. Academics. Creatives. Part of the conspiracy trap, though, isn't it?"

"How do you mean?" She nudged his arm so he'd look at her.

He did and smiled. "The lion's share of these guys *are* smarter than most people. Better minds. Better educated. So, there's already a fundamental, perchance justified, feeling of superiority. The fact that most people don't believe, can't wrap their little minds around the—what to *these* guys are obvious truths and facts—that all becomes additional proof it's a room of smart people. 'We're so smart, we can see things other people can't.' The allure of having secret knowledge, of knowing something most don't, is quite powerful."

Katie couldn't deny this. It *had* been somehow satisfying: knowing more than the average person. After only a few weeks of research, she'd already learned more about recent history and politics than most people. Still . . .

"Powerful enough to fabricate the knowledge?" She narrowed her eyes.

"Maybe." He clasped his hands together behind his head, leaned back, and closed his eyes as if to nap. "The problem with most of these Truther sites—most websites in general, in fact—is that anyone can put up any 'knowledge' they want. No peer review necessary. No proficiency or education required. No accountability. Click Save and you're in business."

More people filed back into the lecture hall. Maybe more of a crowd than she'd figured earlier. Keynote speaker and all.

Katie sank back in her chair, too. Still holding out that whatever was supposed to happen here today just hadn't happened *yet*. That someone—maybe Benevolus552, maybe someone else—would walk up and hand her secret 9/11 files or a check for fifty grand to cover her father's legal expenses. Something like that. *Yeah, right . . .*

"Hey." She turned to Max.

"Yeah?"

"Thanks."

"For what? Spending the day with you?" Max gave her that lopsided smile again. "I ain't one of the dummies," he said.

The keynote speaker was on stage.

He'd been a professor of cultural studies at Kent State University. Now, Dr. Compton was an "award-winning" author, an "expert," the host of some online radio show that claimed "millions of listeners" worldwide, and so on. Katie didn't know about any of that. It all sounded good, but it wasn't like the guy had worked at the Pentagon or something.

He was dressed better than the other presenters. Wore a suit and tie like a business guy, like Paul Cobb. And his slide show was super pro. Smooth. He spoke with complete ease and confidence. Way this guy talked, he'd maybe give Mr. Ward a run for Teacher of the Year.

Dr. Compton had already done twenty minutes on the latest fallout regarding the 9/11 Commission Report. The report itself was old news, 2004. But as the US government's official record of what happened that day, it was six hundred pages that people still interested in 9/11 were always focused on. Katie had her own dog-eared, highlighted copy at home. Mostly Compton recounted how members of the commission, including the chairs, later claimed the investigation had been hampered by the White House, that resources had been pulled, that hundreds of pages had been deleted from the final report.

Throughout, Katie listened intently. Hoping—as she had with the other two panels—to find some new sliver of information that somehow supported her dad's ghastly claims. Some of it fit. That explosives may have been used, that the 9/11 Commission may have been obstructed by the White House.

But there'd been nothing specific yet today about the planes. The passengers. Anything about airports or Cleveland.

Mostly, she could only claim to have found a very generic confirmation of deception. The White House *had* lied about what transpired that day. One hundred percent. And not telling the entire truth was a lie, right? If that single line-in-the-sand made her a Truther, then maybe . . .

Dr. Compton was now ticking off a list of information and questions left out of the Commission Report. Challenging the government to trust its own citizens with, well, the Truth.

"Numerous sources," he expounded, "including other governments, as well as news services such as the BBC, have established that six of the nineteen alleged hijackers are still alive today. That several of the men accused less than a day after 9/11 were merely imposters with invented names. This was recognized years before the Commission Report was released, yet there is no discussion, not one word, of this discovery, or even its *possibility*, in the report. Friends, we must forever demand from our government the truth, the whole truth. And nothing but the truth."

"So help me, Dr. Compton," Max whispered beside her.

Katie elbowed him discreetly.

"Building 7," Compton continued, as a slide with the familiar footage of the building collapsing appeared behind him. This was the mostly-forgotten *third* building to collapse in New York that morning. "Forty-seven stories high. Tenants included the Department of Defense, the CIA, the Secret Service, and the IRS. No plane hit this building on 9/11, yet it still collapsed and several employees saw explosions from inside. In addition, numerous New York firefighters claim to have heard explosions in this building. A building not even *mentioned* in the Commission's report. Not one word. What do we deserve? What must we demand?"

The room murmured various responses involving the word "truth."

"The *whole* truth," he directed. "And nothing but. Molten steel, running underneath and through the rubble of the Twin Towers, burning for months in some spots, according to eyewitnesses at Ground Zero and confirmed via thermal imaging. Given that steel melts at 2,750 degrees Fahrenheit and airplane fuel can't generate temperatures within even a thousand degrees of that, only *thermite* explosives explain the molten steel. But was the steel rubble tested for thermite? For the residue of nuclear-based explosives?"

"No," several voices shouted back from the audience.

"No, the rubble was shipped as quickly as possible to China and Korea as scrap metal. Despite protests from the FBI and the Association of Fire Fighters that crime evidence was clearly being destroyed. Once again, this is not mentioned in the Commission's report. Not one word. What do we deserve? What must we demand?"

"The whole truth," the crowd returned.

Compton smiled in approval. "And nothing but." He resumed, "The company in charge of security for the World Trade Center, and United Airlines, was Stratesec. A company whose board members included President George *Walker* Bush's younger brother, Marvin, and his cousin and CEO, Wirt *Walker*. And yet this remarkable family connection is not mentioned in the Commission's report. Nor the 'workmen' employed in empty floors and offices in the weeks leading up to 9/11. Nor the fact that one elevator shaft was unexpectedly closed for weeks for 'renovations.' Nor that bomb-sniffing dogs were inexplicably *removed* from the towers five days before the attack. Nor the power shutdowns in the towers on the weekend immediately preceding 9/11, as security cameras were blacked out, and numerous witnesses report seeing workers laboring throughout the buildings. Not one word. What do we deserve? What must we demand?"

"The whole truth." The crowd synchronized now, picking up on the game.

"And nothing but."

"He's really got 'em going now," Max noted beside her.

"You wanna get out of here?" she asked. And she wouldn't blame him if he did. It was getting a little too rowdy, border-line scary. He had them now, Dr. Compton. Even half had her. They could leave, and if Benevolus552 didn't get the hint, didn't really want to talk, so be it.

"We can stay," Max said. "I'm good."

Compton continued down his list, supporting his claims with pictures and videos flashing behind him. Some she recognized from her own research, some were new. Each point ended with a mandate and the group's more-and-more thunderous rejoinder: The Whole Truth.

Several men arrested when two vans filled with explosives were discovered in New York on the morning of 9/11. No mention in the report. "The whole truth!"

US bureaucrats warned by the FBI not to take commercial flights that week. No mention in the report. "The whole truth!"

Hundreds of millions made on Wall Street when a handful of secret investors purchased atypical and massive stock options on the assumption that the stocks of American Airlines and United Airlines would plunge in early September. The records of those transactions destroyed under orders from the government. No mention in the report. "The whole truth!"

Osama bin Laden, the FBI's most-wanted man even before 9/11, exposed by numerous sources, including the French government, for meeting with the CIA in Dubai two months before the attacks. What was discussed at this meeting? Unknown. No mention in the report. "The whole truth!"

More than a dozen military drills being run across the US the morning of the attack, including simulated hijackings and a plane crash into a building. No way for air traffic controllers to tell fiction from reality. No mention in the report. "The whole truth!"

Claims that Flight 93 landed in Cleveland and—

Katie jolted up like someone had nudged her with a Taser.

"Passengers," Dr. Compton continued, "were witnessed being led to an unused military hangar and held for questioning.

Again, no mention in the official report. What do we deserve? What must we demand?"

"The whole truth!" the crowd responded again. Louder, much louder, and more as a single voice. A giant's voice.

The speaker's next points were mostly lost to Katie as he cycled through the missing air traffic control tapes, dubious phone calls, shortened black box recordings, and unreleased flight manifests.

She'd read about the Cleveland allegation many times before. It was the cornerstone of her dad's entire allegation.

Planes landing. Passengers being led off.

A thousand planes had landed quickly and chaotically that insane morning. Tens of thousands of passengers. Flight 93, however, was the plane that'd gone down in a Pennsylvania field. *Of all the specific planes to be spotted* . . .

If her dad's story made any sense, it surely had something to do with *that* plane. Benevolus had also specifically mentioned Cleveland. Here was a keynote speaker, some kind of 9/11 expert, bringing up the same possibility. Suddenly various flight paths and times of departure and transponders being turned off rushed into her head. She needed to—

"You okay?" Max whispered beside her.

She stopped thinking, refocused on the room, on Max. The lecture hall was loud, she suddenly realized. *Really* loud. "Yes," she said over the din. The audience applauded now, Dr. Compton waving his hands in thanks. A picture of his newest book and video loomed enormous behind him. Many in the crowd were already moving in to talk further, get a signature, take a pic.

I need to talk with that man, she thought. *What else does he know?*

She started to get in line with the others but then spotted Benevolus moving through the crowd, *away* from Compton. Walking with another man, heading up their way. He nodded at her, kept walking toward one of the back doors.

"What's that supposed to mean?" Max asked.

She'd stood. "I guess it's time to talk."

Benevolus552 and the other man waited.

At the end of the hall, at the far edges of the crowd emerging from the conference room. Katie and Max walked casually toward them. She thought right away of telling Max to hang back, give her some needed privacy, but there was safety in numbers. *Right?* It'd gotten weird before in a hurry. If Benevolus had a new friend, she needed one too.

This second man was tall and pale with glasses and short reddish hair.

He wasn't introduced. "Hey," he said, sizing up Katie and Max.

Katie nodded. Didn't feel the need to introduce herself or Max either.

"So you decided to show up," said Benevolus. His voice had gone low and deep, secretive. He looked past her down the hall.

"You said there'd be people who could help my . . . help me. People who'd have answers."

"Your dad still locked up?" the new guy asked.

Damn it. She hadn't thought about how quickly it would get so personal. Wasn't sure she wanted Max hearing this. No, she decided. She didn't. "Hey, Max." She turned. "Could you . . . ?"

"Yeah, no problem." He backed away slowly. "I'll be over by all the books and tchotchkes." He looked at Benevolus. "I'm on the hunt for a Rudy Giuliani bobblehead."

Benevolus shook his head.

"Thanks," Katie said, stepping between them as Max bowed slightly and wandered back toward the merch tables. Katie watched him go. Smiled. Then she looked back at the two men waiting. Two adult men. This was so weird. "Is it just you two?" she asked.

"Others got spooked," said Benevolus. "Your dad's arrested. That's scary enough. Wanted to see if you'd even show up. If the first meeting had been some kind of a setup. Anyhow, any new developments?"

"No. They told me he's 'making progress,' whatever that means. And then gave me a bunch of shit about keeping away from conspiracy theories."

The two men exchanged wide-eyed looks.

"Yeah, right?" Katie prodded. "So what the hell am I doing here?"

"Who gave you shit?" the new guy asked.

"Guy named Paul Cobb. Works with Veterans Affairs. Says all the 9/11 talk is just fueling my dad's paranoia."

"I'll bet he does," Benevolus said. "Wanna know what fuels mine?"

Katie nodded while the second guy shook his head.

Benevolus continued, "The info I've been getting. Info from your dad."

"I don't understand," Katie said.

"He's figured out a way to *keep* sending us info. He must have known this was going to happen. Planned for it."

"How is that even possible?" Katie frowned.

"Can you get pictures?" the second man asked, ignoring her question. "Pictures of your dad. In the hospital."

Katie recoiled, the very thought making her stomach clench. She was still processing this wild claim Benevolus had made. Was this guy serious? Pictures? She wasn't some sort of ninja paparazzi super spy. And the last thing she wanted was for anyone else to know her dad was in that place. "Why?"

"We thought we could start spreading the word about what's happening to him. Engage the community on this. Picture's worth a thousand words, right?"

"I don't know. That's kinda personal. And your 'community'—from what I can see—is two guys."

"Hey, we're taking a big risk trusting you. There are more people ready to get involved, but we need more time. And a little more from you. Your dad told you to trust me, right?" Benevolus looked around. "We won't use names or anything yet. Just a 'source,' 'ex-military,' that kinda thing. You have my word. Enough to let the Powers That Be know we're aware of what's going on."

"But I haven't seen him in weeks. If I take the pictures, they'll know who did it. And then I'll never get to see him again."

"Your call," the new guy said. "All of this is your call. If it's too much, we understand. But anything you can get us tells us more about what's happening to your dad. Doctors' names, anything more on the Veterans Affairs guy will help. We'll check it all out best we can and use it if everything looks kosher."

"I'll try," she said. "The doctor's name is, um, Ziegler."

"Good," Benevolus said. "Info like that. You know how to get ahold of me."

"We done?" the second guy asked.

"Wait! What? No." Katie reached out and grabbed

Benevolus552. "We're not anywhere *near* done. You told me if I came here, you could help us."

"Not yet," Benevolus said, tugging his arm back.

"What is it you want, exactly?" the other guy asked.

Katie scowled at him. "I want . . . to know if you have *any* substantial proof my dad's not a raving lunatic."

"Yes," he said. Then he nodded in farewell to Benevolus and stepped away to join the crowd down the hall. Katie watched him leave in wide-eyed horror. Did he really have something? Who was this guy?

"Go do your thing." Benevolus552 stopped her racing thoughts. "Let us do ours."

Just like that, Benevolus was gone too.

Max approached carefully.

"Everything you hoped for?" he asked.

"Is it ever?"

He shook his head. "There's a documentary or something up next."

Katie checked her phone. It was moving in on four o'clock. Maybe best to leave. Call the day a washout. But she really wanted to talk to Dr. Compton now more than ever. Demand some answers. Some *real* answers. Not more Truther bullshit. Her head felt like someone was clobbering it with a bag of wet dirt all of a sudden. "Hey, I need some fresh air," she decided. "My head, I don't know. I don't feel so great."

"Sure." He thumbed toward the floor-to-ceiling windows and outside. "We could—"

"Some 'alone time' fresh air, if that's okay with you? I don't mean to be a bitch, but . . ."

"Nope, you're good."

"Would you check and see if the line for Dr. Compton has died down? I really need to talk with him before we go."

Max looked uneasy. "I guess."

"Thanks." She squeezed his arm and sped down the hall, away from the small crowd toward one of the back exits. She needed to move, to breathe. To relax.

Outside led to the side parking lot and a long, narrow bluff of grass and a few trees out back where she might sit or pace for a bit before deciding next steps. The bluff another hundred feet past the building and a couple parked cars.

She breathed deeply, briefly rubbed her eyes and cheeks. The sun was still high in the sky and felt good on her face. The artificial air and cold were already evaporating off her body. *This was a good idea*, she decided, looking up.

Then, from behind, the hands grabbed her.

18

Katie couldn't move.

Weight from behind had completely pinned her whole body. Fingers over her mouth. Her own hands fought back—discovered a monstrous arm around her waist.

Her throat raged against the clasping hand. Produced only a muffled grunt.

She'd been drawn into a nook behind the building. Her body stiffened, struggled, but the collapse came sooner than she ever imagined. She felt weightless suddenly. Apart from her body, as she had been the night the police had come to her house when all this started.

Now to meet some terrible end. Without ever knowing the truth. About her dad. Her mom. She scanned the parking lot, the hillside, the hotel in the distance. This was where it was going to happen? These were the last things she'd ever see.

"Katie, relax." The voice was at her ear, clear and distinct. Decidedly, like the hand, male. "You're safe."

Safe? In what possible way? She felt her physical self returning. Her mind raced a hundred different directions. He'd said her name. What was this? Benevolus? The government?

"I'm a friend of your father's," the man said. "I'm here to help. Do you understand? If you scream, I'll go. I will not be able to help you then. Do you understand?"

Katie's whole body was shaking.

"Katie. Do you understand?"

She nodded against his hand, his top finger pressing up painfully into her nose. She felt the grip release around her waist and mouth. The pressure easing away. Katie turned slowly.

She recognized him immediately.

Tall with a buzzed haircut. Bigger than she remembered. More muscled up close.

The man from the bus stop. The creeper from across the street.

Her legs wobbled. She gathered breath to scream. To fight.

"Katie." He held up his hands in peace. "Your father sent me."

She'd pulled her cell phone free to call 911, but now she just watched as he retrieved a packet of cigarettes from his top pocket. "I'm sorry about scaring you." He surveyed the parking lot and lit up. "I knew you'd seen me the other night and figured walking right up to you today would freak you out even more. Your old man can punch me in the face for it later, okay?"

"How 'bout I punch your fucking face right now?" Katie fought to control her breathing while he, on the other hand, took a heavy drag on his cigarette. Nice. "Who are you?" she asked.

The man blew smoke out of both nostrils. Waited until the cloud had cleared the space between them.

"I'm the Dragon," he replied.

The dragon may come for you.

Her father's words in the hospital. She'd taken it as 95 percent babble.

And 5 percent as a warning of some kind. A threat. The dragon will come for you and do something terrible. But then—as *everything* he'd said that day now filled her mind again to be reprocessed—her dad had followed with: *Your father should know you're alive.*

If the Dragon was a real thing—which was obviously the case—then she also had to accept what he'd said next. *Your father should know you're alive.*

How were the two connected?

Had Scott Wallace been trying to say . . .

"Are you my father?" Katie asked. Why wait?

The man choked back a reaction over his cigarette and smoke burst from his mouth. "Am I your—what? Are you crazy?"

"You tell me," she said. It had taken less than a minute for fear to officially turn to rage. Good. "Who are you? And don't *ever* fucking touch me again."

"Already apologized for that. And, I won't. The name's Collison and I've known your dad going on twenty years now. We served together in the Army." He held out his cigarette. "*Dragon*'s an old Army thing."

"My dad sent you? How exactly did he manage that when he's in the hospital?"

"By *not* contacting me. We keep in touch. Weekly. Quick call or email to make sure everything's cool. If I ever didn't hear from him, I was supposed to check in. On both of you."

"That's weird. This"—she waved her hands to indicate the two of them standing at the back of the building—"checking on me like this, is weird."

"Affirmative. But we need to talk freely. And you're not alone too often."

"Um, how long, exactly, have you been stalking me?" She *knew* she'd seen him before. Must've been around the library, or somewhere near the Claypools' . . . "How do I know you're my dad's friend?"

"You don't," he admitted. "But if you could zip it shut for about two minutes, I'll tell you what I can and be on my way. You wanna call the police or your boyfriend or the nerds inside, knock yourself out."

She crossed her arms. Bit her mouth shut. Waited.

"Four weeks ago, your dad failed to check in. I looked into it and found out what had happened. Then tracked you down, like your dad had asked me to if something like this ever happened. That was the first order of business. The next was to support plans he'd made for some information he had. Information that other people wanted, that he wasn't willing to give up yet."

"What information?"

"After the Army, your dad went freelance with one of the bigger security-contractor companies."

"TERNGO Global Security," she stopped him. Happy to know something.

"There you go. Did a couple years with them. During this time, *something* happened."

"On 9/11?"

"I don't know anything about that. Most of his work with them was overseas long before 9/11. Keep in mind, I've never seen any of this info myself. All I know is that *something* happened during his time with TERNGO. Something that scared the shit out of him. And that there's evidence. Some kinda files, documents, pictures. Of something bad. Involved TERNGO, for sure. US military, too, I suspect, based on things your dad said. Told me if anything ever happened to him, this information needed to be taken care of. And that *you* needed protection."

Katie scowled at him. "Only one who's threatened me so far is you."

"Is that true?"

"Yeah. I mean, there's this one guy, Paul Cobb, who's been asking weird questions. He works for Veterans Affairs. That's what he said, at least."

"I'll look into it. The thing is . . ." He took another long drag. "If this info is as big a deal as your dad says it is, there're a lot of people who'd do about anything for it."

"I don't have this info or have any idea where it is. If it exists at all. So, how am I involved? Where's the 'danger' for me?"

"You're what's called leverage." The man smiled. It wasn't a good smile. "They're probably hoping he'll ask you to retrieve some of this evidence. Or maybe they'll use you to threaten him, convince him to play nice. You're the only family he's got."

"Who's 'they'?" Katie protested. "This sounds ridiculous."

"True. Doesn't mean it ain't happening. Could be TERNGO. The government. Some third party looking to sell whatever all this info is to the highest bidder." The man shrugged. "Take your pick."

"So, then, what are these 'plans' you two initiated? Where's all this supposed info, if you haven't actually seen any of it? I have people telling me my dad is still sending them information from inside the hospital. Is that you?"

"No. And I told you, I didn't 'initiate' anything. I'm doing a favor for an old friend. Your dad's stored most of this data away with someone he trusts."

"Who?" Did he mean—

"Not your new buddy Benevolus. His only role is to

disseminate the info. Meantime, that info—whatever it is—is in the possession of your dad's computer guy. I don't know who that is. But my understanding from mutual friends is that, based on specific dates determined by your dad months ago, dates even triggered *by* his arrest, certain info is to be leaked out to the world. To warn away the guys coming after your dad for all of it, I suppose. From what your dad told me, the parties involved don't want this info out. Ever. Others want all of it out now. Your dad had other ideas."

"You said 'most of it' is with this computer guy. Where's the rest?"

"He told me he kept backups and some critical data for himself. Somewhere safe. With data keys that opened up the most damning evidence. Never told me where. As I said, some are going to think you do know. Or that you soon will."

"Well, I don't."

"I believe you. But my job is to keep away people who might think differently."

"That's touching, but I can take care of myself."

"I imagine you can, if you're anything like your father."

She almost scoffed. The idea of her dad taking care of himself . . . "How well do you know my dad?" Better than she did? Not that this was a high bar.

The man grinned. "Scott and I been through hell and back a dozen times, and trusted each other with our lives more times than that. Katie . . ."

"Yeah."

"I'm not entirely sure what your dad's going through right now, but Scott Wallace is a genuine hero and a patriot and, more importantly, a damn good man. Yeah, I know he had some bad years. The drugs and stuff. But if he thinks this information is worth protecting, or worth releasing, or whatever, well, I'll do whatever I can to help."

"And you don't know anything specific about 9/11?"

"Nope." He shook his head. "I wasn't working with him then."

"Do you know anyone who was?"

"No, sorry. And my advice to you is to stay out of all this as best you can."

"That'd be easier if I didn't feel like I was being stalked all the time."

He winced. "Okay, point taken. In that case, I'm gonna vanish again. You call me if you need anything. Anyone scares you, looks at you funny, something don't seem right, I'll be there as soon as I can." He gave her his number.

She still wasn't entirely sure if she should thank him or call the cops.

"How does this end?" she asked.

He flicked his cigarette away from them onto the parking lot. "First thing is to get your dad free, by scaring some people with the information he has. He'll fix things from there. Always could."

Katie pictured her dad half-asleep on the couch. Tried imagining him fixing anything.

"Sorry again for the . . ."

She waved his apology away like swatting a fly. The anger had mostly drained out of her. Replaced with the overwhelming feeling of a world much, much too big to deal with.

Katie looked back to the convention center, back toward the seminar and Max. Wondering more than ever about the "Whole Truth" and what that even meant anymore.

When she turned back, the Dragon was gone.

"Everything okay?" Max asked.

He'd been standing outside the door before she even got there.

"Yeah. Sorry, didn't realize I was gone so long."

"Not a problem. I just didn't see you and this place is filled with, you know, interesting types. But, you're all right? You look—"

"Christ, YES! I'm all right," she snapped, because there apparently still was some anger left in the tank. "I'm *okay*. I'm *fine*. Everything is good!"

Max's eyes went wide with surprise. "Um, sorry. I didn't . . ." Whatever he might have said next was dropped. He opened the door for her. "Line's dead. You want to try and see Compton now?"

"No," she decided. The excitement she'd felt about talking to this guy had deflated. All these people—her dad, Benevolus, the Dragon—had the same answers.

None.

Nothing but hints, recycled and reframed to disguise how little real information there was. Would Compton really be any different? Most of his talking points she could find as easily from other people on YouTube. The bulk of his speech had been on something written in 2004. There was nothing new here, nothing substantial. Besides, she was still freaked out about being snatched. How easily someone had—Katie shook her head. "Let's go home."

Max paused, waiting to see if she was sure.

"I've seen enough," she confirmed.

He let the door shut and they walked together toward his car without another word. Katie looked around the parking lot, curious—half terrified—the Dragon was watching. She'd forgotten to ask him how he'd followed them here.

She stopped outside Max's car. Max hadn't even blinked at her little outburst. Hadn't gotten mad or hurt. He deserved something.

"Max."

"Yes, ma'am?" He looked over the car's roof between them.

"My dad is in a psychiatric hospital, and it might help get him out if I can prove 9/11 conspiracies aren't completely insane."

That was enough. He didn't need to know the rest. No one did.

Max nodded, got in the car.

She got in too. "You think that's weird?"

"Wanting to help your dad? No, it's not. If it were my dad, I'd try to prove black was white."

"Is that what I'm doing?"

He shrugged. "Probably. I don't know, Katie. If you wanted, maybe I could help you work through some of the grays. Does that sound fair?"

She leaned over and kissed Max on the cheek.

"What's that for?" he asked.

She thought. "Looking out for me."

His whole face had flushed again. She was half tempted to kiss him again, on the mouth even, and see how bright red she could make him.

"You date much?" she asked.

He snorted. "I was eleven my junior year of high school. What do you think?"

"Bet all those college girls are making up the difference now."

"Oh, for sure," he replied, starting the car. "Fish in a barrel."

The Claypools waited in the front room.

It wasn't even eight o'clock yet but they, it seemed, needed to talk. Curfews. Checking in. Responsibility. Legal obligations. Consequences.

Her new foster parents were calm and fair and Katie still wanted to throw them both through the window. But she kept quiet and nodded and said "sir" and "ma'am" a lot and apologized in all the right spots.

Mrs. Claypool finally moved on: "Ms. Dorsey called this morning. Some encouraging news. You're scheduled to visit your dad on Monday."

"Really?" Katie couldn't believe it. And felt irritated she'd been made to sit through that whole lecture before getting this significant information.

"Maybe you should take it easy tomorrow," Mr. Claypool suggested. "Stay in."

"I've got a pretty big paper due next week," she replied. Too quickly, too desperate. She'd already made plans to meet Max at the library. *Bring it down*, she thought. *They'll get suspicious.* "I was going to hit the library again," she added more calmly, and honestly. No need to get precise with *which* library.

Mr. Claypool started to say something, stopped himself, and smiled at her pleasantly instead. How many conversations had he had like this, with how many lost children?

"The girls are watching a movie downstairs, honey," Mrs. Claypool added quickly.

"Thanks, Mr. and Mrs. Claypool," she said, backing out of the room. "I'll do a better job of checking in."

They both smiled, satisfied for another day at least, and Katie retreated downstairs. There, C.J. and Zoe watched some animated thing with subtitles. A deck and small spread of five tarot cards was on the table in front of Zoe.

"Sup?" Zoe said as Katie plopped down on the couch beside her.

"Long day." Katie sighed. "How's the future looking?"

Zoe glanced at the cards. "Depends," she replied. "You want to do a reading?"

"Ahhhh, can you do one about the past?" she asked.

"Sure can." Zoe recollected her cards into a single stack.

Katie shook her head, surprised. She hadn't really expected Zoe to offer a reading.

"No?" Zoe smiled.

"No thanks," she replied.

Tarot cards were bullshit. But in case they weren't . . . she wasn't so sure, just now, that she could handle any more cryptic clues about the past.

The car drifted down the dark pathway like a pursuing shark. The faintest swerve. Dirt popping beneath its tires. Trees running on either embankment gently patting at the sides of both doors.

He'd spent the day among the enemy. An undertaking he always detested, but a necessary one in the greater struggle. And for good reason. You never knew what you were going to discover.

Take this girl, for instance.

A survivor of 9/11? One who'd escaped the "greater conspiracy."

The notion was intolerable. Offensive. He'd already pulled over to vomit.

Oh, but here she was, all the same. Emerging like some new-formed goddess, some demon, from the recent rumors. Rumors that'd become emails and texts. The new pictures of her on the camera. It was a travesty. What information could the father possibly have? There was no way such half-truths should be put into the world. Period.

The drive from Philadelphia had been long. It was already Sunday. There was still too much work to do.

Something would need to be done about the father.

Something would need to be done about the girl.

Hopefully nothing too violent.

Not this time. Not again.

Hopefully.

19

They'd moved to one of the larger tables for more think-ing space. Her notes were spread out in half a dozen different piles. Perfect for a quick glance if needed.

The morning had focused on the practices and scope of direct, cross, and redirect examinations. Analyzing objections. Securing depositions, motions to terminate or limit. Evidence preservation of documents, data, and "tangible things." Max was a pretty good teacher. Katie wasn't sure she understood all of it, but she'd definitely gotten enough to not make an ass of herself in front of Wren.

But enough to prove black was white?

Now it was her turn. To somehow teach Max everything she knew about airports and airplanes, and mass murder. She'd tried a half-hearted run-through days earlier with Zoe and C.J., but this was different. This was Max. The kid who'd started high school when he was nine.

He waited patiently across the table. Phone away, both hands on the library table, sitting up straight, trying not to look bored. Perfect practice for Marilyn Wren, who absolutely intimidated the shit out her.

Katie started simply, slowly, with the four planes.

Tangible. Factual. Indisputable. In any telling.

Flight numbers. East Coast departure airports. (Two from

Boston, the other two from DC and Newark.) Their various West Coast destinations. (Three to Los Angeles, one to San Francisco.) Known times of departure, the official passenger totals. Their official point of hijacking: when each plane had changed course. When the planes' four transponders were manually turned off. When the air traffic controllers knew something was wrong.

"And the transponder basically tells the air traffic guys where the plane is," Max confirmed.

"Exactly," Katie nodded. It'd been his sole comment so far. "And they were turned off on all four planes. From five minutes for Flight 175 up to thirty for Flight 93. No one knew where these four planes were."

She pulled out the flight paths copied from the Commission Report. "This is the official version of the flight paths as determined by the 9/11 Commission. Pulling together info recovered from the flight recorders, radar images, and so on."

"Okay." He studied the four flight maps.

Katie laid her other printouts down on top of them. "*These* are flights paths as determined by secondary radar records, eyewitnesses, and transponder data."

"And they're, I see, slightly different. How does this help your argument?"

"It establishes discrepancy, confusion, as to where the four planes were. Some of these trajectories imply differences by as many as forty miles."

"Sure, if you give these secondary sources the same weight as the government's findings. And in all cases, there is agreement on the final destinations of all four planes."

"How do we know, for sure, those are the same four planes? It's possible that the two planes that hit the World Trade Center were decoys, fakes, that replaced the original flights. That these replacement planes were loaded with special explosives and run by remote control. And so was the plane that hit the Pentagon. And a fourth drone—one heading to DC—was shot down by US forces over Pennsylvania once the delays in getting military air support could no longer be justified."

"Katie . . . that's way out there."

"I know." She smiled weakly. "But plenty of people believe it, and it's the only way to hold my father's argument together."

"Okay, okay. I presume—in this scenario—the plane-switching took place when the transponders were turned off. Planes reroute. New custom evil-plan planes take off in their place."

"Yes." She held her humiliation in check. He was just doing his job.

"And the original planes?"

"Flown to Cleveland and de-boarded there, according to the original flight paths and known air traffic that day. And numerous witnesses at the airport." She dropped a new picture on the table. A huge hangar with the word *NASA* across the top of the building. "They were brought here, to an abandoned NASA hangar, for processing. Their DNA collected, their luggage already taken for later evidence."

"Okay, but in New York, at the Pentagon, *and* in Pennsylvania . . . they recovered pieces of planes, personal luggage, and DNA connected to the original planes."

Katie shook her head. "You mean engine parts that don't match the parts of the 767 planes that officially hit New York. Parts then quickly buried in landfills. Or did you mean the terrorist passport found, in mint condition, lying on top of what was left of the World Trade Center? How difficult would it be for someone to plant luggage and DNA? Witnesses from that morning disagreed as to what any of the four planes even looked like. Some said they were small military jets, black, or even planes without windows."

"Meh, witness testimony. There's film of these planes hitting. That's fact."

"Objection, Your Honor. With the likely manipulation of digital images, the credibility of photo and video evidence is routinely dismissed in court. Besides, many experts believe the footage actually shows military-style planes hitting the World Trade Center, and *not* commercial 757s. As to the other two planes, not a single witness saw Flight 93—the one that went down in Pennsylvania—do *anything*. Not one single person. And the few witnesses at the Pentagon all offer conflicting reports. Several described the plane as a small commuter jet, not a 757 by any stretch. Some didn't even see a plane."

"The missile crap."

"I'd appreciate it if you don't refer to my points as 'crap' while I'm presenting them. This isn't easy for me, you know."

"You're right. *Mea culpa*. Will your points grant that some witnesses *also* saw a Boeing 757?"

"Yes, but there is no film of a Boeing 757 hitting the Pentagon, fact boy. Not a single frame. My high school has forty goddamned cameras on twenty-four-seven, but the Pentagon, the most important military building in the history of the planet, didn't have any cameras operating that day? That's impossible. Impossible. And to ask Americans to believe that is . . . insulting. The cameras that *were* operating, in several nearby buildings, were confiscated by the FBI on 9/11 and have never been shown."

"I have a question."

"You always do." She sighed. "And I suppose that's why I'm putting up with this. So, thank you."

"Why all this hassle? Look, for the sake of your argument, I'm going to buy the premise for a moment. Darth Cheney and his cronies want the oil, weapons sales, fascist America, and so on. They plan the attack as some sort of false flag, and so on. Okay. So my question . . ."

"Go on."

"Why drones and missiles and fake planes? If I'm going to kill these passengers anyway, might as well keep them on the planes. They'll die there, too. Commercial jets can *also* be flown as drones. Easily. The plane galleys could be stuffed with anything from tactical nukes to a thousand crates of dynamite in about an hour right beneath the unsuspecting travelers. Why the charade? Swapping planes midair, collecting DNA, herding people through secret terminals. It's an extra opportunity for something to go wrong. You don't think the bad guys—whoever they are—want to keep things as simple as possible?"

Katie slumped. She'd struggled with the same question. A lot. "Maybe they figured, the messier it was, the harder it'd be for anyone to figure out what really happened. Maybe it had something to do with how the planes had to be rigged with explosives. Or unloading the passengers made it easier to manipulate the phone calls supposedly coming from the planes . . ."

"Those were fakes?"

"Many suspect so. They claim those calls shouldn't even have been possible. Early cell phones in airplanes. Those calls that did make it through are filled with guys giving their full name to their own loved ones—'Hello Mom, this is Max Thompson calling'—other callers giving only generic information, nothing too personal. Stiff, cold. Some claim it's the result of voice morphing technology. Or maybe people providing info under orders. You can hear one of the flight attendants being told 'You did great.'"

"Probably a colleague giving much-needed support on the most important call of her life," Max argued. "And of course some calls would sound weird. People were terrified. Terrorists had taken over their planes. Passengers had been stabbed, murdered. How would *your* call sound?"

Katie shivered. Had no answer. Couldn't begin to imagine what those people were going through. She looked away, hoping to stop thinking about it.

Damn it, Max.

"Let's move on." He'd recognized he'd struck a nerve. "So, tell me about these witnesses who say a plane landed in Cleveland. Who are they?"

Her dad, for one. But she could not bring herself to say this to Max. Not yet.

"Cleveland's mayor," she replied instead. "He even specifically said it was Flight 93 that landed."

"He misspoke on a crazy day. People screw up."

"Heck of a number to drop randomly. He's on record saying that *before* Flight 93 went down. Before anyone, including him, should have even heard of the flight. There are other witnesses, too. Regular people."

"So, where are the original passengers and crews in this scenario? Killed?"

"Yes. A popular Truther theory is that after military drones replaced the original flights, the original planes were dismantled, pieces buried deep in the Atlantic, and the passengers . . . yes, they were killed."

"Again"—Max shook his head—"*any* real proof?"

Again, her dad. Claimed he'd seen them. Helped one of them. Claimed . . .

"I'm sorry," said Max. "It's a lot to take in, Katie. And a little stupid."

Katie started to object. Had no idea how. Because Max was right.

"But it's also possible, I suppose." He studied the flight maps. "You've gathered a lot of info. I don't know how much is hornswoggle. Most of it, I assume. In any case, your mission is to minimize the conjecture and hone your story down to facts. *Fact* facts. Those that'll best justify your dad's beliefs. Would be nice to collect a few more from your old pal Adam Healy."

"Who the hell is Adam Healy?"

He lifted a piece of paper off the desk and handed it to her. It was a Freedom of Information Act request letter she'd written to the FAA, the Federal Aviation Administration, requesting information about the flight recordings. "What's this?" she asked.

"Freedom of Information Act. Signed into law in 1966, as code . . . 552."

"Benevolus552." Katie gasped. "His real name is Adam Healy? How do you know that?"

Max grabbed his phone and waved it at her. "At the root beer place, I got a look at his cell phone. Brand, model. That's why I really went for his onion rings. When he came into the lecture hall, it was pretty easy to pinpoint—"

"You hacked his cell phone?"

"He hacked your friend's laptop. Seemed fair. Maybe we could, I don't know, stop by and convince him to tell you more about what he knows. If anything. What do you think? About contacting Benevolus, I mean."

"Not yet. I haven't decided yet about working with him at all, you know. He's . . ." She stopped, stared at Max a little harder. "You really think my story is stupid?"

He rolled his eyes. "Unsurprisingly, that's all you heard. I also said it was 'possible' and just needed to be honed." He stood. "Need to powder my nose. When I get back, let's maybe look closer at these Cleveland witnesses. Then you're going to impress me with how much you learned about securing official depositions."

"I'll do my best," she said.

"I know you will."

Katie watched him go. Happy for the first time in a long time. Reassured, too.

Because she knew he'd really meant it.

The man came into the restroom whistling.

A random tune Max couldn't place.

He couldn't see the man yet. Only hear the whistling.

Max zipped up, turned away from the bank of urinals, and walked to the sinks. There, the man ended his whistle on a note that trailed off like a falling bomb. He was washing his hands. Clearly too old for a typical graduate student.

He looked at Max in the mirror as Max approached. "How's it going?" he asked.

"Good. You?" Max replied.

The man rinsed his hands. "Busy, busy. You know how it is."

Max swiped his hands quickly under the faucet. Nothing happened.

"Days like this," the man said, flicking water into the sink, "bet it's tough to stay focused. I remember what it was like.

Distractions. Recreations. To really get that gold star, a promising young man like you, you know what he needs?"

"A cape?"

"Focus."

"Focus. Got it."

The man balled up and tossed his paper towel. "Guess that's my fortune cookie for today."

"Then *xiè xiè nǐ bāng wǒ*," Max said—ignoring the waterless faucet, the paper towels out of reach—and stepped away from the sinks.

The man stared at him.

"Means 'thanks much,'" Max explained and hurried for the exit.

"Any time," the man's voice said from behind.

Max hovered by the table. Fidgety even for Max.

"Everything cool?" Katie asked.

He nodded. "Yup, yup. Got thinking is all. So, back to it. How else do you back up this Cleveland thing?"

"I don't know." The answer was, again, *my dad*, but not an answer she was going to give. Not to Max. "There's TERNGO."

"Who's that?"

"TERNGO Global Security. A defense contractor. Private security. They were maybe there, in Cleveland, that day."

"Why do you think that?"

"Anonymous source."

Max smiled with his eyes, clearly knew exactly who she was talking about. "Okay, TERNGO. What can you do with them?"

"I don't know. See if there's any demonstrable record of them in Cleveland that day. But that's not exactly the kind of info that shows up on Wikipedia. If those records even exist at all. This whole thing is probably only a wild-goose chase."

"Will your 'anonymous source' go on record?"

"No," she said quickly. "Not now."

"Someone else from TERNGO, then? Someone who will go on record to corroborate your first . . . source?"

"We'd need a list of employees," she agreed. "From 2001." How many names would her dad remember? "Are there records of things like that?"

Max reached for his book bag. "Let me work on that." He removed his laptop.

"Can you really do that?"

He grinned at her. "Ask Adam."

Katie shook her head. "You're a bad boy, Maxwell Thompson."

Max stepped away with his laptop.

"Only when I focus," he said.

Tomorrow, I see him.

This belief now filled her whole head. And enough of her heart.

It'd been more than three weeks since the last visit. As far as she could remember, she'd never gone more than a day without seeing him before. Though, really, what did that matter? Before, when he was always around, she honestly hadn't paid much attention to whether he was there or not. They were little more than roommates. Sharing the same space and appliances. A few throwaway words of "How was your day?" and "Did you see the Ravens won again?" and hollow nonsense like that. A few presents on birthdays and Christmas. A few shared hours in front of the TV. A few nights sitting out back and quietly watching the fireflies gather alongside the trees behind their house. Not much more.

But in this new reality, she missed him. Each day she found herself thinking of those times beyond "not much more." The day on the pony, maybe. Or when he'd assembled a small soccer goal in the backyard, even played goalie for her for a couple nights. Making omelets together, or gazpacho. Or even gutting fish together. Yes, when he'd taken her to work that one time. When he'd danced silly to that one song she kept playing. Hikes in the woods, always testing her sense of direction, so proud when she always got it right. Proud when she kept playing after getting hurt in soccer, "wiped some dirt in it," the way he'd taught her. Even those nights sitting out back and quietly watching the fireflies—maybe somehow more than passing shared time after all.

Though he would never win Father of the Year, he'd always provided enough for both of them and supported her as best he could. He deserved better than this. There *had* been good times. He *was* a good father.

But, then, why was she so terrified about seeing him? Of trying to sneak a picture of him for Benevolus552? Of sharing the list of TERNGO names Max had found?

Because of what her dad might say. What he might do. The last time, his arm . . .

She held the frame. The faded picture of a different man than the one she remembered now. The man in the photo was a stranger. The girl, too. As much a stranger as the pictures of the passengers she'd memorized.

All two hundred and thirteen pictures.

What—if anything—did this stranger see?

Worse, what did he maybe do?

Tomorrow, maybe questions would finally become answers.

No matter how terrifying those answers proved to be.

20

He sat up in his chair. No handcuffs. No restraints. A man alone in a room thinking about his day. A very *blue* man. With blue sweatpants and a darker blue lightweight sweatshirt. Even his slippers were blue.

Other than the blue man and his chair, the room had a second chair but was otherwise empty. No windows to jump out of. No sheets or phone cord to hang oneself. No saltshakers either. Gloria Dorsey and a large male orderly loitered outside the open door. Just in case.

Her dad looked thin. Hadn't spoken yet. Only stared straight ahead at something clearly not in the room.

"It's good to see you," Katie said to him.

But this was a lie. Looking at him now, she felt something new and terrible.

Pity.

So very unlike the all-too-familiar anger or disappointment or contempt. For his fragility. His weakness. His enslavement. He was so pathetic and small, she could hardly stand to look at him.

I'm a monster, Katie chided herself. She looked back to the door, wondered how much longer she'd have to stay in the room before they came to collect her. All those days, weeks, fighting to see him, to help him in some way—and now that she was in the room, she found herself counting the seconds until escape. *What did you think this would be like?*

"I'm staying with a family named the Claypools for a while," she said, to say something, anything. "I wasn't sure if you knew that or not." She waited. "They're actually kinda nice. There are two other girls. Staying there for a while, you know?"

Babble. All the questions she'd planned embedded deep in her throat. The info he had. The things he'd done. That Tuesday morning in 2001. Cleveland. Her mom.

But she couldn't find those words.

And the man sitting next to her wasn't helping much. In five minutes, she'd be shuffled out the door. How many more weeks, months until she saw him again? How much time lost?

Now or never, she thought. *If you can't do this, stop pretending. Let him do his time, and you do yours too.*

"I met"—she leaned closer to whisper—"the Dragon."

He sighed heavily. She couldn't tell if that was good or bad.

"I also saw Benevolus."

His eyes, and only his eyes, finally moved. Glared at her, almost.

"We met, and . . ." Katie stopped talking, finally registering the urgency behind his face. He was *warning* her. Not to talk.

Okay . . . if they couldn't talk, she had other agendas today that might still work. Her hand shaking, she reached for her book bag, which security had gone through in the front room, and withdrew a stack of homework she'd clipped together. School essays and a couple tests. She went through the small stack and found what she was looking for.

Six pages Max had printed out for her. The names of

TERNGO employees who'd worked there in 2001. How Max had gotten them, exactly, she didn't really know or understand. Something about getting into their accounts-payable records. Her dad's name was on the list: SCOTT T. WALLACE— further proof he'd worked for them during this time—but was it submittable? The other six hundred names Max had managed to pull were the names of strangers.

She held up the first page in front of her dad. Pointed to the first name on the list, waited for a reaction. Nothing. She drew her finger slowly down the page, pausing briefly at each new line.

His eyes slowly followed the path her finger traced. Blinking, half-lidded, his focus retreating with the effort it took. He closed his eyes.

Katie turned the page. He looked at the new names.

Gary Fuenmayor—the man Cobb had asked about—his name was on *this* page. When Katie's finger reached it, her father looked away, used his whole hand to push the page away.

Okay . . . she set it aside.

Next page. She read them, too, to herself, caught between the sheet and her dad's face with each name. Fifty more names. Nothing.

Two pages later, a soft moan escaped his lips. Katie's finger froze. The paper stack trembled in her hand as she looked at the name that had triggered her father's grunt.

Jason Bohenek

"Yes," her dad said. "Find . . . him." His voice like a rasping zombie.

The name meant nothing to her.

"Okay," Katie replied. "I'll try."

On the final page, he only gave a sad chuckle at seeing his own name.

She quickly put all the papers away, then turned back to see what Dorsey and the orderly were doing. Couldn't see them in the doorway.

She snapped two photos of her dad with her phone.

"Do you need anything?" she asked, sliding the phone away. Her pity gone, replaced by a weird new sense of solidarity. A feeling of hope, almost.

Her dad shook his head. His hand had moved again, this time reaching for hers. He squeezed tightly and held on as his eyes closed again.

They sat like that a long while.

Until the orderly came in and took her dad away.

Katie couldn't find Jason Bohenek anywhere.

Those who showed up online clearly weren't the right guy. A graphic designer, a zoologist. A high school cross-country runner in Arkansas. *Damn.* She'd wanted this victory. It'd been an hour.

She sighed and glared up at Max to both admit defeat and, bluntly, to see if he could do any better. He noticed her stare and looked up from whatever he was working on.

"Bohenek. N . . . E . . . K?" he asked.

"Yes, and thank you."

"Please. You're saving me from an otherwise tedious afternoon. You don't even want to know."

"I didn't." She frowned at him. "But now I kinda insist."

"Fiddling with semiprimes and a little reading about Willy Wonka being a serial killer."

"You were right."

"Told you." He turned his laptop so she could see what he was doing.

"Think you can find this guy?"

"I do." He'd opened a small black window on his laptop and she watched as he typed:

```
run maxweb.hal9001
for (i = 0; i <= spider.get_NumOutboundLinks() - 1; i++)
        if (!seenDomains.Contains(baseDomain)) {seedUrls.
Append(url);}
        long i; bool bingo; for (i = 0; i <= 4; i++)
    {bingo = spider.CrawlNext(); if (bingo!= true){ break;
```

It was like watching someone good play piano, all ten fingers moving at once, the code appearing faster than she could read it:

```
        spider.put_CacheDir("c:/spiderCache/");
      spider.put_FetchWebFromCache(true);
    spider.put_UpdateWebCache(true);
    {bingo = fly(Jason Bohenek (1), TERNGO (2) security,
risk management, military, veteran ); if (bingo!= true){ break;
pclose(pipe); return result;}
```

He hit the last Return with a flourish of his thumb.

"What is that?" Katie asked.

"It's your basic custom web crawler," he replied, reviewing the code. "Search engines—Google or Yahoo, whoever—show you only what they want. Their results are manipulated for the highest payer. I prefer to search and report myself. This one'll crawl around anything that's been online for even a minute. Company intranets, proto-sites, property records, court records, phone books, annual reports, whatever."

"You made this yourself, didn't you?" Katie asked.

Max typed "crawl" onto his little black screen. "Would you care to do the honors?" he asked.

"Corny McCornster." Still, she reached over and hit the Enter key on his laptop. Words began scrolling on the screen faster than she could process. It looked like flickering lights. "Why didn't we do this to start?" she asked.

"You wanted to do it yourself."

Katie smiled. "How long will it take?"

"Long," he replied. "But it'll run without us watching and it's tethered to my cell so we're not stuck here. Buy you lunch?"

"No thanks," she said.

"K."

"But I wouldn't mind a walk."

Jason Bohenek, it turns out, was head of security for Brown & Plotsky LLP, one of the larger lobbying firms in Washington, D.C.

He'd been that—according to an intercompany memo someone had put online to honor his own new job—for three years following a "distinguished" decade in the military and another with TERNGO Global Security and Risk Management, then several years running his own security outfit. He'd also appeared on a Brown & Plotsky internal company phone list as "J. Bohenek" and got a single mention in an industrial-exhibitions trade journal regarding security at the 2016 Environmental Strategic Advisory Conference.

Katie and Max now stood in the main lobby of the Symmes Building, of which Brown & Plotsky leased twenty floors. The other four floors were occupied by Chevron—the giant energy company that had eventually absorbed Unocal, the principal player in the 2000–2001 plan to put a new oil pipeline through Afghanistan. The building was gorgeous, mostly a glass palace of open windows and balconies. Everything else in white marble: the vast floor, the walls, two enormous hundred-foot pillars at the front doors. The guards' desk was marble too.

"Sorry, guys," the security guard at the desk said again. "But that name is not in our directory."

"Poppycock," Max grumbled.

Katie angrily clenched the edge of the cold marble between them and the security guard. Knew he was totally lying. She hadn't driven all this way to get stuck in the lobby.

"Is there anything else we can help you with?" His face indicated he was done with both of them. A second security guy behind him smirked accordingly.

"If you could do one more thing, please," Katie said to the guard. "Call your head of security and tell him Scott Wallace's daughter would like to speak with him."

"That's not really—"

"Please call and say 'Scott Wallace's daughter would like to speak with you.' Then we'll leave."

Robocop picked up an unseen phone behind the desk. He turned and stepped away so Katie couldn't hear what he was saying. The other guard had flexed up and came toward the desk in case she and Max might suddenly decide to jump over the counter and attack them both. *What a hero.*

"Yes, sir," she heard the guard say before hanging up the phone again.

She and Max exchanged hopeful glances as the guard approached silently with his arms crossed and stared down at them. He looked a little like he'd just smelled a fart.

"Is Mr. Bohenek on his way down?" Katie asked.

The fart-smelling guard thumbed toward a row of benches opposite the bank of elevators. "Wait over there," he said.

"Appears Mr. Bohenek's on his way down," remarked Max.

21

Bohenek led them across the street to a large city park.

This park was mostly trees, mostly empty.

This man, Bohenek, was mostly scary. Tall and dressed in a dark business suit, his tie black, his eyes hidden behind equally-black sunglasses. And he sported an extreme military haircut like he was still serving. He glanced back at Katie as he walked. "Not sure what you expect me to tell you," he said.

Katie quickened her pace, almost jogging, to keep up. "Were you with my father on the morning of 9/11?" She'd already gotten him to admit the two worked together for TERNGO. Told him her father was under psychiatric care. Bohenek's first question had been if her dad was dead.

"*That's* what this is about?" he replied.

"Yes."

"Sorry," he said. "I'm no longer an employee of TERNGO. I signed significant and indefinite nondisclosure agreements. Your father did too. You maybe want to remind him of that, sweetheart."

"Are you afraid of the information he might share?" she blurted, mostly ignoring his derogatory "sweetheart" comment.

Bohenek laughed. "Me? Not at all. I couldn't care less. And I doubt anyone else does either. Doesn't mean they won't sue his ass or ask the feds to keep him in jail for obstruction of national this-or-that."

Katie tried a different approach, forcing her jaw to soften. "Look, the best way to get him out of that hospital is to prove that at least *some* of what he's claiming is true, and you're the first person who—"

"Maybe it's best if he stays in that hospital awhile," Bohenek said gruffly.

"Excuse me?"

"Your dad's not well. Hasn't been since, Christ, I don't know, going on twenty years. Tell the truth: he ever kick the drugs?"

Katie's hands were trembling. No answer came.

"I didn't think so." Bohenek smirked, pointing toward a bridge to their left before heading that way. "The last half year we worked together, guy could barely tie his bootlaces and a lot of us were covering his ass big time. It was only a matter of time."

"He was a great soldier," Katie snapped, following. "A war hero."

"Yeah, actually he was," Bohenek agreed. "One of the best. We crossed paths overseas a couple times, for sure. And he was a good contractor after, when I knew him even better. For a while."

She glared at him. "So what happened?"

"How would I know? Ask him." Bohenek had stopped partway across the bridge. Below them, water ran down a dozen huge steps, an enormous tiered fountain that slashed down the hill. "Listen, I'd like to help your dad out, really. But not sure what it is you expect me to tell you."

"How about the truth?" Why was this so difficult for everyone to understand?

Bohenek gripped the concrete side of the bridge. Smiled.

"The truth? Is that all? The truth you're looking for is mostly classified, I'm afraid."

"What *can* you tell us?" Max asked, startling Katie. She'd almost forgotten he was there. She looked at him with wide, nervous eyes. What was he doing?

"I mean," Max went on, "can't we do the old she-tells-you-what-she-knows and you, like, blink twice or something?"

Bohenek stared at Max from behind his black shades. "Who are you again?"

"Chauffeur, mostly."

Bohenek shook his head, looked out at the park below. "Your dad was a hell of a soldier." He sighed, staring at something far, far away. Finally, he spoke. "You got three minutes."

Max and Katie exchanged excited looks.

"You worked with my dad on the morning of 9/11," she said again.

Bohenek nodded.

"What were you doing?" she asked.

"Classified." He shook his head again.

"Were you in Cleveland that morning?" she tried again.

Bohenek nodded.

"Were you working at the Hopkins International Airport?"

Bohenek nodded.

"Were you working for the US government?"

"Classified."

"Were you working for TERNGO Global Security?"

Bohenek nodded.

"Were you providing security that morning?"

"Classified."

"Were you involved in crowd control that morning? The passengers?"

"Classified. But, yes."

"How so?"

"Operation changed. We were on-site and got asked for assistance when things turned that morning, so we joined crowd control early. It was an intense day."

"I can imagine."

Could she do more than imagine? Was there any way that—

"We done?" he asked.

She chased away the next thoughts. "To be clear," she resumed, "you were already there and 9/11 just kinda happened."

"Correct."

"That's quite a coincidence."

"Not really. In my line of work, I was probably going to be *somewhere* significant that morning. It happened to be Cleveland."

"Okay, when you got these new instructions, how many planes did you supervise that day?"

"I don't really remember. Six or seven, if I had to say."

"Do you remember any of their flight numbers? Type of aircraft?"

"No. A couple of big 747s. 757s. Four, five hundred passengers rerouted, all in. A lot of people landed and passed through. How in the hell does any of this help you?"

"My father claims . . ."

Bohenek turned and Katie swallowed, again feeling the humiliation surge up inside her, the fear, the doubt. She hadn't shared this level of crazy with Max yet. She hadn't even really wanted to believe it herself. It was one detail in a billion details. It wasn't important, to get her dad free. It wasn't necessary to the story she was trying to build. It wasn't.

And yet . . .

"Did you see," she continued, "or are you aware of—a woman handing Scott Wallace a child that day?"

"What? No. Why?"

"To protect the child from whatever was going to happen next."

"To protect . . . from what? That's absurd."

"Probably. But these are my father's claims. Is it *possible* that he's telling the truth?"

She could feel Max frowning at her in puzzlement.

"No, why would . . . no. On 9/11? That's . . ." Bohenek crossed his arms. "You got one minute."

"Fine. Then please cut the yes-no-classified business and answer the questions. Is it possible he's telling the truth?"

"No."

Katie sighed. "Were you with him the entire morning?"

"Sweetheart, if Scotty says it happened, then I don't know what to tell you. The answer is no. Sorry, but the guy was high as a kite that morning. *That*, I remember."

Not as absurd a claim as she wished. But not what she'd come for.

"What did happen to the passengers then?" she asked. "*After* they were escorted off the planes, I mean."

"No clue. They probably rented cars and drove home or stayed in Cleveland a couple days until the flights were allowed back up. How in the hell would I know?"

"Witnesses at the airport, both travelers and personnel, claim hundreds of passengers were detained for hours that day. Held up by government officials. Debriefed."

Bohenek shrugged. "Like I said, it was a crazy morning. Bomb scares. Possibility of other hijackings. I suspect a lot of people were questioned."

"Did you question any passengers?"

"Not one. Wasn't my role."

"Whose role was it?"

"Wouldn't know. Our responsibility at that point was exclusively crowd management."

"'At that point.' What about *before*? What were you and my father doing at the Cleveland airport in the first place?" she asked. "Hadn't you really been brought in *only* for crowd control?"

"Okay, we're done." He'd started to move away.

Katie grabbed his arm. "Were the passengers killed?"

"You're out of your mind, kid," he snapped and yanked his arm back. "Whatever fairy tales your old man is telling you about 9/11, or anything else for that matter, you best put 'em in the trash with his crack pipes and rolling paper. This is the biggest load of shit I ever heard."

"What do you mean, 'anything else'?" Max stopped him. "What other 'fairy tales' you suppose he's telling?"

Bohenek shook his head and then turned and pointed a finger right at Katie's face. "I'm not exactly sure what your dad's up to, what his game is here—if he even has one beyond being batshit crazy—but I'm not wasting one more minute with this. Or you. I ever see your skinny ass again, I'm calling the cops."

"You may be summoned." Katie's voice came out trembling, and she tried again. "You may be summoned to appear in court and testify about that morning."

"Good luck with that," he sneered. "Once more: I see you here again, I'll have you arrested. Copy?"

"A tad excessive," Max mumbled. "But I suspect the press will enjoy that story."

Katie ignored Max, kept on Bohenek. "If you could—"

"Safe trip home," Bohenek stopped her. He'd also put a hand in his front pants pocket, opening his jacket some, showing a holstered gun within.

A gun.

Katie stepped back. She'd never seen one as close before.

"An HK45, huh?" Max said, coming between them. "Sweet piece. Double action, right?"

Bohenek smiled, and it was somehow the scariest thing he'd done yet. "The chauffeur, huh?" He'd turned to look out over the cascading water below. Dark swells spilling in the just-setting sun. "Time for you two to get the fuck out of here," he said.

"So, 'skinny ass,' did you learn anything useful today?"

Katie and Max followed the outskirts of the park back to Max's car.

"I confirmed my father was at the Cleveland airport on 9/11."

"But can you prove it? Are there records, electronic directives, that you can get from TERNGO? Will Bohenek go on record to help corroborate your dad's story?"

"His position on that was rather clear there at the end."

"Undeniably. So then, where's that leave us? You, I mean."

She shrugged.

"And what's this deal with a woman and a child?"

"Nothing." Katie stopped walking. Stood staring at Max. "Why are you doing this?" she asked.

Max stopped also and looked back. "Make the world a better place?" he replied.

"Nice bullshit answer. Seriously—two weeks ago, you

didn't want to have anything to do with all this conspiracy bullshit."

"It's not about any of that to me, I guess. You and your dad clearly need a break. I'd be a total orc if I didn't try to do *something*."

She studied him. A discussion for later, perhaps. And how much did she even care *why* he was helping? Could she have explained her own motivations any better at this point?

"Also . . . to make the world a better place."

Oh. He was serious about that. "Is that what we're doing?"

"I sure hope so," he said quietly.

"So what now?"

"Tough when everyone's holding out on you. It'd be nice if someone could give you something real to work with. What about Benevolus? Maybe go directly to him and demand real answers? Up to you."

"I assume you know his address?"

Max laughed. "Yeah, but he's not running the site from his home. I checked. He's clearly renting somewhere. Has the Truther site servers there."

"That's nuts, isn't it?"

Max grunted. "Oh, I don't know. Most of the servers I use for my game stuff are offsite. Easier for space reasons, gives me a line of privacy. Probably a small ISP, couple of clients. Adam seemed relatively web savvy. Didn't you talk to him the first time via your friend's laptop? If you contact him again, I could probably follow him straight to his home base with that."

"You think? It was pretty complicated. We had to get on this game, Champion Arena."

"Built on a Linux kernel–based operating system, yeah.

196

One step above counting one, two, three. When you want to do this?"

"Now," she said. "I'll let Gianna know we're on our way."

Max sat in front of Gianna's computer, bookended by the two girls.

He'd already disabled the video and audio input—no one would be seeing or hearing them *this* round—and was working through her registry and new scan logs.

"What's the flash drive for?" Gianna asked, pointing.

"Tomfoolery," he said, working. "Let's just say: this will find him before he finds it."

Winter was curled and purring, eyes mostly closed, in Katie's lap.

"Okay." Gianna looked past Max at Katie, her gaze wild with excitement. *Oh, great.* Katie had feared this would happen.

"You're supersmart, aren't you?" Gianna said.

"Me?" Max replied. "Yes. So I'm going to leave these viruses on there for the moment, if that's okay with you. I'll set up a program that'll wipe them out in a couple days. Cool?"

"Cool. So, *Max* . . ."

"Yeah?" He kept typing, still didn't look up.

"What are you doing on the twentieth?"

"Okay," Katie snapped. "Let's let the guy work, please."

"Of May?" Max asked. "That's a long time from now; I couldn't tell you."

"It's less than three weeks away."

"G . . ." Katie dropped her head sideways, pleading.

"Prom," Gianna continued. "Clara Barton High. You should come."

"Enough already," Katie said, her voice warning.

"You need a break," Gianna pressed, her smile ear to ear. "Don't you think she needs a break, Max?"

Max's eyes stayed on the computer. But there was no missing the smile in his voice. "Yes, actually. I do."

"Aces!" Gianna beamed. "I knew I liked you, Max."

"Not going," Katie said.

"So don't. I'm inviting Max, not you."

"I'm not exactly the prom type," Max said.

"Everyone says that," Gianna replied. "That's what makes them so fun. Hey, anyone ever tell you that you look a little like Evan Peters?"

"Yup," he said, still working. Katie shook her head, focused on Winter. Gianna leaned back in her chair too, mercifully ending the Jersey Inquisition.

Max continued to work for another five minutes, then looked back. "All set. The input mic is physically killed," he said as Katie and Gianna pulled closer. "So you guys can talk if you want to. You ready?"

Katie nodded.

He opened the browser on Gianna's laptop and typed in: Benevolus552. A new window with the Arena game automatically opened. They watched as the computer logged itself in without them touching a thing. Max nodded in appreciation.

Beside this window, another dark screen showed dozens of vertical lines shooting by. Max focused entirely on it. He'd dragged the curser into the chat field and typed: Need to see you.

"MEET AGAIN AS BEFORE?" The computer voice came out of the laptop again.

Max typed: No.

"THEN WHERE?"

Max typed: Will let you know.

"YOU SHOULD—"

Max clicked the voice, window, and game off. Watched the screen on the right.

"You got him?" Katie asked.

"Yup," he said.

22

Benevolus552—a.k.a. Adam Healy—ran his web kingdom from out of a rented property in Canton, a mostly industrial area north of Baltimore. It was a run-down brick building with boarded windows, faded crumbling walls, and a short lawn of tall grass and trash, surrounded on all sides by buildings that looked exactly the same. The one car on the deserted street had no tires and rested upon concrete blocks.

"He's definitely in there," Max decided. They sat in his car, parked down the street. Max had his laptop out, taking turns between tapping the keys and his chin. "Or *someone* is. Data packets flying all over. Somebody's running a lot of equipment in there."

Katie nodded, trying again to build the courage to get out of the car and bang on the building's enormous front door. Happy to stall while Max played hacker. She checked her phone. It was almost nine o'clock. Curfew in an hour, but they couldn't have come any earlier. Max had run tests on the IP he'd tracked and found that almost all of its traffic was at night, in early morning, and on weekends. And on one of those nights, early mornings, or weekends, this guy had met her maybe-father and . . . *and what? Shared something worth locking him away for?*

Next to her, Max shut his laptop and the sound brought her back to the present. "You up for this?" he asked.

She turned to look at him. Felt as if she were someone else, watching them both from outside the car. "Trying to figure out what to say to him. What I'm willing to share."

"You'll know that when it's time," he said. "Trust yourself."

"Who else, right?"

Max's face turned serious. More serious than she was used to seeing, anyway. "I suppose," he said. "Main thing is to try and figure out what your dad gave to him. This evidence. Files of some kind, if they truly exist. And remember, you'll have the advantage simply by showing up here. It'll totally freak him out. He'll realize he's underestimated you."

"Underestimated *you*, you mean. Hey, Max . . ."

"Yeah?"

Katie swallowed. "I might say some things in there that . . . There's a part of this I haven't shared with you yet."

"Don't worry about me," he said. "I'm not here to judge." Forcing a smile, he added, "Ready? The sooner you're done with Benevolus, I think, the sooner you're done with all of it."

"Doesn't that depend on what we find here?" Katie got out of the car. She looked up and down the empty street. Night's shadows had formed between the neglected buildings to cast patches of darkness on the uneven sidewalk.

They walked toward the building: Katie in front, Max trailing. Up the concrete steps onto the dirty porch where a rusted bed frame lay against the side of the house. She knocked on the door. It was like hitting solid steel. Maybe it *was* solid steel, she realized, noticing too that the door had several locks. She knocked again. With the side of her fist this time. More of a bang.

Heard movement inside, then locks turning.

She couldn't wait to see the look of total surprise on the guy's face.

The door opened partway and most of Benevolus552, Adam Healy, stood in the dark space between.

"Figured it was you," he said.

So much for the element of surprise.

Katie and Max stood on his porch, borderline gaping at each other.

"Your dad told you how to find me," Benevolus said.

"Yeah, he did," Max replied quickly. "He thought it was time you and she should meet."

"With the trusted consultant in tow, I see. Cute."

"I try," Max said.

Benevolus552 shook his head, looked up and down the street, and waved them inside with a final swipe of his head. Katie and Max stepped into the building.

"My car cool out there?" Max asked.

"Probably not. Come on." He relocked the door. They followed him through several dark rooms and up a rickety stairway.

"Anyone else here?" Katie asked as they climbed.

"Not tonight."

Katie noticed several security cameras and motion detectors tracing their journey up the steps. "Heavy-duty security," Max noted out loud.

"Rough neighborhood," Benevolus said. "Half the buildings are empty. Some have squatters, dealers."

They'd reached the second floor. Benevolus552 smiled and pushed open the first door.

From the outside, it looked no different than the other doors in the hall, but inside they could see how its single outer lock connected to and operated three bolts. Beyond the door, half a dozen servers blinked in a tall computer rack and several tables supported another half dozen desktops and laptops, along with several monitors of various sizes. Shelving ran up one wall filled with wrapped cable, older model computers, and assorted odds and ends. The opposite wall was covered in hundreds of notecards and printouts. The room was lit with overhead fluorescent lights someone had crudely wired to the ceiling. Above it all, another security camera.

"Cool setup," Max said. He'd made a beeline for the shelf of computer equipment. "Wow, a Commodore 64? Triumph Adler. Tandy Radio Shack."

"TRS-80, yeah. Boxes of the old-school stuff seems to collect here. You know computers?"

"A little," Max said, and Katie turned away so as not to laugh. "These still work?"

"Most of them."

"My dad had one like that," Katie said. "His didn't work."

"This?" Max patted the Commodore's nubby dark keys. "Where'd he get it?"

Katie shrugged. "Brought it home from some flea market. Thing was gone a week later." She briefly imagined him browsing that flea market alone. As he'd done so much else.

Katie had wandered over to a framed poster on the wall that caught her eye; browned pages with old English-style printing, and a cartoon she recognized from bumper stickers and history class: a snake cut into pieces and the words JOIN OR DIE. "*The Plain Truth*," she read aloud, leaning close to decipher the small, old-fashioned print. "Ben Franklin wrote this."

"One of his earliest radical essays. Called for a citizen militia to form and combat the lies and threats of tyrannical government. Printed and distributed the brochures himself. There's a guy who understood what true freedom requires."

"A kite?" Max asked, smiling. He'd moved from the older computers to better check out the servers.

"A platform." Benevolus552 gestured at all the room's equipment. "And the balls to use it." He sat in his extravagant workstation chair and pointed at the folder in Katie's hand. "What'd you get for me?"

She first brought out the thumb drive from her front pocket. "Pictures of my dad," she said. "At the hospital."

"Okay, great." He laid the drive on his desk. "What else?"

"First, I'd like to know more about what he told you."

"No, no, no. That's on him. If he's not telling you, there must be a reason."

"They have him drugged out of his mind and locked away twenty-four-seven. How's that for a reason?"

"He's clearheaded enough that he told you how to find me."

"Maybe so." She kept Max's lie alive. "But that took a ton of effort, let me tell you, and his intention was certainly that you and I should work together on this."

"You think so, huh?"

"He didn't send me out here for the view."

Benevolus552 sighed. Turned around and worked on his laptop a few seconds. "Your dad was in Cleveland on 9/11," he said as, on several of the monitors, two different emails appeared. "These are his instructions directly from TERNGO that day."

"Neither one of these says anything about Cleveland," Max argued, squinting at the one screen. "*Or* 9/11. It's a simple purchase order."

"Unless," Katie said. "Unless they're in some kind of code."

"Correct." Benevolus552 smiled. "Watch." He hit another key and both emails instantly changed to show travel arrangements, hours, dates, commanding officer.

More proof her dad was there on 9/11?

Or something he'd invented in Photoshop in ten minutes?

"He gave us several of the ciphers TERNGO used in 2001, along with his original e-mails from that week."

The monitors flashed with new life.

"These," Benevolus said, "are pictures from inside the NASA hangar at the Cleveland airport. Images he nabbed that very day with a digital camera. They're time-stamped."

"Isn't that easy to fake?" Max asked.

"We had the original files checked out."

"Isn't that easy to fake?" Max asked again.

Benevolus552 ignored him. "Look at the people."

"I am," Katie said. A cluster of maybe ten people standing in a shadowed corner of an enormous hangar. "But you can't see their faces. It's taken from across a dark room."

"That's a pilot," he pointed. "Right there. Clear as day."

"So what?" Katie asked, stepping back from the monitors. "I don't see how it proves anything."

"Hey, you came to me. What're *you* bringing to the table this round? Anything?"

Katie considered walking out. Escaping these blurry pictures and magic emails.

She didn't.

"I have these." She extracted three paper-clipped letters from her folder. "I'm getting legal affidavits from witnesses who were there that day. People who saw private security. Who saw a plane being unloaded. Who saw the buses taking them away again out a back exit."

Benevolus552 had been reading the letters as she spoke. "Getting or got? These are just emails discussing the possibility." He focused on Katie. "But . . . this isn't bad. Two of these names I've never even seen before. Okay to put these emails online?"

"Why?"

"Create interest. Get people talking about the site, eventually about your father."

"Thought the idea was to release everything all at once. Aren't you afraid of also getting locked away before that happens?"

"I've made plans for that. I wouldn't just vanish."

"That's what my dad thought."

"And he hasn't vanished, has he? Here we are. So, can I put these up?"

Katie thought. Her dad had said to keep the pressure on them. Who, exactly, she still didn't know. Would this, in any way, help? Was this really putting the pressure on anyone? *Anyone but me?* "Okay," she said. "But no names. Not yet."

"Fine." He set the letters aside. "What else?"

"Tell him about Bohenek," suggested Max.

"Who's that?"

"Jason Bohenek. Another TERNGO employee," she said. "Security work like my dad. He was there that day, too. Admitted it to us earlier this week."

"He go on record? Will he?"

"No. And no."

Benevolus shook his head. "Guess we can go 'anonymous source' again. Not very sexy. Got anything concrete to connect this guy to 9/11?"

Katie pulled another sheet from her folder. "TERNGO employee records. Bohenek's name. My dad's name."

Benevolus reached out to take it. "Where'd you get this?"

"Her dad," Max answered.

"And Bohenek's name was also on one of the emails you displayed," Katie said. "He was there that day. They both were."

"Not bad . . ." Benevolus nodded, then turned back to his computer and tapped a few keys. "Since we're on TERNGO, your dad clued me in to *this* guy." A face appeared on one of the monitors. A silver-haired lawyer type. "Know him?"

Katie squinted at the photo. Max leaned in, too.

"That's Gary Fuenmayor," she said. "My dad's used his name before. I looked him up. But all I know is he worked at TERNGO when my dad did."

Benevolus nodded. "Major player there back in the 1990s. Retired 2010. Does mostly consulting now."

"So what's the big deal?" Max asked.

"He's likely America's next National Security Advisor. Currently making all the rounds in Washington. Vetting underway. Safe to say, your dad's not a big fan."

"He ever tell you why?" Katie asked.

"Claims Fuenmayor's crooked. Big time. Claimed to have the motherlode on him. Classified emails, reports, communication logs. Bankroll accounts and secretly recorded conversations. More images. Enough to bury not only Fuenmayor but all of TERNGO, even implicate the US military."

"This TERNGO 'motherlode.'" Max's voice had gone a little flat. "It's all connected to 9/11 or . . . something else?"

"We only talked about 9/11."

"Yeah, but did he—"

"Only talked about 9/11. I got a sense there was more, though. Yeah. And that 9/11 was the tip of an iceberg."

Katie frowned. "If he has all this info, why didn't he release it ten years ago?"

"Could be Fuenmayor was rising too high in the government food chain for your dad's comfort. Could be it took this many years for your dad to build his case. That's what he said. Of course . . ." He blew out a big breath. "I imagine the bank statements he showed me also had something to do with it."

"What bank statements? What are you talking about?"

"Oh, come on." Benevolus grinned. "All that money?"

Katie looked at Max and then back at Benevolus. "What money?"

"You really don't know, do you?"

Her stomach had knotted into a thousand-pound ball. "Know what?"

"Your dad's still on the TERNGO payroll."

"No, he's . . ." Katie didn't understand the point he was trying to make. "He works for the park service."

Bank statements and single transactions suddenly appeared on the monitors. Receipts made out to Scott T. Wallace. *Dozens* of transactions going back years. "He's a 'consultant' earning two hundred thousand dollars a year."

"That's not possible."

Katie stared at the records on the screen. Scanned documents from 2016, 2011, 2008 . . . even some old-style checks that'd been endorsed, processed. "How many? How long?"

"Twice a year, every year," Benevolus said. "Ever since 9/11."

23

"You're lying," Katie said.

What else to say? This new claim was as ridiculous as the rest.

"Think what you will. Guy handed me a stack of bank statements and payment receipts and I scanned 'em." He patted the nearby scanner. "As straightforward as it gets."

"Maybe . . ." She thought. "Maybe it's some kind of pension or something."

Benevolus laughed. "Hell of a pension. It's hush money. They're paying him, and others too, probably, to keep quiet."

"He come here a lot?" Max asked.

"Only twice. First time to check out our setup—that's when he showed me the money transactions and encrypted emails—and once more a couple weeks later to work out some technical details before receiving the rest of it."

"What kind of details?" Max pressed.

"Gearhead talk. Appointing unique encryption keys and safe data transfers. He had me working with someone else, wherever the bulk of his info is stored. They set it up so I'd get fed pieces over time. 'My way, my schedule.' That's what he said. Only way he'd do it."

"You ever meet his tech guy?" Max asked.

"Nah. Tried tracking him. Every time the new files arrive.

But whoever he's working with is better than I am. For now, at least." He turned to Katie. "*You* have any idea who he's working with?"

Did he mean the Dragon—Collison? No. That guy, her dad's alleged friend, had also claimed someone else was running the technical side of things . . . Katie was still trying to process what Benevolus was saying about the payments. About her father. About the *three million* dollars he'd maybe received during the past fifteen years. All the while, the two guys in the room kept staring at her, waiting for her to say something. No words came.

"No, this other guy is news to us too," Max started slowly as Katie looked at him with thankful eyes. "So, other than the very-forgeable bank stuff and these unclear photos here"— he pointed back at the monitor with the shots of the NASA hangar—"what else did he have? What's actually in these files he's sent you?"

"For a couple weeks, only names and numbers. Every two or three days they came. And always with specific directions on where we should then place this info. Public websites. Chat rooms. Blogs. Movie-review sites. Crazy stuff, but he'd said it would start like that. So we set them as ordered. I gotta tell you, we'd almost given up on the guy—figured he was messing with us, you know? It was meaningless info—but we played along in case he was testing us." He'd turned to find and display a file. "Then *this* showed up."

"What's that?" Katie asked, knowing now it could be about anything.

"Okay, on the morning of 9/11, the FAA and the government ran several training exercises. Conflict-management scenarios among military and commercial airlines, including faked hijackings."

"I've read about those," Katie said, scanning the words appearing on the screen. "Added to the confusion that morning for sure. Intentionally, some believe. But what's that got to—"

"Here's something you probably haven't read about. Not when the government's done everything it can to kill this story completely. On the morning of 9/11, the Secret Service and the CIA received text messages from an unknown source warning that the White House and Air Force One were targets too. A source using presidential transmission codes, something only a handful of people have. This source *also* used the identification codes of Air Force Intelligence, Military Intelligence Corps, Naval Intelligence, the Marine Corps Intelligence, as well as the intelligence services of the Department of Energy, the DEA, *and* the State Department. Not one single person, not even the president, is authorized to have even two of these codes. Whoever this was had a dozen."

"And these here are the transmissions that included the codes?" Max asked, leaning into the screen for a better look.

"Three of them, yeah. No one official *ever* talks about these codes being sent that morning. Not one word in the Commission Report, in memoirs. The original news articles with White House confirmations regarding this incident have since all been scrubbed. Reporters who pursued this story have been fired. But that doesn't change the facts. Either someone got hold of the algorithms and cracked America's most-secret codes, or someone had operatives infiltrating each one of these branches. In any case . . ."

"In any case," Katie said, "someone was putting the United States on notice."

Benevolus552 grinned. "A warning that someone else was now running the show. Basically, an electronic coup d'état to go along with the actual physical attacks. And if you think a bunch of guys living in caves in Afghanistan had the capability to—"

"So what's this have to do with TERNGO? With my dad?"

"TERNGO Global Security and Risk Management provided third-party consulting that day for the crisis training going on. The kind of service they routinely provide. Watching the watchmen, as it were." He grinned at Katie. "You still don't get it, do you? I got these transmissions from your dad."

"Who got them from TERNGO," Katie concluded. "So, then how'd TERNGO get them? If they—" She stopped talking. Shook her head in disbelief. "TERNGO *sent* them," she said.

"Correct." Benevolus leaned back, genuinely satisfied. "There was a lot of electronic chatter that morning. Encrypted chatter. These files here prove beyond a doubt that at least three of the messages traveled *within* TERNGO broadcasts."

"Maybe someone was piggybacking on the electronic communications," Max suggested. "Maybe TERNGO is an innocent carrier here."

"Yeah, maybe." Benevolus shook his head. "But if not TERNGO, then whoever it was would have to first bypass mega-secure private channels. So this is the proverbial smoking gun, guys. One of them, anyway. These are the raw feeds from within the TERNGO network. Scrambled covert channels. Covert channels your dad was recording that morning."

"So what?" Katie stared at the meaningless binary numbers, even as their possible meaning formed in her mind. "Are you saying that TERNGO Global Security wants to take over the world or something?"

"Not at all. I'm saying they're maybe working for the guys who do. Whoever threatened the United States that morning did so through *these* transmissions. Some shadow government within our own claiming control? NSA, CIA? Something more international, maybe. Federal Reserve. The kinda people looking to increase America's hold, the banks' hold, on the world. TERNGO is part of a larger corporation named Plainview Inc. that's made hundreds of billions off the wars since 2001. With Fuenmayor in Washington, that could become several trillion."

"Like Cheney setting up his old pals at Haliburton," Katie said. "Can you prove those transmissions are connected to TERNGO?"

"Already have. If we give this to the FBI today, they could too. But we can't."

"Why?"

"Because he doesn't trust the FBI," Max replied. He'd wandered over toward the rack of servers. "Right?"

"Why should we?" Benevolus asked behind him. "Maybe *they're* the ones working with TERNGO. It's 100 percent fact the FBI deliberately blocked and canceled several investigations related to known Islamic extremists in the months and days leading up to September. Why would they do that, I wonder?"

"Then give it to the *Wall Street Journal*," said Max, turning.

Benevolus replied to that idea with a deep, exaggerated laugh.

"Let me guess, they're in on it too?" Max said.

"You've been working on this awhile with her, right?"

"*Her* being Katie, yes? I have."

"You got any unanswered questions? Say, about Bush's comments and actions that day, or the hundreds of Saudis flown secretly out of our country on September 12, or the FBI being pulled off certain leads, or, say, these codes here."

"Absolutely. For sure a lot of unanswered questions."

"Well, then, wouldn't it be nice if our press did its job?" Benevolus said to both of them. "I mean, asked these very questions, dug around. Except anyone who does is fired, run out of the profession as a quack. Dan Rather was one of the most respected newsmen in the business until he started talking about 9/11. They got rid of him real fast. That's why the Internet is so important. Instead of getting our information from one source, we have access to experts and voices who otherwise wouldn't be given airtime; we have sites like the Plain Truth; and we have six billion people with cell phones, recording and sharing everything that happens. You can't hide the truth anymore."

"Power to the people," Max agreed. He'd pulled his phone free and was holding it up in front of his face. "And yet . . . I can't even get one bar in here. Trying to text my mom. What's the deal?"

"We're jamming you." Benevolus smiled proudly, nodded toward some unseen gadget. "Security, man."

"I understand completely." Max tucked his phone back away.

Katie still gazed at the codes and transmissions. "What are you going to do with this?"

"Whoever sent these transmissions—and it sure looks like it was TERNGO—was directly involved in the execution of 9/11," Benevolus said. "The first order of business is to triple validate these, of course. But it's looking pretty solid."

Max spoke. "If your basement floods and a frog's swimming in your basement, does that necessarily mean the frog flooded your basement?"

"Max . . ." Katie shook her head.

"What do you mean?" Benevolus asked, genuinely curious.

"Let's say these threatening codes *did* come from TERNGO—worst case. Maybe they were taking advantage of the chaos of 9/11 to send a message. Thought it was safe. Islamic terrorists attack. Might've seemed like a good time to remind a client how vulnerable they were. Almost a sales pitch."

Benevolus snorted. "There was a whole lot more than a sales pitch going on that day. Isn't that right, Katie? Let's not forget the elephant in the room here."

Katie grimaced.

"'Cause you're right," Benevolus said. "Payoffs and unreliable eyewitnesses and complicated transmissions recordings and flight paths don't come close to flesh and blood." He fixed Katie with a serious stare. "Scott Wallace told me he had that kind of proof. The flesh and blood kind. The kind that changes the whole world."

Katie cast a nervous look at Max. Even though she'd warned him.

"Hey, let's stay focused on TERNGO," Max said.

"He hinted," Benevolus kept going. "Hinted *strongly*, there was a survivor that morning. One of the passengers. A little girl." He was staring at Katie again. "So let's cut all the bullshit. Are you this mystery girl?"

Katie looked over all the monitors. The encrypted emails and blurred photos and puppet masters of the world. She sighed.

"If there is a girl," she said, "I'm her."

"You got anything to prove that?" Benevolus552 asked.

His manner was careful. Borderline unenthusiastic.

"Not yet," Katie replied. She'd tried unsuccessfully not to look at Max, who stared at her. "But he told me . . . he told me

I am *not* his daughter. That a woman, one of the passengers, handed me to him on the morning of 9/11."

"That's . . ." Benevolus552 hunched down into his chair, covered the bottom of his face with his hands, thinking. "That would be, I mean, he'd hinted but . . . Jesus. Do you have any idea what that would mean if we could prove that?"

"One moment here." Max held up his hand. "We can scarcely substantiate her dad was even at the airport on 9/11. And even if you could, it doesn't confirm *you* were or that—what?—you're one of the children from the airplanes? And even if you prove he's not your dad with a paternity test, so what? Won't mean a thing unless you DNA-test against all the passengers who died that day."

Katie stared back, unable to respond. She knew he was right, had reached the exact same conclusions. But this guy, Benevolus552, he had the bank records, the transmissions . . .

"Who are you kidding?" Benevolus laughed at Max. "You really think the government is going to provide her *real* results? The real DNA?"

"Yeah," Max said, some anger in his voice. "I do."

He looked straight back at Katie, who had to look away.

"We'll file you under 'sheeple' then," Benevolus said.

"And I'll file you under 'codswallop.'"

"Sure, I get it," Benevolus sneered. "I'm just the big dumb cliché in all of this, right? Nerdy white dude surrounded by monitors in his mom's basement kinda thing. Well, guess what—I got a real job, a wife, and two little kids. I don't give a shit about yard work, so my free time is spent here doing this, trying to get to the bottom of very real issues. The militarization of our police. What corporations are putting in our food. Why the United States accounts for 4 percent of the world's population and *20 percent* of its prisoners. If that makes me a cliché, then okay."

Max made an impatient noise in his throat. "You don't really want the truth. You want whatever data fits your hypothesis. It's confirmation bias. DNA test says Wallace isn't her father? Great news for you, fits the yarn, blog all night long, *Sic Semper Tyrannis*. But when a DNA test says none of the known passengers are related to Katie in any way, *then* the tests are clearly fake. You can 'expose' them as a lie or ignore the unfavorable data altogether." He shook his head. "It's an unreasonable way to seek truth."

Benevolus ignored him and turned to Katie. "Do you have anything else?"

Could she tell him about vague memories of yelling and dark rooms and being shoved at someone?

"No," she said. "Max is right. If the passengers were taken off the planes, are there recordings of that? Anything beyond these questionable photos and a few witnesses who may have seen 'something'? Eventually, I'll need to test my DNA with surviving family members."

"What about the rest of the info?" Max asked. "The information Wallace hasn't shared with you yet. That he's doling out so carefully. He give any idea what it is?"

"No," Benevolus said. "He wouldn't get into specifics."

"Any generalities then?" Max asked.

"He told me only that the forthcoming information buried TERNGO and threatened the US military, so he had to be careful about how it was revealed. And he warned me lives were at risk."

"Whose?" Max asked.

"His. Mine, if I agreed to get involved. And . . ." He looked at Katie. "Yours. Said he feared for his daughter's life. And now,

now I sure understand why. My God, if you're really a survivor from one of those planes, no one can find out until *everyone* finds out. That's the only thing that might keep you alive."

Katie hadn't thought of that. Hadn't even imagined the possibility. She'd felt pressure, had been scared. But would someone really use murder to try and silence any of them? To erase her, the same way they maybe tried to erase her sixteen years ago?

"Knock it off," Max said to Benevolus in a tone Katie had not heard him use before. She blinked, re-grounding herself in the moment.

"Sorry to get all hardcore," Benevolus said. "But you don't think this scares the shit out of me too? That I'm not at risk? Let's get all the cards out, man. They've done this shit a hundred times before."

"Done what?" Katie asked.

"Let's just say, people who speak the truth . . ." He waved his hands to indicate the room, monitors, them. "They have a funny way of no longer being alive."

24

Benevolus552 pulled up each face one at a time. A go-to slide show he kept with him like some sort of talisman. Or warning. For himself and others. The first face was a heavy-set black man with glasses and a gentle look that Katie liked immediately.

"This is Barry Jennings," he narrated. "Deputy director at the New York City Housing Authority, and the last known employee to escape Building 7 before it collapsed. He's on record with claims he'd heard several explosions from the lower floors *before* the collapse and, more shocking, that he'd had to step over dead bodies during his escape."

"But why would . . ." Katie knew no casualties were reported in Building 7. Fire damage collapsing the building was one thing. *But bodies?*

"His testimony was never pursued," Benevolus said. "Or even addressed by officials. And when the government released its initial—inconclusive—report on the collapse of Building 7, he was nowhere to be found. He'd died, causes unknown, days before the report was released."

Another face. A younger, bald white man. "Kenneth Johannemann. A janitor in the North Tower who testified to several explosions beneath, then throughout, the building immediately before its collapse. Died of apparent suicide."

Another face. Younger guy, goatee. Looked a little like her dad. "Christopher Landis. Operations manager for the Virginia Department of Transportation. One of the first on the scene at the Pentagon on 9/11 and took hundreds of never-before-seen pictures that called into question the damage done to the building, the wreckage found, and mysterious vehicles and persons on-site during the attack. He'd started delivering these pictures to Truthers developing a film called *PentaCon*, but committed suicide a week later."

A woman. "Katherine Smith. Department of Motor Vehicles employee who sold counterfeit IDs to 'Middle Eastern men' under investigation for their possible involvement. These same men were seen in the towers in the weeks before 9/11 as 'plumbers working on the sprinkler system.' She was found burned alive in her own car."

"My God." Katie brought her hand to her mouth.

"You've made your point," Max said.

Another face, another woman. Benevolus clearly wasn't done. This victim was a middle-aged white woman with bangs and glasses. Kinda polished, pretty. "Deborah Palfrey. Ran a deluxe prostitution ring in Washington and had major clients in the FBI and CIA. She claimed to have information regarding what the government knew *before* 9/11. She also specifically told friends and news sources she was *not* planning to commit suicide and intended to, quote, expose the government, end quote. She was found hanged in her shed."

Another face. A middle-aged man standing between two attractive teens, a boy and a girl. "Philip Marshall. An airline pilot who penned several Truther books and was working on another with never-before-shared evidence when he reportedly shot his two kids, his dog, and then himself. Now, how a right-handed man shot himself in the *left* temple is not a detail the authorities want you to think too much about."

Katie shivered in the dark room. Would they really kill a man and his whole family simply for questioning the official story?

Another face. A bald, smart-looking man with a goatee. "Paul Wellstone. Senator from Minnesota and the most outspoken opponent of Bush's post-9/11 Patriot Act. Within a year of 9/11, he was dead. Plane crash. Want more? One of the two pilots onboard was the same man who reportedly gave flight-simulator software to one of the alleged 9/11 hijackers."

Were even US senators being warned to keep quiet? And, if so, what might happen to a Park Services worker and his teenage daughter?

Another face. A pretty blond woman—

"Beverly Eckert," Katie said.

Benevolus nodded, slid a triumphant glance toward Max. "Tell him."

"Her husband was killed on 9/11," Katie said to no one but herself. "She didn't believe the official story and became the figurehead of the victims' families demanding full disclosure. Testimony under oath. Declassified records. Independent investigations. Brought lawsuits against the US government to get it."

"Sounds familiar," Max said.

"The US government offered her money—millions—to sign some papers and go away quietly like most of the other victims' families."

"But she said no," Max said.

"Claimed her 'silence could not be bought.' And then, she was dead. Killed in a commuter plane crash a week after visiting the White House to discuss 9/11."

"You honestly think the government murdered her?" Max asked, his skepticism clear. "Murdered everyone on the plane she was on, too?"

"I . . . ," Katie said, glancing behind her. Almost as if she'd gotten turned around, forgotten where she was. Looking for the exit. "I don't know what they did," she said. "I need to get out of here."

"Let's 'get,' then." Max started for the door.

Katie followed quickly. Desperate to escape. Caged on all sides by computers, printouts. More information. More lies. More death.

Max unlocked the door, led her out with his arm.

Benevolus552 had jumped up behind them, following them out of the room. "Wait. Wait! What should I put online? I mean, what do you think? What's okay?"

Katie stopped at the top of the steps and turned back. "You've got the emails. And the pictures I took. Use those, but no name yet. I already fuzzed out his face."

Benevolus552 shook his head, disappointed at that disclosure.

"Can you do anything yet with the codes that were transmitted?" she asked.

"Need to confirm a bit more, but soon. Yeah, that's major." He stared at her. "And what about you?"

"What about me?"

"What can I say about, you know, *you* being . . ."

"Nothing," Max replied.

Katie scowled at Max, then looked at Benevolus. "Say that . . ."

People who speak the truth. They have a funny way of no longer being alive.

"Say that an anonymous source, a government witness, claims a child was saved that day. One of the passengers."

"That all?" Benevolus looked hopeful.

"Isn't it enough?" Katie said.

She took the porch steps two at a time. Almost running.

"You sure about all this?" Max pestered behind her. "How do you know this guy won't use your name? Make you and your dad Internet-famous forever in a single post?"

Katie didn't reply, kept moving to his car. Had to escape. Before she heard any more horrible tales from Benevolus. Before she agreed to anything else. Before someone came along, killed her, and made it look like a suicide.

She stopped with the door half open, spoke over the roof. "All those dead witnesses . . . Do you really think—"

"Oh, come on, Katie. Those people weren't killed by conspirators. This is what I meant about confirmation bias. Some 9/11 witness dies young or in an accident and the only possible explanation is that it's part of the cover-up. How many examples did he show us?"

She swallowed. "Maybe half a dozen."

"And how many people witnessed the events of 9/11?"

Katie looked down at the street, realized he'd trapped her easily.

"Thousands." He answered for her. "More when you work in all the people who escaped the towers and the Pentagon, the emergency personnel, news people, crime scene investigators, airport employees. Ten, *twenty* thousand people. Half a dozen questionable deaths? In sixteen years? There were more suicides by people connected to Maryland University during that time. What'd *they* know, I wonder? Statistically speaking, it appears that 'knowing the truth about 9/11' is actually a health gold mine."

"You believe my dad's story?" she asked.

"Not at all," Max said.

Katie shivered in the dark, wanting to collapse. Or to scream.

"But that's irrelevant," he continued. "You need to be concerned about the people who *will*. And I don't mean some judge or Marilyn Wren. I mean people like Healy back there who don't give a damn about your dad, or *you*, beyond getting the story they want. That Truther echo chamber that'll keep your name and face on slide shows and grammatically-challenged YouTube videos for a hundred years. You're worried about government conspirators coming to get you. Your real concern should be the people who get all caught up in these conspiracy theories. I don't believe Jack Ruby shot Oswald because some shadow government told him to. I believe he felt it was his civic duty to avenge Oswald's murder of Kennedy. I'm worried about the Jack Rubys out there." He breathed deeply. "Maybe it's a good time for you to get out of this. Let your dad and the legal system work out the rest. Benevolus, too, if he wants."

"But if it's true—what he says, I mean—it'll be bigger than an echo chamber. The whole world will know. Even if the regular press won't pick it up, the Internet, regular everyday *people*, can still spread the truth."

Max shook his head, opened his door. "Katie, most Americans can't locate Afghanistan on a map. A third can't name our last vice president. After fifteen years at war, half can tell you who the Taliban are. The *people*? They're watching funny cat videos and free porn. Your friend Gianna spend a lot of time on WikiLeaks?"

"Gianna's a merit scholar and probably going to Columbia for free. How 'bout you leave my friends out of this discussion?"

"Sorry, went personal only for shorthand. But you see my meaning, I hope. You would need a ton more concrete evidence *and* a week-long series in the *New York Times* to *maybe* see it gain mainstream traction. Healy's website won't cut it. He's smart and precise and also genuine, I think, about wanting to hold our government to a worthy standard. I do, too, by the way. But that doesn't mean he has the ability, or the necessary ethos, to assess and circulate a story like this to the world."

"Ethos? Whatever. You still think he's a joke."

"I think anyone can hop on Google and consider themselves an expert on something in fifteen minutes. The Warren report on Kennedy's assassination was nine hundred pages long and had an additional twenty-six volumes of supporting materials. You really had to earn it in 1964 if you wanted to be a conspiracy guy."

"Or girl."

"Exactly. Don't know how much he's really earned it, is all. His faith in the Internet somehow bringing everyone together is the exact opposite of what's really going on. The vastness of the Internet allows people—no matter what their views—to crawl into the world's smallest teapot of those exact same views. Visiting only the websites and people that agree completely with your take, everyone spouting the exact same stuff."

He got into the car. Katie slid into her seat too.

"Does he piss you off," she asked, "because you disagree with his research methods, or because he's a Truther?"

Max grunted. "Remember what I told you the day we met?"

"That I was the Chiefest and Greatest of Calamities."

"That too." He smiled. "I told you I didn't believe we live in some evil, shitty country. And nothing I've seen these past weeks with you changes that. I believe we're as close to good guys as this world has. We make mistakes, sometimes dumb and self-serving mistakes, bigoted mistakes, bullying mistakes."

"But?"

"But, to paraphrase: the United States is the worst country on Earth." He clipped his seat belt into place. "Except for all the others."

"You really believe that?"

"I have to," he said. "In ways I can't . . ." He stopped himself. "Look, can you name a country that *saved* more lives worldwide than we did yesterday? Fighting everything from disease to genocide. You know we send a billion dollars a year to North Korea—*North* Korea—to help them fend off famine?"

"We've also killed thousands of people with drones, and hundreds were civilians. We export more weapons than any nation that ever existed. We've been at continual war since 1941. What other country can claim *that* distinction? But I guess that's all for the sake of protecting American lives, right? So what's your take on the death penalty? Or the criminal justice system in general, for that matter? Or a murder rate five times higher than Europe's? Doesn't seem like the government's done much to deal with *those* threats to American lives. So I'm sorry if you don't see how the country I just described might have done something awful on 9/11. You know, for all your brilliance, you've got some major blind spots when it comes to the home team."

He thought about that. "I guess I do," he admitted. But his voice was not defensive, more stumped. Like he'd had his shit called for the first time in a long time.

Seeing him at a loss didn't feel satisfying. Here she was slinging death tolls around as talking points, to make herself look smarter. It wasn't as if she'd lost sleep over any of these tragedies. She was merely using them to win an argument, barely registering their real impact. It hardly put her in the running for the moral high ground.

She decided to throw him a lifeline—no need to let him sit there and stew. "So, for the sake of argument, let's say our government *wouldn't* be involved in something like this. What about TERNGO, then? You okay with an evil corporation? What if they're pulling all the strings?"

"Couldn't pull them all," Max said. "You know that. For events to transpire the way you've proposed—substituting planes, eliminating witnesses, concocting evidence—someone on the inside, the government, would *have* to be helping."

"So, then, you're totally sure that's impossible?"

Max didn't answer. At this rate they'd be sitting in his car in front of Benevolus's secret lair till sunrise.

"How come I don't piss you off?"

"What do you mean?"

"No stalling, genius. You know exactly what I mean."

"You've only been at this stuff a few weeks. It's easy to get swept up in all the 9/11 jargon and conflicting reports and misinformation out there. That's what always drives a lot of this conspiracy stuff. Half the information you need for the truth is deemed too classified to see, and the other half is more info than any one person could possibly wrap their head around. So, I get why it's all very believable at first. Even appealing in some strange way."

"You think I'd believe differently if I spent more time on it? If I 'earned' it?" As if she had that kind of time. She tried to give the kind of look Marilyn Wren could summon so easily. "Have *you* 'earned' it?" she asked. "Your views on this subject, I mean."

Max looked at her. Made some grumbly boy sound. She wasn't sure if it was a concession or a deflection. Maybe both.

"Okay, then," she said, figuring that either way this counted as an argument she'd won.

After a moment he asked, "Your dad know much about computers?"

She was happy he'd changed the subject.

"Basic stuff. Why?"

"Trying to figure out a couple things. One, how tech savvy your dad is, and two, who his contact might be. This other computer guy no one seems to know. When you talk to your dad again, you think you could ask him specifically about that? Who his computer contact is? How they share data? If—"

"Thought you wanted me out of this."

"I do." He sighed. "That's the other thing I'm trying to figure out."

Katie reached over and gently squeezed his leg. He dropped his own hand to cover hers.

It was too dark to see if he was blushing.

He watched the two teenagers sitting in the car.

Camping out in the empty building across from Plain-Truth.com proved more advantageous every day.

He zoomed in for a better picture of the girl.

Again, Kaitlyn Wallace.

Later, he would print the pictures and put them in the folder with the others he'd taken in Philadelphia and near her high school.

"So many lies," he said in the dark, empty room.

Too many.

"Soon," he said.

The car made a tight U-turn and the two liars pulled away.

The transmitter securely in place beneath them.

He put the camera down and eyed his rifle.

"Very soon."

25

"This"—Max handed back the pages—"is an interesting affidavit."

Katie took the letter and read it again. "If only we had this yesterday. Benevolus should love this."

Typed and notarized testimony from Mrs. Sara Murtha all the way from Rochester, New York. Katie had found Murtha's name in a newspaper article regarding her experiences as a passenger on 9/11. Two emails later, she had this. And it was more than interesting. It was magnificent.

Two simple pages on how Murtha and other passengers had been forced to land in Cleveland and then were led off their plane (Delta 1989). How they'd been directed by guards and security who clearly weren't with the airport. Plainclothes men with assault rifles. Detained, questioned, logged. How she'd clearly witnessed other passengers being led off *another* plane in a single group and directed quickly to the large NASA hangar at the airport. How she'd lingered, seen those same passengers loaded onto "military-looking" buses.

Magnificent.

And—maybe—nonsense.

Katie couldn't decide. Felt so tired. Too tired. Her mind stuffed with so many questions, random bits of data and speculation.

"Think it will help?" she asked. "Or is it ridiculous?"

Max shrugged. He seemed less into enduring her today than usual. Something in his voice, his energy. "You finally have a witness on record. Notarized. Official. Supports some of your dad's claims in a fashion. That's a win, counselor."

"But?"

He shook his head. They'd hunkered together in a deserted back corner table of a local fast-food burrito place. The restaurant was mostly empty, the workers making their first hopeful moves toward closing. "*But* nothing. Present it to Wren and see what she says. Your job is only to present the strongest case you can. The outcome is ultimately out of your control."

"What do you think about Murtha's story?"

"I'm not your judge, Katie. And I'm not Marilyn Wren."

"I'm asking Max Thompson. Your job was to shoot holes in this case, remember?"

"Barely."

"C'mon, Max. What do you think?"

He sighed heavily, genuine disappointment painting his whole face. "Fine. Why land at the Cleveland airport? There must be a dozen military bases and a hundred empty fields between the East Coast and Ohio. Why risk a major airport?"

"Hiding in the open, maybe? Easier to get lost in all that chaos. Harder to do at some vacant military base. Especially if it wasn't the military or government conducting this operation, but some rogue faction *within* the government using foreign agents and outside contractors."

"Contractors like your dad."

She swallowed. "Yes."

"Okay, so then why not park *in* the giant NASA hangar? Why let hundreds of witnesses watch you unload outside?

Seems a profound waste of, well, a giant hangar. Doesn't it?"

"The hangar was probably already full. There're reports NASA had a KC-135 aircraft on-site that day for gravity experiments. Also, Boeing often uses NASA hangars to store its experimental military shuttles."

"So then, maybe *that's* why your dad was in Cleveland. And it had nothing to do with 9/11. Fits what Bohenek claimed. Maybe your dad was ordered, as an employee of TERNGO, to provide security for one of those shuttles. Getting ready for some classified test, or to move it, or who knows. *Then*, 9/11 happened and they were asked to help."

"So why his horrific story about the passengers? The woman, her little girl?"

"I don't know." Max took another sip of his soda. "But neither do you."

"You know, I finally picked up one of those DNA tests at Walmart."

He sighed. "That could maybe answer *one* of your questions, Katie. But would prove nothing about what happened on September 11, 2001."

"God." She flopped her head into her arms on the table. "My brains hurt. I can't even process, you know. It's too much."

"Lost sight of the forest for the trees."

"I guess," she said. "Let's talk about something else."

"Fine. If you had three apples and one pumpkin and four oranges and three more apples in one hand and four apples and three oranges and two coconuts and one more orange in the other hand, what would you have?"

"You're not well."

"What would you have?"

"Six . . . *ten* apples, eight oranges and, what, two coconuts and, and a pumpkin."

"Yes, anything else?"

"What? No." She recounted. "No."

"Large hands," he said.

"Har, har."

Max smiled broadly. Held up his hands.

"There's a point here, yes? We're making some kind of point."

"A reminder, is all," he said. "Sometimes the best answer is the simple one."

"Couldn't you just say Occam's razor like everyone else?"

"I almost cited Solomonoff's theory of inductive inference," he replied. "The apples seemed more fun."

The Claypools were not happy.

So not-happy, they'd been waiting at the front door when she and Max pulled up.

Max got out of the car before Katie even had a chance to intervene, and then he politely took the blame. Worse, the Claypools responded by inviting Max into the house. Said they "wanted to talk." They might as well have said: "Wanted to Humiliate," or "Wanted to Make Sure You Never Ever Missed Curfew Again, Young Lady."

Mr. and Mrs. Claypool took either side of the couch and sat, leaving a coffee table between them and two chairs where Katie and Max could sit. Katie spied Zoe passing slowly in the hallway on her way to the basement. A quick and curious look at Max, no doubt. But also a supportive—and much-needed—wave and eye roll. Katie managed not to smile back and turned her full attention back to the Claypools.

"I want to apologize again," Max was saying, clasping his hands together and checking out the house.

"Well, let's let that..." Mr. Claypool started, then restarted. "Katie tells us you've been helping her with some school report."

"Ah, yes," Max said carefully.

"You go to Maryland?" Mrs. Claypool confirmed.

"Freshman, yes. Pre-law."

Katie had turned to gaze out the bay window behind her and Max, into the darkness outside. Her mind wandering while Max fibbed some generic answers to questions about his family, background, and career plans. Maybe he was right. Maybe it was time she let her dad and the courts work this all out. Maybe she'd given enough. How could she possibly—

"We have some concerns that . . . May we ask what school project this is you two are working on so energetically?" Mr. Claypool asked.

Max replied, "Well, I'd say—"

"No," Katie stopped him, turning back from the darkness outside. "You may not."

"Katie." Mrs. Claypool tilted her head kindly. "We have some idea what you're working on and it's a commendable thing. Our concern is that—"

"That's a private matter, Mrs. Claypool," Katie interrupted. "With all respect. And whatever assumptions you've made about what I'm doing with my own personal time are, I admit, yours to make. But I'm not going to share them with you. I'm not doing anything illegal."

"Katie." Mr. Claypool held up his hands. "We're not trying to invade your privacy. Have we once pestered you about personal matters beyond the rules of this house?"

"No," she admitted. Even felt bad, some, blasting these two. "I'm sorry."

"Gloria Dorsey stopped by earlier," Mr. Claypool said. "She explained some things. Gave us more information than before."

"Oh, I'll bet she did. Anything to keep us quiet. Why was she even here?"

"She's coming to pick you up tomorrow morning. To see your father and—"

And then Mrs. Claypool started screaming.

26

"A face." Mrs. Claypool gasped again struggling to catch her breath. "Right there!"

She stood pointing at the window behind Katie and Max. Her husband had already darted (quite deftly too, Katie noted) to the front door, hurrying out onto the porch, as Max looked outside, pressing his face against the windowpane with his hands cupped around his eyes.

Katie's heart raced as if she'd been the one who'd seen the face. She'd seen Mrs. Claypool recoiling into the couch, her eyes wide, the gaping-mouthed scream. And when Mrs. Claypool had screamed, Katie had known from the woman's look that it was about something in the window right behind her, and she'd spun around. And had seen . . .

Maybe something. A shadow?

The back of someone retreating into the night?

Had she imagined it? Had Mrs. Claypool?

Or *had* there been someone standing there in the dark behind her? Watching. Someone who'd likely even been right there when she'd been gazing out the window a minute earlier.

"Who?" Katie asked. "Did you recognize who it was?"

Mrs. Claypool shook her head, waved her hands, as if chasing away the memory. "No, no. It was . . . a horrible face."

"Horrible how?" Max turned.

"Odd," she replied. "Blurred. The features were all washed out. Like I imagine a ghost would look, I want to say. I know that sounds silly."

"Not at all." Katie moved finally to join her on the couch. Realizing how much it'd shaken her. "Can I get you anything? Water or something?"

Mrs. Claypool shook her head. Outside, Mr. Claypool passed the window.

Zoe and C.J. appeared in the hallway, clearly only now feeling like it was safe for them to intrude. "Um, everyone okay?" Zoe asked.

"No, no. Nothing." Mrs. Claypool patted down her pants, looked up at the girls with a forced smile. "Were you outside? No—no, of course you weren't. What am I saying? I'm sorry to startle everyone. I just, I've made a big deal over nothing."

Katie looked across the room at Max, who shook his head at her once. He knew the same thing she did. It wasn't nothing. *This* was far from nothing.

"I'm sure you're right," Katie lied.

She rubbed her face, trying to focus. Something Mrs. Claypool had . . .

"You said something about seeing my father?"

She sat in the hospital conference room alone this time, waiting. Picking at the sides of the table for something to do. She'd been waiting for almost an hour. Even stuck her head out into the hallway twice to let the security guard know who she was waiting for: Dr. Ziegler. Her father's psychiatric physician. He evidently wanted to talk to her as soon as possible. The mysterious face in the Claypools' window had left a hollow fear deep in her gut. Along with even more confusion than before. And now this.

Finally, the door opened behind her, and Katie turned.

The first man to enter was heavyset, early fifties with a dark, neatly-trimmed beard. Glasses pushed up onto the top of his head. He was wearing a traditional white doctor's jacket. Ziegler. She recognized him from the hearing.

"Miss Wallace," he said, holding out a hand. "Very sorry to keep you waiting."

Katie stood. "It's okay. Is my father—"

She stopped, withdrew her hand, as she saw the second man. Paul Cobb.

"What are you doing here?" Her eyes narrowed to dark slits.

Cobb only nodded politely as if saying hello, pulled the door shut, and claimed one of the many open chairs. "Dr. Ziegler invited me."

"We'd like to allow you to see your father again," the doctor said. "On a more regular schedule, I mean."

Katie started to speak—particularly bothered by the word *allow*—and Ziegler stopped her.

"Before we can do that, I'm hoping you can help me sort a few things out. This is delicate." He sat with an audible sigh. "I don't want to discomfort or embarrass you. You know about your father's delusions regarding 9/11, yes?"

She let the word *delusions* pass. "I guess," she said.

"He has recently shared other, ah, claims," Ziegler said. "And he's growing more adamant about one in particular. One we were hoping you could shed some light on."

"Who's 'we'?" She glared at Cobb. "Him?"

"We're only trying to help your dad," Cobb replied.

"You've got that one on repeat, Mr. Cobb," Katie said.

"Not sure we even need you here to say it. What are these new allegations about my father?"

"Would you like to sit?" Ziegler asked. "And they're not allegations. It's an idea he has, a revelation during his therapy that may, or may not, be true. And it's important that we, and he, know the difference moving forward."

Katie sat. "What is it?"

Ziegler looked at Cobb again and then said simply: "Your father believes that you are not his daughter."

"Okay." She kept her voice steady and emotionless. Of all the topics for them to bring up today! But she knew Cobb was watching and hanging on her every word . . . Did they know what she was planning? The security guy hadn't dug around in her bag much today. Was it purely coincidence? Was there such a thing anymore?

Ziegler leaned forward. "I'm sorry to have to ask this, but were you aware of this belief? Has he mentioned it before?"

"Hints here and there." She decided to focus on answering their questions, to keep her mind on that. "Nothing serious."

"Why do you say 'nothing serious'?"

"Well, because he was always drunk or high at the time."

"'A drunk is just an honest man talking,'" Cobb remarked casually.

Katie turned. "Well, then, there you go."

"So he could be telling the truth," Ziegler said.

"He could," she agreed.

"Would you mind if we took a DNA test?" the doctor asked.

They knew! They had to know . . .

"No thanks," she managed.

"Don't you want to know?" Cobb asked.

"Not sure it matters at this point," she lied.

"It could help us with your dad, I think," the doctor pressed. "We're trying to establish a foundation of reality for him."

"Also," Cobb added, "if he's *not* your father, people might wonder where he got a little girl. You might have been abducted or, who knows." He spread his hands, ever the helpful bureaucrat. "It's possible to get a fake birth certificate. We'd have to track down the original paperwork from Vital Records and the Department of Health to be sure. I know that must sound absurd to you. But your dad's finally getting all these other legal issues behind him. It would be nice to settle this little matter too."

"Got it. I'll think about it. May I see him now?"

The two men exchanged a look.

"Yes," Ziegler replied quickly and led them out and held the door as she stepped into the long hallway. "Thank you again, Miss Wallace." The doctor waved politely and headed off in one direction, as Cobb motioned she should follow him the other way.

"We're just trying to sort all this out, Katie," Cobb said.

An unexpectedly cold fury rose up within her, whiting out all her careful reactions, her cautious accusations. "It's sorting out," she said, her words clipped. "And when it does, everyone will know what happened here, Mr. Cobb. And what happened before."

He glanced back at her but didn't stop his slow, casual amble. "What happened before, Katie?"

She ignored him, and they continued down the hall past the security guy, who swiped the door to let her back to where her father was. But she found she wasn't quite done yet. She turned to glare at Cobb. "When everyone finally hears the truth about what my dad knows, about what I now know, that's when everything changes." She stepped into the next wing. He'd stayed in the doorway, ready to vanish back again into whatever dark cave he inhabited when not pestering her. "Starting with that smug look on your face."

She expected one of his infamous smiles. Instead, his expression had shifted to something cold and hard. And certain.

"Good luck, soldier," he said.

And then the door shut between them.

"What's she doing?"

"Appears she's applying a cheek swab. To see if daddy's really daddy."

"Not going to be a good week for her."

"She can handle it."

"How's this help us, sir? We've already done the tests ourselves. We know the results."

"Heat always generates more heat," Cobb noted, watching the video.

"Let her burn a little?"

"Let her burn a lot. She can handle it."

"So you keep saying. And if she can't?"

"Then you can say I was wrong."

"With pleasure, sir."

Cobb studied the girl on the screen. "This morning, a classified memo appeared as a GIF on, of all places, a Home Shopping Network chat room. Someone sending us a message. Let's rattle her some more. Keep the pressure on. See what other messages shake out."

"How much heat, sir?"

"A One for now."

"That all?"

"Just want to scare her a little. A One should do the trick, I think."

"And if daddy gets pissed? Tries to scare us back?"

It was a question Paul Cobb had thought a lot about lately.

"We have other numbers if it comes to that," he said.

27

Katie looked at the building where her mother had maybe saved her life.

The NASA Glenn Research Center.

Not the *real* building. That one was six hours away, shielded behind half a mile of various gates and barbed fences and security. And her emails and calls to the airport and the research center requesting a tour of the facilities, specifically the enormous white hangar, had gone completely ignored.

So these virtual versions were all she had. Google Earth. YouTube videos of some kid's aeronautics class. A segment on *Jeopardy*. Bird's-eye views from a hundred miles above, then ten, then eventually inside. In each case, the hangar was being photographed ten or fifteen years *after* 9/11. Imperfect comparisons. But still the same building. A colossal white structure tucked in the back of the airport, far from the everyday passengers and flights. Far from inquiring eyes. The NASA letters in bright blue on top, covering half of the roof, probably visible from space.

He'd been in this building. Scott Wallace.

NOT her father.

The paternity test results had been ready in two days, as promised on the back of the over-the-counter kit. The verdict in digital black and white.

The reactions of anger or loss or betrayal weren't there as she'd anticipated.

Your father should know you're alive. He needs to know.

Something about that 0%.

Probability of Paternity: 0%.

One hundred percent not her father.

One hundred percent.

She'd almost forgotten, or given up believing, that such a thing was possible.

Squinting into the glow of the Claypools' computer, she used the 3-D rendering on Google, tried duplicating the exact path—and sensation—of landing at the airport and then being taxied to the NASA hangar. Of sitting and waiting, of getting out, being directed out under armed escort, and walking inside. Tried imagining where the "military buses" would have been waiting. Behind the hangar? Inside? Waiting until the interrogations were done, when the personal belongings and DNA samples had been collected. Why not collect them later, after these people were killed?

Each scenario she imagined only brought more questions. Questions that always seemed to come into her head in Max's voice.

Max, whom she hadn't seen in days. Ignoring his few polite texts with generic "hi-busy-talk-later" responses. She didn't have time for Max. Couldn't see him. Or anyone else, for that matter. Texts and calls from Alexis and even Gianna had been similarly brushed off, including something about Winter wandering off—not unheard of—and several variations of "Are you okay / do you want me to come over?" She'd totally skipped the last two days of school. "Sick."

Sick in the head, mostly. Imagining these things. These horrible things. Looking at harmless videos of experimental planes and replacing the planes with lines of people. Terrified people. Confused. Furious. Powerless. Being ordered this way and that. Cell phones confiscated. A man sweating in his thousand-dollar business suit. Or an older woman with bad knees limping down the air-stairs ramp. A couple of school kids wide-eyed and anxious. The veteran stewardess and her pilot whispering to each other that "something's not right." The mother carrying her infant daughter . . . all of them. Two hundred souls. All ages and shapes. Led from their plane without knowing why. Knowing, maybe, only that America was "under attack." That they were now a small part of something bigger. Something very bad.

Focus, she thought for the fiftieth time. *Remember.* Remember being here. This place. Those doors? *No.* That wall? That ceiling? *No.* Something about the lights. Remember something about . . . remember being in her arms. The others crushing in. Remember seeing his face, his face for the first time as she hands you to him. Katie clicked from one image to the next, back to the map, three videos running at the same time—*REMEMBER*—approaching the towering wall of tinted windows—*REMEMBER*—the methodical framing and roof beams inside, like the gray bones of some enormous whale—*REMEMBER*—another picture—the ceiling two hundred feet above totally lost in shadows, security moving along the planking.

Remember.

That memory, however, remained narrowly out of reach. A moment, a single breath away. But never close enough. Lost forever. If it'd ever been there at all.

Probability of Paternity: 0%.

Katie pushed back from the computer table. Covered her face with both hands and moaned. Eyes closed in that new darkness, she let the images—the pictures and maps and videos of the hangar—continue to play in her mind. Each iteration getting darker and blending into a fully-realized room. She could see that room now better than the one she was actually sitting in.

Was she really there?

"Kit Kat, you okay?"

Katie dropped her hands, leaned back to find Zoe standing at the bottom of the basement steps behind her. "Yes," she responded.

"C.J. and me were gonna walk down to Walmart for something to do. Wanna go with?"

Katie smiled. "No, thanks. But, hey . . ." She tilted her head. "You believe in past lives, right?"

Zoe nodded. "I do."

"Do you ever try to figure out . . . what you were before? Like, I don't know, tap into a past life?"

"Of course," Zoe said, clearly curious as to where Katie was going with this. "It's called regression memory. People do it all the time. I've studied it. Why?" Her eyes were bright. Interested. "You wanna dig around a past life?"

Katie'd spun her chair fully around to face Zoe, clasping her own hands tightly. They were shaking. But she wouldn't be alone, doing this. Zoe and C.J. would be here. Gianna was a five-minute drive away and would jump at the chance to check up on her. "What if I wanted to dig around *this* life some? Can you do that?"

"And miss out on Walmart?" Zoe said, sighing loudly.

And you're now crossing the bridge, crossing, the cool water of the stream trickles beneath your feet, crossing over, the sun warm against your face. Three. (Zoe's words drifting within the gentle music.) *You're relaxing, deeper. Your whole body is relaxed. You are safe. Nothing can harm you. Relaxed. The universe protects you. Two . . . You are safe here. Your whole body is at peace. One. On the other side of the bridge, what do you see? Tell me.*

Grass.

Look at your feet. What are you wearing? Tell me.

Sandals. Red sandals.

Describe the other side of the stream. What does it look like? Tell me.

Another field. There's a small house. Farmhouse. And trees in the distance. A party.

Walk toward the party. You are relaxing. Everything is at peace. The universe protects you. You are safe here. Who is at the party? Tell me.

Kids. Lots of kids. There's, there's a piñata hanging in the tree. Music, a band. People. A tractor. A pony. My dad.

You're relaxed. You are safe here. Look down. What are you wearing?

My blue dress.

What are you doing? Tell me. You're relaxed. You are safe here.

I'm on a horse. A pony. My dad is standing next to me.

Nothing can harm you here. Nothing can hurt you. How do you feel? Tell me.

Fun. Happy.

Good. Feel your body relaxing more and more. Do you want to go into the house? Do you want to go into the woods? Nine . . .

The house.

And you're walking toward the house, crossing the field, the grass beneath your feet, walking, the cool wind against your face. Eight. You're relaxing, deeper. Nothing can harm you. The universe protects you. Seven . . . (Zoe's words continuing in the same cadenced progression, counting down as Katie imagined the house closer and closer, its door opening.) *You are safe here. Your whole body is at peace. One. Inside the house now, what do you see? Tell me.*

My new room! It's painted yellow.

Look at your feet. What are you wearing? Tell me.

Sneakers—my new white sneakers.

Describe the rest of the yellow room. What does it look like? Tell me.

My bed. Toys. Bear. Books.

Good. You are entering the room. Walking into the room. Who is in the room with you? You are relaxing. Everything is at peace. The universe protects you. You are safe here. Who is in the room? Tell me.

My daddy.

Look down. What are you wearing? You're relaxed. You are safe here.

Purple shorts. The flower shirt . . .

What are you doing? Tell me. You're relaxed. You are safe here. What are you and Daddy doing? Tell me.

A book. He is reading a book. Time for nap. No play.

You're relaxed. You are safe here. What book is he reading? Tell me.

Go, Dog, Go. "Do you like my party hat?"

Nothing can harm you here. Nothing can hurt you. How do you feel? Tell me.

Sleepy. Smart. Funny.

Good. Feel your body relaxing more and more. Stepping away from the house. Do you want to go into the woods? Nine . . .

No.

Crossing the field. Into the woods. Eight. Do you see an opening in the woods, a path to follow? Tell me.

No.

Nothing can harm you here. You're walking toward the woods.

No, no, I can't.

And you're leaving the house, crossing to the woods, the breeze trickles through the trees gently, closer to the woods, the shade cool against your face. Seven. You're relaxing, deeper. Your whole body is relaxed. You are safe. Nothing can harm you. Relaxed. The universe protects you. Six . . . Do you see an opening in the trees? A path? Tell me.

Yes! Yes . . .

You are safe here. Your whole body is at peace. Five. Walking toward the path. On the other side of the field, what do you see? Tell me.

More trees. Dark. Too many trees.

Step onto the path. Everything is at peace. The universe protects you. Four. You are safe here.

I can't.

You are safe here. Your whole body is at peace. Three. Walking onto the path. You're relaxing, deeper. Two. Stepping into the woods. You are safe here. Following the path. Your whole body is at peace. One. On the path, what do you see? Tell me.

More trees. Dark. Too many trees.

Stay on the path. Look at your feet. What are you wearing? Tell me.

Feets. Toeses. PJs.

Describe the path, describe the woods. What does it look like? Tell me.
Dark. All dark.

Walk down the path. Who is on the path? Who is in the woods?
You are relaxing. Everything is at peace. The universe protects you.
You are safe. Who is in the woods? Tell me.

Mommy.

You're relaxed. You are safe here. What are you doing? Tell me.
Hiding.

Why? Why are you hiding? Tell me. You're relaxed. You are
safe here.

Mommy is yelling. Fighting. Mommy is crying.

How do you feel? Nothing can harm you here. Nothing can hurt
you. How do you feel? Tell me.

Crying. Scared.

You are safe here. Your whole body is at peace. Walking onto the
path. You're relaxing, deeper. Stepping into the woods. You are safe
here. Following the path. Your whole body is at peace. On the path,
what do you see? Tell me.

Mommy fighting with the man.

Why are they fighting? Tell me.

Mommy doesn't want me. The man doesn't want me. She's
crying. Bad words.

Who is saying bad words? Tell me.

Mommy and the man.

About you?

Yes. NO, Mommy!

Everything is at peace. You are safe here. The universe protects
you. What do you see? Tell me.

Mommy is holding me. She's crying. She's . . . it's dark.
Mommy is shoving me at him. At Scott. Everyone is screaming. Bad words.

Who is on the path? Who is in the woods? You are relaxing.

People. I don't know them. Mommy's bad friends.

Mommy is gone. Mommy is gone?

Everything is at peace. You are safe here. The universe protects you. What do you see? Tell me.

Daddy. Scott. Daddy has me. Bad words.

He is crying. He is holding me. In the dark.

Please . . .

I'm sorry.

Katie stared up at the ceiling for a long while, enfolded in the room's darkness, before looking around again. First she saw Zoe, sitting at the end of the bed at her feet. Dressed in black. Beautiful and mysterious with the flickering candles lit behind her. Her smile broke through the room's shadows. Then Gianna, staring at her as if she'd just levitated off the bed.

"Fuuuuckkkk, girl," Gianna breathed. "Welcome back."

Beyond Gianna, C.J. sat cross-legged on the floor, staring back wide-eyed. Katie brought up her hands and rubbed her face. She grumbled into her palms.

"How you feeling?" Zoe asked quietly.

"Stupid," she replied.

"Oh, beautiful, why would you feel that?"

"Did I sound stupid? I thought . . . I don't know. I don't even know what I was saying."

"You did not sound stupid." Gianna strode forward, sitting on the bed. She turned to Zoe. "This is so much better than going to a shrink. You know that, right? You totally have to take this shit on the road."

Zoe accepted G's words with a soft smile of appreciation,

then squeezed Katie's calf. "You were *amazing*. And some part of you knew exactly what you were saying."

Katie sat up. "I don't remember everything I said."

"Not a problem." Gianna held her phone up. "Recorded for *your* ears only."

"Oh, God." Katie rolled her eyes. Maybe she was still under. Maybe none of this was real.

"How do you feel?" Zoe asked, getting up to turn on her lamp. "Remember, you're safe now. We're just talking. How do you feel? Tell me."

"'Tell me.' Ha. I remember *that*." Katie rubbed her hands together. "I feel, I don't know. Lost? It's hard to describe. It's not a bad feeling for once, though. More like—I feel apart from the world, disconnected in a good way for once. An afterthought, kind of. Is that weird?"

"Of course not," Zoe said.

Gianna interrupted, her voice quiet now, almost sad. "You saw your dad. Even said 'Scott' at one point."

"Yeah." Katie sighed. "Yeah. It was him I saw at the end. Him and her. My mom." Her mouth felt a little dry, even saying it. *My mom.*

But how would she have known the name "Scott" on 9/11? If he and her mother had just crossed paths for the first time, if there were only a few minutes to spare . . .

"Was that a memory?" she asked, directing her question to Zoe.

"Maybe," Zoe replied. "Maybe not. Memories are funny things. They get all jumbled up sometimes. Tangled with other memories. Often with invented memories."

"Why would people invent memories?"

"To fill in gaps," Zoe replied.

"Or replace worse memories," C.J. added quietly.

The other three girls turned to her.

"That too," Zoe agreed.

That same afternoon, a package arrived at the Claypools' house.

Capt. S. Wallace & K. Wallace
c/o Claypool Residence
5281 Pinehill Drive
Ferndale, MD 23749

Postage only, no return address. A brown box big enough to hold a basketball. "Didn't know your father was in the military," Mr. Claypool said, handing her the heavy box.

Katie didn't know how to respond, so she didn't, beyond a thanks. Then she took the box upstairs, closed her door, and laid it on the bed. Who had sent this?

She grabbed a pen from her book bag and used the tip to puncture the tape holding the box closed. Inside, a smaller box and more tape to split free.

When she opened that, the smell hit her.

Katie gagged, covering her mouth.

Inside the smaller box was a thick, dark plastic bag. Rolled closed on top.

She'd somehow stepped back from the bed and it was only with great effort that she forced herself forward again, then carefully took hold of the top of the bag. Rolled it back. Slowly. The girl frozen above her horse seemed to turn, to watch her as she worked the bag open.

Inside was . . . she wasn't sure. The reek was even stronger. The room no longer smelled like lavender. She didn't yet quite understand what she was seeing.

But then she did.

With one hand to her mouth, mere fingertips somehow holding back the scream, the turning in her stomach, she used the other hand to grab hold of a top flap and shift the box violently.

No head—*Where's the head?*—gone or smashed—but she knew.

It was a cat.

. . . Its white fur flattened and wet . . .

Katie turned away to vomit but only dry-heaved. She grabbed hold of the chair to steady herself. To think. *No, please, no.* Her phone? Frantic. No clue where she'd—in her back pocket, and she pulled it free. *No, please, no.* It took three swipes to make her password work.

"Hey," Gianna's answered. "How are you doing after this morning's—"

"Did Winter come back?" she gasped.

Silence on the other end.

"G?"

"Not yet," Gianna replied. "I meant to tell you this morning but then you wanted to get hypnotized and shit and I forgot. Mom and I even drove out to your house a couple times earlier this week. But you told me she does this sometimes, right?"

Who? Who would do this? Bohenek? Benevolus552? Paul Cobb? *Who?*

"Katie?"

What had she done? "I've—" Katie gabbled. "I've got to go."

Closed her phone and let it drop.

She wanted to scream. An anguish and rage so loud that the whole house came up to see what was the matter. To call the police. Gloria Dorsey, even.

But she couldn't. These people would only complicate her life further. Ruin everything she'd been working on. So close to understanding, to *knowing*, what really happened that day. They'd maybe even somehow blame her or her father for Winter's death. Use it as another excuse to keep them *both* locked up. No. She could see that future like she was looking at it through a telescope, small and far away and perfectly clear.

No. *That* future that wasn't going to happen.

She closed the box, resettling the tape as best she could. Screams would have to wait.

You want to scare me away? Threaten me? Hurt me?

Katie retrieved her phone from the floor.

Not until I hurt you first.

28

Katie and Gianna sat in Gianna's car in the school parking lot. Students trickled in around them, the first bell only a few minutes away.

"I can't tell you how much I appreciate this, G," Katie said, taking the keys.

"How worried should I be?" Gianna asked. "About you, I mean. Not the stupid car."

"I know what you meant. And you shouldn't be worried at all. I'll be back by the end of school."

"Let me go with. You won't even know I'm there."

Katie shook her head. "Nope. Something I gotta do alone."

She had to get back to Washington. Had to confront the only other person besides her dad—besides Scott Wallace— who'd for sure been there that morning. She hadn't even told Max what she was doing. No reason he needed to be involved in this part. Or any of it, if she could help it. Not anymore.

Why should anyone else suffer because of her?

"You gonna get through this?" Gianna finally asked, the words coming out like they'd been bottled up, under pressure. "Your last pre-calc grade was, well, 'unexpected.' And you look, I mean . . ."

"Thanks a lot."

"Tired. And like you've been crying all night."

She had been. "I'm fine."

"You worried about Winter? Was it that hypnotism shit? Did something else happen?"

Katie laughed nervously. "Oh, no. No, it's not . . . just all the stuff with my dad is all. Really. The court case. Stuff at the hospital. And it all takes time. Energy. More than I ever imagined it would. I just need a break."

"I get it," Gianna sighed, instantly contrite. "That was selfish, stupid, of me. I can't even wrap my head around what you're going through."

Katie couldn't either, really. Would she ever?

"You're fine. Truly. This is weird and new and you've been great. Guess yesterday was a bust, in terms of actual hanging out. I'll try to make some real time soon," Katie said. "For you and me. This weekend."

"Come to prom next week."

"Yeah, that'll solve everything."

"It will for a couple hours. You still hanging with Max?"

"No, it's not like that. We're . . . no. You should probably head in."

"Yeah." Gianna looked back toward the school. "Sure you don't need me to—"

"Go," Katie laughed, pushing her elbow. "I'll be fine. This is no big deal."

She watched Gianna open the car door and thought: *I'm just going alone to confront a creepy, gun-wielding mercenary who threatened to have me arrested, who likely played a part in the biggest scandal of the millennium. No big deal.*

Gianna leaned down toward the open window. "Hey," she said. "We'll find Winter tonight, okay? You and me."

No we won't. Katie held back a sob.

"Yeah, yeah," she managed. "Now get to class, young lady."

Gianna stuck out her tongue playfully.

But when Katie pulled the car away slowly, she looked back in the rearview mirror to find her friend still watching her, her face in the distance no longer playful.

Now it was troubled. Scared.

Katie turned out onto the main road, her gaze shifting to her own reflection in the mirror.

Her expression looked a lot like Gianna's.

She was ready to get arrested if that's what it came to.

And even more ready to demand more information from Jason Bohenek.

The lobby of the Symmes Building, where Brown & Plotsky LLP manipulated the whole world and Jason Bohenek provided them the security to do so, was much less impressive the second time Katie walked through it. The high ceilings and white marble and fancy fountains were all ignored as she stomped straight toward the security desk.

The same two men from before were working. Perfect. And the larger of the two was already coming around the counter to stop her advance. Even better.

She held up a hand in warning. Prepared to scream her lungs out the second this security gorilla touched her.

"Miss . . ." He was holding up his own hand, indicating she should stop walking. His other hand rested on his belt where his gun, a Taser, and a canister of tear gas were all hooked like he was Batman or something. "This is private property and I am ordering you to depart."

"Call the cops," Katie said, looking the gorilla right in the eyes. "Go ahead. See what I tell them *and* the papers." She'd never stopped moving forward and had reached the front of the desk with the gorilla standing beside her. "I'm here to see Mr. Jason Bohenek."

"He's not here," the fart-smelling security guy said. He looked a little less aggressive today. More curious, actually. Almost as if he'd been expecting her.

"We played this game last time. Why don't you get on—"

"No, seriously." He stopped her, his gaze even more intrigued. "He's not here."

"I'll wait then."

"You'll wait a long time. He's on a leave of absence."

"Bullshit."

"Think what you want, but that's what we were told. Haven't seen him in three, four days." He looked at the gorilla, who mouth-breathed back.

Gone? Why? "What's that mean?" she asked.

"It means he's not here," the gorilla said.

There was no way this was coincidental. "But I need to get ahold of him," she said to the first guy. "It's very important. Do you have a contact number, his cell? Or a home address or anything?"

"I'm sorry." And this time, it truly looked like he was. "There's no way we'd give out personal information like that. Best I can do is take your info and make sure he gets it when he returns."

"Which could be weeks."

"Or longer."

Katie looked down at the snowy marble floor. "He's really not here?"

"Really," the security guy replied. "What's the best way to reach you?"

"Please tell him Kaitlyn Wallace needs to see him," she said. "I'm sure he knows how to find me."

He nodded.

"Miss." The gorilla beside her got all puffed up again. "Now that your business is finished, I'll escort you out."

"I'll walk her out, Steve," the first guy said. "Take the desk."

The gorilla hesitated, then shrugged. Evidently taking the desk won out over intimidating a minor. The two guards switched places.

"Miss Wallace." Her new chaperone gestured toward the door. "If you don't mind."

She thought about making a scene of some kind. What if they were lying? Was Bohenek watching her from some security camera, maybe from one of the hundreds of frosted windows and offices overlooking the lobby? She looked up hopefully, saw only hundreds of tiny shadows.

"He's really gone," the guard remarked. And there was something about the way he said it.

They walked quietly together to the front of the building. The enormous glass doors slid open as they approached and he led her outside before stopping at the top of the steps.

"What's this about?" he asked, his gesture taking in both her and the building behind them. "Seems like it's a pretty big deal to you."

"It's private," she said, head down.

"Okay. Well, so you know, it's maybe not that private. You're not the first one to come looking for Mr. Bohenek this week."

"What do you mean?" Katie looked up.

"A couple of guys came on Friday. Day after you were here, in fact. Looking for him as well. He was already gone, though."

"Gone."

The guard looked at her steadily. "Miss Wallace, he never came back after seeing you."

Fresh alarm spiked through her. Was he implying—? "We left him at the park." She pointed. "Seriously. *That* park."

"I believe you. But no one's seen him since. It's all a little strange, even for this place."

"Could you describe these guys who were looking for him?"

"Hard guys. Suits. Pros. They all look like Bohenek, you know. Scary dudes."

"Why are you telling me this?"

He shrugged, his grin almost embarrassed, but not quite. "Guess I'm nosy. Seemed like you might know what it was all about."

"It involves stuff from a long time ago," she said. "Something important he probably knows something about."

"So, how'd you get pulled into it?"

"That's what I'm trying to figure out."

He nodded, started back into the building as the doors opened again. Then he glanced back. "If he comes back, I'll tell him you were here."

"But he's not coming back," she said. "Is he?"

"I wouldn't," he said and went back inside.

"Hello, stranger," Max answered his phone. "Thought you'd left the country or something."

"A lot of that going around," Katie replied, checking her rearview mirror. "Bohenek's vanished."

"The TERNGO guy? What do you mean 'vanished'?"

"I, ah, I drove out to see him again."

"Katie, why?"

"Had some more questions."

"You could have—"

"Didn't want, or need, you there. Sorry. What if they got rid of him?"

"'They' who?"

"The people at TERNGO. That Fuenmayor guy, maybe. Someone working with Paul Cobb and the government? Who knows. There are a whole lot of people who don't want Bohenek talking."

"Katie."

"Yeah?"

"That sounds . . ."

"Paranoid?"

"A bit."

"Then do me a favor," she said.

"Anything."

"I need to find this guy again. Can you do that? I mean, like, search the web again. Like travel plans somehow or other known addresses or, I don't know."

"A guy like Bohenek will be hard to find. Again, maybe now's a great time to finally back out of all this. You have enough. You've done *more* than enough. Present to Wren and call it a day."

"They killed Winter."

Silence on the other end of the phone.

"My cat. They mailed me . . . they killed Winter."

"Katie, I . . . I mean, who did? How do you . . . Katie, I'm really sorry." She could hear the hurt in his voice. "Should you call the police or something?"

"What would they do?" Her voice was shaky. "Anyhow, I've got to find Bohenek. Subpoena him. I've got to. I did a

DNA test on my dad and . . . oh, yeah, ha, my dad. So, Scott Wallace is not my father. Zero-point-zero. That's what it says."

"I'm sorry."

"Don't be. It answers a lot. Everything, I suppose. So I need to track down Bohenek, and *then* we go back to Benevolus. The real press, even. Once I can . . ." She felt the energy draining from her body, the words and meaning slipping away. What now? "Look, can you find this guy or not?"

"I'll try," he replied.

Katie blinked tears. "Good. I . . . thanks, Max. You're . . . I don't know what I'd do without you. Thanks."

"Yup," Max sighed. "Now, will you do something for me?"

29

They took 70 West out of Baltimore and drove for three hours.

Neither one of them spoke. Not once.

Silences with Max, she thought, had become more and more important, more healing, and she let this long one envelop them both in its comfort and simplicity.

To just *be*. How long had it been?

No questions. No research. No arguments. No hurdles. No drama.

No tomorrow. No yesterday.

Even when she realized where he was taking her, she said nothing. Let the world pass by her window, anonymous and detached, the morning sun warm on her face.

Eventually, the signs: *FLIGHT 93 NATIONAL MEMORIAL*.

Eventually, turning into the park and the long drive up the winding road.

"Why?" she asked then.

"I don't know," he admitted. Trusting her even with his doubt.

She reached out and took his hand.

Katie and Max drifted slowly from display to display. There were maybe twenty other people in the outside portion of the info center. A park ranger, a skinny guy in his late twenties, meandered among them.

She had arguments for each display they stopped at. Evidence of some kind that those who'd made the displays were "lying." The discrepancies with the official flight path in the MAYDAY! display. Suspicions about the calls that'd been made from the plane. The buried news reports about abnormalities in the crash site wreckage.

But she kept all of that to herself. Read, reflected quietly, shuffled on. Like the other visitors.

Those few who did speak used whispers. Any sound was connected to unseen tranquil things: crickets in the surrounding fields, the occasional squawk of a crow, a flag clanking against a flagpole somewhere.

She stepped with Max toward the next display.

This one was of the crew and passengers. Five rows of eight pictures. She recognized every face. Most of the forty names too. Had already spent long, late hours with each of them, especially the women, looking for one who might have had a child onboard that day, one who might—

But that had been weeks ago, she realized. An idea she'd never really allowed herself to get attached to. Not really . . .

Katie stepped away from the exhibit of pictures and toward the indoor exhibits. She and Max moved as they had all day. Quietly. Unhurried. Just being.

They came to the huge display covered in notes. A hundred little white cards with the scribblings of visitors. Some of it was in beautiful cursive, some with misspelled words, some clearly written by children. Notes to the dead.

We will never forget. Forever in our hearts. Love you.
You are HEROES. Thank you.

RIP. God Bless. Dozens of little cartoon hearts.

May You Rest in Peace. Thank you for being brave. I'm so sorry. All Heroes.

God Protect you and God save America. To all family and friends. Thank you.

Katie took a blank note. LEAVE YOUR MESSAGE, it read.

"What should I put?" she whispered.

Max smiled. "You'll know. No rush."

Katie watched him take his own card, tap the pen against his chin, and then write. She thought about the forty people on that plane. And all the people on the other planes, too. Strangers. Or not. Suddenly that didn't matter.

She wrote three words: *We miss you . . .*

Then she tacked the note to the wall and stepped back to inspect it among the others.

Max put up his card beneath hers. She couldn't see what he'd written, but didn't want to snoop either. Fearful her curiosity would get the best of her, she tugged at his arm to move on.

Outside again, they stepped into the chapel area. There, half a dozen people sat quietly among the rows of pews overlooking endless fields and rows of trees as the American flag fluttered high overhead. A pathway led away toward the actual memorial. Katie and Max followed it.

The long, dark pathway led them along a low, sloping black wall for a quarter mile. Nearly sixteen years before, the FBI had tossed up temporary fencing along the exact same line to keep onlookers away from the crash site. Today, the fence was gone. Only green fields on the other side. Every fifty yards, the black wall recessed into a flat nook, each niche filled with its own assortment of tiny American flags, flowers, rosaries, friendship bracelets, stuffed animals, pennies, crosses, small potted plants.

In the distance, she could see the enormous memorial marking the end of the curving trail, a long white wall touching a cartoonishly blue sky.

Katie leaned into Max, touching shoulders. "What did you write?" she asked, the words out before she could stop them.

"On the card?"

"You don't have to tell me."

"Tell you when you're older."

Closer, she saw that the memorial wasn't a long white wall at all, but forty *separate* monoliths. Each massive square stone stood alone, engraved with a single name—each rotated at a slightly different angle, so that from afar, the display had the appearance of overlapping into a single structure. Forty standing together as one again in this new reality.

"My God," Katie said. "It's . . ."

"Yeah," Max said beside her. He had no words either.

To the left, at the far end of the monoliths, they ended opposite another row of white columns running parallel with the main "wall" for a while and then continuing another twenty yards or so into the field beyond. Between the two walls and blocking the field beyond was an enormous wood gate—the gate of a fairy-tale giant, each vertical slat as twisted and distinctive as the hundreds of trees in the distance. Behind the gate, a grass trail that led back out to the field they'd passed. There, at the end of the long track, hundreds of yards in the distance, was an enormous boulder. A monument unto itself.

Katie wrapped her fingers around the edges of the gate's thick wood slats, cold and glossy to the touch. She knew the boulder marked the original impact site. The hole she'd studied in dozens of pictures. The supposed end of Flight 93. The hole that'd been quickly backfilled by the coroner and FBI. The hole that had looked nothing like any other crash site. The hole that baffled, even incensed, many Truthers.

And yet, she didn't care one bit about any of those claims or suspicions. Not right now.

Katie sighed to herself, aware that she'd probably uncovered Max's agenda. Max, who'd already turned and started walking back toward the engraved monoliths.

She followed him eventually, trailing slowly in his sinuous wake, stopping at each structure. Most had flowers and items laid against their bases. She caught up at the seventh.

SANDY WAUGH BRADSHAW

One of the five flight attendants. Katie could have discussed any of them. A mother of three, two not much older than Katie had been in 2001. She'd recently started working part-time to spend more time with them. She'd dutifully called US Airlines to report the hijacking *before* calling her own family. According to her husband, one of the last things she'd said to him was that she was boiling water to throw at the hijackers when they stormed the cockpit.

Again, the now-familiar arguments and mistrusts involuntarily sprang to mind, as easily as the Spanish words on her study-guide notecards.

1. An absence of—

No.

Not now.

She let them recede. It didn't matter that the story was disputable. It didn't matter if the passengers bravely stormed the cockpit or sat in their chairs thinking it was all a drill. Or had never even gotten on the plane. If the hijackers crashed the plane or if the Air Force shot them down. If they died here or in Cleveland. Or somewhere else. Even if they were now hidden under new identities on some island near Scotland with the grandchildren of *Lusitania* passengers. None of that mattered.

Forty people were gone. Forty families shattered.

And just at this one stop, three children without their mother.

She continued to the next stone.

And the next. And the next.

They sat together on a picnic table beside a small lake.

Behind them was the memorial parking lot. Ahead, beyond the lake, stood a huge thicket of grown trees that ran lengthwise as far as Katie could see. A fish jumped and water rippled out toward them beneath a newly-setting sun. It didn't suck.

"When did you decide to bring me here?" she asked.

Max thought before speaking. "Some scientists," he started. Paused. "Believe conspiracy enthusiasts are the result of a genetic trait bred into us millions of years ago."

She made a face. "Are you gonna ruin this and start being condescending?"

"Not at all. It's a compliment. It's a positive trait that increases survival probability."

Katie puckered her mouth, curious.

"Okay." Max started waving his hands about. "Take Cave Guy One. It's two million years ago and he hears some rustling in the tall sub-Saharan grasses and he thinks, 'Oh, that's the wind again.' And Cave Guy Two freaks out, jumps back, and shouts, 'Look out! It's a saber-tooth bear thing!'"

Katie smiled, even as her attention sneaked over Max's

shoulder to rest on a man in the parking lot.

"Sure, everyone laughs at Cave Guy Two. Because 99 percent of the time, it *is* only the wind. Eventually, this guy looks and sounds like a goof."

"But that one time . . ." Katie nodded. The thin older man with a camera . . .

"One time it's *not* the wind."

"And Cave Guy Two gets a five second head start."

"Uh huh. So guess who has more offspring in the long run."

"Cute," Katie said, but her attention was still fractured. The old man pointing his camera at them. "You ever gonna answer my original question?"

"I don't think what you're doing, what you've been doing, what *we've* been doing, is wrong."

That focused her. "Oh, lucky me!" She turned her full attention back to Max and clapped her hands slowly, mocking.

"I'm serious. Searching for the truth. Trying to *see* something, to *solve* something others haven't yet seen or solved. I know sometimes when I'm working on a project, a puzzle, a whatever, I'm prone to losing myself to that matter fully. So much so that, on occasion, I may forget the bigger issues of *why* I'm doing it. For *whom*." He shook his head. "Recently, I've been very focused on a difficult project and it wasn't until a—what else should I call it?—a 'human element' was appended to the scheme that I stopped being all Vulcan. That's when I truly started conceiving effective solutions, outcomes, my most-useful function within said project, and so forth."

"You don't think I've got enough of a 'human element' in this?" Katie looked away from Max, back toward the parking lot. The man with the camera was gone. "The man I thought was my father my whole life—isn't. The government or some evil corporation might have killed my mother." Had the camera guy even really been there? Was she jumping at the wind?

"Yes, I know," he agreed. "I guess we're here in case they didn't."

"What does that mean?"

"You've, we've, spent a lot of time reading blogs and sitting in libraries. I wanted to remind you, and me too, what 'real' looks like."

She studied him, then turned back to the lake. Was any of this real anymore?

"What's 'being all Vulcan' mean?" she asked.

"You know, *Star Trek*." He'd lifted his hand, splitting his fingers apart oddly. "Like Spock. Long on logic, shorter on emotion."

"My dad—" She paused, caught the slip. How many more years would she do that? "Anyhow, he likes all that stuff," she said. "*Star Trek*, John Carter, something called the Vorkosigan Saga?" It was the first pleasant thought she'd had about her father in almost two months. "Maybe I should bring some of his paperbacks to the hospital. He might like that."

"Bujold's great. You wanna swing by your house and pick them up?"

"Could. He had some books at work too. In his locker, piled up with a bunch of other crap. Maybe he was in the middle of reading those when, you know. I wonder if he can even read with all the stuff they have him on."

"I bet just seeing the books would help lift his spirits." Max flicked a small stick at the lake. "So what kinda crap was in his locker? More books or . . . ?"

"Some clothes, newspapers. Some old cassette tapes, candy. I was out there looking for clues, you know."

He smiled. "Find any?"

"Not one."

"Maybe you did and you don't realize it yet."

"Dirty shirts and candy?"

He grinned. "But what *kind* of candy?"

Katie smiled back, grabbed hold of his closest hand.

They sat quietly again just watching the lake. The tall trees shifting in spring wind.

"Hey," Max said.

"What?"

"I think . . . that is, there's something I've been meaning . . ." He stopped again.

"You silver-tongued devil."

"Something I'd really like to tell you, and, it's . . ."

"You're married."

Max narrowed his eyes. "No."

"Vulcan?"

"This is not, I admit, how I imagined this talk going."

Katie leaned in and kissed Max on the cheek. Like before. Almost. This time, however, her lips lingered, opened slowly against his skin, before she drew back. And her right hand slid up his neck, pulling him closer for the real thing.

"Wait," he said.

She slumped forward in a thousand pounds of *are-you-kidding-me*.

"I just, I don't think . . ." He was bright red again. But not in a good way.

"What? What is it?"

"Can we . . . I think it'd be best if we, you know, stay friends, until this is all over."

Katie frowned at him as if she were staring straight into

the sun. "You're a piece of work, Maxwell Thompson."

"I just—"

"One, whatever *might* have happened there wouldn't have changed your so-called friend status, friend. I wasn't going to rip your pants off, you know? It was just gonna be a little kiss."

"Sure, I know." His face looked like a STOP sign. "I'd never think . . ."

Shit. What was she even thinking? Verdict: she hadn't been.

For the first time in a long time.

Which was . . . was kinda wonderful, actually.

"And, two," she resumed, "this may *never* be over. Not for me. Or him. Never."

Max clasped his hands together, turned out to the lake. "Okay," he said. "Sorry."

"Nothing to be sorry about. It's no big deal."

She stared at the lake with him again. Waiting for something to happen. A fish to jump. A passing crow or deer.

"You go to *your* prom?" Katie asked.

"I was twelve," he replied.

"So, no. You, ah, wanna go to mine, *friend*?"

"Who with?" he asked, turning.

Katie's response was her middle finger held between their faces.

"Will you be making such lewd gestures at the prom?" he asked.

"Probably."

"Yes, sir?"

"Got some good news this morning, and wanted to tell you personally. We got him."

"Which 'him,' sir?"

"Wallace's web contact. Isolating the exact location as we speak. Not easy—as expected, this guy's no amateur—but the cyber team assured me we can be outside his door sometime in the next few hours."

"You tracked him down using Healy's servers?"

"Indeed. Healy received a small packet of data this morning that, on first look, appeared to come from one of his own servers. Sending data back and forth to himself, as you suspected from his hardware setup. Here, take a chair. On closer digital analysis, it was data originally delivered from another source in pieces and reassembled on a final trigger within the guy's own system. *He* probably doesn't even know that's how the info is arriving."

"What's the plan?"

"We'll stake out the location first. Learn what we can from online transmissions. Eventually, I suspect there's hardware we'll want to confiscate."

"Be careful when you decrypt. My impression is that Wallace will suspect something like this and he'll have worked in some nasty—"

"We can handle it."

"I tried tracking this guy myself. I'm telling you, there're going to be mines all over the encryption. Maybe I could be on hand to—"

"We'll take it from here, son."

"Sir, may I make a final suggestion, then?"

"Yes?" Paul Cobb smiled.

"You have the data. Or will, assuming all goes well. Perhaps it's a good time to stop trailing Wallace's daughter. Close that portion of the case."

"The exact opposite, young man. This coming week, in fact, is when things could get really interesting. First, Bohenek is still unaccounted for, and if you think he's the only entity connected with TERNGO who'd love a crack at Wallace—or his daughter—you're not as smart as they say. Your new pal Benevolus552 just posted his 9/11 crap about the ex-mercenary and his teen daughter, after all. Plenty of people will figure out it's Wallace."

"Then shouldn't she have real security?"

"Second," Cobb continued, ignoring the question. "When we *do* get ahold of that data on Adam Healy's servers—and we will, thanks to you—it's probably going to be rigorously encrypted, password-protected, and scrambled. Still need to find those encryption keys. There's got to be something Wallace left, a clue. Something the daughter says or does. We're gonna have to push pretty hard on Wallace now. She might come in handy if—"

"How hard, exactly? On her dad, I mean."

"Not your concern. Prom tomorrow?"

"Yes."

"Good. Keep up the good work. That's all."

Cobb's guest stood to leave, then turned back. "Sir, what if I don't want to do this anymore?"

Cobb's smile was easy. But firm. "We can talk about that later. Meanwhile, try to relax. No one ever said running the world was simple."

"Is that what this really is?"

"Something like."

30

Katie really wanted to hate the prom.

Had spent years, in fact, expecting to take perverse pleasure in how much it sucked. Final proof that high school was
nothing more than hell with more fire drills.

But damned if Gianna wasn't right. Katie was actually having fun.

Or at least not feeling gloomy. Or worried. Or afraid.

Gianna wouldn't allow it. Hadn't left Katie's side all night,
shepherding her and Max through the crowds and beneath the
swirling lights from table to table, dance floor to gabfest as if it
were *Katie's* party and Gianna was the grand hostess. Making
sure Katie was in good spirits. It helped that her best friend
approved of Max, included him completely, made him smile—
blush a couple of times too. Gianna also knew enough to let
Max spin the story he wanted as to where he went to school and
so forth. Everyone was extra friendly tonight, playing the part
of sociable adults if only for a few hours. Jocks and nerds doing
group pics together. The bitchiest princesses in the school telling marching-band girls how pretty their dresses looked, and
totally meaning it. And in that spirit, it was fun to see people
being nice to Max.

It was fun too, she admitted, just seeing Max. Like this.
Not hunched over one of this many laptops (she'd counted

three) or a pile of books. But talking to his peers, her class-mates, over the thumping dance music. Making friendly jokes with Alexis's and G's dates. Being cordial. Being kinda awe-some. Even now telling a riveted table about the time he got chased by a bear.

Oh, and he'd shaved. Katie couldn't believe it when he'd pulled up in his car. The half-formed beard all gone. Not sur-prisingly, he looked younger, more baby-faced for sure. But for the first time—how ironic—she'd sat beside him in the car and imagined what he'd look like as a grown man. He'd worn a simple black tux like most of the other guys. He'd brought her a pretty wrist corsage of baby's breath and white roses.

Katie straightened the corsage on her wrist, smiled. She wore a Prussian blue dress with spaghetti straps and embroi-dered flowers running along her waist. Mrs. Claypool had got-ten ahold of it somewhere. It was actually fairly stylish.

Gianna and Max were right: it was nice not thinking about . . . other things. The first time in weeks she hadn't been focused on 9/11. Her father's incarceration. The impending trial. The corruption of the United States government. Her mother's possible murder.

These things could wait.

Even if only for a few hours.

Neither she nor Max had brought up any of that. Instead, they talked about various bands and "best" ice-cream toppings and anime films and weird past teachers and some online game of intricate puzzles he was working on. Like normal people.

Like people from September 10.

"Hey," she said quietly, and Max turned instantly. As atten-tive as Gianna was being, she still didn't come close to Max. He'd gamely assumed the role of her escort, giving himself over to her every whim. No wisecracks. No argument. The perfect prom date. "Let's dance some more," she said.

He raised an eyebrow playfully, smiled. Waved bye to the table. She pulled him into the crowd of dancers, where they joined the juniors' ring of bodies, the seniors gathered more toward the center. It'd been so long since she'd given herself over to music, she'd forgotten how freeing it was; how easy to lose herself for a while. Escape. Disappear. As she'd done for most of her life.

She moved so easily tonight, relaxed. Max did his best, shifting from side to side, bopping his head playfully, no worse than most of the guys. She got closer than the first time they'd danced tonight. Close enough to brush against him, close enough he was blushing again, laughing nervously even, with a protective hand slipping against her hip for a little distance between them.

She reached up to straighten his bow tie.

"Do I look silly?" he asked.

"Not at all. You look perfect."

"Well." He dramatically readjusted his cuffs. "Thank you for noticing."

Katie smiled and slid both her hands around his neck.

Max muttered, "Not quite a slow song yet."

"Slow enough." She pulled him against her.

He put his hands back on her hips stiffly, and she chuckled.

"What?" he asked, panicked.

"Shhhh. Just stand there and look pretty."

"Yes, ma'am."

She looked up at him. "Thank you," she said, moving one hand to his chest.

"For?"

"This. Tonight. Right now, this."

They continued to rock slowly back and forth.

"Well, thanks for inviting me."

"I said shhhh." She smiled and rested her head against the top of his chest.

He shhhhhed.

While the others danced wildly around them, they stayed together like that for the next two songs. Katie's one hand moving along Max's shoulder and chest. At some point, his hands had found each other at the base of her back.

"Hey," Max said. "You maybe wanna get something to drink?"

Katie looked up at him and smiled. "You know, you look a little like James Bond tonight."

Max blushed. "Ha. Like Daniel Craig? Or more like a George Lazenby thing? It's funny you—"

Katie leaned up to kiss his lips. Briefly. But enough.

Max squeezed her back and stepped away.

"I need to tell you something," he said.

She shook her head. "Not tonight. Tomorrow. And some water sounds great."

Over at the drink tables, she and Max worked their way through the line for two cold water bottles. She wiped her brow with the side of her bottle.

"Any chance you'd . . . the after-party at Bryce Robbins's house?"

Max's shoulders slumped a little. "Ummm, thought you didn't want to go to that."

Katie shrugged. "Maybe for a little bit?"

"I don't know, Katie. What about the Claypools?"

"I've got until one. There'll be like ten people there. No big deal."

He blew out a short breath. "Sure."

"Everything okay?" she asked, puzzled.

"Hunky-dory."

She squinted at him, as if she could read his mind. "No shit?"

"No shit."

"Then why you acting so weird?"

"Tell you when—"

"When I'm older. Yeah, yeah. I'll be older at Bryce's, you know."

He smiled. "Then you're in luck."

The plastic mask was slick and warm against his face.

Filled with hours of his breath. Hours of waiting.

He'd parked in the back row of the lot, trunk facing the low hill that separated the school from the highway. Facing the boy's Saturn.

He watched them again.

He liked her blue dress. Even liked the way her shoulders looked with her hair up like that. She looked older than before, dressed like that.

Good. He wouldn't have to treat her like a child.

Next they would go to some park or motel or party and do what teenagers did after prom. And that's when he'd have his chance.

To end her lies. To end all the lies.

The boy's car backed up and pulled off slowly into the night.

He turned his key.

31

Katie sat on the steps of a massive backyard deck. The fire pit burned close, warm. The heated pool beyond, unoccupied for now, flickered in ghostly blue light with mist hovering over its surface. The small gathering of "maybe ten" had escalated into "maybe thirty," no doubt abetted by the fact that Bryce Robbins's parents were MIA as usual. Half a dozen kids sat together in the surrounding wicker chairs, talking, getting high. Everyone else was inside, chilling in the basement, playing music that drifted out to the deck. A few couples had already sneaked upstairs.

Katie wore a zip-up golf jacket that Max had commandeered from the Robbins' front closet. Rubbed her hands together in the cool night air. Max was inside somewhere, hopefully drumming up something to drink. Gianna and Alexis were inside too, so aside from the murmuring pool crowd, Katie was alone. Which gave her time to think again. Night thoughts.

Eventually, Max plopped down beside her, passed over a filled cup.

"Lemonade?" she asked, chasing away the thoughts, looking into the cup.

He held up his own drink. "I suspect its intended purpose was to mix with the vodka, but thought we'd go for it straight."

She took a sip. "Nice find. Thank you."

"How's everyone out here?" he asked, nodding over to the smokers.

"Guess they're fine," Katie shrugged. "Who knows?"

"Yeah," he agreed. "You don't smoke, do you? Like pot, I mean."

"God no. Won't ever drink either. I see how they affect my dad. Do you?"

"I like wasabi almonds too much," he admitted. "That's about it."

"Fierce."

"Yeah," he said again, clearly fighting back a yawn.

"You poor thing, you wanna go?" she asked. "We could—"

"Nope, I'm fine. Second wind coming. No rush ending this night. It's been a good one."

"Yes." She stared out at the fire pit, then added, "I wish my mom were here."

Max said nothing.

"Not *here* here. I mean . . ." She tried explaining, patted her dress against her bent legs. "If she could see me tonight, I mean. Know that I was—I don't know. Either mom would be fine, actually," she added. "You know what I mean?"

"Maybe," he said. "I'm not sure."

"Well, there's Mom Number One. The 'hero' who maybe died on 9/11. Who maybe saved my life. She would be great, right? But then there's Mom Number Two. The 'bitch' who maybe abandoned me, like my dad always told me. The addict, the failure. And she would be *not* great, but I don't care which one, honestly. I just . . . it would be nice if she saw me tonight. My friends. My dress. My date."

Max shook his head.

"I'm serious." She'd put her cup down and leaned into Max. "Whichever one she is. Tonight, it doesn't matter."

Max stiffened beside her.

"What?" she asked.

"Nothing."

"Yeah, right!" She punched his shoulder lightly. "What?"

Max sighed. "I think you should prepare yourself for the possibility your dad was telling the truth the first time. That she was a woman with drug problems who left."

"I have. I *always* have." She sat back again, looked up at him. "So, then, what do *you* think happened on 9/11?"

"Thought we were taking a break tonight."

"Past midnight," she argued. "It's tomorrow now."

"Fine," he said. "I think a well-funded, well-motivated team of radical militants sucker-punched a sleeping giant. I think we financed and trained these exact same militants for twenty years to pester Russia and China, and they finally targeted the West. And I think there was some cover-up afterward by our own government to downplay the direct involvement of Saudi Arabia, an 'ally.' Maybe to downplay our own incompetence. Probably both. But I also think your dad was involved in more than 9/11. I think he's using *that* event to misdirect others, or even himself, from something else."

"Why would you even think that?"

"Something Bohenek said, to start. The guy was shocked you were even asking about 9/11 and not about something else. I wondered then what that 'something else' might be. And Benevolus made reference to your dad having all sorts of info on TERNGO. Including info not related to 9/11. He said 9/11 was only 'the tip of an iceberg.'"

Katie shook her head. "Isn't 9/11 iceberg enough? There

must be a reason so many people believe the US played some role in that day."

"Fear," he said. "How's that for a reason?"

"Brilliant."

"Sometimes things just happen. Sometimes no one's in charge. That's scary for a lot of folks."

"Ah yes, I see. Please, Dr. Thompson, do go on."

"First, you're kinda being an ass. Second, I will. Nietzsche and Voltaire were right: 'God is dead,' and if he's not dead, the twentieth century chased him away for a while. The grand Clockmaker in the sky, the Big Guy pulling the strings for thousands of years . . . gone. When's the last time any of the people here tonight went to church?"

"You want them to go to church?"

"My point is, people like believing there's *someone* in charge. That there's a point to all of this. A *reason* why people are dying, starving, fighting, whatever. It might not be a reason we understand, but they need there to be a reason. And for thousands of years, God—whatever the hell that means—provided that reason. There was a grand plan to it all. Well, he's gone now. And so is that imaginary plan."

"And we replaced God with the worship of conspiracy."

"Didn't we? Because now we've all got 'a reason' again. An explanation. For the dying and starving and wars and hurricanes and accidents and winning and losing. Only, now it's the Freemasons controlling everything. Or the Bilderberg Group. The Illuminati. The New World Order. Satanists. Communists. Monsanto. Haliburton. The Federal Reserve. Reptilians. Rockefellers. TERNGO."

"Take a breath," she said, cutting him off. "What's your point, Max?"

"Sometimes there *is* a bigger plan at work. I know this, believe me. But sometimes, also, shit just goes wrong. Sometimes levees break. Disease spreads. Sometimes terrorists kill."

"Max, I don't want—"

"And sometimes moms just leave."

Katie gripped the edge of the stairs, freshly-painted fingernails digging into the deck. Her attention fixed again on the glowing fire pit, crimson flames dancing beneath the flush of yellow.

"Hey," Max said softly beside her. "I'm sorry. I didn't mean . . . I shouldn't have said that."

"It's okay."

"Katie, seriously. I—"

"It's fine. Drop it." She looked at him. "You were right, I never should have brought it up."

"I'm sorry."

"Say that again and I'm tossing you in the pool."

"I'm sorry."

Katie shook her head, then leaned it against his shoulder.

They sat like that, still and quiet, for many minutes.

Until the porch door burst open behind them.

It was Alexis. With her long blonde hair pulled up into a high coiffure *très* Marie Antoinette, she looked seven feet tall.

"What's the matter?" Katie asked, looking up.

"I can't. I just can't." Alexis paced back and forth behind them. The students in the wicker chairs had turned to watch her, too. "And Gianna . . ."

"Alexis!" Katie snapped. "What is it?"

"Eddie," her friend replied. "He—oh my God. I can't even. Did you know about what happened over at Evan Quinn's last weekend?"

"Evan? Ritual sacrifice wouldn't surprise me."

"Sheila Faller was there." Alexis covered her face, began sobbing.

"Ohhhkay." Katie separated herself from Max. "Where's G?" she asked.

"I . . . don't . . . know," Alexis managed, sagging against Katie with enough force to prove *her* lemonade had been the mixed kind.

"Let's take a walk," Katie said. "We'll talk."

Max had stood too. "Okay if I tag along, make sure—"

"Just us girls," Katie said. "We'll be fine. Back in a little bit. Then we can call it a night and find some wasabi almonds."

"Okay." Max held up a hand. "I'll be here."

Katie was alone.

Shadowy trees wavered high above the split-rail fence behind the Robbins' yard. A mostly-full moon floated overhead and warmed the night's otherwise total blackness. Outside the fence, in the side yard where Katie had let Alexis talk and talk, a row of tall bushes marked the line where the property ended. From here, she could see the cluster of cars parked unsystematically throughout the long gravel driveway.

Katie watched Alexis step back through the gate into the yard, on her way into the house. She needed a few more minutes alone, though. To decompress.

Still, she was happy to have briefly filled Gianna's customary role of drama control and meltdown prevention. Quite successfully too, she thought, considering the hour and the amount of drinking Alexis had done. And on prom night, no less; always extra stress on couples.

Not her and Max. What was prom compared to exposing global corruption and saving the world for democracy? Even his comment about her mom hadn't ruined anything. In fact, standing here now—and while listening to Alexis, if truth be told—Katie had been thinking about what he'd said. Wondered how valid it was. Had she embraced this 9/11 business only to explain her mom's leaving?

Not to be settled tonight in any case.

Besides, tonight was about escaping all that.

So she'd asked Alexis to send Max out.

Because it really was time to go. Where they went, well, that was still to be decided. Tonight was about holding hands. Maybe even more kissing. She suspected even the reddest blushing couldn't be seen in the dark.

Katie smiled to herself.

A sound from behind made her turn. Something in the bushes.

Someone moving in the bushes.

She lurched back, startled. Not really sure what she was looking at.

What the—

She stumbled backward, gasping. But any scream she would have uttered was caged too deeply. And there was no breath coming back to set it free.

A man emerged out of the bushes, out of the darkness.

A man with no face.

32

Katie tried the truck's door handle again.

Nothing. He'd locked it.

He. The man with no face.

Who kept one hand on her still, shoving her against the passenger door. His other hand both held the gun and rested along the top of the steering wheel.

A gun. Other than Bohenek's gun, she'd never seen one up close before.

And this one had just been in her face.

I'm going to die. As long as she squirmed and fought, however, he couldn't get the key turned with his right hand. *For knowing too much? Not enough?*

She'd gotten a scream out. One or maybe two. Before he'd grabbed her mouth from behind, before he'd jammed the gun into her side and shoved her into the pickup.

Had it been enough? Did anyone know she was gone?

I'm sorry.

He wore a mask. A thin, cheap plastic mask that washed out what he really looked like underneath. His hands were gloved.

She looked around the cabin of the truck for anything that she could use later. If she lived.

He pushed back harder and her head slammed against the side window.

The whole world turned sideways with pain. She reached up to hold her head.

They killed her. Killed all of them.

He drew back his hand. The truck started.

They coasted slowly into the night. Into the blackness ahead. He hadn't turned his headlights on. They passed the line of other cars. Passed Max's car. Seeing her friends' cars fired her up again, and she cursed and screamed. His gloved hand grabbed her whole face.

"SHUT UP!" he warned. "Or I'll . . . I'll kill you."

"Then fucking kill me!" she screamed back.

Lurching forward, she grabbed for the steering wheel.

His elbow struck her in the throat.

She fell back. Sobbing. Gasping for air.

"That's what you get," the voice muttered through the small slit in the mask. "You and all the liars."

"Who?" she gasped. *Focus!* "Who, who's lying?"

"YOU'RE ALL LIARS!" he boomed. His muffled voice filled the whole truck.

"Please," she said. It was the only word that came to mind.

He laughed. It was a sound she knew then that she would never forget for the rest of her life. However long that might be . . .

"Why are you doing this?"

"You and I are going to have a little talk. All about your daddy's lies. Lies that need to stop."

"Good, good," she gasped. "That's all I want, too."

"You'll understand now, won't you? They all will."

"I do," she tried. *Keep crazy man talking . . .* "They will. I do understand. Please let me go and—"

He turned to her. The monstrous non-face staring at her in the darkness. Katie shuddered. Collapsed back against the seat.

"He's shut up now too, you know," he said.

Her dad? Max?

"Who? Who did . . ."

"Your friend Benny552." He looked at the clock on his dashboard. "Or he will be soon. He won't be spreading your dirty lies anymore."

"Good," she agreed, playing along. "I told him not to. I told him it was all a mistake."

The faceless man shook his head. "More lies."

He turned again to look at her.

And behind him, she saw something moving. Someone running at the car from out across a lawn.

Max.

Of course it was Max.

Katie screamed his name. Saw the look in his eyes. The absolute fear.

The man in the mask turned. Enough.

Something cracked against the driver's window.

Katie grabbed for the steering wheel again. Pulled with both hands.

Pulled as hard as she could.

The truck veered. The man with no face shrieked.

Katie bent forward, covered her head. Knowing that at any second he would fire his gun by accident or design. Any second, she'd be dead. Her face and brains all over the dashboard.

Skidding sideways off the road. She braced for impact.

Something heavy, a tree, slammed the back of the truck and she plunged forward. Tossed against the dashboard. Instinctively grabbing out at the driver to steady herself.

She heard the driver's door open, heard the man tumble out onto the street.

She flinched as someone shouted. Garbled words.

Then nothing.

She looked up. The man with no face was gone.

The door opened and she screamed. Whereas before she could hardly make a sound, now all she could do was scream.

"It's okay," the voice said, and she recoiled in terror. Shaking against the far door. *Max, it's just Max, it's just . . . Max?* Katie looked again.

Her prom date, her friend, stood in the opened door, holding out his free hand for her to keep still. His other hand held his cell phone. "Stay there," he said. "Stay down."

"Max? Oh my God. Are you—"

"I'm fine." He glared down the road, gasping for air himself. "And you're amazing." He spoke next into his cell phone. Thumbed the screen without even looking. "JupeOne calling Mr. Bones. JupeOne to Mr. Bones."

Katie could not hear what the person on the other end was saying. Her ears were ringing. She tried the door again. The back window was cracked.

"Stay still," Max said again to her, and then spoke into the phone. "Got a twenty-three on foot. Repeat, a twenty-three on foot. Heading west on Bridgeport Road. Affirmative. Yes, sir, white, five-ten, one-sixty, middle-aged. Dropped a nine millimeter pistol. Unloaded. Yes, sir. But consider armed and dangerous. Yes, sir. She's secure, sir."

Katie stared in shock as Max listened to the person on the other end.

"Is that the police?" she asked. *A twenty-three?*

Max held up a finger. His eyes—broken, defeated eyes; eyes

she'd never imagined on Max, not him, not ever—didn't leave hers. "Yes, sir," he said and put the phone away. "Are you okay?"

"What's going on, Max?"

"I'm sorry."

(I'm sorry.)

"Was that the police? You called 911?"

"Help is on the way. We're going to take care of this."

"Who was that, Max? Who were you talking to?"

He looked down. "Katie . . ."

She pulled at the passenger door again. When it wouldn't open, she slid out awkwardly toward him. The whole truck was slanted, she realized. Half off the road and down into an adjoining ditch.

"You should really stay where you are. It's safer."

"Get the hell out of my way, Max."

He stepped back.

Katie stumbled out gracelessly onto the embankment. "Who were you talking to?" she asked again. "Give me your phone."

He sighed. "Katie. Damn it."

"Give me the fucking phone."

She lunged forward and snatched it from his hand. He didn't resist.

She found the last call, hit redial. It rang only once.

"What now?" the voice on the other end said. "We've already got a team on the way."

That comment made little sense, but what made even less sense . . .

The voice.

"Paul Cobb?" she said.

Max looked away. The phone call terminated on the other end.

"What the hell is going on?" She felt the whole street, the black landscape and trees, shifting left and right. She reached out to the truck for something to keep her standing up. "Tell me!" she shouted. "Tell me the truth!"

"I was assigned to protect you," he started, reclaimed his phone.

Katie staggered backward. "You were *what*?"

"To watch you, I guess. It's hard to . . . I . . . it's complicated," he finally said.

"No shit!" She couldn't breathe.

"Katie, stop." He reached for her.

"Get away from me! Who even *are* you?"

"I tried to tell you. I did." He inhaled deeply. "My name *is* Max Thompson, Katie. I *am* a law student at Maryland. And I *am* only seventeen. Everything I told you is true."

Katie trembled with anger, pain, loss. "What about everything you didn't tell me?"

"Katie . . ."

"That was Paul Cobb, wasn't it? You're working for Paul Cobb."

"I can't . . . I can't say anything about that, I'm sorry. But you gotta believe me, they're the good guys. You have to believe that."

"I don't have to do anything." She stiffened as he stepped toward her. "Get away from me!"

Headlights swept down the road. As Katie turned to watch the approaching car, she noticed Max's hand had dropped inside his jacket again. Where he'd put the masked man's gun.

"Have they come to kill me?" she wondered out loud.

"No, Katie, listen to me. You—"

"SHUT UP!" she turned, fists clenched. "I don't have to listen to anything you say, Max Thompson or whoever you are!"

Max wilted, his whole body gone lifeless. "Fine," he said. "Just—fine. Here's Gianna," he said, looking past her.

It was. Gianna's car, Gianna driving.

Katie ran to her. Stopped the car twenty yards down the road.

"What the fuck?" Gianna asked through the lowered window. "Alexis came in like a lunatic. Said Max needed me to—" Her words cut off as she finally saw Katie's face. "What happened?"

Katie opened the passenger door. "Just go," she said.

"Katie, what's going on?"

"GO!"

Gianna looked forward, pulled away from the wreck, from Max. "What about . . ."

Katie punched the dashboard.

"Going," Gianna said and kept driving.

Katie turned away as they passed Max. Left him in the faint glow of the abandoned truck's cabin lights. "Jesus."

"Now you wanna tell me what the fuck is going on?" Gianna asked.

"No."

"Then wanna at least tell me where we're going?"

Katie focused, head clearing for the first time in too long, shutting out everything else she'd just discovered—it was too much to process, anyway. She zeroed her thoughts on something small, something the man with no face had said . . .

"North Baltimore," Katie said. "And drive fast."

"Okay." Gianna looked over, clearly puzzled, a splash of baby's breath still in her coiffed hair. "May I ask why?"

Katie took a deep breath. "We're gonna try to save some guy's life."

Gianna brought her car to a shuddering halt in front of Benevolus552's downtown building.

Katie jumped out and ran barefoot up the crumbled concrete steps to the heavy door. The same door she'd first knocked on hardly a week before. With Max beside her. Yet that night already seemed a lifetime ago, if it'd ever happened at all. Max—whoever he was—was another ghost now. Another person to forget and lose in the swirl of a lifetime of lies and manipulation. Everything he'd said. Everything they'd done.

Gianna ran around the front of the car. "Katie!"

"What?" Katie turned, banged on the door as before.

"Are you serious?" She looked up and down the street. "This place, I mean, shouldn't we call the police or something?"

"No!" Katie shouted. "I told you, we can't."

"Because they're working 'with the government'?"

"Maybe. I don't know." She'd raced to one of the porch windows. Barred with steel. Boarded too. The windows higher up, barred as well and out of reach anyway. *Damn it, Adam!*

Gianna had drifted to the right. "We could check around back," she said, peering into the space between the two buildings. "But seriously, Kat, this is totally rape city back here."

"Let's go." Katie came back down the steps, followed Gianna, who'd already started toward the back of the building. "He's gotta be inside somewhere."

"What's that stink?" Gianna asked.

Katie stopped moving. Smelled it too.

Fumes. Gas fumes.

She noticed the garage now. Nestled on the side of the house at the end of a narrow concrete driveway. "Come on," she said. It was dark, the single-car garage door hidden in the shadows. But the smell was stronger the closer they got to the shut door. And the sound. "Listen. There's a car running. Do you hear it?"

Gianna nodded. "Totally." Her eyes were completely round. "He's killing himself in there, isn't he?"

"No," Katie said. "He isn't." She slammed her fist against the door. "Adam!"

Gianna covered her mouth, understanding finally hitting her. "Katie . . ."

"We gotta get this door open!" Katie'd found the handle, pulled. No luck. Exactly like pulling the truck's door handle. Both of them locked by the same man. "Look for something!" she shouted. "Something to break the wood."

"Try the back and maybe find a window."

"They'll be barred too." The toxic vapors inside, the carbon monoxide, escaped from beneath the old garage door. Invaded her nose and mouth. "Jesus Christ!"

"I'll get my car. Smash the door."

"You'd hit the car on the other side. You could kill him, and the door still might not even bust. Wait!" Katie looked for it. "Where is it? The door opener thing. The damn keypad!"

Gianna pulled out her phone, lit up part of the concrete walls. "Wait . . . no, no . . ."

"There!" Katie shouted. She snapped off the keypad cover. "Keep your light on it," she said.

"You know the code?" Gianna asked.

No.

Max could totally do this. Max, whoever he really was . . .

Katie squeezed her whole face in frustration. "Fuck!"

"You always figure out all my passwords," Gianna said. "Come on. What do we know about this guy? The Ben Franklin stuff."

Katie's finger hovered over the tiny number pads. Tried 552 and hit Enter. Nothing happened. "He's super secretive. Doesn't even use his real name. How am I—" *Shit, shit, shit!* "When was Ben Franklin born?" she demanded.

"How the hell would—"

"Look it up. Quick!" Katie paced in place, waiting while Gianna's thumbs flew. Listening to the running car inside. Another "suicide." Another victim of the world's greatest lie?

"1706," Gianna shouted.

Katie pulled out her own phone for fresh light. Typed the numbers and Enter. Nothing. "Is that Julian or Gregorian?"

"What the fuck are you—oh, yeah, the old dates are all different . . ."

Katie checked the date herself with her own phone:

January 17, 1706, Gregorian date.

January 6, *1705*, Julian. Which Franklin would have used!

She tried 1705. Nothing.

"Damn it!"

The fumes from inside the garage were leaking out from under the door, surrounded them both completely. "Um, what year did they pass the, um, the Freedom of Information Act?"

They both typed.

"1966!" Gianna shouted triumphantly.

Katie tried. No go.

"Shit," she said. "He's really dying in there. We have to call the police. My God, G, I should have called the police twenty minutes ago. I should have—"

"Ben Franklin, right?" Gianna tried 1776. Enter. Nothing. 1790 (died!). Nothing. KITE—KEY—100. Nothing. Nothing. Nothing. Katie slammed both her fists against the garage. Hard enough to scream out in pain. This man was dead because she'd come to him. Gotten him involved. He was dead for wanting to share the truth with the world, for—"Wait."

"What?"

Katie's thumbs flew over her phone: *the plain truth franklin.*

"Try 1747!" she said. "1747!"

Gianna put in the numbers—the publication date of Franklin's *Plain Truth* pamphlet. Enter.

The garage door grumbled.

Opened.

Exhaust fumes poured out into the night. Katie choked against them, then stumbled into the garage. Toward the sputtering old car within.

Pulled the driver's-side door open.

Benevolus552, Adam, lay lifeless in the front seat.

"Help me!" she screamed.

No need; Gianna was already beside her.

With four hands and a lot of cursing, they yanked the man free from his car, THUMP, and then across the garage floor. Dragging him like he weighed a thousand pounds.

Katie's eyes burned and she kept gagging against the thick smell of exhaust fumes. But they kept pulling. Until he was on the grass.

"Is he . . ." Gianna kneeled over the still body.

"I'm calling 911." Katie hit the digits.

Gianna had an ear pressed over his mouth. "Katie, I don't know if he's breathing."

"Nine-one-one," the voice said on the phone. "What's your emergency?"

33

"We're here to see Scott Wallace," Katie said.

"I'm sorry, miss," the nurse at the reception desk began with a forced smile. "You must have an appointment to—"

"Good morning," the attorney stopped her. "My name is Marilyn Wren. Mr. Wallace's acting attorney. I am formally requesting to meet with my client instantaneously or this facility and you will be charged with the fullest torrent of civil and criminal indictments possible by Maryland and federal law."

The nurse stood behind her Plexiglas barrier, her hand darting for the phone. "I—I'll need to contact Dr. Ziegler," she stuttered. "I can't—that is, he'll need to—"

"Excellent, thank you. And please notify Dr. Ziegler that if I am not conversing with my client within an hour, as is his lawful privilege, I will hold a press conference right outside your front door, where we will be discussing Mr. Wallace's personal military history, as well as the role of Veterans Affairs, and his specific reasons for incarceration and treatment within your facility."

"One moment, please." The nurse held up a trembling finger.

Wren nodded cordially.

"Thank you," Katie whispered to her.

The lawyer turned, leaned one elbow on the counter and curved her brightly painted pink lips into a thin smile. "You saved a man's life," she said. "I figure that's gotta be worth something."

Katie was alone with Scott Wallace—the man who'd raised her.

Marilyn Wren stood outside the conference room with the independent doctor and physiatrist whom she'd hired and brought along. They'd taken blood and urine samples and performed a mini physical on her father. Even given him something to help counteract the drugs he was on. Now Wren and her doctors were waiting outside the door, guarding it.

Scott Wallace, no longer handcuffed, sat in a chair at one end of the table. He'd stayed quiet throughout the examination. Eerily still. Even now, he looked only half awake, his pupils dark and wide. Maybe the drugs Wren's doctors had given him weren't as strong as the kind the government used. As before, Katie wasn't sure if he knew she was in the room. He hadn't yet spoken to her or looked directly at her once.

Katie stood across from him, her hands tapping nervously at the tabletop. This looked like the same room where Paul Cobb had brought her a month before, but it wasn't. She let silence lie between them for a long time. Too long.

Soon, Wren would open the door and say it was time to go. Then she'd be forced to leave without learning anything. This whole scene—reaching out to Wren prematurely, storming the hospital—was to get one thing. Just one thing.

"I know you're not my father," she said quietly, slowly. He looked up at her, and for the first time this morning, something like recognition crossed his face. "I took a DNA test the last time I was here and—"

"I know," he said. His voice was gruff, filled with dirt. "The swab."

"Good for you," Katie snapped, anger surging to the surface faster than she would have expected. "Did you also know someone tried to kill me last night?"

He lowered his stare, then his whole head. "Katie, I—"

"Some man, some lunatic or, who knows, some *agent* of the *government*, kidnapped me at gunpoint last night. Held a pistol to my head. Said he needed to stop me from telling lies. To stop you."

"I never—"

"He was probably going to kill me."

He said something, his voice too soft to hear.

"What was that?" she challenged.

"I'm sorry."

"NO!" The anger flared again, white hot. "You do *not* get to say that to me. Your sorries don't mean shit. Not anymore."

"I never—" He tightened his mouth, a vein jumping in the side of his head. "I never meant to—"

"Never meant to what? You asked me to get involved. You practically ordered me to. 'You and me together,' you said. 'You and me against the world,' or some other shit like that. Remember? When you were burning your arm like a goddamned lunatic? When you were dragging me down into your crazy hell!"

"I was protecting us."

"I almost died last night. And the same man almost killed Adam Healy. Benevolus552. Your Truther buddy. You remember him? You promised him all this information and then they tried to kill him. Tried to make it look like a suicide."

"'Almost.' Then he's still alive?"

"Yeah, he's alive. Barely. No thanks to you."

"Katie." Her father wiped a hand over his face, turned haggard eyes to her. "I don't know what I can say. You have to understand there's something going on here. Something bigger than both of us."

"Well, that's why I'm here, *Dad*. To understand. You're going to tell me everything you know. Not in half-truths and hints and garbled riddles. You're going to tell me what really happened that day."

He flinched, his face shutting down. "I can't."

"You can," she said. "And you will." Something in her voice—something new, something stronger—caused him to look totally at her again. "Or I'm walking out of here, washing my hands of all this. And you're on your own. I can't do it anymore. I won't." Now it was her turn to pause, her blast of strength already giving way to a sob that lodged in her throat, making it difficult for her to speak. "I need you to tell me the truth, Dad. I just need the truth."

The truth! she heard in the back of her mind. *And nothing but the truth.*

He looked away. "It's all so—" He cut himself off. Tried again. "You can't ask me to do that. You don't understand."

"Good-bye." She started for the door.

"Katie!"

Her hand was on the doorknob, and she turned to glare at him. "No, you tell me what really happened. Now! Tell me the truth about you, about me. If the next words out of your mouth are anything but—"

"She looked different than the others. Something, something in her eyes. She knew." He closed his eyes in memory.

"She knew. What was happening."

Katie had dropped her hand, realized she was drifting back into the room as he spoke. "And what was happening?"

He shook his head, but he wasn't looking at her anymore. He was staring at the wall, reliving a decade-and-a-half-old memory. "She, they were . . . I was, *we* were, supposed—I can't—we were there to provide support, and it went sideways. They brought them in. In sets of twenty. All of them. This long line. It was dark. I remember it was dark."

Katie's own voice was quiet again, and she edged forward another step. "Who brought them in, Dad?"

"She carried the girl in her arms. I can't." He grimaced, his face going hard again, the hint of the soldier he once had been. "She'd gotten away from the others somehow. Gotten past them, gotten to me. And she begged me to save you, to save the child. She knew what was happening. And I didn't. Not really, not—not all of it. But they took them off the trucks, and—" He stopped, flinching again in his seat, his eyes opening wide.

"Trucks?" Katie frowned at him. "Trucks, Dad? Or were they planes?"

"She begged me to take her. I was—I couldn't, but—why didn't I?—to save her child. And I—my God, Katie, how could I ever? And they killed her. Killed all of them. Why didn't I save you?" His last sentence came out in a cracked noise of agony.

Katie came up to the chair beside his, sat, and grabbed his trembling hands. He was staring right through her, his gaze eerily vacant. "I'm right here, Dad," she said. "Everything's—"

"I was up at the farm, at—at Parker's Farm. And that's when I saw her. This mother holding her daughter just so, just so. And then it came to me again. All of it. How I—I told her no.

I told her to get back with the others. Nothing I could . . . Why didn't I? I knew what would happen. The massacre. I told myself they wouldn't, that these villagers wouldn't be . . . The passengers . . . the warlord's men had promised . . . but I knew. Like she did. Like . . . They killed her. I'm sorry."

Katie sat back, trying to track what he was saying and not following at all. "What are you talking about? I don't understand, Dad. You have to help me understand. What villagers?" She paused, trying to redirect him. To get clarity.

Three different stories. Finally clearly converging.

Something overseas, in the war.

Something about 9/11.

And, now, Parker's Farm, where he'd been the morning of his total freakout.

All invented? All true? The only connection . . .

A mother and her child.

"Dad, did someone hand me to you on 9/11?"

"I wouldn't take her baby." He shook his head fiercely. "I couldn't. I *didn't.*"

"Dad?"

I'm not your father. I'm sorry.

They killed her. Killed all of them.

Tears streamed down his cheeks. It was the first time she'd ever seen him cry in grief. But when he turned his gaze on her again, his eyes were finally clear.

"Did. Someone. Hand me. To you. On 9/11."

He shook his head. "I'm sorry, Katie. I'm so sorry."

All other sound seemed to desert the room. She wanted to scream. And maybe she was screaming, and didn't know it.

Her father's eyes refused to let hers go. "Drugs," he whispered, drawing in a haggard breath. "I took . . . the kind you don't come back from. Fell in with this group, group of people, people like me, all living in this one house. Your mother was one of them. This house in DC and we . . . she and I, for a while . . . but we were all of us in this mess, nobody kept track of . . . I was in and out of the place for a few years, working for TERNGO and . . . Well, one night, she just left you there. Split for good."

He let his gaze drift to the wall behind her, seeing rooms she could not see. Would never see. "I don't know. You were two and a half, three . . . There was nothing I could . . ." He grimaced, the smile bitter and lost. "Why didn't I? So . . . so, she was gone. And, well, years before, she'd put my name down as the father on the birth certificate and I'd never objected to that lie because . . . she'd asked as a friend for help and, well, I did love her as more than a friend, I guess . . . Never knew who your real father was. She wouldn't say. And so, yeah, when she left, walked out on you, I took you. I did. This time, I did take you. This time, I . . . I saved you. Saved us both. And took you away from . . ."

He broke off, his shoulders hunching forward.

Katie could only stare at him. It was a variation on the tune he'd sung before. The mother who'd left. But a house filled with drug addicts? And what, if anything, did it have to do with 9/11?

Her head began to pound, her heart thudding so loudly that surely her dad could hear it, even over his own broken sobs. Was the 9/11 business all some wild fantasy he'd invented? All that work for nothing? Like the doctors and foster parents and Paul Cobb and Max and everyone else she knew had warned her.

No! There was proof. Pictures. Emails. The secret codes TERNGO transmitted. She knew he'd—

"Dad, I know you were in Cleveland on 9/11," she said, her voice by far the calmest thing about her. "I know you were there."

He brought his hands to his face, wiping away the tears, hiding himself from her.

Without 9/11, you're just another girl whose mom took off.

"Was I there?" she asked. Needed him to say it again. "Was my mother on that plane?"

"I don't know," he muttered. "I can't."

"Was TERNGO behind 9/11? Were you working with the government?"

"Please, I can't." He looked up again, his eyes oddly bright. "I told them: Let me out. Let me out and then I'll show everyone the truth about those who committed these crimes. But they, Fuenmayor, they buried all of it. They want too much." And just like that, his face went darker, sanity peeking out at the edges. He leaned forward, this man she'd never seen before, never in person. This man was a soldier. "Protect yourself, Katie. Remember what I told you? Remember who I said would protect you. You promise me that, okay? Promise me you'll stay safe until you can get me out of here."

They killed her. Killed all of them.

Katie shook her head, chasing away the words there.

Invented? True? A mixture too muddled to separate? How could she know the difference when he couldn't?

"Dad, I can't get you out of here. You . . . you really do need help."

And that quickly, he lunged for her. Cutting off Katie's scream with strong arms that—

Simply hugged her. Pulled her close.

Like he was any father and she was any daughter.

"I love you," he said, his face muffled against her shoulder. "I didn't know. You have to . . . God, I love you so much, Katie."

Katie shivered against him.

This person who was a stranger. A madman. A murderer? Dad.

"I love you too," she said.

Small waves broke white against the Inner Harbor pier where Katie walked with Marilyn Wren, red bricks beneath their feet. Katie carefully placed and matched her steps to touch every other one. Still trying to focus, to bring some order to a world turned upside down and inside out.

"Is he insane?" Katie asked simply.

"Outside my expertise, I'm afraid." Wren reset her paisley scarf against the breeze. "He's clearly been heavily sedated. Michael, my medical expert, was somewhat amazed your father could even speak. I'm curious to see what the toxicology reports come back with, but that will take a couple days. There was also . . ." Wren paused.

Katie waited. Took a big breath.

"Michael believes there may be evidence of, well, some kind of physical abuse. Bruising. Not from the restraints. "

Katie looked down at her feet.

"I know how that must sound. We'll need to—"

"I think I'm done." Katie blew out a long breath. "I think all of this . . ." She trailed off. She didn't know what to think anymore.

"Maybe that's best," Wren agreed.

Katie turned, somewhat surprised. She'd assumed Wren's cooperation today meant the lawyer was now willing to fight the good fight to the bitter end. That she'd argue for Katie to keep going.

"You're not the same girl who came into my office a month ago." Wren put a comforting hand on her shoulder. "*Shell-shocked* is the term that comes to mind."

Katie twisted her lips. She hadn't even told Wren about being abducted. About the man with no face. About Max. Only that she'd helped save a potential witness connected to the case from an "accidental" death. Only that Adam Healy was alive and well and thankfully ready to provide whatever evidence he could. Only that she was close, so close, and wanted to present to Wren as soon as possible. To be done with it. To get it all out of her head once and for all.

But Wren was giving her a free pass from all of it.

Saying it was okay to quit.

"My dad will be fine." Katie tried the idea out. "He'll get better, eventually get out."

"Eventually, yes."

"Then it was all for nothing." An echo of her anger flared, Katie's voice bitter and hard. Maybe she didn't want to quit after all. "All of it."

"It feels like that sometimes, I know. But you tried, which is more than anyone else did. And your dad, someday when it's time, he'll know it too. That matters, Katie. "

Katie blew out a frustrated breath. She'd found half-truths and half-lies and evidence supporting much of his story. Not all, maybe not even most. But enough to gnaw at her. She gritted her teeth in frustration. "I've got hunks of this solved but still can't bring it all together. I'd hoped he'd fill in the gaps. But—now there are more pieces on the table than ever. I think the confusion is it's three different puzzles on *top* of each other."

"How do you mean?" Wren's voice was kind as she withdrew her hand.

Katie chose her words carefully. "I think he was witness to, or part of, something bad *before* 9/11. Something that drove him to drugs and alcohol. Something involving TERNGO and the military. Something that has a lot of people nervous. And I think he's confusing this event with things that happened on 9/11, his very-real role that day. I think the hugeness of 9/11 absorbed these other terrible memories and he's been struggling with that confusion all these years. A confusion that escalated a few months ago when this guy, Fuenmayor, at TERNGO started making national news—and then came to a head when my dad saw a random mother and her child at some park. An emotional flashback of some kind."

"Very common in sufferers of PTSD. Sounds to me like you've got all this figured out just fine."

"But none of that can actually help him." Katie stared out into the harbor. Watched two sailboats bobbing, deserted and lonesome on their moorings.

"Tell you what," said Wren. "Present to me everything you've pulled together. It might be enough to get you what you need."

"I need Paul Cobb's head on a stick, is what I need."

"The Veterans Affairs guy?"

"He's much more than that. He has to be." If Max was . . . whatever he was, surely Paul Cobb was something even worse. "He's the real reason, I think, why my dad is locked away. Why I was . . ." She trailed off, thinking about the man with no face again. Knew she'd be thinking about him off and on for the rest of her life.

The man with no face was still out there somewhere. Looking for her.

"Cobb probably knows more about what's going on—what's *really* going on—than anyone." She startled Wren with a voice stronger than before. "He told me from Day One this had little or nothing to do with 9/11. And, yet, my dad's still locked up. Why? If Cobb really doesn't care about 9/11 . . . what *does* he care about?"

Wren sighed. "Katie . . ."

"Could we force him into court?" Katie continued. "To share what he knows?"

"From what you've told me, this guy could lawyer up behind military council for years. National security, classified this and that. Even *I'd* have trouble getting evidence from a guy like this."

Katie shook her head. "I don't want evidence anymore. I want the truth."

"Sorry. I'm in the evidence business."

"Then I really am done, I guess. I have so little that approaches real evidence. Healy won't cut it on his own. There's no way." Unless . . . *Remember who I said would protect you.* Unless she could believe a man who'd just now admitted to her that he'd lied to her every day her entire life. A man whose grasp on reality was fragmented at best.

Could she? Would she dare?

"Well, that's a happier face," Wren noticed, sharp eyebrows lifting. "Know someone else who can help?"

More to herself than to Wren, Katie said, "I know a dragon."

"Even better," Wren said.

34

Paul Cobb's head was entirely cocooned in a canvas backpack.

He was also tied to a metal chair in the center of the room, his legs secured with zip ties, his arms bound behind his back. There was no other furniture. Just a small diesel generator humming in one corner, connected to a pair of lights draped over some ceiling rafters. And two large buckets, one already filled with water.

And three men in ski masks.

The Dragon and his two "friends."

Katie had not been given their names, and she hadn't asked. Their faces were hidden, but she'd been allowed to see them earlier. An older black man with a shaved head and a terrific smile, and a ripped Hispanic-looking guy with killer biceps and funky scars on his arms.

All she'd had to do was call the number the Dragon had given her in Philly and they'd taken care of everything else. Finding Paul Cobb. Bringing him here.

Breaking probably a hundred different laws.

"Now or never," the Dragon whispered. "We can all still vanish and this never happened. Or . . ."

Or . . .

Katie looked across the room at Paul Cobb again.

How different her life had been before she'd met him. Was it fair to blame Cobb? Was it fair to ask the Dragon and his pals to do this? To commit *treason*? She found it hard to care about such things. Not anymore. Not when people were trying to kill her. Murdering her cat. Torturing the man who raised her. Filling the world with more lies.

"I'm good," she said.

The Dragon motioned to Biceps Guy, who went for Cobb. Katie had stepped backward while the masked man removed the backpack from their prisoner's head.

Paul Cobb leaned over and spit on the ground. Then he looked up, squinting into the light, clearly sizing up the masked men. "Gentlemen," he nodded. Then he saw Katie. "Miss Wallace." He didn't sound surprised. "Pretty dramatic, kid," he said. "Gotta admit, I never predicted this."

"Me either." She wondered if her voice had even made it across the room to him.

He must have heard her, because he smiled. "Do you have any idea how much trouble you're in? A hundred people from Homeland Security are probably already waiting outside."

"No one is outside," she told him, her voice sharper. Clearer. "Everyone here—including you—got scanned for tracers by professionals two states ago. We're here alone. For as long as it takes."

Cobb nodded, almost approving. "Okay," he said. "But there's no way you're getting away with this. Whatever 'this' is. You, and your father—" His lips tensed, not quite a smile anymore. "You figure whatever info your dad had in his little files is going to save you both from life behind bars? Then you're as crazy as he is."

"But you don't really think he's crazy," Katie said, taking a step forward. "Do you? If my dad doesn't have anything you want—if he's just gone off the deep end and you only want him to get better—then why are there traces of sodium amytal and scopolamine in his system? Why evidence of bruising? He was tortured, wasn't he? To get to these 'little files' you don't care about. If you don't think he has real information, dangerous information, then why'd you have Max spy on me? Why'd you send someone to kill me and Healy?"

Cobb stared at her. The smile gone.

"The attacks on you and Adam Healy had nothing to do with me," he said. "In fact, we apprehended your assailant ten minutes after he ditched you and the truck. His name is James David Hauk. Based in Florida mostly. Dishonorable discharge in 2005 after a year in the Army. Bit of a drifter. Last four, five years, he sometimes poses as a Truther on websites and at events, then tries to scare away folks as some kind of self-proclaimed 'patriot.' Thinks any criticism of the official story is a sin against the victims, the troops who died after, and against his country."

"You seem to know a lot about him."

"Like I said, he's in custody. It appears he's been stalking Adam Healy for months, eavesdropping on Healy's emails and phone calls from right across the street. Then you showed up. Claims he first noticed you at the Philly convention."

The red-haired guy who'd been with Healy?

"Overheard some stuff thanks to a listening device he picked up at some website called The Spy Store. You three assholes oughta check it out." Cobb nodded toward the three men.

Ah—so Hauk hadn't been anywhere near them at the convention. She'd never seen his face.

"In any case," Cobb concluded, "he claims he was only trying to scare you—and Healy."

"Scare? He knocked Healy out and put him in his car with the gas running," Katie snapped.

"Yes, well, he'll be going away for a while."

"Don't need me as a witness?"

"No, we're good."

"What if I call the cops? Tell them what really happened the other night. Or about what you're doing to my dad."

"So call them. I gotta tell you, from where I'm sitting, I'm fine with that. There's this thing called leverage, and you've got far less than you think."

Katie bit the tip of her thumb. Studying him. Would anything she learned from him now have any value? And if not, what was the point in all this craziness? "Who do you work for? What agency? Homeland Security?"

"I am, as they say in the movies, 'not at liberty' to share such information. But, Katie, you have to hear me on this: we're the good guys." The same thing Max had said, over and over. "Honestly, I'm willing to cut you a break here, if you agree to end this. No harm, no foul. I just walk. Whatever your father has said, whatever these men here have gotten you into . . ."

"I called them," she said. Cobb stopped talking.

"They're helping me because I asked them. And my father knows nothing about this."

He nodded. "Then you're definitely in way over your head, Kaitlyn. You really are."

"Probably," she agreed. "But it's a feeling I've gotten very comfortable with these past few weeks. Thanks, in part, to you."

Paul Cobb looked away—perhaps reconsidering options. Perhaps conceding to himself that intimidating her was no longer an option.

"What happened on 9/11?" she asked. "What does my father know?"

He shook his head. "Goddamn 9/11. This has nothing to

do—Look, I told you this when we first met: I wanted to help your dad, to help you. The offer still stands. But not like this. You can't do it like this, Kaitlyn."

"I really don't like when you say my name," she said. "Any version of it."

"Fine. We'll call you Fred. But you should know, I'm still trying to make this right."

"Me too."

"What is it, exactly, you want?"

Such a simple answer. It almost sounded dumb to say it out loud.

"The truth," she said.

"Let's talk alone," Paul Cobb said.

Katie froze. Alone? What was his angle? He might . . . he might what? He was tied to a chair with three ex-military types standing ten feet away.

"I can give you more information if it's just you and me. Maybe the kind that'll get us back on the same page. Sort this out, end it, in a way everyone wins."

"Let me guess. With my dad and me in jail for the rest of our lives? No, thank you."

"Come on." Paul Cobb's smile was back, but cleaner, more real. "You wanna deal, let's deal. But I'm not sharing state secrets with these three."

"What makes you think I'm not simply going to tell them, and the whole world, everything you say anyway?"

"Maybe you will," he said. "But that's my deal."

Katie looked at the Dragon and his friends. Nodded. They headed for the door.

She turned back to Cobb. "You got five minutes."

"Don't suppose you got any gum?" Paul Cobb asked.

She shook her head.

"First thing, this has nothing to do with 9/11. Nothing. I've been trying to tell you that all along."

"I know my father and other TERNGO employees were at the Cleveland airport that morning. I've seen emails, secret codes transmitted."

"But that's not why *I'm* involved. Or why we're interested in your father."

"Then what does it have to do with? What does he have on you?"

"Me? Nothing. He has information that—how do I say this?—would compromise many other people."

"Too vague."

"International corporations."

"TERNGO. This is about the codes transmitted on 9/11. The security codes warning of some kind of overthrow of the government."

"News to us. We first found out about that when we scrubbed it off Adam Healy's servers while you were meeting with him."

Katie sighed in disgust. Had Max done that? Had Cobb and his men been lurking outside the whole time they were there?

"Fine, don't believe me. But I'm telling you that was not something we knew about, nor something we were looking for."

"So I'll ask again: what *are* you looking for?"

He blew out his lips, frustrated. "TERNGO's been working with Uncle Sam for more than thirty years in the Middle East, going all the way back to Afghanistan in the eighties. During that time, situations have arisen."

"What kind of *situations*?"

"Classified. But I'll remind you, a five-hundred billion dollar opium trade runs out of Afghanistan. That's 80 percent of the world's heroin, and you may have noticed heroin is quite popular again. That's a lot of off-the-record cash someone's getting. The kind that can be used to fund global initiatives *without* congressional knowledge. Buying weapons for unofficial allies, for instance. Certain parties within our government have been able to carry out all sorts of covert projects while several private companies get very, very rich."

"And TERNGO is one of those dirty companies. This Fuenmayor guy."

"That's right. And Scott Wallace decided to uncover all of it."

"Why's my dad"—what else to call him?—"so invested in bringing these people down?"

"Based on our investigation, we suspect your father was a witness to something during his military service overseas. Something that changed the nature of his relationship with everything, I think."

Killed her. Killed all of them.

"What's this 'something'?"

"Classified. Sorry."

"Did he see people killed? Was he witness to some kind of massacre?"

Cobb went a little more still. "Why would you ask that?"

"Let's say I have a hunch."

He paused, seemed to come to some decision. "Yes, that's what it's looking like."

My God.

"Did he . . ."

"We don't know the role he, or anyone else on his team, played. Possibly because some major players, including high-ranking US military officials, implemented a very costly cover-up. If such a massacre was exposed, this whole crooked operation would collapse. All we know for sure is Wallace has been collecting data on certain companies, certain persons, since those alleged events. Maybe enough information to establish what really happened."

"And you want to stop him."

"No," he said, impatient now, "we want to *help* him. The problem is, his goal, we think, has always been to reveal this information in a way that only incriminates specific guilty parties while protecting those who were merely in the wrong place at the wrong time. Those who were following orders."

"US soldiers."

Paul Cobb nodded.

So this was it. Scott Wallace's big secret. US soldiers and contractors involved in some kind of massacre and cover-up. Horrific enough on its own, and now entangled in his head with unrelated horrors. Had she really spent all this time merely chasing a red herring?

"Then what about 9/11?"

Cobb groaned. "We're looking into it, the security codes thing. But I've seen nothing else to indicate your father, or anyone else for that matter, has any legitimate evidence on 9/11 being some kind of 'inside job.' If we ever find such evidence, I'll be the first to look into it. I give you my word."

"As one of the good guys."

"That's what I tell my kids."

"When my dad gets out, he'll be the one who decides how that evidence gets shared—"

"Well, that's actually the other thing I need to tell you." He stopped whatever threat she was going to invent next. "We already have your dad's files. All of them."

Impossible.

"We tracked his source, the man doling out data to Benevolus on your father's behalf, and confiscated the original data files. We did this a few days ago, in fact. Same day as your prom. Those payments your dad's been receiving from TERNGO for years? Turns out most went to pay for all the encryption work, special hardware, et cetera. Plus, a half-million-dollar educational trust fund in the name of one Kaitlyn Wallace."

"What?" Katie fought to breathe. A half-million—

"Oh, you didn't know about that, huh? Well, there you go." He shrugged, making it clear that Katie's secret wealth was no concern of his. Though he was probably quite pleased he'd dumped more on her plate for her to try and swallow. "Anyhow, as we speak, all your dad's files are being decrypted. There's nothing he has that we want anymore."

This, she now believed. It was the way he'd said it, she supposed. Now what? Her brain still trying to process whatever this trust-fund thing was. Katie wished she had something to latch onto. Max . . . "Max helped you do all of this."

"The entire operation is classified. The thing I'm trying to make clear to you is that once these files are decoded, you and your father, with all due respect, are no longer calling the shots. No more wild threats about leaking sensitive national security intel. We'll be the ones deciding how to use the information for prosecution. As we should have been from Day One."

"There's that 'we' again. Who do you work for?"

Another smile. "We're done here," he said. "I've told you as much as I ever plan to. Tried to give you a sense of the bigger picture. You're a smart girl, so I hope you'll do the right thing."

"Me too," she said. "But not yet."

Cobb's lips tightened. "I'm not going to tell you anything more."

Katie picked up the canvas backpack. "The guys out there might try and make you."

"Figured. Won't be the first time." Cobb shifted some in his chair, sat up, held his chin up so she might replace the bag over his head. "My God." He looked up at her. "What did your father do to you?"

Taught me to fend for myself more than I should. Taught me to solve problems. Taught me to question everything. Taught me there was only one person you can ever truly trust.

"He raised me." She pulled the bag down.

"This isn't going to work, Katie," Cobb said, his words only slightly muffled.

Katie stepped back.

"Good luck, soldier," she said.

"Get what you needed?" the Dragon asked.

Katie sighed. "I don't know. What he says makes sense, I admit. But I'm still doing mental gymnastics to pull it all together. And I can't tell entirely if he's lying to me."

"We'll take care of that," he said.

"He said he's not going to talk anymore."

One of the masked men laughed. "Oh, please." He shook his head. "They all say that."

"At first," the Dragon agreed. "But eventually he'll talk, and in a way that we know it's the truth as he understands it."

"Meaning?" Katie asked. "You—torture him?"

"Persuade him. No sleep. Little food. Keep him unhappy. Eventually . . . it all depends."

Katie couldn't even imagine. This wasn't some movie or show on Fox. This was a human being in the next room. A guy with kids. A guy with a disarming smile and a penchant for peppermint gum.

Is that what this becomes? What I become?

Maybe she should be the one wearing a plastic faceless mask.

The Dragon saw her hesitation. "It's entirely up to you. But don't think they haven't done worse to your dad."

"Mr. Collison." She'd used his real name. Couldn't imagine calling him anything else right now, when everything was hidden and nothing was certain. "Even knowing that, I don't think it's right." She imagined her dad. Locked in that hospital. What had they done to him? Paul Cobb and his team of monsters. Breaking laws. Deceiving the world. Mistreating—maybe even torturing—her dad.

For the truth . . .

She needed more information. Needed to be able to go to Wren or the courts or the newspapers and end this. Get her dad the real help he needed. "How long would it take?" she asked. Couldn't believe she was even considering this.

"He's trained. A real pro. Could take days."

"Or weeks," one man said.

Katie stared, aghast. She couldn't bring herself to imagine ten minutes. "What happens if we let him go?"

"Nothing," said the man with the arm scars. "Like he told you. He walks, lets it drop."

"We take his word? He said they already have these files my dad had. We have nothing to scare him, nothing to blackmail him with."

"Even so," the Dragon said, "I *do* think he'll let this go. Let *us* go. Reason One: he's embarrassed we grabbed him so easily."

"Oh, that's undeniable," the bald man said, pulling his mask off.

"What's Reason Two?" Katie asked.

The scarred man took his mask off too. "He's one of the good guys," he said.

Katie looked at the others for confirmation. They nodded in agreement. "I'm maybe starting to think that too," she said and closed her eyes briefly. "But what if we're wrong? What if I'm wrong?"

"You're arrested, vanish into juvie," the bald man said. "And we're hunted down with the goal of 'termination with extreme prejudice.'" He chuckled. "Course, for us, that's not unusual."

Katie shook her head at this strange world her father had seemingly lived in for years. Men joking so easily about torture, being hunted, being killed. Men with scars and no names. Men hidden beneath ski masks and canvas bags.

No wonder he drank, smoked pot. No wonder he was so . . .

Alone. Lost.

Broken.

"Let Cobb go," she said.

35

A day passed. Then two.

Katie had retreated to her bedroom, expecting the worst. Not eating. Not really sleeping. Ignoring friends' calls and texts. Claiming to be too sick to go to school, or to talk. Awaiting Homeland Security or some local SWAT team or the NSA, the FBI, the Cub Scouts—someone!—to swarm the Claypools' house.

For kidnapping. For treason.

Yet no one so much as knocked at the front door or even sent a certified letter.

Three days now.

The Dragon and his men had been right: Paul Cobb wasn't coming for her. Maybe because he *was* one of the good guys. Knew Katie and her dad were working for justice, trying to help save the United States from—

No. How could he or anyone else ever think such a thing?

I wasn't saving anyone from aaaannnnything. I was saving myself from foster care. From further humiliation. From the memory of a mother who abandoned me. Merely replacing her with something else. Even if that meant blaming the government for murdering three thousand Americans.

Katie curled deeper into her bed, fetal, completely drained.

The flying cowgirl—she'd named her Ruby—loomed above

her head. No longer falling off the horse or on the horse, but lifting away from the horse as if pulled by some unseen force. Drawn back to some distant mothership or another dimension as the horse galloped away to its own world, too. Ruby and reality separating for good. Disconnected. Indifferent. *That's all I want*, Katie thought. To detach completely again. Get back to the feeling she'd had the night Paul Cobb and the police and all her dad's problems—real and imagined—had first come to the door.

She'd not yet decided whether to present anything to Marilyn Wren.

The known lies and uncertainties that fit Scott Wallace's version of 9/11. All those time charts and flight-path maps, sworn affidavits from witnesses, communications from TERNGO, transmitted codes hinting at a full scale coup d'état. Even if she could pull it off, what would it accomplish? Would it really expose the government? Undermine TERNGO and this Fuenmayor guy? Would any of the info actually make it into the mainstream news and change how people looked at 9/11?

Would it even get Scott Wallace out of that hospital?

She'd admitted to Wren that her dad's story was primarily a psychotic diversion from something else. Would Wren even take her case anymore? *Free my fake dad?*

Her dad. A man who'd dragged her into . . . what? Delusions. Paranoia. She couldn't pretend there weren't still suspicious facts and testimony related to 9/11. But were such discrepancies evidence of a conspiracy—or merely the result of the confusion of war, combined with the messiness of everyday governing? Would presenting her information to Wren answer that question? Would presenting it to *anyone* ever, truly, answer that question?

Closing her eyes, the image of Ruby the cowgirl burned faintly into the darkness, Katie didn't think so. All this uncertainty was just a horse to fall off. To free herself from . . .

She lay quietly, trying not to think about what she should/could/would do tomorrow.

And when tomorrow came, she did it again.

A quiet knock at her door. Timid.

Mrs. Claypool or C.J.

Katie had been awake for hours but hadn't moved from her bed yet. She glanced at the clock. 7:18 a.m. Her room was dark, but sunlight already flushed the one window behind the drawn shades. It was Sunday. Why was someone waking her? They'd done such a terrific job of keeping away for most of the week. Maybe it was Cobb and—no, four days now, and it was a Sunday. They didn't arrest you on Sundays. Did they?

Knocking again.

She slid from her bed, dragged to the door, and unlocked it. It was Mr. Claypool. His eyes worried. His hands clasped together. "Good morning," he said. "I'm sorry to knock so early."

"No, I was already—is something wrong?"

Could be anything at this point. Really, anything.

He looked back away from her room. "Could you come downstairs for a minute?"

Katie blinked nervously. *Oh no. Who's downstairs now?* Mr. Claypool was already heading back down the hall. Damn. She followed. Bare feet on the wooden floor, sweatpants tucked around her heels. Down the steps, she could see the front door was open and sunlight coursed onto the front hallway, casting long shadows.

At the bottom of the steps, Mr. Claypool stepped aside and indicated she should continue toward the door. "There's something on the porch for you," he said, speaking in a morning whisper. "And a note."

Katie slipped down the last two steps. No, no! What could they . . . ? The last time, they'd—but she saw right away it wasn't a box. It was . . .

A pet crate? The fold-up polyester kind with the mesh windows and zippers and stuff. Sitting out on the porch. And something moving inside.

Oh, no, she thought. No, no, no. Gianna must have felt bad about Winter "running away" and . . . or maybe the Claypools found out about that and . . . Another cat was the last thing she needed.

She stepped out onto the porch and stared down at the crate. The cat inside, pacing back and forth—parading, really, as cats do—was white with a dark patch on its head like Winter. *But I don't want to think about her again. Not ever.* The cat purred up at her. What idiot did this?

Katie sighed and crouched down.

Then fell down onto her ass beside the crate.

The cat didn't look like Winter.

It *was* Winter.

Her hand reached slowly for the door's zipper and pulled it back. The cat, Winter, stepped out and onto her thighs. Purring. Rubbing back and forth against her.

"Yours?" Mr. Claypool said behind her.

She turned. "I . . . yes, sir. I think it is. But . . ." *But I buried her. She was murdered*—"Where did you find her?"

Mr. Claypool stepped out fully onto the porch. "That"—he pointed at the crate—"was sitting on the porch when I got up this morning. That's all I know."

"Oh." It was all she could think to say. She focused on stroking Winter's back.

"I'm sorry, didn't mean to pry," Mr. Claypool said. "The note, I mean. Happened to see it."

Katie found it taped to the right side of the crate. A notecard.

LIBRARY—5 P.M.—CODA

Max? she thought first. No, why would he? Wishful thinking. Cobb? . . . *What happens at 5:00?* "CODA?" *Like in a music piece—*

"What's his name?"

Katie startled. Replayed his last sentence, catching up with the real world. "Oh, she's Winter. My friend Gianna can take her again and . . ."

"Winter's welcome here as long as you need to stay."

Katie felt tears coming again. Maybe she was already crying. "Thank you," she said, standing with the cat.

Mr. Claypool breathed out deeply, a strange look in his eyes. It was clear he still had something to say.

"Mr. Claypool?"

"I can't pretend to understand what you've been going through, Katie. I can't. I could tell you some stories about myself as a boy and some of the things I had to make it through but then I'd sound like what I am: an old man with stories."

"No, sir. You—"

"If I may," he stopped her. "So, I can't pretend to truly understand what's been happening to you. But I know enough to recognize when someone could use a hand, and I'm not sure Lisa and I—not sure we've done too good a job helping you."

"You've been great." She smiled. "Really." Winter squirmed against her chest.

"I'd like to drive you to the library tonight, if that's okay with you."

"Mr. Claypool, you don't have to do that. Thank you, but I'm probably . . . I shouldn't even go. I'm done with all that."

"Uh huh." Mr. Claypool reached out to scratch the top of Winter's head.

"Mr. Claypool?"

"Yeah?"

"What do you think about when you think of 9/11?" she asked.

Mr. Claypool pulled his hand away. "Oh, well."

"I'm sorry, I didn't mean to . . ."

"No, it's okay. I suppose it's been a while."

"Yes."

"One of those things that seems like only yesterday, too."

Katie looked at him, waiting. Happy to wait.

"I remember . . ." He looked past her, thinking. "I remember the guy in the next office, Bruce Fairchild, had this little TV in there, and called a bunch of us in. First time I'd ever heard him curse and I knew then that today was going to be different. And I remember driving home early. Not even noon yet. And the skies, looking up at the skies, half expecting planes to be falling out of the clouds as I drove out of Baltimore. Except there were no planes. None. For miles in every direction the whole drive home, and I remember feeling fear. Real fear. Like we were all living in some other world now. Living *in* history, you know. That place where bad things happen. I came home and Lisa was at the TV and the towers had collapsed by then and—and she was crying. And we didn't even know anyone in New York or anything but still, the enormity of it all. The sorrow. Knowing that all those people . . . and seeing what New

Yorkers were already doing. To make things right again. The firefighters and police and all the rest. And I just remember holding her, and we were both saying everything was going to be all right." He laughed. "I guess I cried some then, too."

Katie breathed deep. Had closed her eyes as he spoke, trying to imagine them together.

"Drive you down at four, four-fifteen?" he asked.

Katie looked up, looked him in the eyes. Kind, strong eyes.

"That'd be perfect," she said.

The symbolism of the meeting spot was not lost on her.

The Thurgood Marshall Law Library was where she'd given up so many weekends, done so much work, worked so many hours. And where she'd met Max, of course.

It has to be Max, she decided as she left Mr. Claypool in the parking lot (knowing he would follow her, watching from a distance, even though he'd promised he'd stay in the car). *Who else would have asked to meet here?* If someone else had been following her, some government agent, some Truther or even *anti*-Truther stalker, they wouldn't pick the library, instead of some park, her school, Ground Zero in New York. *No, it has to be Max.* Though she'd hoped—sworn—never to contact him again. What game he'd been playing, whatever role in this enormous charade, she wasn't interested in ever finding out. That was one mystery she had no need to solve.

But then Winter had appeared, resurrected. And the note. And the promise of "coda." An end. *The* end. If such a thing were possible. *Does anything ever truly end?* she wondered, coming up the library steps at 4:58 p.m. *Or does the past always stick like glue to the present and future?*

She crested the top step to the second floor and froze.

It was Paul Cobb.

Sitting in a chair by her favorite study cubicle. Legs outstretched and crossed at the feet. He even held up a hand to say hello.

She thought of turning and running, but only for an instant. She scanned the rest of the floor. There was no one else. Five o'clock was always a quiet time in the library, especially on weekends. Katie slogged forward.

"Figured you'd be invited too," he said, checking his watch.

"You didn't arrange this?"

Paul Cobb shook his head. "Was told to be here at five o'clock. That's all I know."

"Max?" she asked. She stepped closer, prepared to flee, scream, fight again, if needed, but all she saw was a laptop on the desk.

He shrugged. "One would assume. Why don't you take a seat?"

"I'll stand, thank you."

He made a popping sound with his tongue, checked his watch again.

Katie looked away. The next minute ticked by like weeks in solitary confinement. The kind of confinement her dad was in. What she'd be in if Paul Cobb decided to arrest her or—

Katie heard footsteps drawing closer. She didn't want to be happy to see him. She didn't want to react at all. She didn't want her heart to surge in her chest, her throat to close up, her hands to clench. There were a lot of things she didn't want.

Max walked up the stairs to join them.

"Hot damn." Paul Cobb nodded in approval. "Five on the dot."

36

Max still looked like Max. Technically. But there was something different about the way he moved, carried himself. He wasn't as loose, as restless. He was rigid. Formal. *He's nervous*, she thought. Afraid? It wasn't an emotion she'd ever imagined on him. What the hell was he doing?

She'd taken a step back as he approached, strangely choosing to be closer to Paul Cobb than Max. At least she finally knew what Cobb wanted, who he really was. Max, on the other hand . . . What was his agenda?

What had it ever been?

"Thank you both for being here," Max said, glancing at them both quickly. Not making direct eye contact with her.

"Didn't leave me much choice, Mr. Thompson," Paul Cobb said.

"No, sir. I think it best if—"

"That's Winter, yes?" Katie interrupted. "On the porch this morning."

"Yes." Max looked at her. "Entirely."

Katie's eyes brimmed, the tears as unexpected as they were angry. "How did—"

"Can we discuss that later?" Max asked. "Right now we need to—"

"There is no later," Katie snapped. "Not for you. Not for

any of this. You tell me right now everything you did or I'm walking out and you two assholes can play catch-up all you want. I don't give a damn anymore about any of this." This last was addressed to Max. "So tell me, what did you do?"

He sighed, glanced at Cobb. "I was ordered . . ." He turned back to Katie. "I was ordered to scare you. To scare you away from all of this. This business you supposedly 'don't give a damn about' but still, somehow, wouldn't leave alone. Not to scare you away from some 'truth' that would topple the government. But to protect you until your dad's claims about other things got sorted out. To protect you from guys like Bohenek. Guys like Hauk, the other night."

"*Protect* me? By pretending to murder my cat? By killing some poor other white cat?"

"I didn't kill any cats!" Max's voice was exasperated. "As a matter of fact, I drove all over the state—animal shelters, Baltimore's animal services—looking for a Winter look-alike that was already dead. And it wasn't easy, let me tell you. I finally found one in Salisbury, but I had to use some dark hair dye to—"

"What is *wrong* with you fucking people?" Katie looked between the two.

Paul Cobb held up his hands. "Hey, don't ask me. We assumed he'd just killed your cat."

Katie let that pass. "Where was Winter all this time?" she asked.

"With me," Max said. "My apartment. She's been fine. I grabbed her outside Gianna's one night. I was gonna give her back once everything calmed down."

They stared at each other, both carefully deciding crucial next words.

"What are you?" she asked, breaking the silence. "I mean, you're what? Some kind of spy or something?"

"Um." Max looked at Paul Cobb. "No," he replied. "But that's a bit of a technical answer. I was recruited two years ago—"

"Max," Paul Cobb warned.

"I was recruited two years ago to serve my country," Max continued. "I'm a good programmer, probably a better cryptologist, and the plan was that with a lot more training I would one day join the digital front lines of Homeland Security. Hitting the bad guys on the digital front: financials, communications, data security. It was something I wanted to do. Then you . . ."

"Me, what?" Katie asked.

"I really *am* taking law classes at Maryland. To better understand international finance and regulations. When you started working here, it was seen as an easy opportunity."

"To spy on me?" Katie said, looking only at Max.

"You were the only one your father was talking to at the time and . . . well, some hoped you'd be able to help resolve this quickly. And, yes, I agreed to help. It was also presented as a way to help protect you. Which—"

"What a good little soldier boy you are," she sneered.

"Sometimes," he said, turning to Cobb. "Sir?"

"Yes, Max?"

"I warned you what would happen if you tried to open her father's data."

Cobb nodded, his eyes on Max.

Katie scowled. "What? What happened?"

"It vanished," Cobb replied. "Deleted itself even as we were trying to decipher it. Once it started, the more we tried to stop it, the more data it destroyed."

"Until, I suspect, there was nothing left," Max said. "As I predicted. Everything on TERNGO. Drug trafficking, maybe. Evidence of a massacre that involved civilians, contractors, the US military. Maybe even something on 9/11."

"You're right," Paul Cobb said, standing. "It's all gone. So what is it we're doing here today, kid? You want me to kiss your little pink ass and tell you what a genius you are? That the data was booby-trapped by someone smarter than us, that we screwed up? Because you can forget that. This whole operation is over. The intel Scott Wallace may or may not have had is now irrelevant. I'm still not entirely convinced it was ever valid in the first place. We've already moved on to a hundred other problems. And Wallace and his daughter here aren't our concern anymore. You tossed away a bright future, kid. You really did."

"*You* fired *me*." Max held out his palms. "What future you talking about?"

"I told you then we'd talk again when you got your head out of your ass."

"That could take decades, sir," Max replied.

"So, then I'll ask you again," Cobb said. "Why are we here?"

"Because Scott Wallace had a backup," Max said. "Of everything."

"A backup?" Cobb's voice sounded strained. "Bullshit. We looked everywhere. *You* looked everywhere."

"Katie found it," Max said.

Katie tensed. "What? I don't know what you're talking about."

"The cassette tapes in your dad's locker." His smile was a little more lopsided. A little more like the real Max. "All that super old hair-metal stuff. You told me what you'd found when you were looking at his work."

"Jesus H. Christ." Paul Cobb plopped down again.

Katie's eyes went wide.

The cassette tapes. Sitting right in front of everyone for months.

Max explained: "When we went to Adam Healy's place, you mentioned your dad came home with an old Commodore 64 computer once. Those used cassette-tape data recorders. Back in the day, data was stored on regular old cassette tapes, *any* cassette tape. All you have to do is put a little piece of Scotch tape over the ridge up top and the cassette becomes record-able again. For music *or* data. Anyhow, he stored all his backups on those tapes. The files were encrypted, but he had all the encryption keys saved on another cassette, which he'd hidden inside one of the pickup trucks at his job."

"Old Rusty," Katie said. "Phil Lampert said my dad always liked driving the oldest truck they had. He'd been safeguarding his data."

"Only truck that had a tape player," Max said. "Just had to hit eject and there it was. As a private citizen, I mean."

"Right," Paul Cobb snorted. "Wonder how many years a private citizen gets for burglary."

Max just laughed. "For stealing an old copy of *Pyromania*?" He swung his backpack around and pulled out a stack of cassettes. Eight held together with a rubber band. "These belong to your dad," he said to Katie.

"And I won't take those, why?" Paul Cobb wondered.

"Because these are merely the hard copies of digital files that were posted online again this morning, for when Scott Wallace is ready to share it in the way he sees fit."

"So you put the files online," Paul Cobb said. "We'll find them again."

Max nodded. "Maybe. Of course, the files live online on about ten thousand different sites, split into a million pieces that reassemble and move every time someone visits these individual sites. It will reassemble on the servers of every international major news service, however, only when Scott Wallace says it should—or if anything ever happens to him, Katie, or me."

"Or Winter," Katie added.

"Right." Max nodded at her, even smiled a bit. "Or Winter."

"This actually is treason," Paul Cobb said. "You'll go to jail for the rest of your life."

Max hesitated for the first time. Then he tilted his head, thinking about it. "Another maybe. Since you fired me, I did most of this as a private citizen and broke no confidentiality or security agreements. Though I'm sure you can always use the Patriot Act to get me if you really wanted."

"In any case, this makes our relationship *difficult*."

"I hoped it might," Max said.

Paul Cobb scratched the back of his head. Stared up at Max, also thinking.

"I'm going to leave now," Max said. "Thank you again. I . . . I'm truly sorry to both of you for the disappointment I've caused. Please believe in all cases it was always with the best intentions." He turned and looked at Katie. "I'm really sorry."

Then he turned and walked quickly away, down the steps. Gone.

Katie stood gaping after him for a very long moment, the stack of cassettes in her hand.

"Well, that was . . . interesting," Paul Cobb said behind her.

Katie looked back at him as he stood.

He withdrew something small out from his jacket. A packet of gum.

"I'll talk to my dad," she said. "When he's well again. He'll . . . we'll get you as much information as he's able to give. On the massacre, I mean. Then you can go after the real bad guys, whatever that even means."

"It's hard to tell the difference sometimes," he agreed. "We'll try to sort them out as best we can."

"I believe you," she said.

"Thank you."

"Did you really fire him?"

"Max? Classified," he replied. "But I'd be a total shit if I didn't admit it was because he was looking out for you and your dad instead of focusing on his assignment."

Katie nodded. Despite herself, she blushed.

"You want some gum?" He offered the pack.

"Sure," she said. "Why not?"

"So," Paul Cobb asked, watching her. "Now what?"

Katie took the gum, slowly unfolded the wrapper.

"I know, right?" she said.

37

Katie sat in the lobby of Marilyn Wren's law office. A small stack of folders rested in her lap. Everything she'd pulled together over the last six weeks. Everything about 9/11.

The receptionist answered the phone while smiling pleasantly at her. She tried smiling back. It wasn't as easy as she'd hoped. She looked up at a clock on the wall. Officially, she still had a few minutes to bail, to walk out the door and leave Ms. Wren alone for good. But she knew that choice was no longer on the table.

Nine-Eleven was no longer hers to believe or disbelieve. It was beyond her, a day whose truth she would never fully pin down. All she could do was present the evidence she'd gathered and hope it was enough to convince Wren—enough to convince the judge. Everything else was out of her reach.

The office phone buzzed again, a different sound than all the ones before, and Katie jumped. The receptionist took the call, said "Yes, ma'am," then hung up.

"Ms. Wren can see you now." He'd lifted his hand to indicate the next door.

Katie stood with her things.

"Do you need a hand, Ms. Wallace?"

"No," she told him. "Thank you. I've got this." She opened the door and found Wren waiting down the long carpeted hallway.

"Good morning." The attorney led her into an adjoining conference room. "Can I get you anything?"

"No, ma'am," she replied. "Thank you." Katie entered the beautiful room and Wren shut the door behind them. "Will anyone else be joining us?" Katie asked, putting her things on the table.

"No, it's just us," Wren said. She took a chair at the top of the table. "Start whenever you're ready."

"Yes, ma'am." Katie tried to breathe evenly. Tried imagining worst-cases *and* best-cases. Tried not imagining Wren laughing at her.

They killed her. Killed all of them.

Her father's words still echoed in her mind. But none of that pain or regret or fear could be shared with Wren. Because she couldn't prove that specific memory was connected to 9/11. More likely, it stemmed from some other tragedy in her dad's life.

She didn't know. Might never know.

But there was other pain and regret and fear from 9/11 she could share.

"Scott Wallace," she began, "was admitted to the Ventworth Mental-Health Facility on April 20 and diagnosed as dangerous to himself and society due to violent delusional psychosis and advanced paranoia. Per hospital records, this diagnosis stems specifically from Mr. Wallace's views regarding the tragic events of September 11, 2001. His suspicion is that the full and true story of 9/11 has not yet been shared with America's citizens, that the official story regarding nineteen Islamic terrorists is a deception masking the true culprits, namely a group working within the United States government and/or its business and military partners. I am not asking today that you believe this alternative story to be true. I am asking you only to consider if the facts presented here sufficiently create within your mind the possibility this alternative story might be true. Is there enough reasonable doubt that Mr. Wallace's beliefs are rooted in a dangerously unbalanced mental state, but rather, based on evidence available to every citizen? Evidence I will share with you here today."

Marilyn Wren made a note on her pad, studied Katie for a moment, and then nodded for her to continue.

Katie began like this:

"On the morning of September 11, 2001, the skies over the eastern United States were what pilots call 'severe clear.' A cloudless blue so vast, you think it might never end . . ."

The courtroom was quiet. Everyone waiting for the judge to enter.

Scott Wallace—her dad—sat directly in front of Katie this time. Close enough to reach out and squeeze his shoulder. (Which she did.) He looked awake this time too. Determined. He looked good.

Wren and her doctors had been conducting drug tests every single day since the first visit when they'd discovered traces of so many state-prescribed medications in his system. He was mostly clean now. Only the barest minimum, as agreed to by Wren's doctor friends.

To her dad's right sat Mr. Schottelkotte, the attorney. He and Katie had met several times in the past week and talked for almost three hours the night before. He caught her looking his way and winked encouragingly.

The judge entered the room at 3:00 p.m. as scheduled. It was the same woman from before. Her black robe trailed behind as she crossed swiftly to her bench. Katie stood with everyone else as the judge's eyes scanned past those at the table to glance over the small crowd gathered this time in the visitor's gallery.

Katie peeked backward to see them, too. Wren was stunning and polished, as always. More so, somehow, in an actual courtroom. She sat with a paralegal and one of the expert doctors she'd brought in. Plus Phil Lampert. And Adam Healy.

Gloria Dorsey and both Claypools sat in the next row.

And Gianna, who flashed a thumbs-up at Katie.

"Mr. Schottelkotte," the judge said, sitting. "I've reviewed your request for a preemptive re-evaluation of the case regarding Mr. Scott Wallace. And I note that you've submitted the necessary letters of grievance and condition with the state mental board and county court. May I remind you, we're time-tabled to examine Mr. Wallace's case on the fourteenth of next month."

"Yes, Your Honor," Schottelkotte replied, still standing. "But we feel that—"

"You contend," she stopped him, "information has emerged to substantiate the argument that Mr. Wallace has been unfairly interned under compulsory medical supervision, and that . . ." She paused to look over her glasses to papers on her desk. "Pursuant to the cases *Fraley v. the Estate of Oberholtzer* and *O'Connor v. Donaldson*, among others you've listed here, his immediate release is to be deliberated immediately. Do I have this right?"

"Yes, Your Honor."

"And you'll be presenting various affidavits and documents, character witnesses Philip Lampert and Kaitlyn Wallace"—the judge looked straight at Katie—"the patient's daughter, as well as Adam Healy as some form of 'expert' to present much of this evidence. Is that right?"

"Yes, Your Honor."

"Mr. Healy as an expert on the matters in question?"

"Yes, Your Honor. Per Federal Rules of Evidence, and prior to any testimony, we will verify his competency in the relevant field through an examination of his credentials."

"Please be seated," she told the court.

The room shuffled and settled noisily and quickly as Katie sat with everyone else.

"Ms. Wren." The judge acknowledged Marilyn Wren in the audience. "Always nice to see you."

"And you, Your Honor."

The judge said: "Are you here in some sort of . . ."

"Official capacity?" Wren finished the question. "Not today, Your Honor. I am, however, now working with the Wallace family and Mr. Schottelkotte on a promising civil case. Potentially significant breaches in public mental-healthcare protocol as perpetrated by several organizations, including Ventworth Hospital, and government officials. Misuse of pharmaceuticals, misdiagnosis, and physical abuse."

"I see." The judge sorted some papers on her desk. "Well, the Wallaces are in capable hands."

Wren smiled back.

"Please proceed, Mr. Schottelkotte," said the judge.

Schottelkotte nodded to the judge, but then bowed slightly more to Katie.

Katie breathed deeply and stared up at the judge.

Her dad had turned slightly to lift and place his hand onto the short half-wall between them. Katie laid her hand over his and squeezed.

And she did not let go when Schottelkotte stood.

"Good morning, Your Honor," he said.

Max returned on a Saturday. Five or six weeks after the hearing.

Mrs. Claypool had come upstairs to say he was at the door. Katie found him sitting out on the porch steps.

"Shouldn't you be in jail or something?" Katie asked, stepping out onto the porch. The setting sun felt good on her face as she looked out over the neighborhood.

"Probably," he agreed. "Looks like Cobb's dropped it. You want me to go?"

She shook her head. Gripped the banister, closed her eyes against the summer warmth.

"I wanted to . . . to apologize," he said, after a moment. "With Cobb there, I couldn't really, you know. Anyhow, I wanted to say—"

"I miss you," she said.

Max looked up. "No shit?"

"No shit."

He looked down at his feet, sitting quietly.

"I know you tried to tell me a few times. What was going on," Katie said. "I know that now."

"Didn't try hard enough."

She considered that. "Maybe not."

"How's your dad?"

Katie looked down at him. Sighed deeply. "He's good. He's . . . better. He's at the Cassidy Clinic. Pretty nice place right outside of Annapolis. We diverted a fraction of my 'college funds' to get him the help he needed. They're, ah, they're working on his PTSD, his addictions. A lot of things. But it's voluntary, you know. He's there by choice now."

"That's great," he said. "I'm really . . . you did great."

"Sure I did."

"Katie, seriously, what you did was— "

"I told him what you did, you know. The cassettes and all. He seemed impressed."

Max laughed. "Well, it wasn't easy."

"Guess not. And he wants to work with you and Cobb when he's ready. He really does."

"Not me," Max said. "I don't do that kind of stuff anymore."

Katie sat next to him on the step. "What kind of stuff?" she asked.

His smile was tired. Maybe a little sad. "Saving the world."

"Is that what we were doing?"

"That's what I thought."

"And now?"

He shrugged. "I don't know. Gonna travel, hit some gamer and hacker conventions over in Asia. Figure it all out there, maybe."

They sat quietly again.

"In Pennsylvania, the memorial . . ." Max looked directly at her. Like he used to. "Remember the cards we wrote?"

Katie nodded. "Of course. I didn't see yours."

"'Thus be it ever, when freemen shall stand / between their loved home and the war's desolation.'"

She looked at him. "Who said that?"

"It's from the 'Star Spangled Banner.' One of the verses no one knows anymore."

Something shifted in her chest, lodging behind her rib cage. It hurt, but it felt good too. It felt right. "You're a true patriot, Mr. Thompson, aren't you?"

"I thought so. I believed in this country. Our core values. I still do, I think. If that's a patriot, then okay. I just . . . I wanted to help somehow, always have, so when they approached me . . . I said yes."

"But not now."

"It's tough to be a 'freeman' without the full truth."

"So you don't think we have the truth?"

"Do you?"

She looked back out over the street. "How could I dare to claim such a thing? Our leaders lie every day. Our news lies. Our own families." She turned to Max. "Our *friends*."

He lowered his head.

"We even lie to ourselves," she allowed. "How could anyone ever possibly know the real truth of anything? When you get to the point where it seems like *everything* could be a lie."

"*Scio me nihil scire*." Max smiled.

"I take Spanish, not Latin."

"'I know that I know nothing.'"

"Cute."

They watched in silence as a pair of kids went by slowly on their bikes. The two boys eyed Max and Katie suspiciously. Max chuckled.

"How's everyone here?" he asked.

"Good, good. Actually, C.J. is back with her mom. She headed out last week."

"No kidding. That's great."

"Yeah. It is."

"And you?" he asked.

"I'll be with my dad again when he's better. We're hoping the end of the summer."

"And your . . ."

"My mom?" Katie stilled next to him. She shook her head, thinking. "I guess I'm still at that everything-seems-like-a-lie point."

"Yeah," he nodded.

She drew in a long breath of summer. "I suppose I could hire a detective or—something. Find out who she really was. Where she is today. There's still those transmissions, and the chance something really did happen on 9/11. But something involving me and my mom? I doubt it now. Is 'a chance' enough? I could ask Cobb to help me take a blood test against all the passengers. To know 100 percent. But isn't 99 percent enough?"

"For most people."

"The truth and lies are so tangled, I don't know if I'll ever know what really happened. Or if I even want to. Today, I'm just a girl flying off the back of a horse."

"Huh?"

She looked at him. "At this point, whatever the real truth is about any of it—9/11, my mom, my dad—it won't change how I feel. Who I am and what I do. That's pretty much just on me. I'm not the same person I was the day my dad got put in that hospital. Just like he's not the same person he was the day he witnessed some horrifying massacre. There are people whose lives are going to be forever changed by something that happens to them later today, stuff they never wanted to happen, could never have predicted. And then they'll argue about What happened or Why and never ever reach agreement on either.

Not even with themselves. So, what do you do *after* the buildings fall or the doors slam and there's nothing but silence left? Maybe that 'after' is what counts. Your actions, your feelings. Maybe that's the only real truth we ever get. And maybe that's enough. Makes all the 'I don't know' not so scary."

"Fair," he said. "So then, what now? For you, I mean. What do you think you'll do?"

Katie's mind raced through the list:

TERNGO. Fuenmayor. Following up on 9/11 with Paul Cobb.

Max. Her mother.

Rebuilding a life with her dad.

Me.

Katie smiled at Max.

"I don't know," she said.

Author's Note

On September 11, 2001, Al-Qaeda (a militant Islamist group with global reach and aims) coordinated a terrorist attack on the United States by hijacking four commercial jets to crash into high-profile American targets. The operation took two years and half a million dollars to prepare and execute. The result: One plane crashed into the Pentagon; two others were flown into the World Trade Center (causing both towers and another nearby building to collapse); and the fourth plane crashed in a Pennsylvania field during a struggle between the hijackers and passengers. In all, nearly three thousand people were killed. Al-Qaeda claimed full responsibility.

These are the events as recounted by the US government, other governments, the general media, and numerous reputable scholarly books and qualified investigations since then.

Yet more than one third of Americans believe it is (in the words of a Scripps Howard poll) "somewhat" or "very" likely that "federal officials either participated in the attacks" or "took no action to stop them" because they "wanted the United States to go to war in the Middle East."[1]

Governments have a long record of not disclosing the full truth to their citizens for a variety of reasons, and the events

---

1   Karlyn Bowman and Andrew Rugg, "Public Opinion on Conspiracy Theories," AEI Public Opinion Studies, November 2013, 1-29.

of 9/11 are among the most complicated, mysterious, and challenged in American history. This novel aims to explore those complications, mysteries, and challenges. Several characters in this novel support alternative versions of what occurred on 9/11—ideas many readers will find absurd or offensive. I merely hope to use these ideas to explore the causes and effects of conspiracy theories, as well as questions about civic duty and the nature of truth.

I teach high school English, and many of my students look at 9/11 the way I once looked at the Vietnam conflict: with curiosity but little understanding of a time "before" me. My freshmen were not alive when 9/11 occurred. Still, they and my older students have many questions about its history—including, of course, "the conspiracy stuff."

More than fifteen years after 9/11, the biggest national event yet of my lifetime, I wanted to write about it. To learn about it. I wanted to introduce a new generation (the one I'm currently teaching, the one to which my own sons belong) to that day and to the Truther phenomenon that followed—which permeates, in different forms, almost every tragedy that has befallen us since. And ultimately, I wanted to write about Katie and Max.

Included here is a partial list of sources that I used in my research. Inclusion in the list does not imply endorsement, only recognition that the source supplied material related to this novel.

Few works of fiction regarding 9/11 have escaped the criticism that they are exploiting the victims. To those who feel I've done so here, I can only apologize and state that the exact opposite was my sincerest intention.

Selected Bibliography

Books

Bresnahan, David M. *9-11 Terror in America*. Brightwaters, NY: Windsor House Publishing, 2001.

Chossudovsky, Michel. *War and Globalisation: The Truth Behind September 11*. Oakland, CA: Global Outlook, 2002.

DiMarco, Damon. *Tower Stories: An Oral History of 9/11*. Solana Beach, CA: Santa Monica Press, 2007.

Dunbar, David, and Brad Reagan, eds. *Debunking 9/11 Myths: Why Conspiracy Theories Can't Stand Up to the Facts*. New York: Hearst, 2011.

Gaffney, Mark H. *The 9/11 Mystery Plane and the Vanishing of America*. Waterville, OR: Trine Day LLC, 2008.

Griffin, David Ray. *The New Pearl Harbor*. Ithaca, NY: Olive Branch Press, 2004.

———. *The New Pearl Harbor Revisited*. Ithaca, NY: Olive Branch Press, 2008.

———. *The 9/11 Commission Report: Omissions and Distortions*. Ithaca, NY: Olive Branch Press, 2004.

Hartwell, Dean T. *Planes without Passengers*. Seattle: CreateSpace, 2012.

Kay, Jonathan. *Among the Truthers*. New York: HarperCollins Publishers, 2011.

Meyssan, Thierry. *9/11: The Big Lie*. Melbourne, FL: Carnot Publishing Ltd., 2003.

National Commission on Terrorist Attacks. *The 9/11 Commission Report: Final Report of the National Commission on Terrorist Attacks Upon the United States*. New York: W.W. Norton, 2004.

Ruppert, Michael C. *Crossing the Rubicon*. Gabriola Island, BC, Canada: New Society Publishers, 2004.

Ryan, Kevin Robert. *Another Nineteen: Investigating Legitimate 9/11 Suspects*. Seattle: CreateSpace, 2013.

Spencer, Lynn. *Touching History*. New York: Free Press, 2011.

Spiegel, Der. *Inside 9-11: What Really Happened*. New York: St. Martin's Press, 2002.

Summers, Anthony, and Robbyn Swan. *The Eleventh Day: The Full Story of 9/11*. New York: Ballantine Books, 2012.

Tarplay, Webster. *9/11 Synthetic Terror: Made in U.S.A.* San Diego: Progressive Press, 2005.

Woodward, Bob. *Plan of Attack*. New York: Simon & Schuster, 2004.

Wright, Lawrence. *The Looming Tower: Al-Qaeda and the Road to 9/11*. New York: Vintage, 2007.

Zwicker, Barrie. *Towers of Deception: The Media Cover-up of 9/11*. Gabriola Island, BC, Canada: New Society Publishers, 2006.

Websites

www.911blogger.com

www.911conspiracy.tv

www.911day.org

www.911families.org

www.911memorial.org

www.911myths.com

www.911proof.com

www.911review.com

www.911scholars.org

www.911truth.org

www.911truthnews.com

www.911tv.org

www.ae911truth.org

www.debunking911.com

www.emperors-clothes.com

www.infowars.com

www.nps.gov

www.pentagonmemorial.org

www.pilotsfor911truth.org

www.prisonplanet.com/911.html

www.reopen911.org

www.scientistsfor911truth.org

www.standdown.net

www.tributewtc.org

About the Author

Geoffrey Girard is the author of several books, including *Project Cain*, a 2013 Bram Stoker Award nominee for Superior Achievement in a Young Adult Novel. He has degrees in English literature and creative writing. He currently lives in Ohio, where he chairs the English department at a private boys' high school.